THE OFFERING

THE REAWAKENING SERIES
BOOK 1

LAYLA MOON

Cover Design: Layla Moon

Interior Design & Formatting: Layla Moon

Editing and Proofread: Brittany | BLD Editing

Illustrations: Night Rose Art

Illustrations: Christina Hennessy

This is a paperback novel.

ISBN: 9798876015419

THE OFFERING

THE REAWAKENING SERIES
BOOK 1

LAYLA MOON

BOOKS BY LAYLA MOON

THE REAWAKENING SERIES

The Offering - Book One

DARK TABOO ROMANCE

Twisted Friction - A Dark Taboo Romance (foster sibling)

Twisted Friction - A Dark Taboo Romance (full sibling)

BOOKS COMING SOON

After the Rain - Book Two in The Reawakening Series

Title to be Announced - A Feminine Rage Anthology

Title to be Announced - A Dark Stalker Romance

Title to be Announced - A Dark Psychological Erotic Romance

and more...

To stay up to date with Layla Moon, book signings, new releases, tours, behind the scenes and giveaways visit

www.laylamoonauthor.com

CONTENT WARNINGS

This book contains **explicit adult content** and is for mature audiences only. The story contains **heavy dark matter** that may be concerning for some readers.
Due to issues outside of the author's control, content warnings can no longer be placed within this book.

The author has noted **some** of them, highlighted on the *next page.*

However, there is a full list of them on her website.

SEE HERE FOR C.W's

CONTENT WARNINGS

__Please note these have been abbreviated to avoid the book being removed from the platform.__

Intention To K!ll The Main Female Character
Kn!fe play
Non Consensual and Dub Consensual Interactions
Bl00d Play
Taboo (no bl00d relation)
Degradat!on
Severe Scar!fication With Intention To Harm such as;
Gen!tal Scarif!cation/Brain Bleed and Stroke
Su!cidal Thoughts
Su!cide/D3ath

Your mental health matters as always, please stay safe within your reading limits and reach out where needed.

Layla Moon is here for you, every step of the way.

PLAYLIST

Shadow - **Livingston**
The Offering - **Sleep Token**
Figure You Out - **VOILA**
Sugar - **Sleep Token**
Breathe Into Me - **Red**
Hold My Hand - **Lady Gaga**
Use Me - **PLAZA**
No Time To Die - **Billie Eilish**
Take Me Back To Eden - **Sleep Token**
and more...

For the girlies that just want a masked stranger to make a good girl bad.
The Shadow Man is waiting for you.

PROLOGUE
NEVER UNDERESTIMATE THE POWER OF YOUR IMAGINATION

I t goes without saying that we should never underestimate the power of our imagination.

My nightmares of a dark figure haunted me relentlessly. Watching me. Always watching me.

How could anyone possibly sleep after what I saw? They couldn't. Though it wasn't the first time something went bump in the night in Sayville. Not with the crime rate in that city. Nor with the roommate I had, my best friend. She was a wild, bright and beautiful woman, spending most of her nights making a dollar at the local club—the one where clothes are taken off— and bringing strange men home for a little extra cash.

I loved her, though, and I didn't let her lifestyle choices make me think anything less of her. I accepted her for who she was— kinks and all. But aside from her noises, there were other sounds keeping me awake every night. *The sounds... the voices... the smells.*

Sleeping terrified me—so much so that I was falling behind in my studies. Watching over my shoulder became muscle memory, and truth be told, I was exhausted. Closing my eyes quickly became my biggest fear—which was weird because I collected dead things for a hobby—well, an aspiring career. *If I can finish it.*

Spiders, insects, and butterflies alike hung beautifully on my bedroom wall, others in glass containers. They all watched me in my sleep, but *they* didn't scare me. My nightmares did.

They always started the same.

First, it was the thick smell of musky cologne mixed with blood, pine, and moisture. A scent that I could never again omit.

Then there was the spine-splitting chill whenever *it* appeared. A sensation that I could never again unregister.

Next was a shattered breath tearing through my skull from one ear to the other. A sound that I could never again forget.

Finally came the haunting sight of a black figure in a mask that resembled the Grim Reaper. A sight that I could never again obliterate from my vision.

My nightmares were a diabolic monstrosity, and I couldn't tell you how many times I questioned if what I dreamt was real... or if I was just hallucinating. When the nightmares first started, that stoic figure followed me everywhere like a shadow. Always in a metallic, horned mask and a long black cape. It appeared in all the places I had been that day, just out of reach—almost out of sight—then it would disappear.

Every. Single. Night.

My secular deliriums. The figure never caused me harm in the nightmares; it just watched.

When I had my first nightmare, it was standing on the curb on the other side of the bus—the same one that I had taken home the night after my shift at the cafe. Then it just... disappeared. In my second nightmare, it was standing in the corner of my room as I was studying. In my third, it was sitting at a buffet booth at the local diner while I celebrated Tilly's birthday. I was sure that it was indeed a nightmare, because I didn't *really* see him there... *Did I?*

Every time I shut my eyes, there the caped figure was. But it wasn't there when I opened them. That was how I knew it was just a nightmare. *But if that is true, how did my hairbrush move from my bathroom counter to my bedside table while I was sleeping?*

How was it that someone—or something—in a nightmare could actually unlock a window, even when you had changed the lock time and time again? I knew I wasn't thinking straight. That they were just nightmares, figments of my imagination due to exhaustion from school. Stress, maybe.

They *were* just dreams, after all.

Or so I thought.

I knew I locked my window after the first time it happened. I did the same routine as every other night; I pushed the block of wood up against the edge of the window so that it couldn't open from the outside. I even recorded myself doing it. That's how much I doubted myself.

But like clockwork, the smell of moisture, blood, and pine stirred me into my slumber. I remember it like it was yesterday. It was so vivid. Its presence sent that familiar chill up my spine as it stood at my bedside, the same way it did every night, tenderly brushing my hair with its excessively long, black-painted fingers, then with the brush. As it groomed me, the brush clinked against the metal rings on its fingers.

The moonlight had beamed from the window and cast a glint over its metallic, mouthless skeleton mask. Its thick black cape pooled around its feet, and the sharp goat horns of its mask curled out from the hood.

The stoic figure was a *man*. That much became clear over time. He was big, tall, and gloomy. Lean, muscular, and had a painted torso that glowed under the green amulet dangling around his neck.

The eye holes of his mask were empty, soulless, hidden by a thick layer of mesh. He was absolutely terrifying. But he was always quiet, gentle, and tentative. He never spoke to me or hurt me. In the nightmare, he appeared content yet somewhat provoked as he trailed his fingers over the delicate areas of my neck, right along the part you would squeeze if you wanted someone dead.

I tried to wake up. I really did, because it felt so real. But it was just a dream.

He was like the human version of Death that I'd read about in books, but without the long scythe. And he wasn't of deathly bone form. He had flesh. He was *human*. I knew it was different from the other nightmares.

Because when I opened my eyes, *he* was already halfway out my window, giving me one final glare before he fled.

The shadow man was *real*.

CHAPTER ONE

IF YOU'RE GIVEN A CUP OF CHAMOMILE TEA... MAKE SURE IT'S ACTUALLY CHAMOMILE TEA

"E eh! You're home early," my roommate Tilly blurted in a shriek. It was hard to avoid her perky breasts wiggling around under her shirt as her arms splayed out wide to embrace me, almost knocking me over as I walked in the door. I should have been used to that. It didn't matter if it was in our apartment or out in public, she was always braless. *Why did I have to have big boobs? I can't wear nice clothes like her.*

"I've only been gone a few hours." I laughed, letting her continue to squeeze the post-assignment stress out of my body. It was my hardest one yet, leaving me famished and drained. *Holy heck, I'm starving.* I needed food, stat. I couldn't help but mimic her smile as she wrapped herself around me. Her grasp pulled away all my worries almost entirely.

"Still not sleeping, babes?"

"Not in the slightest," I deadpanned. She had no idea about the real reason I wasn't sleeping. Tilly thought it was just my studies keeping me up at night. That was what I told her. She thought that was why I had panda eyes from studying too hard.

And why I had frayed, untamed hair and lived off more coffees than I cared to count. But that wasn't the reason my complexion was weathered.

I had hopes and dreams of graduating college in a few weeks —which I had recently been undeniably failing. The truth was, I hadn't had a wink of sleep for three weeks. Three whole painful weeks. Not since that night.

The shadow man.

He watched me as I slept. Who knew where he truly was.

All I knew was that he was real.

He broke into my room, even when I changed the locks on the window. How does someone sleep after that? And who would believe me if I told them? *No one.* Not if you heard the commotion that happened in our building complex. We lived in the slums. It was everyone for themselves, and if you couldn't fight, you stayed indoors, like I did. I couldn't fight—I didn't have a mean bone in my body. I cried over a paper cut, for heaven's sake. Tilly, though... well, she could take a whole football team with one fist and still be the last one standing.

What if the shadow man goes into her room? What if he... touches us? In that *way. What if—*

I pushed aside my intrusive thoughts. Tilly was my favorite part of coming home from college or work at the cafè. She was my safe space, and I'd have lost my mind months before if it wasn't for her.

She would think I'd gone mad if I told her there was a strange, shirtless, masked man with too many six packs of muscles, dressed in a cape with black-painted skin breaking into my bedroom window at night. *Actually, no*—if I so much as whispered something about a masked man coming into our apartment, I think she would just about have an orgasm on the spot. Tilly was freaky like that, into things I had no business lurking around. So, I kept my stupid nightmares in my head where they belonged.

"I'm sorry that you're not sleeping," she furrowed, pushing me aside and smacking me on the rear-end. I yelped, and she held me at arm's length. "That's for leaving this morning without saying anything!" Tilly waved her index finger in front of my face and tsked at me.

I rolled my eyes and scoffed. *How am I the one in trouble?* I had snuck out of the apartment before she got up because I knew she would make a scene about my birthday like she always did.

"You know I hate being fussed over, Tilly. It's just a birthday." I swallowed and my cheeks flushed at the memory of the night before. Banging on walls, moaning, groaning, and heavy breathing. And yelling. *So much yelling.* "And besides, you had... company."

I bit my lip and my mind trailed off. Curiosity always got the better of me. I wondered what it would be like to kiss someone the way she did—I'd seen her kiss a guy before. He left after spending the night in her room, handing her some cash and giving her a long—*very long*—wet, tongue-swirling kiss. And then he was on his way. Though that was only the half of it; they were doing way more than just kissing before that. No different than any other night, really. *I ought to buy a decent pair of earphones to block out the sound.*

Sex.

It was Tilly's regular pastime, a new fling showing up every other day of the week. Sometimes more than one. That's how we could afford our place. *I guess, from this perspective, you could call her a lady of the night. But I'd rather just call her Tilly.*

Maybe I'll die a virgin. I was loyal to my bible. Sex was so illicit to even think about it. Not that it stopped me. I often trailed off, imagining what a penis looked like. What it would taste like. What it would feel like to have one inside my vagina.

But what man would want me? I was just a boring, pasty white, twenty-one-year-old girl with a poor sleeping habit, big breasts that never fit into bras and thighs as wide as a planet. The chaffing ... oh, the chaffing. I may have woken up twenty-one, but I felt incredibly past my time. I was nothing like Tilly. *Come on, girl, focus.* I pushed away my intrusive thoughts again as the ache between my thighs began to tingle.

"Mmm. Yes, I did." Tilly's tongue darted across her lips. "But that's no excuse to sneak off without me wishing you a happy birthday. Luckily for you, I love you, and you can make up for it," she said deviously. I rolled my eyes at her and she crossed her arms.

"Oh, gosh. What crazy scheme have you whipped up this time?" I asked, waiting for her to answer, but her response was a self-satisfied, almost seductive looking smirk turning up her plump, sable lips. *Seriously? Why does she have to look* this *good?*

"You're not going to make me watch *Fifty Shades of Grey* again, are you?" I hated that movie, and she knew it. *Okay. Fine, I lied.* I didn't *hate* the actual film... I just hated the way it made me feel.

Hot.

Flushed.

She'd made me watch it for my last birthday in the hopes that she would convince me to meet a guy and have my first kiss, or maybe even lose my virginity. But I was having none of it. Simply put, I wasn't ready. I still wasn't sure if I was. Not unless I met the one—you know, the perfect one. Mr.

Perfect. Mr. Fairytale. Fairytales didn't exist for girls like me, though.

"Nope! No movies. No staying in. We are going out tonight! No ifs or buts about it!"

Crap. My mouth dried. She chuckled as I shook my head. *Out? In public? At night? No way.* It was bad enough that I had to change my shifts at the café because of... *him.* Going out at night willingly was not exactly on my to-do list. Besides, I didn't go out or party like she did. I didn't even have Facebook or TikTok.

I always kept my head in books, studying hard to finish my degree in Entomology. Boring, I know. I stayed home, and when I wasn't there, I was working most mornings and every Saturday at the café. I had church on Sundays like good girls did. And when I wasn't at either of those places, I was in the library. But I knew the day would come that I would have to do something other than *be boring.* I sighed loudly, drawing my palm over my face. *Seriously? Am I really considering this?*

She was panting with excitement. I could practically hear her head ticking away, deciding which slutty dress she would put me in, what makeup she would throw on me, and what crazy alcoholic beverage she would pour down my throat.

"Fine. But I'm *not* drinking," I demanded with a stern voice, not that it sounded like it. *Pipsqueak.*

"Oh my god! Fuck yes, bitch! I'm so excited! You have no idea how long I've been waiting for this moment!" she squealed. Despite me mentally scoffing and rolling my eyes at her, I couldn't ignore how her beautiful ebony skin radiated in glee. *She's been waiting for this night for a* long *time.*

My twenty-first birthday.

"I think I have a pretty good idea. And watch your mouth.

My gosh," I scoffed as I moved from the doorway and inside, stumbling over my own feet. Tilly cackled, sticking her tongue out mockingly, and then we both fitted into a laugh. She loved teasing my innocence and my two left feet. It was weird that we were friends; so very opposite.

I caught a glimpse of my reflection in the mirror in the foyer, the warm shade of rose on my freckled cheeks blossoming from my incompetence and my illicit thoughts from earlier. That tended to happen a lot. I hated it.

How can I go out like this? The black bags under my emerald eyes made me look at least ten years past my expiry date, the lack of sleep clearly visible. My frayed black hair was scrunched up in a loose bun on the top of my head, left unbrushed and unwashed for days—weeks, even—with two-day-old sandwich crumbs in it.

"I know the *perfect* place. You don't have to dress up too much, but," Tilly paused, offering another giggle as she looked me up and down, "you'll need something other than what you're wearing. And a shower." She finished the last part of the sentence with her hand swishing in front of her nose.

"Okay, okay. I get it. I'll go scrub up."

I'd showered, if you count using a wet cloth under your armpits, but I hadn't washed my hair in a week or two. The thought of showering was terrifying, mostly because I couldn't see my window from the shower. And if I couldn't see the window, I couldn't see if anyone had broken in.

Even though I hadn't seen him since that night, it didn't mean I didn't think about him. *Why did he stop after I saw him? What if he comes back when I least expect it?*

I checked the living room for Tilly after cleaning myself up for quite possibly the longest time I'd ever spent in the shower. I'd decided not to let *him* deteriorate my life any longer, so I let my body and mind space out under the hot water. She wasn't in there, so I checked her bedroom.

"I don't have to dress up too much, hmm? Knowing you and the look on your face alludes me to believe you're telling fibs, Tilly," I tsked, seeing the grin on her face as she stammered around her closet, flicking through the gazillion dresses she had. Revealing ones—outfits she wore to work. She pulled one out for herself, tossing it onto her unmade bed. A sigh of relief struck me that she hadn't picked one for me.

The thought of showing skin made my stomach churn. *Who wants to see a chubby girl in a dress? No one.* I envied Tilly. She could wear anything. Anything she threw on suited her, whether she was dressed up to the nines or in her PJs.

Thankfully, my oversized t-shirt saved the day, hiding the rolls of my stomach—my go-to around the house, and out of it. I tried to wear loose clothes as much as I could to flatter my appearance and "fit in" to avoid the judgment. I paired it with my nicest jeans. You'd never catch me dead in a dress. *No, no, no.* Or in shorts.

"I'd rather shoot my own foot than to see you wearing anything like," she paused and pointed to my shirt, "*that!*"

"What did you have in mind?" I regretted the question as soon as it spilled from my mouth. "And no, I'm not wearing one of *your* types of dresses. Please, Tilly."

"Don't worry, babes. I wouldn't make you do that. I would never," she comforted me.

"Okay. I'm a little nervous, though."

"Don't be. I promise, you'll love it. I wouldn't take you anywhere I didn't know or trust."

Her words were genuine, so I nodded and accepted that she would look after me, even if she was a wild one. We had lived together since we started college a few years earlier. Two very different individuals with two very different lives, tastes, and interests, but we were two peas in a pod.

"Thanks. I trust you. I just need to shake off my nerves." I doted on her so much. You could call us Yin and Yang. Tilly grinned ear to ear, and I couldn't help but mirror her infectious smile.

"I have just the—"

"No alcohol, remember?" I cut her off. I didn't need another cause to alter my attention.

"No. No alcohol." She smiled. *Why is she smiling like that?*

"Ready?" Tilly finished the last few twirls of my hair with her curling iron. I nodded. She spun me around to face the mirror, losing my balance. *Wow, dizzy.* I brushed it aside, blinking over the random cloud over my eyes until I could see a little clearer. *Why can't I see straight?*

I swallowed and my eyes widened, not quite able to comprehend the person looking back at me in the bathroom mirror. It was a liar at the best of times, but this was the epitome of catfishing. My eyes were seductively shaded in soft browns, fading into a golden shimmer in the middle, above my iris'.

Tilly took my tea cup from my hand and placed it on the counter before fondly holding me at arm's length, looking me up and down. The glint in her dark brown eyes was practically glowing.

"Hey, I was still drinking that," I deadpanned. She had boiled and strained us quite possibly the best tea I'd ever had. It tasted like strawberries, and was far better than the crappy chamomile tea I usually drank for my nerves.

"You are incredibly beautiful, Esme. Inside and out. Never forget that. You are so pure. Any man would be the luckiest man in the world to have you, to claim you as his queen. And you, in this dress? Mhmm. Girl, they'll be groveling at your feet."

Claim.

How absurd.

"Thanks." I giggled, and she copied. *Why did I giggle?*

"Ha, it's true! Look at you," she ordered. I craned my neck back to the mirror. My already-flushed cheeks had a darker pink tone right to the edges of my hairline, somehow highlighting my freckles. She had gone above and beyond to shape my face with her makeup to contour my face. It was like I had lost ten pounds just sitting there. I was... beautiful. "Here. I got you something."

"Tilly, you really didn't have to get me anything," I scoffed, but I couldn't help but admire her generosity. She knew I hated gifts.

"Babes, tonight is a *very* special occasion. It's not every day you turn legal age." She handed me a large white gift box with a beautiful green bow on the top. *My favorite color. Of course.* The month of May—the emerald, and the color of my favorite butterfly.

She knew me too well, though it wasn't exactly hard to notice; they were all over my room. Taxidermied butterflies of various species, and the many drawings I crafted, mostly of the Emerald Swallowtail. I pondered on a thought, remembering that some had gone missing, but it didn't bother me as much as I thought it would. I felt unusually carefree.

"Tilly! This is... " I gasped, opening the box to reveal a beautiful black satin dress, even though I had made it very clear to her that I was never going to wear a dress unless it was for my wedding. *Especially a dress like this; short and tight. With my belly? No, thank you.* "Beautiful, but—"

"Shh. I'm not taking no as your answer. You're wearing the damn dress," Tilly snapped over me and mischievously looked down at my breasts before continuing. "Here." She filled my empty tea cup again, and I sipped at it while she waffled on about me needing to stop dressing like a forbidden fruit.

"A fourth cup of tea? I'll be peeing like a racehorse," I exclaimed as I put the dress on anyway, because why not?

"It's making you feel better, isn't it? You just got dressed in front of me and you didn't even notice," she said with a cocked brow.

Wait? I did?

I did.

Didn't that just make the butterflies in my stomach flutter? It made me think a little less about the shadow man. I was so grateful for her. She made the bad days good and the good days better. Even though I loved her tremendously, I knew I couldn't tell her about him. To be quite honest, I don't think I even want to admit that I saw him, that he was real. Because that would mean I'd have to convince *myself* that he was. And I had spent so long telling myself that he wasn't.

"Oh, shit. I did too."

"You just said shit!" Tilly pointed, laughing at me for my slip-up. I had never sworn in my entire life. We both fell into hysterics. *I don't swear. This is hilarious. Why do I feel so weird? I felt light and carefree. *Is it the tea? That's definitely not chamomile tea.*

And just like that, we were out the door and calling a cab, dressed to the nines and ready to *hit the clubs*. Or whatever it was that people said.

CHAPTER TWO

DON'T JUDGE A BOOK BY IT'S COVER, ESPECIALLY IF IT HAS MR. FAIRYTALE ON IT

*A*m I... *dreaming again?* I could not believe I was outside a nightclub. Me. In a dress.

A tight, short dress.

With bare legs showing. And arms.

Now, I know for a fact that I *should* have been shaking by a leaf in all my nerves and anxiety—the music was loud and it irritated my ears, even outside, and more so as we skipped the queue and walked into the building through a draped curtain—but I wasn't. There was not a single goosebump or sliver of anxiety present. *Why?*

What was in that tea?

The smell of BO and cigarettes was the first thing to hit my senses. The place was dark and flashing all the colors of the rainbow to whatever upbeat music the DJ had on. It was a slow-beat, steamy type of song.

"Tilly?"

"Yes?" she replied. There was guilt in her tone. *I knew it.* She had done something to it, the stinker.

"What was in that tea?"

"Chamomile... " she answered eventually.

"And?"

"And... something to help with your nerves."

"What was in the tea, woman?" I demanded.

"Weed." *What?*

"When will *it* go away?" My heart raced a second before lulling again. *Will I go to prison? What if I get kicked out of school if they find out I'm on drugs?*

"It's been a while now. It should start fading soon... if it hasn't already. I'm sorry,"

"Well, shit."

"Are you mad?"

"No," I replied truthfully. Because it was true. I wasn't mad. *Actually, I should probably thank her.* It was the calmest my mind had been since my nightmares had started.

But she was right—the stuff in my system was wearing thin because when I actually paid attention to where we were, my stomach flipped into a knot at the erotic visual. Looking straight at me was a pair of perfectly designed, artificial breasts, planted snug under the skin of a skinny blonde girl.

Wait? Why is she naked?

"Wait. Is this... " I wailed, taking way too long to put together that we were in a strip club. *Her* strip club. "Oh my gosh, Tilly. You brought me to your place of work?!" I quivered, some of my nerves finding their way through my docile veins.

A stripper is standing in front of me. And I'm on weed. I have whoopi drugs in my blood and *I'm in a naughty club.*

Ha. Funny.

I craned my neck around to see another, and another, and

another. All naked. Of course, that was in Tilly's bag of tricks all along.

"If I told you where we were going, you'd have never come out!" she snickered, offering me a playful smile. "Plus, we get free drinks! Come on."

"You drugged me to come out?" I asked, following her further into the club, not entirely focusing on anything other than her.

"No, but I guess that worked too. I only gave you the tea because you were so rattled up. Everything stresses you out lately, and I hate seeing you that way. I just wanted to help you. I worry about you, Esme. I'm sorry. I also didn't think it would hit you this hard. But look, on the plus side, you look absolutely banging."

She had a fair point. It *did* help me. As much as I didn't want to be out in public with so much skin showing—*or at all for that matter*—I needed to suck it up. After all, Tilly had gone to so much effort for me. And I really did look quite outstanding. It *was* my twenty-first birthday, after all, and I really needed a night off. *Forget about the stalker and the nightmares. Forget about college. Forget about work. Just enjoy the night. Be different. Do something different.*

For once in your life, just be normal and have fun.

"It's okay. Let's just... enjoy the night?" I smiled. and then Tilly yanked me, leading me through the rest of the club.

"Oh, you will. I promise." She giggled. Eyes immediately locked onto us around the room. The place was packed. My cheeks flushed, and I almost stumbled. *Oh my gosh. Two left feet. Focus.*

I gulped down the reality of what was happening. I was on drugs that made me think and act a little slower, and I was having a case of *forget me feet*. I followed Tilly's footfalls one by one, paying close attention to the way she walked.

I had already nearly fallen to my feet getting out of the taxi just a moment earlier. If I wanted any chance of getting that kiss and ticking that off the bucket list, I was going to have to learn how to walk the walk and talk the talk. *Okay, Esme. You've got this.*

Left, right, left, flick the hair, right, left. I could see a bar on the other side of the last of the crowd. We pushed through them and my hand parted from hers. I felt something firm shift under my feet, across my path, and I tripped right over it.

Crap.

Thud.

Hello, darkness...

The beats and thumps of music faded into nothing. Darkness enveloped me. Tilly looking down at me was the last thing I saw.

Wow, this dream is nice for a change. I was blessed with a handsome, fairytale man leaning over me to give me a fairytale kiss to bring me back to consciousness like sleeping beauty. He had beautiful blond hair, blue eyes, a tailored suit with a cutting-edge razor blade jaw-line, perfect white teeth, muscles, and the voice of an angel. He was perfect. Mr. Perfect.

Mr. Fairytale.

Soft, lulling voices bounced through the air, and I could feel myself drifting in and out of consciousness. I fluttered my lashes, seeing a blurry face or two hovering over me—I couldn't tell. *Why am I seeing two of everything?* I blinked again, noting that whoever was above me wasn't Tilly, because their features were masculine and broad. *Where the hell is she?*

I flinched, startled by the change of scenery. The man's scent tore through my nose like an aphrodisiac; fruity hints of spices, and aromatics with an earthy, low tone... and whiskey. He smelled rich, powerful, and sexy, pulling me entirely from my drift, seeing very clearly the exact fairytale man I had envisioned in my head a mere second before, right there in front of my very own eyes.

Mindlessly, my lips parted, letting out a laugh of disbelief before they closed again. *Yep, I have definitely lost my mind. I must have hit my head pretty hard to conjure someone like him.*

"Miss? Miss?" his sweet voice sang in my ears as I came to once more. *No, you're for sure dreaming.* But I wasn't. He was still there. Very real. Not a fairytale.

I blinked my eyes, not quite believing what I was seeing. Men like him didn't *actually* exist. They were just magazine models that had been artificially generated. The man smirked, sending the butterflies in my stomach into a chaotic spiral.

"Get her some water," he called out—I think to Tilly, but I couldn't be certain. "You hit your head pretty hard there. Lucky you didn't do too much damage." His thumb brushed at the tender spot on my forehead where I'd collided with whatever it was I hit. *What did I trip over?* There was nothing on the ground. I knew I had two left feet, but I also knew I didn't stumble on thin air.

"Wait, you're real?" I muttered under my breath. He laughed, slicking his immaculate blond hair back through his fingers. I was used to seeing people *in* my dreams, but I wasn't used to them coming *from* my dreams. My cheeks burned crimson, and I mindlessly bit my lip. *He is beyond gorgeous.*

"Contrary to your belief, yes, I am."

Tilly ran to my side, passing a bottle of water to Mr. Fairytale. He cupped the back of my neck with one hand, holding it in a way that made the painful thumps throb a little less. *Damn my brain-to-body malfunction. How embarrassing.* He held the water to my lips, and the cool liquid melted the heat racing through my veins.

"Are you alright?" he murmured.

I took a moment to part from his intense blue-eyed gaze, noticing the crowd that had circled me. I was in a heap on the floor with a lovely bump on my head—evidence of colliding with the bar beside me. The music had completely stopped. *For me?* Tilly squatted at my side, perching her soft hand on my thigh.

"Do you want me to call an ambulance, Esme?" *An ambulance? Did I lose a limb?* I shook my head slightly.

"I'm oka—"

"She's fine. I've got it covered. A bit of water, and she will be right in no time," he cut me off reassuringly, yet with a firm edge to his tone.

"I wasn't talking to you," she snapped.

My mouth dried at her hissy response. All I could think about was her not making a scene. She had a bad temper when someone was rude to her or dismissed her in any way. The man turned back to me after glaring at Tilly, cocking a brow and smiling eagerly.

"Are you ready to stand, gorgeous?"

Gorgeous? He thinks I'm gorgeous? Does that mean I could be in with my shot? My first kiss. I giggled. At what, I didn't know. The drugs, probably.

The music started to play again and the crowd went back to what they were doing, the girls on the poles continuing their routines. I swallowed. A half-hearted nod of my head was all I could manage to offer him. My heart was fluttering out of control. He held his hand out for mine with a soft glint in his doe eyes, a direct stairway to heaven.

I paused for a moment, my eyes darting between them and his perfectly modeled hand, coming to the realization that I had never touched a man before. I took his hand with reticence, and he pulled me off the floor as if I were no heavier than a feather. Last time I checked, I was a solid 220lbs.

It shouldn't be that *easy to just pluck me up off the floor without so much as creasing a shirt or messing up his perfectly slicked-back hair.* Seeing Mr. Fairytale from the ground was impressive, I'd admit that. But from a standing position? *Sheesh.*

There was only one way to describe him.

Holy-ever-loving-shit. Mr. Fairytale.

CHAPTER THREE

TEQUILA IS A BAD IDEA. DON'T DO TEQUILA

S hit, he's so hot. Shit, I really need to stop swearing. However, that wasn't the right word for *this* specimen. I stood, swaying as I took him in.

"Easy, easy," he coaxed. There was a lot to drink from that tall glass of water—all six feet of him, maybe six one. He was dressed elegantly, too dressy for a strip club.

As if falling flat on my face wasn't bad enough, I hadn't realized that my facial expression while looking at him was that of a drooling dog when you're holding out a treat for them, just out of arm's reach... frothing at the mouth. He returned the gaze upon me *hungrily*, and I could feel my palms getting clammy.

His tongue ran across his bottom lip before giving it a small bite on purpose. He cocked a brow again, taking a step closer to me before brushing the loose hair across my face behind my ear, examining the bump on my forehead. An involuntary, breathy noise fell from my lips. *Oh, heck, what is happening to me?* He smirked slightly, and I lost myself in his eyes.

He was a business-type man, wearing a faded, dark blue

tailored suit, taut across his arms. His neck was thick, masculine, and struggling against the seams of his button-up collared shirt. I started seeing two of everything again and began to sway more. I couldn't tell if it was from the fall, the marijuana, or the fact that a delicious human being was making me light-headed. Very light-headed.

"Here, come, sit down." He grabbed my hand and took me to one of the empty seats near the bar in front of a pole. I craned my neck for a dancer, but there wasn't one nearby. He sat me down, like a true gentleman would, and took a seat in front of me across a small drinks table. He glared up through his lashes and frowned as Tilly pulled a chair next to me and sat down, interrupting our intense gaze with her *I'm-going-to-eat-him-for-lunch* look. She brushed her hand on my thigh for comfort and went to say something, but he cut her off.

"How are you feeling now? Can I get you anything?" He flicked a brow in an inviting way, and his tone was like a lure. *Is he hypnotizing or what?*

"I'm... I-I don't... think so?" I muttered nervously, nibbling at my lip under his devouring stare. I wasn't sure if he meant a drink, a night away with him, or his hand in marriage.

"Hmm. You're certain?" he asked, and his eyes widened as they darted behind me, trailing from side to side... like he was following someone.

A flash of a malicious smile drew across his lips, but it was gone as fast as it appeared. Something felt off, but I couldn't quite put my finger on it. Unease tickled my veins. *Am I overthinking again?* I had as much social awareness as a log, so I couldn't be certain what to feel. It was like my instincts were telling me to stop talking to a strange man. His tone was... *odd...* and what if every man was the shadow man?

But on the other hand, my body was drawn to him in a way I couldn't explain. There was a need, a pull that I wanted to learn more about. And I really did want my first kiss. I'd never get another chance with a man like him, not unless Tilly made me look like... *that* every day. I plucked up the courage to respond.

"Well, I-I'd like a... a—" I stuttered, stopping my sentence as his jaw clenched. *I wanted to ask for a drink, but why is he clearing his throat and standing?*

He smoothed his suit jacket down before leaning into me, hovering over my ear. I squirmed and drew in a breath. His scent burned my nose, and I saw stars.

"Wait here," he whispered. *Wait? Don't leave.* "I'll be back for you later, princess," he finished with a wink. And just like that, whatever unease I had in my veins was gone.

Princess.

"O... kay."

He turned to face Tilly, and his eyes narrowed.

"Look after my lady properly this time, will you?" he toyed with her before storming off through the crowd and heading toward the direction where he was looking earlier—the entry to the club—where there was a big, buff, tattooed guy. Only half the big man's body stood in between the slit of the curtain. The security guard beside him was not allowing his entry.

My lady?

My... lady.

The breeze from Mr. Fairytale's departure caused me to mindlessly breathe in his scent. I inhaled him so hard that I felt lightheaded *again*. And something tingled between my legs. A little too intense. *What? Why did he smell so good? Am I in love now?*

I'd barely spoken five words to the man, and I was already

catching feelings. He seemed smart, safe, and secure. Like a man. A real man. I giggled when I noticed Tilly. Given her facial expression, she must have had the same reaction to his scent as I did.

"Damn," she uttered in disbelief, bumping her elbow into my side. We both shifted in our seats to get a better view of the men.

"Damn," I mimicked before we giggled again.

Tilly and I swallowed in unison as the big man pinned his eyes on me, cocked both brows, and winked as he held the curtain open for Mr. Fairytale. With it open, I could see that there was another male with them. I couldn't see him fully, but from what I could make out, he towered over the two of them and wore a black leather jacket. *Who is even that tall? That's insane.*

Tilly whistled. "Wow. Esme."

"Hmm?" I asked absently, still focused on the curtain they had departed through.

"What the *fuck* just happened? You need to fall over more often if it gets you *that* kind of attention. Girl, he was eye-fuckin' the shit out of you," she blurted. Normally, I would scold her profanity with a comment like that, but at that moment, I couldn't give two toots.

"I... have no idea," I answered with a smile after a moment of silence. Tilly and I both sat like wax statues, completely dazed by the man, his smell, his voice. Just... *him.* So much so that we both ended up in hysterics again after realizing that we were both in the same predicament. *Bamboozled. Twitterpated. Flabbergasted.*

In love?

I finally caught a breath between laughs, and a short, colorfully dressed bartender hailed Tilly's attention and approached us. He was carrying a full bottle of vodka in his hand

and three shot glasses in the other. Tilly moved out of her seat and began bouncing up and down with glee, her infectious smile glowing once more. I could tell she and the man were quite fond of each other.

"Jesse!" she called out affectionately. They hugged and he sat on the seat opposite me, where dreamboat had sat earlier, and poured some vodka into one of the long, skinny shot glasses before sliding it across the table toward Tilly. She returned to her seat next to me and Jesse's bright green eyes—dazzling with mascara, eyeliner and glitter—met my emerald green ones.

"You must be Esme?" he asked as he poured another shot before dropping its contents into his mouth like water. Tilly drank hers in unison, shaking her head as it went down her throat before turning to me, prompting my answer.

"Uh, hi. Yes. Umm, Hello. I'm Esme," I stuttered my reply awkwardly. *Clearly, I'm still in Fairytale Land.*

"Jesse, Esme. Esme, Jesse," Tilly acquainted us as she wiggled her fingers for more of the liquor and continued. "You'll have to excuse her. She's a little *flustered.*" She waved her head toward me.

"Yes, I saw your... very unglamorous introduction to my bar. You're lucky you didn't dent it. That's a nice bump on your head, by the way," Jesse chuckled mockingly. *His bar?*

"I didn't mean from her calamity," Tilly giggled. "She just met her new man. We've already started planning the wedding."

"I-He... He's not—" I stuttered, the skin on my face burning like the sun. *When is too early to send out wedding invitations?* I shuddered at my stupid brain. "Wait. *Your* bar? This is your club?" I gasped. Jesse was Tilly's boss. Even more embarrassing.

"Yeah," he replied with a grin. My mind wandered into the

abyss again before realizing that I should probably have something for my onset headache.

"Oh. Nice. Sorry to ask, but do you have some Tylenol? I really think it will do the trick for the head."

"Oh, honey," Jesse laughed, somehow humored by my request. "No. Have one of *these* instead." His smile was impertinent as he poured the vodka into the third shot glass and slammed it before me.

"Yes, drink it. You need to quench your thirst," Tilly added playfully. A moment passed and I still hadn't drunk what was in the glass. I wasn't sure if alcohol was the solution to my... *situation*. Nonetheless, it was my birthday. I sure as heck wasn't going to let my two left feet ruin it for me. I raised my glass to my lips and—

"So, twenty-one, hey?" Jesse asked.

I didn't get the chance to drink my drink, or even have the thought to. Tilly had it down her throat before I could blink an eye, wearing a satisfied grin on her glossy lips. Jesse fixated a vexing frown at her, then laughed.

"That wasn't yours, you cheeky bitch. I'll be back. I think we need something better than this." Jesse tapped the bottle and ushered off back to the bar.

"Okay," Tilly called out to him as he left and then faced me with a creased brow, scanning my face. "Are you sure you're okay? I don't *want* to go home, but... "

"Tilly, I'm totally fine." I smiled and nodded, choosing to look at my hands on the table. I mean, it was partially a lie. I *did* have a headache, and I *did* need some kind of relief, but the idea of *him* coming back to see me again was enough of a distraction.

I didn't want to go home. Granted, if I hadn't met him, I would have. But suddenly, I had a reason to stay. He said he would come back for me. *And he called me his lady... and princess, like I was a damsel in distress.* That was enough to send me off into dreamland, and the butterflies in my stomach spiraled—and the ones in my... panties. I shrugged my shoulders.

"Besides, I want to enjoy my night out. You've gone to such effort to make me look this way. I'd hate to ruin it now."

"That's my girl. I'll drink to that." Tilly clapped her hands together excitedly as Jesse returned with a bottle of tequila, a container of sliced limes, and a shaker of salt.

"Ahh, yes. Show me," he gestured to my outfit before pressing on. "I didn't get to see all of you before your face made love with my floor."

I frowned. Tilly giggled with glee and pulled me off my seat. I winced from the sudden shock of going from sitting to standing, but managed. She gestured to all of me, showing off her styling and makeup craftsmanship proudly for Jesse to admire.

My stomach churned from the unfamiliar sensation of eyes on me. I was not accustomed to being admired. Being the center of attention made my skin crawl. Jesse nodded in approval and kept his hand over his chin as her hand glided through my long, bouncy, curled hair she had styled, occasionally humming and smiling as they talked about the brands of hair products and other makeup stuff I had no knowledge of.

I didn't know why, but all I could focus on was each of her fingertips sliding through my hair. I arched and squirmed from the sensation as they ran down to my butt cheek, repeating the process several times. My brain tingled, and a little involuntary noise escaped my mouth again. *Jesus, pull yourself together,*

Esme. Thankfully, the music was so loud, no one could have heard it. *Why am I acting like this?*

"Well done, Tilly. She's fire as fuck. As always, you do amazing!" Jesse whistled and applauded. "You'll be on the big screens soon, you'll see... if I allow it, that is." He creased his brow in disapproval. She had a degree in beauty therapy and cosmetology—even applied for some pretty big time places, but she hadn't heard from a single one of them. Even if she did, I didn't think she would ever leave home. *Or this place.* The nightlife was her thing, as was sex—and money.

"Yep. I know. And it got her the attention she needed to catch a man. *And* he's coming back later. So I must have done something right. I also polished it off with water-resistant setting powder, too, so the sweat won't rub it off when she... and he... if you catch my drift." She chuckled and then performed some kind of victory dance.

She spoke as though I wasn't there. Like I couldn't hear her silently screaming to the rooftops that I was still a virgin. My belly churned and then warmed at the idea of maybe experiencing more than my first kiss.

"Mhmm. Yes, I get it. Uh huh." Jesse nodded, pouring three shot glasses of tequila and pulling a few slices of lime out of the container. "It's only fair that you go first. It's your birthday." He slid one of the shot glasses toward me with a cocked brow and a smug smirk before grabbing the salt shaker plonked it where my hand leaned on the table.

"But—" I objected.

"But? No buts here. Be fucked if I'm letting you out of my club sober, anyway, regardless of how many times you hit that pretty head of yours. Come on, Virgin Mary, let's go," he wailed, his hands moving. "Up, up,up."

"Let's make some memories and then forget them all," Tilly demanded with a laugh. *Alright, alright. I get it, sheesh. Drink till I'm drunk. That probably won't be hard. One will probably do the job, anyway, since I've never had a drink before tonight.*

I pinched by brows, wracking my brain at the three objects before me: tequila, salt and a cut quarter of a green lime. *Am I supposed to eat a lime? Yuck.*

"How do I-I haven't—What do I do?" I stammered.

"Here." Tilly grabbed my hand and pulled it to her lips. "I'll show you." She slid her tongue along the top before sprinkling some of the salt over the wet area.

I gulped. The sensation of her tongue along my skin left me in a state of freeze, and the tingling between my thighs started to surface again. I squirmed in my seat, taking a deep breath to refocus. The salt was stuck to my skin. Then she passed me a lime.

"Lick the salt, down the tequila, suck on the lime. It's easy. Got it, babes?" *Okay, you got this.* Her tone was enough encouragement. *One, two... three.* Fueled by adrenaline and her energy, I went for it.

The salt tormented my tongue, and then the burn of tequila slid down my throat. *Don't throw up, don't throw up.* I shuddered. It felt like I had swallowed a barbed wire. The alcohol's viscous temperature scalded the sides of my esophagus, then my stomach.

And just when I thought it was over, I was hit in the mouth with the sour hit of lime. *What the heck?! Whoever thought of this was in need of a narcotic. People do this? For fun—oh, it makes sense now.* The hit was almost immediate. The warmth in my belly was a *buzz*. One that I welcomed. It was nice. I wanted more.

CHAPTER FOUR

FAIRYTALE KISSES ARE BETTER THAN TEQUILA

"Happy birthday to you, baby girl," Tilly toasted, repeating the same method I had with the drink. *Salt, tequila, lime. Ha, suck on that.* To my surprise, her expression was just as twisted as mine when she got to the lime. I'd thought she would be used to it, given she was in the club five nights a week.

"Not too nice, was it?" I laughed, scrunching my face in sympathy.

"Nope! But fuck it. We're young. We're hot as fuck. We are here to celebrate *you!* Keep them comin', Jesse. We're not done until we fall... uhh... until we fall twice." Tilly toasted, and we clinked glasses. *She has been waiting so long for this moment.*

She sprinkled another row of the salt on our hands. By the fifth round, the salt, tequila, and lime all started to taste like nothing, making it easier to swallow. I shuddered involuntarily, unable to ignore the thought of something feeling *different.* I had a horrible feeling brewing in the pit of my stomach, building and building.

I didn't want or need that. *Not now.* I scoffed. I was finally enjoying myself, but it was an all too familiar feeling, like someone was watching me. *Stop this.* We were in a club with a lot of people around. I looked around, but no one out of the ordinary was lurking or even looking in our direction. And no sign of Mr. Fairytale.

Jesse was tapping away on his phone, scrolling senselessly, and Tilly was watching one of the girls' performances, cheering her on. Everyone else in the place was doing the same. *You're being silly, Esme. Enough.*

Up until then, I hadn't actually had the chance to look at the place. I craned my neck around, seeing some of the dancers walking around, others on their poles. They were nice to look at, but not as beautiful as Tilly. *She deserves more than this place.* I wasn't certain, but I thought that one had gang tattoos—on her face. *No wonder Tilly makes a killing here.*

The more I looked at the place, the more I felt all kinds of wrong.

Dirty.

Misplaced.

I cleared my throat, apprehension becoming more prominent as the feeling of being watched didn't go away. *Maybe I've had too much to drink too soon.*

"Something's not right," I blurted to Tilly, but she shrugged me off casually.

"That's tequila for you, babes."

I shuddered once more, feeling a chill in the air that blew up my spine. My mouth dried in an instant. *No. This isn't happening. Not tonight. He isn't here. No one is watching you. Just shut up and move on.* I waited, minutes passing as I contemplated my next string of words.

"I think I want to leave." I fidgeted with my hands in angst. I wanted to go home. Mr. Fairytale hadn't come back to see me again, so what was the point of staying?

"Nuh uh. We're not doing this. I'm not letting that little introverted voice in your head pull you out of this one. Come on, babe, this is your twenty-first. What's up?"

Not wanting to bother her with my pathetic little fear of *the shadow man*, I thought of something else to tell her. I didn't want to bring him up—ever. I had a hard enough time trying to keep those thoughts—and him—out of my head. I didn't need her adding to it, and I knew she would just make it worse.

"It's just, there's lots of people looking at me." I grimaced, deciding on a lie that she would believe.

"Yes... " She nodded her head and gestured to all of me—my outfit, my hair, my makeup, my breasts. "You're hot as fuck. That's why." And there it was again, the tingle. The flirty comment making that spot between my thighs ache once more. I swallowed, hard. *Crap. This keeps happening.*

"Tilly, I—"

"Yes. She is," Jesse interrupted, plonking his phone on the table and tuning into our conversation. "Hey, why doesn't she come work here? We could use someone like her. She would make me a killing." Jesse's tone was blunt, like I was an object or something money could buy. I frowned, as did Tilly.

"She isn't like that, Jesse," she snapped, but he ignored her and turned his attention toward me.

"I could make you a decent income," he pressed.

"Thanks, but no thanks." I forced a polite smile, my throat thickening at the thought of someone seeing my naked body.

"Ahh, come on, look at you." *Okay, now I really want to go home.* His reply was vulgar, forceful. Like I was being cornered.

I shivered, feeling another chill up my spine, and then a growl ripped through my ears. Instinctively, I inhaled through my nose. My heartbeat was no longer rhythmic as the smell of pine, blood, moisture, and earthy cologne bombarded my brain. My eyes widened, and pure fear washed over my face.

I darted my head around in a panic, looking for... *him*. My heart was pounding in my chest, but no one masked or dressed up like the Grim Reaper was there—only normal-looking people.

"Who are you looking for?" Jesse drawled, repeating the same action as he scanned his club. I shook my head and swallowed.

"Nothing. I mean, no one. I—" Jesse grabbed my arm, cutting me off as he pulled it further along the table. I yelped from the intrusion.

"Come one. What will it take, huh?"

I shook my head, snatching my hand back as his eyes broke eye contact from me to something—*or someone*—behind me.

"I believe the lady said *no*, Mr. Ventry," a soft, masculine and possessive voice behind me growled at Jesse. I turned and let out a sigh of relief, seeing it was Mr. Fairytale and *not* the man from my nightmares. His nostrils flared as he stared Jesse down, who scooted from his seat to stand.

"Whitlock. What are you doing back in *my* club? Don't you and your brothers have your own club to frolic in?"

"Yes, we do. But we have *business* to attend to."

"My guards already had words with your boy tonight. How did you get in again?" Jesse asked nervously. Mr. Fairytale moved from beside me to sit on the chair in front of me and locked his eyes on mine. My lips parted to let out the breath I had been holding.

"There's not a single door on earth that could stop me from *this* fine diamond." He winked at me, and my cheeks flushed. Tilly nudged my side with her elbow again, and I just about melted under the table like a knob of butter on a hot day.

"As long as your brothers don't come in here and start shit, there won't be any problems. Right?"

"Not unless you forget your place, Jesse. I've kept my brothers at bay *for now*."

"Good. You're the good one. Please make sure that—"

Whitlock snapped a glare at him with a snarl, cutting him off. In an instant, Jesse spun on his feet and quickly disappeared behind the bar. My belly swirled with flutters, diminishing all my worry, and then the dizziness returned once more. *Wow, tequila brain.*

"Hello, princess," he purred. I blushed and started twirling my hair around my fingers. "I had to come back to see you before I go out again. I wanted to make sure you're alright."

I panted and bit my lip, getting lost in his words and eyes—again. *Reply.*

Words, Esme.

He reached out and grabbed my arms with both hands.

"Hello?" He trailed over the tender area at my wrists to break my wandering mind. Acting entirely on drunken buzz mode, I muttered a reply.

"Thank you, Mr. *Fairytale*," I giggled, calling his name and swaying a little. I gasped, realizing what I had said. My eyes flung wide open and he chuckled.

"Mr. Fairytale? Is that my name now?" He turned his brow and glared at the empty glasses beside me. I gulped, and my head fuzzed at the alcohol that swam in my belly. "The fairytale that needs to rescue his damsel in distress."

I didn't reply, merely biting my lip. I knew it would be another brain-to-mouth malfunction if I did.

"Uhh. I'm just going to go... over there," Tilly muttered awkwardly. I'd almost forgotten she was there. She was gone before I had the chance to respond. He watched her walking away before turning his attention back to me.

"You fell pretty hard, princess. You really shouldn't be drinking," he continued, his tone firm. I couldn't tell if he was condescending, or genuinely concerned for my wellbeing. I frowned at him, pulling my wrists from his hands.

"Excuse me, *sir.*" I put emphasis and sass on the 'sir' part. "I can drink how much I like. It's *my* birthday, and *my* head that I hit on the bar, so *butt out.*" I crossed my arms and raised a brow. *I don't know where that came from.* The buzz in my belly was mixing with the butterflies, and it was definitely messing with me and my ability to think, see, and speak straight.

He tilted his neck and chuffed from his nose, a slight grin curling from his mouth before he leaned over the table and hovered inches from my lips. I immediately felt small and froze in my tracks. He trailed his minty, warm breath to my ear. I whimpered and swallowed *twice* to lodge the swell in my throat.

Crap.

"Watch that mouth, missy, or I'll have to kiss that attitude right out of you," he whispered.

My skin flared with goosebumps at his flirty threat. I wasn't totally against the idea. I melted into my seat and my cheeks burned crimson, eliciting a deep chuckle to form at the pit of his chest.

"I-I-I... " I fumbled my words. I could barely keep myself together. His shirt could barely hold itself together, his muscles were that taut against it as he leaned over the table.

"You want me to?" he questioned, his eyes burning into mine for my answer. I fanned my gaze around his features. His neck was thick, veiny and broad, the buttons on the shirt's collar done all the way to the top, straining at the seams. I wondered how he could breathe, it was that tight around his throat.

He rolled his sleeves halfway up his arm, revealing a gold watch. *Could he be any more perfect? Wait, did he change? This shirt is a different color, and he is wearing a vest.* He chuckled, instantly pulling my attention to the fact that I had not yet answered him. *Crap.*

"If you stare any harder, I'm going to take that as a yes." His tone was low and seductive before breathing out a heavy sigh. He reached into his pocket to grab something, and then planted his hand on the table. "Meet me here later, then, when you're ready for it." He moved his hand away, revealing a business card.

"But... " *Yes. No. Yes.* My head ran a million miles an hour. At that point, I would quite possibly have done anything the man asked me without hesitation. He was just so... dreamy. *And persuasive.* But that *thing* in my gut was saying no.

"It wasn't a question," he breathed.

"Why?" I asked timidly, and he smirked.

"Because I want to get to know you more, but not in this dump."

"Me?" My eyes widened. *Why would anyone want anything to do with me? Especially a man like this.*

"Yes, you." His gaze drifted hungrily over my body again.

"Why?" I gulped at the intensity of his hunger, nervously looking down at my hands on my lap. My breath staggered, the tension pulling. It didn't add up. *Is he vision-impaired? I'm not a*

model. I'm not the type of girl men like him want. So why me?
He tutted as if he knew what I was thinking.

"Don't do that."

"Do what?" I bit my lip as I fiddled with my hands.

"Dismiss your beauty. You are beautiful, and you aren't like," he gestured his hand blindly toward the naked girls dancing to their hearts' content without breaking eye contact, "these girls. They are merely pathetic, desperate zirconias. But you?"

He stood, stepping toward me and planting his index finger under my chin. I followed it willingly and got to my feet. Even standing, I felt so small before him, not that he was overly tall. Taller than me, by a foot at least, but he was more muscled dominance than height. My chest suddenly mere inches from his, I forced myself to breathe. *Does he have to look at me like this?*

"*You* are a diamond."

A diamond? Oh, good heavens. My lips parted, eliciting a shattered breath, and I swallowed in an attempt to push down the nervous lump in my throat and speak something more than a singular word.

"But... you don't know me."

"I'm trying to," he breathed, inching closer, teasing my body for more, somehow without touching. "I like diamonds, Esme... I know one when I see one. You are *the* diamond. And I'm the gemologist."

Holy shit.

Wait... how does he know my name?

"How did you—" I looked down, and he curled his finger a little firmer under my chin, cutting me off and correcting my contact back to his.

"And I know that *this* diamond doesn't belong here." His

seductive note made me lose my breath again. *I'm going to end up a puddle if he does that any longer.* Acting entirely on impulse, I asked him a question.

"Where do I belong?"

He held the pause for a moment, swapping his gaze between one eye and the other, then my lips, and back to my eyes again.

"With me." His tone weakened me, and before I knew it, his minty-flavored lips were all over mine. His fingers shifted from my chin and curled behind the nape of my neck, pulling me up onto my toes and my chest into his.

Everything ached and throbbed, my core lightening and warming as I fell heavily into him. He took my weight as I became nothing more than goo beneath him as he devoured me with his tongue.

Fuck.

CHAPTER FIVE

THE GEMOLOGIST

"How long are you going to stare at that damn thing before you finally give in?" Tilly glared at me as I thoughtlessly flipped the little black and gold plated business card Mr. Fairytale had given me before that kiss... before he left.

The card didn't have a name or a phone number, just an address. Every bone in my body was telling me that it was a bad idea, but, his kiss, his lips... I wanted *more*. My first kiss, and I didn't even know his name. All I knew was what Jesse mentioned: Whitlock. *I really need to remember to communicate better.*

"You're going to go and see him, right?"

"Huh?" I asked absently. I did hear her, but the rush of *his* lips on mine was putting me through a daze I couldn't break from. I didn't have any capacity to have any other thoughts. I wanted to see him again. *No—I* will *see him again.* She tutted.

"Esme, you *have* to see him again." Tilly laughed as she fluttered her eyelashes with mascara in front of the mirror of the club's bathroom, freshening herself for whatever reason. She was already stunning. "If you saw what I saw when he was kissing you... *Fuck*. I don't even have words to explain that, and I've kissed my fair share of lips."

I glanced in the reflection, seeing that my makeup was still perfection, despite the bump on my head. Thankfully, the headache was no longer present. Turned out, tequila had more remedies than I anticipated.

"I do?"

"You do!" she repeated with a wink. The dirty thoughts of what Tilly did in her room raced through my brain without warning, adding to my already distracted mind. *Sex*. Hot, sweaty, sex. I mean, I'd heard about it and seen it in movies. I knew it was something I *shouldn't* desire. I was to preserve myself for marriage. That's what was expected of me.

What the *Man Upstairs* required. It would be a sin. *I always follow the rules. I always follow orders.* But I didn't think I'd have the willpower to follow them this time. Not with him. No. His lips on mine were... heaven.

Granted, I had just as much regret brewing in the pit of my stomach, but the desire overpowered it. That undeniable itch... something deep within telling me I *needed* more of, but knowing that I *shouldn't*.

That's your moral compass, Esme.

Huh. Was that what that was?

His words circled my mind over and over again.

"With me."

"You are the diamond."

"With me."

The more I repeated them, the more flushed my skin got, the hotter my temperature rose, and the more the delicate area between my thighs ached. The undeniable pulse at my womanhood. Could it be? Could I have found my Mr. Right? *Don't be stupid. You don't even know his name.*

"Yes, I do. I mean, no... but... yes." I could barely mumble the words to Tilly, confused about what answer I needed to choose. My head was spinning with confusion, and it wasn't from the lump on my head. *He* was the lump on my head.

"Oh, for Christ's sake. Give me that." Tilly snatched the card from my hands, pulling me from my train of thought.

"Hey!" I hissed, trying to grab it back. She held it high above her head with her long arms, looking at me with her lips scrunched to the side and both brows lifted.

"Mmhmm. We're going, and that's final. But first, I'm putting some of this on you." She pulled out a lipstick tube. "Next time he kisses those lips, he's going to be covered in your cherry stain." The smell of cherry ran through my nose as she slid a red-tinted shade of lipstick along my lips.

"Now do this." Tilly swished her lips together, and I creased my brow trying to mimic her action, rubbing the red across both lips awkwardly.

"Wow," I gasped, looking at my reflection again. *Sorcery.*

"Amazing how the color of your lips can change your entire look, eh?" She smiled and drew her tongue across her top teeth.

"Tilly, I... this is too much."

She tutted. "Girl, shut up. No, it ain't. It suits you. Plus, I want to see you two kiss again. I want to see his lips stained, so he will never forget you and those voluptuous lips."

Granted, so did I. I wanted that more than I cared to admit. He had left the club with the same tattooed guy from earlier, and we had been in the bathroom since. Stewing in my thoughts.

Red light.

Green light.

Stay.

Go.

Bad.

Good.

Over and over.

Jesse seemed to have some kind of acquaintance with him, as he'd called him Whitlock and mentioned that he had brothers causing trouble. The thought unsettled my stomach. *Maybe my moral compass is right? Maybe he* is *trouble?*

Stupid brain, always looking for problems that are not there.

I lulled the thought, pulling my attention to Tilly again, who was glaring at me with her *you're-off-with-the-fairies-again* look.

"Really?" I muttered, tugging at the inside of my bottom lip with my teeth. She nudged my side again.

"Yes. I knew you would get your first kiss tonight. Look at you. Hell, even I'd kiss you. It was HOT! But far out, girl, I wasn't expecting *that*."

"Neither was I."

"Maybe he will take you home tonight," she toyed.

"Tilly!" I hissed, tsking at her sinful words. *I would never.* Though just talking about it made the spot between my thighs purr like a cat again. It was inappropriate.

"Did you shave?" she asked with a grin.

"What?" My eyes widened.

"Oh, dear," she snickered.

"What, Tilly?" My anxiety flared again. *Was I meant to?*

"You're hopeless. Let's hope he likes hair."

"Tilly! I'm not having sex with a man I just met." *I don't think so, anyway.* "I mean, maybe? I don't know. I have a lot going through my head right now."

I truly couldn't tell if that was a truthful statement or not. For a moment, I wanted nothing more than to make love to him—with him—but I pushed the thought aside. She raised a brow and her mouth parted into an O.

"Did you just say *maybe*? Who is this new Esme? Fuck me, girl, you should absolutely hit your head more often. I think your other *womanly* senses came in when you hit that bar." Tilly laughed, amused at her mockery.

Instead of scolding her for her language, I laughed with her. Because she was right. Something in me was different—the alcohol maybe, or the fact that I had indeed hit my head hard enough to actually wake up and realize that I was a woman, ready to explore.

"I guess... better late than never, right?" I asked, stroking my thumb over the embossed card, considering that I might actually lay with that man. My skin tingled at the thought, activating that little twitch in my ladyhood again. *Is that thing ever going to stop bugging me for attention?*

"Do you have a—"

"Nope! Zip it!" I laughed, shoving her away from reaching for a condom in her bag. "Shoosh your mouth, woman. Be gone with this nonsense." *I said I'd kiss a man tonight. Let's not get too far ahead of ourselves, okay?*

"Okay, okay. I'll just put it in your bag when you're not looking anyway," she teased.

"I know you will. Now, I've had enough of staring at this thing. I'm thirsty—for water! Don't go getting any ideas."

"Roger that... *princess*," Tilly teased, looping her elbow around mine.

Jesse was waiting for us at the bar with a smile. He hadn't charged us once for our drinks. *Staff perks, I guess.* I decided on an icy glass of water for all of five minutes, before eventually caving for something a little... stronger. Not that either of us needed anymore booze to wash out our brains. But I wanted something to take the edge off.

I sat on one of the stools and listened to Jesse and Tilly talking about makeup, work, sex, money, the latest goss, and whatever else they could utter from their lips between sipping on cocktails. I was tiring by the minute as I waited for an opportunity to ask him about my one and only admirer. I didn't know his name, age, or... well, anything. Mysterious Mr. Fairytale.

Finally, Tilly stopped talking to him and asked me a question —something to do with butterflies hanging around our window. I brushed her off with a quick reply. I wasn't interested right that very moment, keeping my full attention on Jesse.

"Can I ask you a question?" I asked.

"Yeah?"

"Earlier, you called that guy by his last name—Whitlock? Do you know him?"

"Oh, yeah!" Tilly barged in, her face screaming to spit out the latest news on Mr. Fairytale. "The guy she kissed! How did I even forget that? Shit, I talk too much. Oh, Jesse. Wow, you should have seen it. Her first kiss!" Tilly finished, fanning herself.

"Hmm. What no way? You kissed him? *Him?*" he asked with a concerned tone.

"Yes," I admitted, abashed. *Why do I feel ashamed for admitting that?*

"Jesus. And you let her?" Jesse rolled his eyes like I had kissed someone I shouldn't have. I hesitated before pressing.

"Who is he?"

"Oh, you know his uncle owns PU$$, right?" Jesse ignored my question, speaking directly to Tilly. Her face lit up like he'd just told her she won a million dollars.

"PU$$? *The* PU$$?" Tilly repeated in disbelief.

"Yep." He popped the *p* and Tilly stood in a flurry, clapping her hands with glee.

"Oh my god! I didn't think—Okay, let's go. Now! I've been dying to go there! But it's by VIP entry only."

"You mean that?" Jesse pointed to the blank business card in my hand. "And bitch, please. You wouldn't last five minutes in there," he playfully scolded, waving her off.

"Wait? This is the VIP entry?" she asked as she snatched the card from my hand, holding it up to his face. "Oh, and umm, excuse me? What makes you so sure?"

"The one and only. How did you get that? Hold on, did he give it to you?" he asked me.

"Yeah."

"Wow. You must be something special. Those cards *never* get given out," Jesse said directly to me before pressing back to Tilly. "And because you're just as slutty as I am. When I say the men and women in there are hotter than the fucking sun, your sweet ass would be on one of those sons of a bitches' dick in thirty seconds flat."

"Hey, I like money... and cock...and pussy too. What can I say? I'm a simple woman." Tilly flicked her hair as if her vagina was a trophy and she was proud of it.

"Tilly!" I scowled.

Uhh, hello? What about my question?

"Don't forget I *own* your ass. I've seen you shake that thing around here. They'll be begging for you to work for them, and I can't pay you any more. And it won't be in their *club*, either,"

Jesse went on, a jealous edge to his voice. "Rich motherfuckers. So don't go getting any ideas, ditching me and working for those fancy bitches."

"I'd never leave you," Tilly leaned over the bar and grabbed Jesse's shirt, yanking him toward her. "You're stuck with me until you rot in the ground as an old dirty man, got it?"

I scoffed. They'd gotten off-topic.

"Who's *they*? Is there another club? Jesse, is he trouble?"

"The Whitlock brothers... And for you? Yes," Jesse retorted. "Anyone would melt you like butter! Look at you. You can barely hold it together after one bloody kiss."

My eyes widened and I bit my lip. *I knew it. That's it, I'm going home.*

"But Caine's the good one. Just stay away from the others, and you'll be fine. Especially the tall one."

"Caine?" I tilted my head, confused, and a self-satisfied smirk turned his lips.

"You just had your first kiss with a guy and didn't even know his name?" He laughed and clapped his hands, rubbing them together. "You're a little flirt in disguise, aren't you? Pity you don't want to work here. You'd fit right in. Why are you asking?"

I shrugged nervously. "I was just wondering. You mentioned earlier about his brothers being trouble, that's all."

"Well, yes, *they* are trouble. Drugs, money, cars, women. The sex parties they have. Or so I've heard. And the charity balls. They are rolling in mullah and women. Apparently, they own a mansion. I don't know for sure. But I do know that with them, there comes a lot of fucking drama. I pay them a lot of money to keep their noses out of my club and stop them from taking my girls. They don't come in here anymore... until tonight, anyway.

As long as you don't go getting that little sniffer nose of yours in any of their business, you'll be fine."

"Oh," was all I could blurt out. My head was spinning with information I could have gone without knowing. *Why did I have to look for a reason to flee? This is why I don't talk to guys. I suck at it.* But Caine didn't seem anything like Jesse explained. And I so desperately want to see him again. Touch him. Smell him. Have se—

"Why are you still sitting here? Off you go."

"Come on, Esme. Please. I've been dying to go there."

They both stared me down, waiting for my answer. *Why do I have to be so easy to coax?*

"Do you know what? Fuck it." I laughed, throwing my hands over my face for swearing. I knew I had a moral compass somewhere, but at that moment, it was nowhere to be found.

I was a new Esme. A *drunk* Esme. And I liked it.

CHAPTER SIX

I'M HALLUCINATING AGAIN

"**D**o we look the part? I feel like we're not dressed good enough," I whispered to Tilly, not wanting to draw attention to ourselves while standing in line at PU$$. We looked very *non* VIP.

The women waiting to get into the club were dressed to the nines. I'd thought I was too, but compared to them, I was chopped liver. They boasted labeled frocks, permed hair, and shoes that cost more than our apartment's rent. Heck, probably the whole complex—*annually*. The men donned tight tailored suits with pointed leather shoes, razor-sharp jaw lines, slicked-back hair, and buff arms.

Like Caine.

"Esme, he's invited you here for a reason. He was well aware of your... dress code.," she tittered, looking directly at my breasts.

"Oh, God," I uttered. *What have I come to? Run. Run away now. This is too much.*

No. Be quiet. I'm going to enjoy myself.

Maybe.

I fanned my face to try and cool my flushed cheeks, which didn't do a thing. The warmth of the late spring air shifted through the busy streets of Manhattan, making me sweat. Tilly had said that she put a special setting spray over my makeup to help with the moisture, which I was grateful for in the condition I was in; curves, makeup, styled hair, and heat did not pair well.

How long does makeup last anyway? It had taken us well over an hour in the cab to get to Jesse's from home, then add the time we were there—*and now here*—for however long that would be. PuS$ was only a brief walk from Jesse's club, but even so, it was safe to say I was in dire need of a drink and a pat down.

I mindlessly started to wander off, thinking about the juicy kiss with Caine—Mr. Fairytale—letting it penetrate my head again.

Penetrate.

What a delicious word.

"You'll be fine. Do you have the card?" Tilly asked. I opened my small clutch, pulling out the card as we stepped another inch forward and waved it.

"Yep."

"Good. We need that to get in."

As we waited, I inhaled deeply, studying the smells that surrounded me—partially because I was trying to see if I could locate Caine's delicious cologne—but the only things I could smell were cigarette smoke and the endless fumes of the city.

"Miss?" an unfamiliar male voice called, startling me. "Miss?" he repeated. I turned around to see a tall man beside me who I assumed was a security guard. *Why has he come this far down?* Tilly and I were at the back of the line.

"Y... yes?" I stuttered. *What did I do? It's the dress code, isn't it? I knew it.*

Tilly peered around me, grinning at him. I knew that grin. She had those *sexy eyes*—the ones she had on when she flirted. The guard stood intimidatingly tall above us, his muscles pushing at the seams of his shirt, holding his clipboard with authority. *What is it with these men and their tight shirts? Did they not know there's a size up?*

He gestured with an arm open, pointing toward the entrance of the club.

"Please." His tone was impatient, as though his job was so hard. *Please what? Cut in line? I haven't even shown my card.* With a cocked brow and a sideways glance, he spoke with his face first—rudely. "*This way*, ladies," he demanded, almost condescending, with no room for objection. Tilly scoffed.

"Us?" I asked with pinched brows. There was a long line. *We couldn't possibly cut through?*

"Yes, both of you. Please."

"Wow," Tilly and I said the word in unison as we walked through the grand double doors. No ID needed, and no VIP card shown. The club was full and buzzing. I scanned over the people to find Mr. Fairytale, but he was not to be found, so we kept moving as the guard pushed us forward.

The club had a seductive darkness with subtle red luminance, keeping the lights low and giving a sense of mystery. Very different to Jesse's strip club. The smells of sweet, feminine perfume, alcohol, and unfamiliar notes stimulated my nose.

The place was covered with leather-padded walls and mirrors, and the entire ceiling was one gigantic mirror overlooking the tops of the women—*stunning women*—dancing on the poles. The furniture was clean, rich mahogany with leather and suede coverings, and the tables were all lit with a candle or two. You could lick the table and not a single germ would be transferred.

No wonder the place was booming. It was stunning.

The girls were not of the shy type; their perky, fake breasts were on display like they were in a museum, dollar bills bunched in whatever crevice of their bodies they could find. The women were outstanding, and I could see why Jesse was fretting that Tilly would leave his dump for the place. If I were a stripper, I would. At least PU$$ wouldn't give you an unknown disease just by touching one of the poles, or the girls.

Not that Tilly was disease-ridden. She just deserved more than Jesse's place. In fact, she was more beautiful than those women. She was a billion dollars more than those *build-a-women*, with their fake nails as long as my dinner knives, fake tan, hair extensions to their ankles, and eyelashes that could set them in flight. They were stunning, truly. But Tilly was *a la naturale*. She deserved to be up *there*, with the girls dancing before us.

I studied her face. She was ecstatic, like she had just walked into heaven.

"Here." The security guard ushered us to a VIP booth with a gold rope across it. We ushered in and he closed the rope and stormed off.

"Oh my god," Tilly brushed her hand over my arm and back to her mouth."What?! I can't believe we're in PU$$ right now... what?!"

We giggled our way into the seats with grins ear to ear. I felt like royalty. It was nice, different.

"I've been trying to get into this place for a very long time, since I first started dancing. I'd never have guessed that of *all* people, *you'd* be the one to get us in here," Tilly exclaimed.

"It's the dress, isn't it?"

"It's definitely the person wearing it." She winked, and I blushed at her comment.

"I'm so nervous, Tilly," I admitted, the butterflies in my belly dancing like a stripper. *Round and round, up and down.*

"We need a drink, stat."

"Pity you don't have any of that tea here," I tittered, and we laughed again, slouching ourselves into the cloud-like booth seat.

My eyes drew to one girl in particular, tucked in the back of the club around the corner, waiting for her cue to come on stage. She was a little curvier than the others... toned, but curvy. A man's voice chimed in over the music and announced her entrance, and the crowd turned their attention and cheered for her. *"Scarlett."*

The music changed to a heavy metal song "Adrenalize Me" by In This Moment, and she immediately reeled me in. The short redhead blew kisses and spanked her bottom as she strutted toward us. I gulped as she took a spot on the pole opposite our booth.

Her eyes teased the crowd as she moved around the stage. Scarlett was obviously popular; the crowd had moved in closer, bills raised in the air for her. Not a single eye strayed from her in the club, except for mine—interrupted by a waitress who had swished toward us with a bucket of chilled champagne and two empty glasses.

She placed them on the table with a professional smile and strutted off to the next table. As she departed, a cold chill tore through my spine again. *Shit. Not again.* Then a shattered breath spun from my left ear to my right... just like it had done last time. *Three weeks ago.*

I gasped, and in a panic, I threw my head around, but no one was there. Panic washed over my face again. *Esme, this has to stop.*

"You good?" Tilly's voice dialed up a notch over the music as she questioned hesitantly, her face looking like I was a crazy person. Instinctively, I inhaled through my nose. *Thank God. No scent of pine.* My heart was pounding. There was so much going on.

"Yeah. I just—" I paused to swallow the lump in my throat and push aside my unpleasant thoughts.

"You look like you need this," she laughed as she poured us glasses of champagne before turning her attention back to Scarlett. I threw the whole glass down my throat, and without missing a single beat, the dancer dropped effortlessly to her knees, her eyes locking onto mine as I watched her dance routine in awe.

Crap.

She had no panties on.

Why am I looking? Stop looking. I couldn't. I could see... *everything.* Clean, tidy, and pink. Glossy.

She rolled her tongue over her lips, and the little flutter started to dance between my thighs as she touched her delicate area before moving into another pose and up the pole like a monkey. Instant buzz and heat. There was no denying the arousal I had for a *woman*. The little voice in the back of my head whispered that what I felt was wrong, a sin. But I couldn't stop watching her.

Tilly was just as in awe as I was. The girls at the other club didn't dance the way Scarlett did. They didn't have their lady bits out on show. *Does Tilly want to do this, too?* I wondered for a moment what she would look like up there.

Without any hesitation, I poured another glass into my flute, and the liquid warmed my throat. The entire glass was gone— again. I needed more. *Stat.* Goosebumps rose on my body. *That must be some good champagne.* Though I had a hunch it wasn't the alcohol.

Wait, what was that? Something caught my eye, but it was gone as fast as it had appeared. I pinched my eyes closed and rubbed the bridge of my nose, trying to pull some sense into myself. I had truly lost my mind; I was seeing *and* hearing things. *Pull yourself together!*

I looked over my shoulder once more, but no one was there. Not even Caine. *Where the heck is he, anyway?*

Maybe my dreams weren't real. Maybe I was in a trance between awake and sleep. Maybe... *fuck.* What was real anymore? I didn't know. *Language, Esme.* Maybe I needed more of that tea. I felt like my head was going to explode, left in a heavy trance of the man from my nightmare three weeks earlier, the lusty thoughts of Mr. Fairytale, and a ridiculously attractive *woman.* Not to mention the fact that I had consumed illicit drugs *and* had my first drink... *And the night isn't even over yet. Am I even Esme anymore?*

I snatched the bottle from Tilly, who was pouring another drink a little too slowly for my liking, and put it directly to my lips, letting a heavy flow of its contents down my throat.

"Jesus, Esme, what's gotten into you? You're all over the place." She frowned.

"I needed a little more than a glass," I admitted, setting the bottle down.

"If somethings going on, you can tell me, right?"

I knew that. But, I just... didn't want to tell her. *But she deserves to know. It is her apartment, after all.*

"Yes, I know. I love you for that. I... " I inhaled deeply, needing to tug away my eradicated emotions as I peel back the visions of *him*. "I need to come clean about something."

"Sure, babes. Anything." Tilly softened with a worried look on her face.

"I've been having nightmares." I hesitated during the last part, and she furrowed. I knew she was seconds away from either laughing or waving me off.

"Oh, is that it?"

"No... well, okay. Listen. I *thought* I was having nightmares." I finished my sentence involuntarily, and we both froze in time. My words had gone astray. She was staring at me like a deer to headlights. "Of a man stalking me."

"A man?!" Tilly exclaimed.

"A man dressed like the Grim Reaper. He—" My hands started to shake, and panic surfaced through my throat. A tear threatened to leave my eye, sitting delicately at my water line.

"Jesus Christ, is that it?"

"Tilly!"

"Sorry. Go on," she grimaced.

"Well, it's been happening for a long while... every night. In my sleep, I revisit my day, and he's there, wherever I go. School, the bus, the cafe. Even when we went out and celebrated your birthday. He was there, too. Watching me. I thought I was losing my mind, that I was seeing things."

"Oh?" Tilly muttered, her tone pressing me to go on.

"I didn't just *see* him. I could smell him, too. And then that became touch. Because three weeks ago, when I woke up from my usual nightmare, he was in my room. He was real."

"And... you said he was in a Grim Reaper costume? Breaking into our apartment with twin lock windows... that high up?" She cocked a brow and narrowed her eyes at the empty bottle. *I knew it. She thinks I'm crazy. I think I'm crazy.* "Girl, you're more drunk than I thought."

"I knew you wouldn't believe me," I sighed.

"Wait. You're being serious? Someone actually broke into the apartment? Why didn't you tell me? Esme, this is serious!"

I looked around again mindlessly—something I did a little too often.

"There's no one there, Esme. No one's even looking at us. Is that why you've been so weird lately? Honey, you're imagining things."

"I'm not. I know what I saw," I huffed.

"No one can break through our windows, babes. Besides, I think I'd know if someone broke into my apartment."

"Yes, well, you've been busy as of late. Banging and crashing and screaming and loud noises have become a norm for our place. You'd think no different if someone bashed my window open."

She is right though. Maybe I am imagining it. Wouldn't I wake up if he broke through the window? If I drink some more, maybe I'll mellow out again. A voice called from somewhere near me, startling me.

CHAPTER SEVEN

ONE, TWO, THREE GEMOLOGISTS, FOUR

"Looking for me, were you?" Caine slid into the booth's seat next to Tilly, looking directly at me. *Same spot, different place.* The lighting above him complemented his features. Belly flutters—instantly. Tilly playfully bounced her eyebrows at me and mouthed, "You're getting lucky tonight."

I scoffed but split into a smile, my cheeks flushed. He was energized, buzzing on cloud nine. He drummed his perfectly manicured hands on the table. An instant wave of release and calm washed over me as I locked eyes with him.

My gosh, the man is ridiculously good-looking. I forgot every train of thought. I couldn't even put something together to say to him without a brain-to-mouth malfunction. That's what he did to me.

"Hi, me," I flirted, holding my hand out for his. He chuckled and tilted a brow, humored by my remark. His icy blue eyes were glistening playfully.

"Caine," he exclaimed as he shook my hand twice.

"Hello, *Caine*."

I already knew his name, but it was nice to hear him finally introduce himself. I could listen to him say his name all day, though I'd prefer to hear him say mine.

"Hi... little diamond," he teased. *There they go, the butterflies, fluttering so hard they feel like they're about to fly out of my mouth.*

Diamond.

"This place is... " I trailed off, not knowing what else to mutter out between Scarlett making me flushed and Caine bringing on more arousal that I definitely didn't need to act on. Who knew what else would stream through my head? *Shambles. That's what!* I cleared my throat. "Nice... we've never been here before," I finally said.

Small talk was all I could offer at that point.

"I know."

"You... know?" I repeated nervously, unintentionally in question.

"I do. I'd know if a girl like *you* ever set foot in here. I've never met anyone like you. Men like us spend years dreaming and praying for women like you. Some of us even go looking. So, welcome. Anything you desire is yours." He stared into my eyes with the same hunger as before. And I was happy to return the gaze. *Wait? Men like... us?*

Suddenly, a very tall, skinny, young, and absolutely gorgeous man wearing a slick black leather jacket and a motorbike helmet propped in his hand approached us. I had to crane my neck to get a good look at him. He was insanely tall. He must have been at least six foot seven, or taller. He was huge.

He slipped his way into the booth next to Caine, immediately glaring at Tilly with a smirk before thumping the helmet onto the table and turning to face him. There was a red flag in my head, something I couldn't quite put my finger on.

"Brother," Caine muttered to him, clearly trying to keep his voice level, but I could detect a hint of annoyance. In the corner of my eye, I could see Tilly mentally drooling. *I give it thirty seconds, like Jesse said.*

Crap. Brother? The tall one. He was trouble... he looked like trouble.

He turned to look at me, and his tongue darted across his lips in a way that made it a little too obvious that he was eating me with his eyes. *Red flag.* But hell, he was hot. *Red. Flag.*

"Who's this?" The guy creased his brow. He was no different than the cocky idiots at school. They ran around like they owned the place, with their cool swagger attitude. Assholes, and yet girls seemed to fall for it every time.

"This is Esme. Esme, this is my brother, Damon. Damon... " Caine introduced, freezing at Tilly for her name.

"Tilly," she was quick to respond, not taking her eyes from the hot shot.

"Tilly, Damon. Damon, Tilly."

"Wanna go get a drink, babe?" Damon persuaded Tilly. She wouldn't need convincing. She was only half a blink away from pulling her panties off there and then.

"Fuck yes. Let's leave these two in peace." She immediately hopped up from her seat and began walking with Damon.

"Wait... " I wailed, catching my breath as it was trying to leave my chest. "What about what Je—" she cut me off.

"Sorry, can't hear you... " Her words faded into thin air, and I had to speak a little louder before she disappeared from my sight completely.

"Don't go far. And don't do anything stupid." I knew she

would, but I had to tell her not to anyway. Jesse said he was trouble, though trouble was her favorite type of man. I rolled my eyes, and in a blink, she was gone.

"Jesus, that wasn't even thirty seconds," I muttered thoughtlessly under my breath. Caine chuckled, and glared at me like I was the last woman on earth.

"Thirty seconds?"

"Oh... Umm. Nothing." I blushed. I hadn't realized I'd said that out aloud. "Just something someone said earlier." *If he stares at me any harder, I am going to lose my words again.*

"Ahh. You mean Jesse?"

"Yeah. He said you... " I froze. *Foot in mouth, Esme.*

He didn't need to know that I was the dumbest girl of all. That despite the warning signs and the very clear word that Jesse had said—"*trouble*", a word that I clearly didn't listen to—I was happily sitting across the table from him with love-struck eyes and a fluttering stomach. *And somewhere else.*

"You... " he pressed with a daring grin.

"Whitlocks are trouble," I admitted. *I can see why people drink.* The buzz in my veins was inviting.

"Did he now?" He laughed through his nose. "Trouble, hmm? The only trouble I see here is you."

"M-me?" My cheeks flushed. I was far from it.

"Yes, you, little diamond."

"I'm not... " I sighed, brushing him off. *I'm no diamond, not compared to* those *girls...* whom I had not paid attention to since Caine sat down.

"What did I say, Esme?" *What?* I studied his face. His brow was pinched as if he was disappointed—hurt, even—and was waiting for an answer to slip from my lips, but nothing left them. "I told you not to dismiss your beauty. I meant what I said." He licked his lips, and I squirmed in my seat, seeing the hunger in his eyes grow by the second.

"But—"

"I want you. Is that so hard to understand?"

"Yes, it is." I flushed, averting my gaze.

"Is it, though? I know you want me just as much as I want you."

What?

Oh. God.

Am I melting?

My brain fizzed. The champagne was hitting me, strong and heavy. Warmth flooded me, and just when I thought my cheeks couldn't get any more flushed, they did. I mustered up the courage to speak again.

"How?"

"Because I can smell it on you." His words fell from his lips like liquid silk. *Oh my god, do I smell bad?* I instinctively turned my nose to my shoulder and smelled for B.O. There was nothing other than the perfume Tilly spritzed on me before we left Jesse's club. Caine laughed deeply again at my innocence.

"No, not there."

He shifted in his seat slightly, and a hand brushed my thigh. My lips parted for my gasp, and I could feel the temperature of my cheeks burning against my skin. The man sent me in a mindless fuzz, like I could perish away at any moment. *How did he know about the moisture between my legs? And it has a smell? Crap, crap, crap.* I had to look anywhere else but him. I couldn't catch my breath.

I needed air. *This is a bad idea.*

"I told you, I like diamonds. And by I, I mean we," he added with a dangerous smile. *We?* My eyes widened. *Why did he say it like* that*?* Panic kicked me into overdrive. My body was screaming at me. *Get out, get out, get out.*

I scanned the club for Tilly. I had completely lost sight of her and Damon. No doubt, she already had her dress hiked up to her waist somewhere. In the bathroom, maybe.

"Excuse me. I need to use the restroom."

Caine nodded and I hastily ushered from my seat and scampered off to look for it, locating it on the other side of the club. The music wasn't as loud as Jesse's club, so it made thinking easier. I nudged my way through the people, slipping into the room.

"Tilly?" I called out. *Nothing.* She wasn't there. My body was pinging with signals to get the hell out and go home.

I shakily pulled out my cell from my clutch and dialed her, locking myself in one of the cubicles. No answer. I tried again. No answer. I realized I had a missed call and a voice message from her five minutes before.

I hit play and my stomach fell instantly. She was yelling in a panic, muffled, and someone was laughing in the background. There was another male's voice as well as a female's, but I couldn't make out what was going on.

"Esme, get the fuck out. NOW! Esme! RUN. *He's* here!"

He?

As in... he he?

My heart pounded. Her distressed voice had broken free from whatever muffled her, echoing like she was in an alleyway. The sound of struggling and whimpering crackled through the speaker.

"What is this? You little slut!" a man's voice shredded.

"No! NO!" she howled again. Without warning, the message ended.

My heart swelled into my throat, freeing tears from my eyes. *This is bad. Really fucking bad. He is here. Fuck. Now I'm here alone. Jesse was right. So was my moral compass.* I paced the stall I was in and slapped the side of my face to stop my sobs. *Focus, woman.* I needed a plan.

My phone dinged, a message with Tilly's location spread over my screen.

"Oh, thank God," I blurted to myself. Tilly and I had set up our phones to automatically call each other in an emergency after pressing the volume down button three times, then after the call it would ping a location. *The reception in the club isn't the best. That must be why I didn't hear her call.*

I punched 911 into my phone, but it dropped out. The screen on my phone turned pitch black, and the dreaded red battery icon lit up.

"Shit," I hissed at my phone. It was dead. I had used my entire battery while doing my assignment at school. I didn't think to charge it before going out.

I peered out the main bathroom door, seeing Caine still sitting at the booth, tapping away on his phone. I needed to somehow get to the front doors without him seeing me. I couldn't ask anyone for help. It was his *family's* club. I couldn't trust *anyone.*

I ducked down with my clutch covering the side of my face and ran to the door. By the time I got out, tears were streaming down my face and my heart felt like it was about to climb out of my mouth. I needed to find someone to help me. I needed to find Tilly, but not alone.

Not a single soul was walking the streets. *What time is it, anyway?* I didn't look at the time when I had my phone. I kept my pace on the footpath, looking for a cab as it was safer than walking, but it was quiet. Too quiet.

The streetlights above me flickered, and the sound of heavy footsteps echoed. My breath left my chest and I turned, but no one was there. I started to jog to the best of my ability in heels, heading back to Jesse's club. But with each step I took, another one followed.

I turned to look over my shoulder again, and suddenly my body slammed right into a solid force, making me ricochet onto the concrete walkway, falling hard straight onto my ass. My head throbbed at the sudden blow of pressure.

Peering up through clouded vision from running mascara and tears, I sniffled. A blurred shadow merged into the night sky before me. He was well over six feet tall. I squinted to focus my eyesight, shuffling backwards in a panic.

"No, no," I cried out, seeing that the figure's face was covered by a haunting, metallic, mouthless mask with mesh-covered eyes. Two large, coiled horns perched from the top of the mask shone under the flickering light. I had lost all the air in my lungs. Fresh tears fell, one after the other.

He panted and clenched his fists, crouching beside my head. Revolt riddled all over him. He was shirtless, and his skin was painted all black. He was dressed in a thick, black, frayed cape.

"Ah," I yelped. Or at least I thought I did. Nothing else would follow. It was then, as he hovered over me, that his scent intoxicated my nose. No different to all those nights. The smell of pine, blood, and musky moisture entwined with another smell. Something like rotting flesh.

The shadow man.

My body was frozen, not a single limb capable of movement other than my eradicated heart as his unsteady, angry breath hitched under the mask. He growled, a sound of rage and something else I couldn't put a name to. *Why is this happening to me?*

His demeanor was if he had every reason to hate me, like I had ruined his entire life and he was hunting me down to break even. But I'd never met the man. I'd know if I had ruined someone's life.

He stepped forward, his heavy boot grazing the concrete underneath it. I bellowed a terrorized scream. But no one was around to help. And by the looks of *him*, no one would if they could.

My nightmares turned into reality. My stalker had me trapped. And I was alone with him. Right where he wanted me.

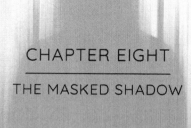

CHAPTER EIGHT

THE MASKED SHADOW

My body trembled uncontrollably and I flinched, catching sight of the knife that he was twiddling in his hand. *Don't look at the knife, don't look at the knife.* Pure terror was racing through my veins as I laid upright on the concrete, trailing my eyes over him.

His skintight jeans buckled at the seams from the pressure of him squatting before me. He didn't move. He didn't speak. He was stoic. And he sat in a way that gave the impression he was only happy to let me study him. He *was* real. And he was more terrifying than I'd remembered.

"Get away from me!" I cried, trying to shuffle back, attempting to make my escape. I only managed to squirm, merely an inch. But my plea was left ignored. His laugh was deep through his nose, directly from his core, and it was downright menacing. My fear was his amusement, his fuel.

He wanted to scare me, for reasons I did not know. A sadistic purr rattled from his chest as he stood, taking another step closer and throwing a leg over me. Still, he didn't speak. Only tormenting slow movements, growls, and grunts, which only made him more terrifying.

"Help! Get away from me" Somebody help!" I cried out again, but no one was around.

He pulled a cloth from the back pocket of his jeans and leaned toward me. I panicked and instinctively threw my arms out to stop him in my defense. But he was too quick. He grabbed my wrists, shoving one back onto the ground and pressing his boot onto it.

"Ow! Stop!" I winced, crying out from the unnerving, unfamiliar pain of a man stepping on my arm.

He left me no choice but to lie flat on the ground. I didn't have the core strength to pull myself up. He twisted his head like he was enjoying seeing me defenseless on the ground. I was no match for him. His knife met the sensitive skin of my arm, and I sobbed harder, the tears burning at the sockets.

"No, please. No, don't hurt me!" I begged. As much as I tried to yelp louder, the sound that left my lips was a mere squeak. "Why are you doing this? I've not done anything!"

I mindlessly went to pry his weapon away with my free hand, and he growled, pressing the jagged edge of his knife into the soft pink flesh, hard—a clear message to not touch, move, or object. I wriggled and opened my mouth to plead again. And because I clearly didn't get the message the first time, he growled deeper, pressing harder into my skin, drawing a thin trail of blood onto the concrete and stepping even harder on my arm.

I snapped my mouth shut with a loud, trembling whimper. The second I did, he released my arm. *Lesson learned. Fight, get hurt. Submit, release.*

"What do you want from me? Money?" I whispered. He didn't answer, but he tilted his head again. "A car?" Again, he didn't answer. He didn't move other than tilt his head the opposite way. *Why is he not speaking?* I didn't even have a car. I didn't even have money—much of it, anyway—certainly not enough to pry off a robber.

But he was no thief. He was a goddamn maniac.

His breath rippled against his mask, like the *Star Wars* movies. That was what he sounded like.

"What do you want? Please... " I begged again. The tears just kept flowing down my face, to the point where it felt like I could fill an Olympic pool. The man sighed as if feeling a sense of relief. The sensation of hearing it was unnerving. And so was the silence. Not receiving an answer only spun me into a frenzy even more. All I could do was cry. *This freak is a professional. He isn't new to this. Not in the slightest.*

I didn't know how it happened. I didn't have time to process it, but somehow his foot nudged under my thigh, and in an instant, he had flipped me over onto my stomach without so much as a struggle. His foot was pressed down at the small of my back, and my wrists were met with the tingling fibers of an old rope, straining at my joints as he secured them behind me.

I wriggled, shuffled, and thrust, but his strength was too much for me. It was no use. He stepped off me before pulling my hair so that my head yanked back, my body straining at the belly. I cried out from the pain of the muscles being stretched so brutally. At that point, I was a sobbing mess. And no one could hear me. I was alone. *What is that noise? Is that footsteps?*

"Help!" I screeched, my breath holding onto a sliver of hope seeing a group of people in the shadows from the corner of my eye.

No.

It wasn't my savior.

It was a group of men walking toward us—*also with masks on*. I squirmed again. It felt like I was choking on my own gasps.

"No! No. Please, no!"

But the shadow man pulled my hair so hard, I had no choice but to maneuver myself onto my feet. I howled from the pain at my scalp and the numbness in my ass from meeting the concrete. The numbing effect of whatever alcohol I had consumed was long gone.

The shadow man pushed me toward the three men in black fabric masks. They crowded me, brushing up against me, tormenting, laughing, and nudging me into the middle of their circle. My body bounced from one to the other as they muttered insolent things that I couldn't fully hear, drowned out by my sobs. The fear had turned entirely into terror, and I could barely keep myself standing anymore.

"I like this one. She's pretty. So was her friend." The tallest male in the black leather jacket toyed. Typical "bad boy" attire, with rings and studded bracelets. *Wait, friend? That voice, that jacket. That's Damon.*

"Mmmm. I think this one is the prettiest *H* has found for us yet, boys. And that smell... " the muscular, tattooed one growled as he brushed my hair with the palm of his hand before inhaling the scent of my hair. "So sweet and innocent."

I shuddered, and as soon as I saw the broad chest, I knew it was the buff man from earlier tonight. The one waiting for Caine out the front of Jesse's club. His muscles were excessive and downright terrifying. He was huge up close, but not as tall as Damon. None of them were as tall as him, though the shadow man was a close second.

It was then that it became clear to me. The men that

surrounded me were the Whitlock brothers. The very brothers that I had been warned about... which could only mean one thing. The fourth masked man must be Caine. My heart sank into my chest as the shortest one became preoccupied with twirling my dress between his perfectly manicured fingers. Turning my attention to him, his familiar scent hit me instantly.

"No," I muttered weakly. It *was* indeed him. It was a setup. *Caine set me up, and now I am probably going to be killed. Or worse... raped. What happened to Tilly? Would they take me somewhere?* My phone was dead, so I couldn't call for help.

I was completely fucked. I hated everything. I hated my whole birthday. All I could do was muffle my tears and let my body be thrown between the three masked men. The fourth—the shadow man—was just standing there with his arms crossed, watching on like a perverted freak.

"Pretty little diamond, isn't she? I knew this one wouldn't resist me. I could smell her desperation a mile away." Caine groaned. "Remember when I said *we* like diamonds?"

Oh, for God's sake. Great.

The shadow man moved into the circle and stood sternly behind me, entwining the rope that was tight around my wrists into his palm and yanking it, slamming my back against the front of his body. My breath left my chest on impact. His body was rock solid against my back, and I could feel each curve of his toned torso on my skin. His shattered, muffled pants fanned against my ear, sending an electric shock through my veins.

I flinched again at his fast movement, my lips parted in a panic. A cloth was shoved into my mouth. My jaw was locked open from the pressure of the fabric. I tried to pry at the damn thing with my tongue, but I couldn't; it was shoved in too tightly.

My lungs bellowed out a fearful cry, but it made *no* sound.

He moved his mask to my neck and drew in a heavy breath through his nose, smelling my scent like it was intoxicating him. Nausea roiled in the pit of my stomach, followed by the never-ending flow of tears burning my eyes.

He pushed me into the front of the muscular man with an elicit groan, and I had no choice but to let my body fall against his. The man rolled my head back by my hair—not as rough as the shadow man, but enough for me to wince at the blow of my tender scalp from all the hair pulling. He tugged it back enough to look me in the eyes, holding the small of my back to balance me.

I froze for a moment, getting lost in eyes that took me by surprise a little. They were the bluest I had ever seen in my life. They tore right through me, and my terror became his incentive. The glint in his eyes under the streetlight was paired with a split second of a sadistic grin, but it was gone as fast as it had appeared.

He took a firm grip on my body, lifting me up with ease and tossing me over his shoulder. He chuckled deeply at my pathetic defense mechanisms. It seemed to humor him as I tried to squirm and cry out for help, but muffled squeaks and a pathetic helpless wriggle were all I could manage. The man was absurdly huge, and all 220lbs of me was clearly not an issue for him.

Regardless, I kicked and punted my legs with all my might, but I saw stars as his arm squeezed down against my thigh. *Wrong move, Esme.* The heavy ache crushed my leg, bruising it instantly. He barely needed to try.

My heart pounded, and I screamed against the fabric harder, catching sight of an open trunk. Without a chance to wrack my brain on what was happening, he heaved me into the trunk of the black SUV with a chuckle.

Twinkling icy blue eyes under a mask were the last thing I saw before darkness.

My breath was heaving, panic and terror marrying each other to the point where I was in a state of fading in and out. *A panic attack, more than likely. How did I get this twisted? How in the fucking blue blazing fuckery shit balls did I go from celebrating my twenty-first fucking birthday with my best fucking friend, to falling over and hitting my fucking head, to flirting with a stupid man in a stupid suit with his stupid hot fucking face, to falling for his stupid trap and being thrown into a fucking trunk by four masked men?*

That motherfucker. I bet he was what tripped me over in Jesse's club.

AND NO FUCKING CELL BATTERY? Are you kidding? I mean, come on. Seriously. Of all the luck.

Gah!

At that point in time, I couldn't care less about my foul language. That was the least of my concerns. The trunk was so dark, I couldn't even see the tip of my nose. Nonetheless, I tried to bang my heels against the enclosed space, and the sound of a snap echoed through the SUV.

I had heaved so hard, I snapped the heel of my shoe. *Great.* The silence tugged at the panic in my belly again, but after pummeling my feet hard against the interior of the trunk for what felt like hours with no response to my pleas, I finally grew tired.

My eyes fell heavy once more, and I floated in and out of a

drift. The SUV thundered, going who knows where. Time had no limit when in a fog. I could tell that it wasn't their first abduction. With the set up they had, this couldn't be new. They knew what they were doing. *Have they been planning this the whole time I was having those nightmares—or reality visions, whatever you want to call them?*

Why?

It was all lies. I wasn't a diamond. I wasn't even a gem. He lied. I wasn't beautiful to him. I was nothing. I was not worth a fucking thing to anyone. I didn't own a car. I wasn't rich. But why me? I owed no one money. I'd never stolen anything. I stayed away from drama. Actually, I stayed away from people in general. *What could these people possibly want from me?*

My eyes fluttered awake again, and I shuddered as the SUV's engine cut off. My heart skipped at least three beats before the doors opened. I counted six seconds between them opening to the vibration of a bassy thud ripping through my ears as each was slammed shut. The footfalls of the men disappeared somewhere in the distance.

They left me. Where have they taken me?

The silence hitched my breath for some time before the eerie sound of a single pair of shoes trailing over stones grew near. A glint of light and idly cool air whispered through the slit of the trunk as it opened. Temporarily blinded by the bright light coming from what I could make out as a garage door, my eyes squinted nearly shut again.

It was morning.

The fuzzy, bulky man hovering by the trunk looked down at me momentarily before throwing me over his shoulder once more. Except this time, I put everything into making my body completely dead weight, letting it fall heavy against itself. The rattle of a chuckle hummed from him, and it radiated into my body.

"Deadweight as much as you like, little one, you're coming with me whether you like it or not. You're *ours* now." His tone was possessive and playful. There was no room for doubting that I was absolutely fucked.

I had been *abducted*.

CHAPTER NINE

BEFRIENDING CONCRETE WALLS

Goosebumps flared my skin. It was freezing. I glimpsed at my surroundings, and it was very clear that wherever I was, I was a *long* way from home. I was being carried through an excessively large garage of polished concrete and a handful of what I assumed to be million-dollar vehicles—all black—and a motorbike. There was an old, crushed car in the corner—remnants of an accident of some sort.

Behind the big steel panel shift door as it was closing was something that only resembled a thriller halloween movie: a backdrop entirely of trees.

Pine trees.

Laced with a dismal layer of fog and sunrise.

Shit.

I attempted to make a mutter of a noise, but all that followed was a squeak. My voice was dry and hoarse from crying and panting for a breath in the hot trunk. And that damn fucking cloth. I had no phone, a broken shoe, I was gagged, tied up, and had no fucking clue where I was, or if the names of those people were even real.

I was in pain practically everywhere, especially my head. We met the opposite end of the garage, and the sunlight had completely subsided behind the panel door. He lowered us slightly, not letting me writhe an inch as he picked up a lit candle, walked a few steps, and stopped at a closed door.

He pried at the handle and walked us in. I could only see the door from the angle I was being held, but I could tell that the room was pitch-black other than the subtle glow of the candle.

The unsettling smells of dampness, urine, and feces filled my nose the further we walked in, curling my stomach into a knot. *Why does this feel like how I imagine a prison to be?* I gagged at the scent, which stimulated nearby gasping and panicked, soft, feminine voices, filling my ears.

We were *not* alone.

Twangs of iron at the fingertips of soft hands haunted my mind, and at each footfall of the man carrying me, more muffled, feared sobs formed. I could hear them getting louder and louder the further we went into the room. *How many people are here?* The glow of the candle finally revealed the contents of the room. It quickly became clear what—or who—else was in the room.

Hostages.

Women in cages, naked. All in their own shelter. Side by side, row after row. Some were bound by old sailors' rope, some chained up against the concrete walls by their wrists, and others curled in the corners of their enclosures. There were many of them—fifteen, maybe twenty.

I screamed against the cloth, more tears burning my eyes again. My chest felt like it was on fire the harder I worked it to bellow. But even then, the man whose shoulders I was perched on did not budge, struggle or grimace.

The women around us were terrified, cold, probably hungry, and lying in puddles of their own secretions. I mimicked their terror. *God only knows how long these women have been here. And what in the fuck were they here for?* The unsettling thought of my own fate, finding out for myself in time sent a shiver up my spine.

The man stopped at one of the empty cages, unceremoniously dropping me onto the cold concrete. My body ached all over. My cry was yet again muffled, but nonetheless, the volume in my own head was loud. Terror washed over my face as he closed the barrier door behind him.

"No. Nooo." It was what I tried to say, but I was muted. Darkness closed in around me as he took himself and the slither of light out the door, leaving me in a heap on the ground and flat on my belly. Gagged and bound. Trapped.

A prisoner.

I squirmed in a disorderly fashion in an attempt to get myself up off the floor, but with my hands tied behind me and no brain-to-limb coordination even at the best of times, there was no way I was going to accomplish it then. Not in the complete darkness, anyway. I tried again, somehow managing to prop myself onto my knees by pushing on my head.

Using every muscle in my body, pushing through the throbs of exhaustion I got onto my feet, taking the weight more on one foot than the other due to the heel that had snapped off. Unease swam through me as I shuffled my way to find my surroundings, blind.

I couldn't see the door, but I had some memory of where it might be from when he dumped me. My breasts were first to meet the cold iron bars. Using my forehead as a pair of hands, I felt my way around, learning the barriers of... *my cage*. It was silent, despite the quantity of women. Too silent.

The three barriers were entirely concrete with nothing else in my cage other than my own snotty breath and tears as company. I resigned to my fate and sank to the floor with my back against the solid, serrated wall of my enclosure. My body trembled as I dropped my head into my knees, letting the tears puddle between my thighs and the cold of the concrete heave through my bones.

"Help me. Please, God. Help me. I cannot bear their pain and sexual desires anymore. I wish to die, ple—" a squeaky, soft young woman's voice whispered in a sob from somewhere, stirring me slightly from my exhausted drift. I caught a trace of light somewhere in the distance, but my eyes fought me to keep them closed. I honestly didn't know if I had slept or not.

Whack.

The wretched sound of metal on metal rattled against someone's cage, cutting off the woman's prayer. My eyes ripped open in a panic at what followed.

"You know the fucking rules. No talking! Do it again and I'll cut your fucking tongue off. Got it?" The threat in his voice was coarse, and by the tone alone, I knew it was Damon.

I didn't know how long I had sat in solitude. *Has it been hours, days, weeks, months?* I had cried so hard, my eyes stung more than they ever had, and my chest was aching, like I had been sat on. I was well past exhausted. *Time clearly has a funny way of escaping when you're confined in small, dark spaces, terrified.*

What did the woman mean? Cannot bear their pain and sexual desires. *Are we sex slaves? Why did she wish she was dead?* I tried to cry out. Pathetic, I knew that. But I had to try something. *I'll be damned if I was going to waste another minute... wherever "here" is.* I had to do something. I tried again, louder. But just like every other time, all that came out was a singular airy note, an inaudible muffle. But the woman must have heard me—or someone did—because someone was shushing me.

"Shh, please. We cannot speak, or else we will get in trouble," a voice whispered. She was closer than the other girl.

I let the sad young woman's words stew in my head for a moment before rolling into a sobbing mess again. The onset heaviness of a full bladder began to knock me. *There is no way I am going to pee myself like an animal. No way. Not today, not tomorrow. Not ever, Esmeralda. Not ever.*

Jesus fucking Christ. I really was fucked. Silence enveloped me again. I couldn't explain the feeling even if I wanted to. The silence was loud.

I stood up, somehow easier than the last time, and stepped forward until there was resistance. *The iron rails.* I trailed my eyes around the place, but there was nothing in sight. It was messing with my mind, I didn't know if my eyes were open or closed. *Just darkness.* And a warm breath. *Too warm.* Too close.

My heart pounded as an unwelcome sensation bubbled in the pit of my stomach, sending it in circles of chaos. I flinched, pulling my body away from the cage door, and the breath disappeared. No footsteps. No light. *What—or who—just breathed down my neck?*

Suddenly, I heard a thud and clang, startling me again as a door slammed closed. My mouth dried and I choked on my own gasp, my tears coming to a halt to focus on whatever was going to happen.

Moments passed of silence and I heard the same door crack open, and a feminine shadow appeared in the light before stepping in and letting the darkness close around her. Stilettos echoed over the concrete, closing the distance, and then a flick of a lighter ripped a shred of light.

I jolted as she appeared right before me. The glow of a ruby red cigarette lit up her face on the other side of the bars. I couldn't make out many of her features other than cat-winged eyeliner and a sharp bob haircut, and the sheer fact that she was eye to eye with me.

I darted backwards in a panic and curled myself up against the furthest wall, in the corner. I sobbed again. There was no way to describe how desperately I wanted to be back home, in the comfort and safety of Tilly's embrace. Back before I had turned twenty-one. Before I knew of the shadow man. Before the nightmares.

All I wanted, more than anything else in the world, was home. But that was the furthest thing from reality.

"Ah," I whimpered against the fabric as she flicked a flashlight to life, pointing it directly at me. I was somewhat thankful I was clothed, unlike the rest of the girls. Unease bubbled in my stomach again as the thought of me being naked —*sexual desires, pain*—made me want to throw up.

"Your turn," the woman snarled, and my body turned cold.

What? My turn to what? Whatever saliva I had left disappeared from my mouth. I tried to gulp, but it was no use. She began to twist and turn a key at the door of my cage, sliding it open. She held the cigarette between pursed lips and pulled a knife from the leather strap around her thigh, hovering it in the air in front of her.

"Come on," she hissed, beckoning me closer, but my feet were concreted to the floor. I was staring at her like a deer would when trying to cross a busy street, headlights pointed at it. "Now!" Her threat was harsh, setting the vomit in my stomach that had been tapping at my throat to pool.

I did what she asked, fearing the consequences of refusal to be much worse than wherever she was going to take me. As I reached the exit to my enclosure, the woman shone her flashlight out, leading the way to the door I was brought in through. The palm of her hand was planted between my shoulder blades, pushing me forward as I made my way to the door with a gasp.

I had two left feet at the best of times, and it was even harder with my hands tied behind my back. Thankfully, I had already taken my heels off, otherwise, there would have been no way I'd have walked that far.

As I got to the door, her hand reached under my forearm, and I flinched at her forceful grip. For such small hands and a delicate frame, she had a lot of strength behind her. *I suppose if you're going to be involved in a group of criminal kidnappers, you have to be able to defend yourself.*

CHAPTER TEN

WHEN SOMEONE SAYS 'YOUR TURN' DON'T EXPECT FLOWERS AND SUNSHINE

The woman led me through the garage and into an elevator. It was bright—too bright—and entirely coated with mirrors. The contrast stung my eyes, but I kept my head down, peering at her in the reflection through my eyelashes.

If you could imagine what a crime-fighting woman looked like, in a movie, she was exactly that. A fighter woman. A bad woman. She boasted feminine power, sex, and control (not that I was familiar with the smell, but I had my suspicions).

I kept my glare inconspicuous, trailing up from her black stilettos to her black latex pants that gripped tightly against her long, toned legs. *Fuck.* My breath hitched at the sight of a gun strapped to her other thigh. *A knife* and *a gun. Who are these people?*

I whimpered a noise of defeat, being so close to a weapon—a weapon that could kill me in the blink of an eye. I could feel my temperature rising and my heart throbbing in my throat. The uncertainty of who those people were, their business with me, and where we were going... every emotion tortured me from the inside, agonizing my every thought.

The woman wore a black laced bra, showing off her fit structure. She looked young in the face—late twenties, at a guess —but her posture and tone of her olive skin made me believe she was older. My gulp echoed through the elevator and her eyes drew to mine. A crease of a domineering smile peered over her cheek.

Her slick, straight black hair carved her face, and the yellow lighting highlighting her features. Despite my fear and angst, the woman was quite beautiful. She reminded me of Tilly. My mind trailed off, thinking of my best friend, but I was interrupted when the elevator came to a halt.

She took me through an overly long hallway—a completely different setting from where I was being kept prisoner. It was no slum, like I had assumed I was going to be taken to. Given the cars in the garage we passed, whoever was behind it all was wealthy. Very wealthy. It didn't take me long to realize that I was in a mansion. *Jesse mentioned a mansion, money, drugs, and sex. Shit. Why did he forget to mention that these people are kidnapping psychos?*

Chandeliers dangled from the ceiling, placed perfectly every two meters. The décor gave the place a classic but modern, inviting tone. We passed many closed doors until we finally reached a black one at the end of the hallway.

Faint echoes of music sounded from behind it, much like the nightclub Caine had invited me to. *No—taken me from.* The woman stopped to look at me up and down, cocking a brow, and a devilish grin curled her lips again as she held the door open and gave me a final nudge inside.

I almost fell to the floor in disbelief. Multiple *stunning* women pranced around the room to the music, completely naked. Like the strip clubs. Some had downright terror written all over their faces, as if they were being forced to perform their acts like puppets on strings, while others were shining in absolute glee, without a single bother that the very place beneath them was a hostage prison.

There was a dimly lit fireplace, a bar with soft neon lights that illuminated the room, and many lounge chairs. Fear tapped at my chest, and my heart skipped a beat. There were four evenly placed tall, cast iron cages in the back of the room. *Is this a sex dungeon?*

Two of them were filled with women who looked oddly like me: terrified, gagged, and tied. Black makeup ran down their faces, cuts and bruises on their bodies. The reflection of fear in their eyes told a story without a mutter of a word. *Were they taken from the club, too? Was the club a lure for women?* My mind couldn't fathom what had happened to them. But it was enough to send my brain into a fog.

I couldn't tell if I was breathing, dreaming, or if I had died in my sleep and been pulled into a realm of another universe. It didn't feel real, but then it did in ways I could not explain. *This sort of stuff happens in movies, in crime stories on television. Fictional stuff. It happens to people who involve themselves in a life of crime, drugs, and whatever else people do in the dark of night.*

Not that I would know. I've never been one to titillate in that world. Unlike Tilly.

Not me. How the hell did I end up here?

I darted my eyes across the room and caught sight of one

woman, crying as she popped up and down on the lap of a masked man on one of the sofas. He had no shirt on, his pants hung around his ankles, and he held a knife at the arc of her thigh, revealing his spectacularly toned muscles, beads of sweat and—*fuck*—a very large... appendage, sliding in and out of the delicate folds of the woman on his lap.

My stomach twisted in knots, and an involuntary squeak muffled in my mouth at the unwelcome sensation between my thighs. *Oh, no. This is absurd.* I mentally scolded myself for a sensation I should not be having. It made me sick that I was experiencing it. Another brain-to-body malfunction. Yet another sin. I needed to change my train of thought. *It might help if you stop looking at his reproductive organ, Esme.*

Crap.

Am I where the woman in the cells muttered about? Most of her whispers were broken prayers. Is she a sex slave? Am I a—Oh, God. Bile rose in my throat.

The numbing sensation of another nudge pulled me from my mental drift as the woman from before ushered me further into the room with a sadistic laugh.

"Ahh, Ruby has brought us another toy to play with. Good. I didn't care for that other cunt," the man with the woman on his lap said, muffled by the same mask as from the street I was taken from. It didn't take a genius to work out who it was. His voice was one you couldn't forget easily. Damon.

My stomach knotted again, but then it rolled to the word "*toy*" as it lapped in my mind, over and over again. *I am definitely in a sex dungeon. Fuck, fuckety fuck, fuck, fuck.* I looked away, seeing that another girl was miraculously crawling about on the bar like some kind of stripper.

I had to really pull myself into my body to realize that she *was* a stripper. The very same stripper from the club I ran from. Scarlett, I think her name was, drunk as a skunk and seemingly enjoying herself. Clearly not a hostage, and unfazed by the freaks in the room. My eyes widened in even more of a panic, my head dizzy with confusion. The whole thing was a complete head fuck, and I was smack bang in the middle of it.

"Hmm. This is the one from the club a few nights ago. Nice."

"Where do you want her until I get back?" Ruby hissed at Damon.

"Put her in the cage. We will deal with her later," he snapped back between lifting the petite woman up and down over himself.

In the cage...

Again.

I couldn't keep up with my own emotions. All of it was so overwhelming, so mind-numbing that it made my very soul ache. Ruby didn't reply to Damon. She just scowled and shoved me to the back of the room where the cages were. I didn't resist, as much as I wanted to. Those people were clearly experienced in whatever system they had running there.

Besides, looking at the cuts and bruises on the girls in the cages, it seemed like resisting would probably have far more consequences than whatever came of obeying. With a harsh shove from Ruby's elbow, I was in the empty cage.

She slammed the gate with a pleased smirk and threaded the thick padlock through the gate. I gasped against the cloth in my mouth as she pulled the knife from her leg. She hovered the blade in a circular pattern, prompting me to turn around. I gulped hard but followed her order.

I flinched from the cold touch on my skin and the knife

tugged at the ropes around my wrists, breaking them free. I rubbed at the red and blue bruises the rope had left behind. I quickly pulled at the cloth in my mouth, discarding it by my feet. The rush of fresh air hit my lungs, giving me a rush of enjoyment as I took an unholy amount of air into my mouth.

I didn't speak. I just stared in fear as I watched the woman leave. I returned my eyes to Damon, his panting becoming noticeably heavier. There I was arguing with myself about all the reasons I shouldn't be watching someone do what they were doing, but having never experienced sexual acts in my life apart from that kiss with Caine, was what was stopping me from turning away? *The smug asshole.* I'd never even watched porn. And I doubted hearing Tilly and her sexual partners was enough to consider it an experience of my own.

Curiosity had the better of me. The woman on top of him was covered in just as much sweat as he was, beads of it running down her bare chest, trailing down the curves of her toned belly. I had a full view of them as she grinded up and down his length.

Suddenly, whatever fear and panic I had were gone. Caught in their sexual entrance, I found myself mindlessly panting a likewise rhythm of the woman, having a tethering case of tunnel vision.

Do I consider myself jealous of her pleasure? No.

Is that a lie? Yes.

That alone is proof that there is something very wrong with me.

The ache in my woman area throbbed. I tried squeezing my thighs together to shut it up, but that only made it worse. It soon became apparent that I was turned on. *Very* turned on. Damon flicked his lashes up, breaking his concentration from the woman as he peered at me. He tugged the mask above his mouth, revealing a wicked grin between his lips.

Shit.

"Leave us. And close the door," he scolded the woman, and she quickly climbed off him and staggered herself out of the room, disappearing into the hallway, the door closing behind her.

Shit, shit.

CHAPTER ELEVEN

THE ROOM I HAD NO BUSINESS LIKING

"Mmm. I can see why he had eyes on you," Damon muttered across the room, pulling himself into his jeans. He tugged at his mask, pulling it up over his head and onto the floor behind him.

His tousled chocolate brown hair with what looked like a heavy amount of product in it flicked up, sticking up high on his head. His jawline was crisp, clean-cut stubble along it. He didn't look much older than me, and far too young to be involved in whatever situation we were in.

He walked closer, still buckling himself away. Whatever fluttery feeling I had before left me quick stat, and fear swiftly returned. My breath swayed and I stood back against the steel bars behind me. Having nowhere to go, I took comfort in knowing he couldn't get inside. Ruby had the key. My eyelids were pushed all the way up, and my lashes brushed against my brows. It was my reminder of just how tall he was.

He draped his gaze down my body, hovering his blue eyes at my feet. They weren't as black as they were the last time I saw him, whenever that was. They were filled with sex and hunger. My mind wondered. I hadn't a clue the day or time, if it was day or night, when I last ate, when I last slept, or even when I'd last showered.

Damon ran his fingers along the bars of the cage, and the other girls murmured under their breaths, seemingly in the same position I was: shrunken against the back of their cages, terrified yet somewhat curious, because let's face it, those guys were no ordinary-looking freaky kidnappers.

The Whitlock brothers all had one thing in common: they were hot as hell. Except for the shadow man. I had no idea what he looked like.

He continued to tap his fingers along the bars of my cage, then onto the next girls', until he got to the last cage before waltzing himself behind the bar. The hostages kept their eyes on him, myself included. I couldn't quite tell if they were watching him because they were terrified, or if they wanted to jump his bones. The sexual tension in the room was pitiful, though. I had to scold myself mentally, because I was part of that tension.

His Adam's apple protruded from his neckline as he downed a glass of water in two gulps, sending a tingle between my thighs.

"Mmm, refreshing," he teased. My mouth tried to salivate, but only dryness returned. I was so thirsty. Within seconds, he was back at the front of my cage, gesturing the glass to me. He fiddled with the pocket of his jeans and pulled out a key—the same as the one Ruby had. I swallowed.

"Stay away from me," I squeaked, flinching back again. I hadn't realized that I had my chest pressed against the bars. He shrugged mockingly and turned on his feet. *No, I didn't mean—*

"Wait," I squeaked.

"Oh, you want this now?" He stopped, glaring at me with a cocked brow and tilted head. I nodded, and he opened my cage.

Keeping him in the corner of my eyes, thirst outweighing the fear, my lips opened for him as he held the glass above my mouth. A singular drop wet my tongue, eliciting a feral groan like I hadn't had fluid for days to glimmer from my mouth. But that was all I was granted before the bastard twisted his hand, tipping the entire glass on the floor.

I sobbed and he laughed, slamming my cage before he walked off.

"Tormenting her already? Without the others?" Ruby hissed, returning from wherever she had disappeared to.

"Ahh, come on, I'm bored."

"Bored? You just had your dick inside some bitch, you fucking idiot. How can you be bored already?"

"I need entertainment." Damon waved her off, moving to grab a bottle of something from the bar. Without warning, Ruby threw her knife across the room, the sharp end plummeting straight into a bottle of alcohol on the wall, inches from where he was reaching. I gasped, along with the other girls.

"Ha, you missed," Damon smirked.

"I wasn't aiming," she retorted slyly. The two carried on like brother and sister, fighting like siblings would. Well, I wouldn't know, as I grew up an only child. But that was how I imagined it: always bickering and fighting like that, neither of them really trying to kill each other, but not entirely trying to avoid it, either.

"Come on, sis, let's drink." I shivered at Damon's words. *Sis? As in... sister? But she was just in here, watching him... what the fuck is going on?* "We have new toys to play with. We should celebrate."

Toy. Is that all I am? Am I not human anymore?

"No, I have a better idea. Go get the other one. Bring her here," Ruby replied, suddenly standing at my cage again and opening the gate.

"Come on! I don't have all day," she hissed at me. I jolted but quickly followed her orders, stepping out of the cage and walking to wherever she was leading me.

I think I had counted how many threads of carpet the floor had by the time he returned. I had stayed standing at the fireplace in silence with my eyes locked on the floor, trembling. The cold sharp edge of Ruby's knife was planted at the small of my back. I was too terrified to speak or even breathe as we waited for Damon to return.

I didn't take my eyes off the floor when I heard him come back, a second set of footsteps accompanying him. I was well aware that he had brought someone with him, as I could hear them muttering, resisting somewhat as they walked in.

"Let's see what kind of *toy* we're dealing with." Ruby's words sent a wave of panic through me. I was in a sex dungeon with kidnappers. I didn't know what was expected of me, other than the possibility of being some sex slave.

"She's jumpy and curious, I know that much," Damon mocked. My eyes widened, and my heart picked up pace in my chest.

"Tilly?" I cried out. They hadn't been able to before now, but the tears streamed down my face. Relief washed over me. Relief that at least she wasn't murdered on the sidewalk after leaving with Damon. But the feeling didn't last long. It quickly churned into sympathy and revulsion, because she was *there*. That meant she was a prisoner too.

"Esme?!" she wailed.

The distance between us was so far, yet so close. I went to embrace Tilly, but Ruby grabbed my arm, holding me tightly against her. The knife pressed a little harder against the small of my back, eliciting a yelp.

"Nuh-uh. Come, back against the wall. Now," she ordered. She gave another nudge with the knife, and I shuffled past Tilly with my head down, walking toward the wall on the other side of the fireplace.

If I had learned anything from the alleyway, I needed to do what they said the first time. *Obey.* There were two metal rings bolted into the wall, high enough that Damon's head could touch. I got the feeling they weren't there for decoration, though. After all, I was dealing with psychopaths.

"Back to the wall." Her threat was firmer this time, if that was even possible. My feet were planted solidly into the floor, and as much as I told myself to move, I couldn't. "NOW!" she scowled.

I jolted, complying with her order with a sob. Ruby grabbed a metal rod from the top of the fireplace, holding it with force under my chin and shoving my head up to meet her gaze.

"This will go one of two ways. You either obey us, or you get punished for not doing so. It's your choice." My throat was too thick to swallow the saliva that pooled in my mouth as she pushed the rod harder under my chin, the sensation tugging at the nerves on my tongue. I winced from the pain. "Let's try that again, shall we?" she snapped, and I offered her a mindless nod. "Good girl."

I inhaled a rapid blow of air and my eyes peeled open. Tilly was completely unclothed. *How... when did that happen?*

"Take off her clothes," Ruby demanded, and my eyes widened. Despite the predicament, Tilly looked like she was in her element; her skin was glowing, and her eyes were smiling.

Is she... turned on?

It oddly gave me comfort. She seemed to possess a fraction of the panic and fear that I felt. Granted, the place was built for her. She *loved* being the center of attention. Naked, controlled, admired. She loved all things *sex*. Clearly, being kidnapped didn't bother her. She had probably already fucked Damon.

I hadn't seen her under that type of lighting before, nor without clothes on. Her body looked amazing. I could feel my cheeks flush from the intrusive thoughts in my head, a sexual tension I didn't know I had for Tilly simmering away between my thighs. She gulped before giving a slight nod, moving quickly to my side.

Damon flopped onto a lounge chair, slouching and crossing a leg over his knee. He had a self-satisfied smirk beaming across his cheeks. *An audience. Great.* Tilly didn't hesitate. She tugged at my dress, slowly, giving me time to process.

I gulped, muttering silently to myself that I was all kinds of fucked up. She was a woman. Women didn't admire other women sexually. That was just the way it was. *Right?* Was there a switch? A button somewhere I didn't know about? A button that turned off sexual desires that shouldn't be felt?

"Please, don't," I mumbled, looking at Ruby.

"Don't speak unless you're begging," Damon ordered. My chin wobbled and Tilly continued. I closed my eyes to try and at least block out something, but it didn't help.

The sensation of her warm, delicate fingers brushing against my skin as she continued to pull my dress up past the apex of my thighs sent me into overdrive. I had completely forgotten about the girls in the cages on the other side of the room until that moment. I'd never been naked in front of anyone. *Ever*. Let alone a room full of people. Revulsion brewed in my stomach. I was losing my mind.

My train of thought was all over the place. I took a deep breath, which Tilly mirrored. She clearly needed no introduction on how to unclothe a woman. She knew what she was doing, and she looked good doing it, based on Damon's facial expression. The man could barely keep himself together. He was like a dog in heat, drooling. *The sick bastard.*

Ruby, on the other hand, stood watching with her arms crossed and her brow cocked, looking content with herself.

CHAPTER TWELVE

JUST A TOY

My lips parted, making an O shape, letting a breathy moan fall out as Tilly's fingers skimmed under the bridge of my breasts to collect a bigger handful of the dress.

The dress was snug over my breasts, too tight to pull effortlessly over the darned things. A little tugging was needed. But then Ruby stepped in, a sly grin over her face as the jagged edge of her knife carved the dress clean in half up the length of it without so much as touching my skin. It all happened so quickly that I didn't even flinch. She tore it right between the slit of my breasts.

My entire front section completely popped right out, and the black dress puddled on the floor at my feet. A tear fell down my cheek. Embarrassed, humiliated, and ashamed... the words barely summed up the horrid feelings coursing through me.

Tilly's brow creased, and she mouthed, "Sorry". A tear pooled at her eye, but didn't fall. I knew she felt bad doing it, seeing me that way, defenseless. Though her sorrow seemed genuine, it wasn't good enough to hide the part of her that was enjoying it.

"Arms up," Ruby insisted. I complied without hesitation. What was the point? It wasn't as if I was going to be granted my freedom if I asked. Given a slap on the ass and a, "Sure, Esme, off you go. Don't tell the cops, though." I at least had Tilly, and I clung to that. I wasn't alone. "Strap her in, Damon."

He was quick to obey Ruby's order. The leather straps were cold against my skin as he tightened them around my wrists before securing me to a chain, linking it to the rings on the wall. It was only then that I realized how small I really felt under Damon. His warm breath fanned over my skin. My arms, even at full extension, were only high enough to touch the base of his jawline if I wanted to.

But I didn't. I let my eyes wander over him while he was attending me, watching his chest rise and fall. How was it that watching the tension of his muscles, working double time to allow something so simple as breathing, be the very thing that tugged at the ache of my womanhood? His body heat radiating onto mine was charging the sparks to life between my legs, and I didn't know if I hated it or liked it.

For a moment, I stopped breathing, letting the sound of my heartbeat thump in my head as Damon's index finger followed the length of my arm. A tear trailed down my cheek as I squirmed against the cuffs, not that it achieved anything.

I was bound to the wall, and I wasn't going anywhere. Though, even if I had my arms free, something in me had me thinking I probably wouldn't run if I had the chance. My moral compass did tend to do that; it was defective. I was caught somewhere between somewhat turned on and repulsed by myself for being turned on.

I took the liberty of blinking up at Damon, seeing he wore a smug look on his face—too smug that he had a defenseless virgin pinned to the wall with no escape, no voice. But who was more turned on? Me? Or him?

"Told you. Curious little thing. Oooh, she's going to be fun to play with," he growled. His finger slid further down, trailing over the peak of my breast, my chest expanding to its full capacity to draw in a fill of oxygen to my brain, but it didn't help.

I instinctively arched my back, letting my neck roll behind me and a breathy moan slip from my lips as his finger met my nipple. He gave it a pinch, and another illicit noise involuntary left my mouth. I squeezed my lips tight to mute myself. *What the fuck is wrong with me?*

My body felt heavy against the straps around my wrists, and the unfamiliar sensation sent a flow of heat between my legs, which only sent a wave of confusion through my mind. I had no control over my body at that point.

"Oh, yes. I like this one. Sensitive little virgin," Ruby stirred. I shook my head in defiance

"How-how do you... know I'm a v-v-virgin?" I stuttered between my turned-on pants, or whatever they were called. Damon moved and his finger planted itself under my chin, his thumb darting across my bottom lip, forcing my mouth into an O shape.

"We can smell it on you, remember?" he mocked before shoving his fingers in my mouth. It was uncomfortable, but I didn't cough or gag.

My heart skipped a beat momentarily, wondering what exactly virginity smelled like. And if he could smell it, did that make me dirty? Unclean? Mindlessly, my thighs gripped tight in an attempt to block the smell. But a sensation of moisture between them trickled in response, and my eyes widened.

Shit. And as though I triggered his mental train, Damon inhaled deeply through his nose. A venomous growl rumbled from the pits of his chest as if my scent was intoxicating every nerve in his body.

"Fuck. I hope H lets us keep this one for a little longer than the rest of them," Damon muttered to Ruby. His tone had changed, a sense of desperation in his voice.

H? Who is H? Is H the shadow man? How many people are in this fucking organization? Damon, Ruby, Caine, the buff guy, Shadow Man, and now H? And a bunch of starving, abused women in the basement—cellar?, Tilly and I included.

"Mmmm, yes. Me, too. She is going to be *fun,*" Ruby agreed with a wicked grin. Whatever good feelings I had were suddenly long gone.

I really needed to remember I was a prisoner, denied my own wants and needs. I was a hostage. It wasn't the time or place to be sexually desired. It was a prison. I wondered if I was even being looked for. *Who will file a missing person's report?*

The only person who would file a report was standing directly across from me. No one Tilly knew would look for us, not with the amount of sexual partners she had. She was messing about all the time, hardly a concern for a missing persons report. And my boss certainly wouldn't look for me. He probably wouldn't even know if I missed my shift. When I thought about it, he probably didn't even know my name. That fucker had treated me like I was nothing but shit under his shoe.

I cursed at my intrusive thoughts, my skin bubbling with a sense of rage. An unfamiliar sensation. Too many unfamiliar sensations had happened so far, and I was losing my fucking mind. *I need to get the fuck out of here somehow.*

Ruby yanked at the ends of the metal rod she had in her hand. A loud metallic twang sounded as the rod extended, doubling in length. Her lips twitched into a smirk, and she held the palm of her hand out. Damon dropped two brown leather cuffs into it, the same thickness as the ones around my wrists.

"Panties," Ruby hissed, directed at Tilly. My heart heaved.

"No—" I protested. *Whack.* I cried out as an abrupt sting planted on my thigh. The rod hit my skin hard and fast, leaving a red line. I went to mutter something but remembered my place. *Shut the fuck up.* I whimpered and swallowed hard.

"Panties," Ruby repeated impatiently. Tilly gave me a sympathetic smile as she hooked her finger between the apex of my thigh and the fold of my stomach. Another tear freed from my eye and streamed down my cheek.

Refusing to look any further, I squeezed my eyes shut, letting her diminish whatever was left of my dignity as she tugged my panties down to my ankles. I shuddered. Ruby placed the rod between the inside of my legs, strapping the cuffs around my ankles. Panic froze me as my thighs parted, and a cool sensation blew between my slit. She pushed the rod's length further and further, stretching my legs open as wide as they could go.

With each click of the rod's locks, I winced from the tension. I gasped, and my eyes peeled open. I felt fluid trickle down my leg. *Fuck. Did I just... pee myself?* I didn't think I did. *Shit.* My cheeks flushed. Ruby's face lit up.

"Look at her. She's glistening for us." Ruby stood back, looking hungrily at my womanhood, which only enticed Damon to look too. *Fuck.* They both lost themselves between my forced open legs.

I wriggled beneath their stares, not that it got me far; I was jammed wide open for them to gawk at. Damon's finger brushed my thigh, mindlessly eliciting a breathy moan *again*. I was quite sick of that happening, but I had no control over it. Besides, it felt good. And that was half the problem.

He slid his index finger along the trail of where I felt the moisture, following it up to my thumping womanhood. I arched my body back, panting at his touch but shaking my head. I hated how much I was liking the unfamiliarity.

He collected the liquid onto his fingertip and drew it to his lips. Panic set in. *No, please don't let it be pee. I couldn't live with myself.* He groaned, loudly. Muttering the word *mmm* over and over as he tasted me.

"Oh my God," I breathed. It wasn't pee. I looked down impulsively. *Shit. His erection.* And didn't that just make the thump in my pussy pulsate a little more?

What the fuck is wrong with me?

CHAPTER THIRTEEN

THERE'S HOT... THEN THERE'S HOT!

How in the *ever-living fuck am I aroused? I am a kidnapped, desired toy. Tied up, naked, legs spread by a fucking rod. Am I that desperate? Who the fuck am I?*

"Now... Fire? Check. Ice?" Ruby hummed as Damon scurried off to the bar. *Fire? Huh? Ice...why ice?*

I should be panicking for my life right now, because who knows what these freaks will do to me? But I wasn't. And I hadn't taken my eyes from the man's junk until then. I was no less a perverted fool than anyone else in the room. I couldn't even bring myself to stop swearing.

"What?" I croaked.

"Check." Damon called out, shaking the ice in the glass.

My eyes darted between Ruby and Damon, then Tilly, who was collectively calmer than I had anticipated. Like she wasn't new to seeing someone restrained against their will.

Damon held out the cup of ice to Tilly, and she grabbed a piece without so much as an inkling of instruction or a glimmer of hesitation in her eyes and then stood before me. I flinched from the intrusive sensation as she slid the cube of ice down my neck, glaring at me like a mother hen to calm me. "Better me than her," she whispered and I nodded. She was right.

The chill from the ice melting into my skin made it flare into goosebumps. An odd feeling, both hot and cold. The sensation was like nothing I had felt before; not like taking a cold shower, or dipping your feet in a cold pool. It was different, and my brain was wreaking havoc, arguing with myself if it was one that I liked or not.

I couldn't answer myself truthfully. But what my *brain* wanted and what the ache between my legs *needed* were two very different things.

I looked anywhere but at either of them. I couldn't. I sobbed through my confusion as Tilly trailed the cube of ice down the apex of my right breast. I panted and tried to wriggle from the sensation, but the cuffs around both ankles and wrists made it almost impossible to move. She pressed it firmly at my nipple and an illicit groan formed in my throat, one I couldn't control. I wasn't expecting her to do anything like that to me, but she did it so easily.

Damon mimicked the groan and I peered over to glance at him...curiosity spiked. My heart pounded out of my chest. *What the—*

Both hands were firmly gripped around his erection, his eyes burning on me.

Both.

Hands.

A twinkle reflected at the tip of his length, and I pinched my eyes to make out the shine, forgetting entirely that I was inexorably staring at a man's cock. My lips parted into a sharp circle, drawing an inaudible gasp. The glimmer was a piercing—no, two?

I could make out that one of them was a thick ring, pierced directly into the shaft near the crease and back out underneath. Between the slits of his fingers as he stroked, another piercing was visible, impaled directly across the shaft.

There was another piercing popping in and out of sight under the palm of his hand, smaller than the other two, under the head of the tip. Unease stewed in my belly. The pain a man would have to go through for a piercing on his member…if he can tolerate not just one piercing, but three, he was not to be messed with.

"Oh, God." I tried to swallow over the lump in my throat. By the look on his face, he was enjoying every moment of my gawking.

"You like watching me?" He asked. His chest panting as he stroked himself, building his orgasm to my curiosity. *Fuck…stop looking.*

I can't.

I didn't have any other word in my vocabulary. Not to mention that I had almost forgotten I had Tilly rolling ice over my skin—I was past the point of numbness.

"Good girl. Those goosebumps are ready," Ruby praised her and shooed her away, taking over, not that I was paying attention. I couldn't stop watching Damon. *Two hands.*

The cool shade of his blue eyes beamed straight onto me like I was either about to be his next meal, or he was going to come and take my virginity. I couldn't be certain at that moment that I'd object to the idea of that happening.

Aren't I supposed to be scared of him? I mean, I was just kidnapped by him and three other masked freaks, who have a bunch of women captive. You'd think I of all people would be screaming for my freedom. But I wasn't.

This silly girl was like a bird to fries. If Damon so much as came near me with that catastrophic thing—I wouldn't even call it a cock, it was a monster—it would destroy me. Especially considering I was indeed what they had called me...*a virgin.*

So why was I considering it? I had to have gone mad. *Am I still drunk, or high? No, it had been...hours? Days?* I mean, come on. Two hands?

TWO?!

My attention vaguely drifted to the sound of Ruby flicking a lighter and holding on the gas, but I didn't look. A building sensation of desire, desperation, and *need* was tapping away at the ache in my womanhood, watching the man stroke his sexual organ as he built his own need...*for something.* His breath intensified suddenly and his eyes darkened, and then I became aware that Ruby was so close to me that I felt another odd sensation; heat.

Tsss.

I cried out as pain shot through my body to somewhere above my breast, later realizing that Ruby had held the hot tip of her lighter against my chest. It left a pink serrated U-shaped mark bubbling on my flesh, amplifying my body into some kind of seizure-like movement against the restraints.

"What the fuck is wrong with you people?" I sobbed, yanking at the straps at my wrists. The tears poured down my face and all good feelings I had frizzled away to the scold.

"We're just warming you up for the big man."

Damon chuckled at Ruby's remark. *The big man? Warming me up? There's worse?* Tilly was silent with her hands behind her back and her eyes to the floor, a tear falling down her cheek.

Ruby held a piece of ice against the burn, I flinched at first, but the pain dwindled away with the melting ice. I dropped my head, keeping my eyes on the floor, and a sharp inhale ripped through my teeth at the sudden change of sensation of something *sharp against* my wrist. I knew it wasn't a knife, but I couldn't make out the object, and I didn't want to look. I kept my head low, weeping at the new wound on my chest. And one I only feared wouldn't be the last.

By the time my mind had the chance to refocus again, it dawned on me that the sharp thing Ruby rolled along my wrist didn't actually hurt, my brain receptors were just telling me it did. Sharp, yes, but not painful. It felt like needles. Ruby rolled the device from my wrist, down my arm, across my collarbone to my neck.

I glared at her in a panic, seeing it was a pinwheel, and it was getting closer to my burn.

"Please. D—" I begged, not letting my tongue finish the sentence, afraid of getting another punishment of some kind.

"Say it again," Ruby hissed with a daring brow arched across her face, lifting her cat wing liner and cutting me off. She was intimidating in every way, shape, and form. And as cold as ice. I stayed silent, holding my breath. *Shut up, Esme.* "Good girl."

She pulled the pinwheel off my skin and trailed her soft, dainty finger across the little white lines the pins left behind against my skin, eliciting a mindless, breathy moan. *Shit. I have to stop doing that.* Why did I keep doing that?

I smacked my lips shut, sucking them into my teeth in my own mental punishment for admitting my obvious arousal to her and Tilly's touch...and watching a man masturbate. It was a sensation I couldn't put my finger on, pleasure and pain, maybe. Curiosity and terror melding together. I was getting quite sick of my fucking head throwing mixed messages. I couldn't keep up. I didn't know if I wanted to laugh, cry, beg for my freedom or beg him *or her* to touch me.

Ruby brushed her thumb around my mouth, and my lips instinctively parted in response, just like Damon had done earlier.

"She's got a pretty mouth, D. I think it would look so much better with something in it," Ruby teased.

"What?"

"Mmmm. Fuck." Damon hissed. My heart skipped a beat or two trying to process what was happening. He was quick to my side, and I worked hard to keep my eyes anywhere else that wasn't the soft, warm, beating rod that was jabbing my belly.

I held my breath as his erection slid up my body to loosen the chain at the shackles on the wall, but not the cuffs. I panted hard, and my nipples swelled. I dropped my hands once more over my breasts, one hand over my pubic area.

"On your knees." He demanded, the heat of his heavy breath ripping down my core and making my skin crawl with both fear and curiosity. I did as he demanded and he moved behind me to secure the buckles on my wrists with a clip, locking the two cuffs together.

"I'll fuck her mouth. But I want *more*. I want to destroy this little cunt," Damon hissed as he forcefully cupped the palm of his hand at my vagina. I cried out but was met with something else I didn't want to admit; *pleasure*. Ruby turned a vexing brow at him.

"No, he will have your fucking head if you take it from her. Not this one," she reminded him.

"But... she's soaked?" Damon's jawline clenched down, trapping the growl with the tension as he gritted his teeth together. I knew what he wanted: *my virginity*. But the way Ruby had said it meant only one thing…there was someone else who wanted it more.

My virginity wasn't someone's to take. It was fucking *earned*. And I wasn't going to have it taken from me without a fight. But being angry wasn't going to solve anything with those people. I was outnumbered. Where did that leave me? Weak.

It was clear that someone had higher authority over them. Someone who was in control of who was coming and who was going. Someone who was on the hunt for innocent victims. Someone who was good at stalking—and opening locked windows.

Only one name came to mind. *The shadow man.*

CHAPTER FOURTEEN

UNHOLY MOUTH

I didn't think I would ever hate a person, not in my entire life. But hate didn't even begin to scratch the surface with that motherfucker. The god damn shadow man, whatever the hell his name was. If that man had a higher control over Damon, then he wasn't someone to be reckoned with.

"Fine," Damon growled at Ruby and he moved his hand from between my thighs hesitantly. "But he better not kill this one too fucking quick. It's not every day a toy like this one comes along for us."

He shifted his cold eyes up and down my naked body, his erection still standing to attention proudly for him, not a care in the world as to who was looking before turning back to face Ruby, who looked as though she was seconds away from cracking his neck.

"You ruin all the fun. Soren should have left you there to rot, bitch." He added.

Wait? It took a moment to gather my thoughts, processing what the fuck he'd just said. The chill down my spine lingered on the word and a thumping beat swelled in my mouth. Like someone had just reefed their hand into my rib cage and squeezed my heart.

Kill...

I froze. Unable to move my body or breathe, I just stood there, letting the word swallow me whole as the weight of it sat heavily on my shoulders. I was incapable of crying even a hint of a tear. Completely numb to my surroundings, their voices faded into thin air, replaced by white noise and stillness. It finally sank in, and the tears came rolling.

They are going to kill me.

But why?

Something warm touched my cheek, pulling me back to the now. It was Damon's wet tipped, pierced penis, hovering at my face. I craned my head away, glancing quickly at the women in the cages at the back of the room. They seemed to be in the same position I was: sexually confused, terrified, and with a ticking time bomb of when they might have their lives taken from them.

Are they hostages for murder too? Is this still a sex dungeon?

Vomit fizzed in my stomach. It was clear that the creep who had put us all in the hell we were in had a type. The girls looked very much like me. Long black or dark brown hair, freckled faces and bodies, with white pale skin. Each with their own indifferences. But they all had one thing *identical* to me. Green eyes. The sick fucking bastard.

Without warning, my head was yanked by the hair and my gaze forced to lock onto his impressive length and piercings. He guided it against my lips, smoothing the wetness over them like a lip gloss.

His fingers knotted my hair and with every inch of force he

had, he thrust right into the back of my throat. Tears fell down my cheeks and I coughed on instinct, but accommodated him quickly. A primal growl freed from his mouth as he rolled his head back. His length doubled in size against the walls of my mouth, if that were even possible.

Suddenly, my O-shaped mouth *wasn't* big enough. I was undeserving of a break to breathe, so if I wanted any chance of that, I needed to stop crying so that my nose had a clear passage. He thrust, hard, until he reached the furthest depths of my throat.

I had all intentions of throwing up, but I didn't. I didn't cough again either; I couldn't even if I wanted to. There was not a slither of space between him and the inside of my mouth for air.

My nose filled my lungs with air, his scent hitting my brain; a dark, hateful desire, heat, and hunger. I instinctively adjusted myself so that I could accept more of him. Suddenly, a hand lodged between my legs and making its way to my pubic area. Looking down I saw Ruby's hand. Pleasure immediately drowned out the terror and fear I had racing through my veins, and my temperature skyrocketed.

I mindlessly dipped my hip to meet her touch, and a muffled moan slipped from my lips. *Fuck. There is definitely something wrong with me.*

"Wow," she exclaimed, which only made my cheeks flush crimson.

"Oh," I muttered inaudibly around Damon. I was soaked, dripping in whatever it was that arousal produced. I wanted to draw my hands over my face in shame. I wasn't fooling anyone but myself. I was tormenting myself, denying my own desires, because what my brain was telling me and what my lady parts were telling me were two very different things.

Ruby made a circular movement over my clit and on impact an unfamiliar, disturbing, yet somehow very welcoming wave of sensations threatened.

"F-fuck." I mumbled as the dribble bubbled from my mouth, feeling something building: a climax—my *first climax*—somewhere in my core, just out of reach. *Is this what pleasure felt like? Why have I not done this sooner?*

I elicited an intense, lengthy, muffled moan around Damon's throbbing cock as my body pushed into her touch like I was going through an exorcism. I had no control over my body at that point; it was doing its own thing. But a release was not something I was granted, yet desperately wanted. *Needed.* I felt like a coiled spring about to explode under them, and they only mirrored the sensation.

Her finger twirled with a little more pressure at the little dot that was my clit, like she had done it a million times before. So gentle yet with such control, building my obsession up and up, and letting me fall again.

"What should we do with her? She's too close." Ruby hummed.

"Fuck, I want to fuck her cunt so bad." Damon hissed his arousal through his teeth, winding himself down. "Don't let this one cum. I want her to be left hungry for H. Got it?"

"You like this, little toy? This is the only thing you'll be good for, a fucking chew toy," Ruby purred, and she licked her lips. I don't know how or why, but their illicit mock only made me whimper and pant harder.

"His toy." Damon added. *His* toy? But what did that me— *Oh god. What is happening?*

"Mmm," I panted as she twirled my clit lightly in a clockwise pattern, alternating pressure. I cried out around Damon's length, and snot pooled at my nose from panting. I could feel pressure building inside of me. *Is that...a climax? Whatever it is that I'm feeling, is close...if only she sped up a little more.*

More.

No.

Yes.

No?

I tried to beg, or deny. I couldn't tell which one of the two had higher demand, but my throat was filled with a cock.

"Her mouth is going to look so good when it's full of my cum." Damon growled as he neared his climax, violently yanking at my hair for leverage. *No? I am not about to drink that am I?* Ah. My scalp tingled as he thrust deeper against the dull ache in my throat. My eyes freed a tear of desperation, panting heavily for more of Ruby's delicious torment...or was my tear from the fact that my mouth was to become a cream-filled donut?

Ruby's hand disappeared, and I was left hungry, desperate, and dizzy. *Wait, come back.*

"Fuck. Oh, fuck!" he moaned before his body stilled and webs of his warm liquid spouted into the back of my throat, over and over again. I couldn't swallow, as he was too deep to contract the muscles. The unfamiliar flavor on my tongue made me shudder. It was salty yet sweet.

With his fingers still knotted in my hair, Damon pulled my head back, all of him leaving my mouth, his piercings clinking against my teeth on his departure. I swallowed twice. There was a lot of liquid.

He forced my gaze up to meet his, and I sobbed vigorously. The reality hit me straight in the face. *I am absolutely going to hell for this.* His signature smirk turned his lips. *The fucking bastard.*

"What a good little slut. Twisted and desperate, aren't you? Sucking off a killer's cock without so much as a blink of an eye. You're going to be so easy to ruin. Just how he likes them," Damon mocked.

Killer.

I stirred into a fit of tears and started to pant. *A panic attack?* My each breath faster than the last but air failing to support me. My brain fuzzed, and starkwhite took over my vision, then darkness enveloped me.

CHAPTER FIFTEEN

STRANGE ROOMS

My first sexual encounter. Divinity and revolt stirred my mind. I was no longer Esmeralda Jane Pierce of Sayville. No longer that sweet young barista at Joe's Café. No longer living the peaceful life of a Christian girl, studying hard with her head in books, drawing butterflies and minding my own business.

No. That girl is long gone. You are a prisoner of sexual fantasies. And they are going to kill you.

I jolted upright, and a sharp inhale filled my lungs as a million visions washed over my head, but I plummeted back against the pillow with a sigh of relief, realizing I was safe in bed. It was all just a dream. I dozed again, rolling over to squeeze my soft pillow. Shoving my nose into it to inhale the scent that was usually a comforting aroma of musky fruits and tangy lemon from my shampoo, the pillow didn't smell anything like it.

Actually, it smelled of laundry detergent. My heart skipped a beat, jolting into an upright position again to let my eyes dart around the room.

This is not my pillow. This is not my bed. This is not my room. Instinctively, I rotated my wrists, believing I'd be tied up. Because I was, the last time I had my eyes open, cuffed to the wall. But I wasn't tied or bound. Not even a mark remained on my body from when I did have the rope around it from the cellar. My head pounded. *What the fuck is going on? Where am I now? I'm not in the cellar.*

· I felt as though I had slept for months, like a bear in a cave, hibernating in the winter months. I spun my head around, seeing the walls in the room were entirely coated black, illuminated faintly only by the moonlight shining through the window. I itched my scalp, trying to recall what my last memory was. *Damon and Ruby. I remember someone bringing me in here, down the hallway. I think.* I couldn't be sure.

There was one thing I did remember. *"He better not kill this one too quick."* Those words again, tearing through my heart like a serrated knife, etching a wound in my brain in ways I didn't know were possible. It only brought my mind back to that night. The shadow man. Hovering over me as I slept before disappearing out my window like a ghost. Appearing again three weeks later to kidnap me with three other people. A sneaky operation, and a very thought-out one at that. Caine was my lure, pretending to be the fairytale man of my dreams, sweeping me off my feet just to put me into his trap. Like a mouse.

"I like diamonds. You are the diamond."

Funny, that sentence had meant nothing to me then at the club when Caine said it. But it was suddenly obvious, that I was nothing but a little token for their appeasement. A collectable item. If he was the lure, the gang obviously needed some muscle. Lo and behold, the guy who carried me around like a bag of potatoes. Then there was Damon. *What the fuck does he have to do with anything other than be an antagonizing asshole? A distraction.* He distracted Tilly with his witty charm. Bile bubbled in my throat.

Gah!

What is Ruby? I couldn't pick it, unless she was in it for the rape-fest too, assuming that's not all they got up to. My mind trailed off. Maybe they killed the girls when they got bored and then found others. Considering the overuse of the word "toy", I wasn't the only one they got to play with. Which left the shadow man as the brains of the organization, the one behind it all. The fucking asshole. What he was doing was sick.

How is he not behind bars? My stomach churned. *He was the one who kidnapped me. He was the one who wanted me in the first place, so why the fuck isn't he here? Where is he now? Nowhere to be seen.* I needed to get the fuck out of there. I leaped out of the bed I was placed in, finding the nearest door to run to and almost falling flat to my face. Mind to limb malfunction, as always.

The darkness in the room made it almost impossible to see. I needed to find a light switch. I made contact with a door. *Oh, please, God, let it be the way out.* I jiggled the handle, kicked at the door, pushed at it, pulled it, yanked it, and hit it, but the handle didn't budge, no matter how hard I tried. My heart pounded.

"HELP! SOMEBODY PLEASE LET ME OUT!" I yelled at the top of my lungs, but the only response I got was my own warm, rapid breath panting back at me.

Fuck.

I tapped my hands against the walls looking for a light switch. Once I found it, I flicked the switch and the black walls sparked to life, a soft yellow light blazing from the chandelier on the ceiling. Darting my eyes around the room, I ran to the oversized arched window that led to a balcony. *Maybe I could jump off and run.*

The window was draped with red velvet Victorian-style curtains on each side and thick, shiny gold tassels, pinning them to the sides of the window. But just like the door, the window's handle did not budge. I froze at the pale white reflection in the mirror, realizing I was still very naked.

My breath hitched, and I shifted my focus to what was on the other side of the window. I was up high and on a very large-scale property, overlooking the same forest of pine trees I saw when I was thrown over the shoulders of the tatted-up hulk when he pulled me from the trunk.

I ran back to the door again, trying my luck at turning the handle once more. *Maybe I didn't do it right.* But I had, it didn't free me this time either. It was then that I noticed a pad beside the door. A digital finger pad. *Of fucking course.* I gave it a tap with my finger and a red LED light flashed at my finger. *Great.* Obviously I wasn't going to be granted freedom. Why would I? They had made it clear I was a hostage. *Fuck.*

But why the change from a fucking cold, dark cellar, to this? Reality set in, and tears began to stream down my face. I sobbed hard between each painful gasp of air, truly letting myself tumble into a miserable weep now that I was finally alone. I slid to the ground with my back against the door, my body trembling through the tears as the walls closed in around me.

After what felt like hours of crying, my eyes left burning and puffy, I got up and took a look around at my new prison. I was somewhat thankful that I was at the very least unbound and alone in a clean room, rather than the rotting cage that smelled like stale pee. Or worse, my lips around an enormous cock. *Be thankful it wasn't your fucking pussy.*

I scolded at my foul language. Up until recently, I had never sworn in my life. After I wallowed in self-pity, I got up and yanked the crisp black sheet off the bed, wrapping it around me so I wouldn't spend another second naked. There was another door on the other side of the room that I hadn't noticed earlier. It was a slider door that concealed a *huge* bathroom. I tapped around at the wall, looking for a switch.

Finding a strip of plastic that felt something like a light switch, I flicked my finger over it. Whatever I tapped at was not a switch for a light. It was a screen, and it beeped to life. Written on the screen were a few prompts.

Shower 1 + more
Shower 2 + more
Bath + more

I flipped the light switch and turned around, seeing there was a huge, black circular stone bath centered in the middle of the room. I creased a brow.

"Pfft." It was completely impractical, and it had no tap. There was a black marble bench top the entire length of the room, complimented by a mirror that sunk into the wall from the bench to the ceiling. The reflection looking back at me was worse than the one I caught sight of in the window. I was as pale as a ghost and visibly exhausted, far from how I'd originally looked at the club. Far from my true self, even. I mean, I'd seen myself anemic. *The sleepless nights have taken their toll on me and my body, but this? This is far worse.*

My hair was tangled and frayed. What was once full of volume and life could now de-thread from a stiff breeze. I even looked like a prisoner. I tugged at the dark circles under my eyes, glowing red from crying so damned hard for so long. And peeking above the sheet wrapped around me was a little raised pink and yellow welt. A burn. Embedded in my skin above my breast from Ruby's lighter.

I winced as I hovered my finger over the wound, immense heat brewing from the surface. Now that it had crossed my mind, the dull ache grew. A tear slipped from my eye again.

The stone basin was fitted with gold tap ware, circular like the bath. I trailed my index finger across the soft, fluffy, deep red and black towels wrapped in a tight bundle under the bench. They felt expensive, much like the rest of the room. It was no ordinary prison cell. Settled next to the basin was a gold basket with a hairdryer, a black toothbrush and a tube of charcoal toothpaste, like I was in a fancy hotel.

And everything was strategically black. I creased a brow and continued scanning the room. The shower was at the back, tucked behind a floor-to-ceiling pane of glass. *Come to think of it, a blistering-hot shower would be really nice right now. To wash away my sins. Let them float down the drain, as well as my self-pity.*

It was a double-headed shower, with no doors or tap, just like the bath. *Why have a bath or shower if you can't use them?* Then I remembered the little prompters on the screen. I ushered back to the screen and tapped on it again.

Out of curiosity, I clicked on the bathtub. The device chimed a melody and opened another menu. I couldn't help but scold myself for fiddling. But curiosity always got the better of me. The screen displayed another section of prompts.

Temperature
Bubbles
Lights
Autofill
Rain fill

I clicked on the rain fill button, and another chime from the screen sounded, followed by a mechanical hum from the ceiling. Then by the sound of water flowing through pipes. I swallowed hard, and my stomach fluttered. *Shit. What the fuck did I just do?* Droplets formed at the little gold metal cavity sunken in the ceiling and fell like rain on a stormy day, straight into the center of the bath. It was loud.

"Shit, shit, shit." I panicked, tapping frantically at the screen in an attempt to turn it off.

The darned thing finally lulled, and the sounds of the water droplets fell quiet again. My sigh of relief echoed through the room. The last thing I needed was to draw attention to myself prying where I shouldn't, or to flood the place that had no escape route. That would be my luck. Temptation was my worst nightmare. I never seemed to have a moral compass when I needed it. Drowning wasn't on my bucket list of ways to go down.

Come to think of it, neither was being kidnapped and held hostage by a sociopath and his group of masked sociopathic buddies who liked to do weird sexual things...

And kill people. That definitely wasn't *on my bucket list.* I scolded myself mentally at the visual of Damon's flushed pink, veiny pierced length in my mouth scrimmaged into my brain without permission. *Again, completely losing sight of that damn fucking moral compass.*

Gah!

I splayed my hands on each side of the basin, leaning closer to the mirror and staring into my tired emerald eyes, quarreling with myself. "You. What the fuck is wrong with you? Get a grip!" I snapped. And with a mighty huff, I swung my arm out, planting the palm of my hand firm against my cheek. The sting pierced my pale skin with friction, leaving a flushed hand pattern where my hand collided. I sobbed again. *There. That should just about do it. Smack some fucking sense into you.*

I took in the view of the room I was held hostage in, seeing that it was huge and, dare I say it, stunning. Despite every inch of the place being completely black, it didn't feel dull or cold. A low sigh fell from my mouth, pushing aside my intrusive thoughts yet again. The room was Victorian-styled, though the building didn't appear old. The Wainscot walls complemented the modern décor with the finishings throughout the room of gold, black, and blood-red.

The carpet was darker than the night sky and as soft as feathers between my toes. I wandered to a closet on the other side of the room, and as I suspected, it too was over-sized and all black, with red LED lighting throughout and gold trims. Both sides of the walk-in closet were blessed with ample hanging space, shelves, drawers, and a glass cabinet with a shelf for jewelry and shoes, but everything was empty.

It made no sense. Normally when people are kidnapped, they were taken to a secret location in a cage like I *was* in, wallowing in their own pee with the fate of being beaten up, raped, and or killed. *So why am I here?* That was anyone's guess. In an attempt to cool my heated face and to shut my racing mind up, I gazed out the window, my forehead propped against the cool glass, unable to feel the late spring breeze that I could only imagine flowed through the pine trees.

Wherever home was, it was long gone. And before I had a chance to stop them, the tears poured down my face once more. *So much for trying to calm myself.*

CHAPTER SIXTEEN

HORNS, EMPTY EYE'S AND A MOUTHLESS MASK

I heard a thud from behind my door, startling me. My mouth dried, and the tears came to a screeching halt. Someone was coming. My heart pounded, and I darted my head from left to right to see where I could hide. There was nothing in the room other than a king-sized bed with a chair beside it.

I can't hide under the bed; my tits would never let me fit. Maybe in the dark, empty closet? No. There are no clothes to hide behind. In a panic, acting on the impulse of adrenaline, the only place I could think of was behind the curtain.

I scurried and twisted myself into it like a burrito. My stomach gurgled at the thought of food. *Mmm burrito. How long has it been since my last meal?* It was anyone's guess, but I knew it had been too long. *Shit, my feet.* The green polish on my toes and my pasty white ankles stuck out from underneath the drapes of the curtain. *Idiot.*

The sound of locks clunking and electrical hums echoed through the air, and the door clicked open. Instinctively, my hand smacked over my mouth to mute my pants, sending a rush of fear and angst through my veins.

Adrenaline was the only thing telling me who or what was on the other side of the door. Terror washed across my face in thought of who it could be, letting the names run a vicious cycle in my brain. Only relying on my hearing and sense of smell, I gasped at the squeaky rotation of wheels echoing across the room, like a cart being wheeled in. The door closed behind it, creating a clap and mechanical buzz as it shut and locked. I waited in silence with my heart in my throat. The sound of faint but calm feminine breaths and a bright flashlight beamed across the room.

"Miss?" a soft, coaxing voice called out. A woman. The unease that fluttered in my stomach almost vanished completely at her tone. *Is she here to rescue me? A police-woman maybe?*

I unrolled myself from the curtain tangle, seeing the woman standing by the door with a perturbed look on her face, noticing my red eyes from crying.

"Help! Please help me!" I squawked loudly, stumbling my way across the room toward her.

She scrunched her face into a genuine sympathetic glare, but it was gone as fast as it had appeared. Her eyes darted from my head to toes more than once, and written all over her face was a look that only sunk my heart. *Repetition.* It clearly was a regular occurrence that she was accustomed to.

She wasn't there to save me. My mind stewed into a vicious torment of just how many women had been here, let alone the women in the cages, wallowing in their own vomit, pee, and dignity. She was dressed effortlessly in a crisp maid outfit with a tight bun perched behind her head.

"Sorry to scare you, miss," she offered sincerely, but her

voice was firm. My lips parted, and my words sat at the tip of my tongue, but she interrupted me as I went to speak. "Please, you must be hungry." She gestured to the food she had rolled on the trolley with an apprehensive look on her face.

I hadn't even smelled it until that moment. The scent of freshly baked eggs and bacon intoxicated my nose. The growl that rumbled startled me. God, I was famished. But the thought of the food being laced with something tapped at my mind. It would be a stupid mistake to eat something I didn't know from a person I didn't trust. Still, it would also be stupid not to eat, because I needed to eat to survive. Either way, I was doomed.

I frowned. The fact that this woman had a way in also meant she had a way out. Nonetheless, I tried reasoning with her again, for my freedom, holding onto the slither of hope that she possessed any morals at all.

"Please. Help me... I—" I croaked but she interrupted me again.

"I'm sorry, but I can't help you," she retorted, holding her hand up, a sense of anguish in her voice. Her tone tugged at my tears, salty droplets falling from my cheeks onto the dull ache of my wound at my chest. I held my breath for a moment to respond to her.

"Why? You're not really going to leave me here, are you? You work for these psychos?" I whispered in horror.

There was another hum at the door. My goosebumps rose, and a chill hit me. *Oh, fuck.* The door popped open and the woman gulped hard, mimicking my own. She scurried back to the door in a panic, like an abused servant would.

I lost my breath as two pale, sharply curled horns peeked out behind the slowly opening door. The very two horns that were attached to my stalker. *The shadow man.*

"He better not kill this one too quick." Damon's earlier words tugged at my heart—a pain I didn't know humans could feel. *He's come back for me. Is he going to kill me now? I am about to die for sure.* My throat narrowed as he stepped into the room.

He leaned against the wall with his arm splayed, and the woman bolted out the door. Terror and panic raced through my veins, so much so that I could piss myself and not even know it. I was *alone* with the man who had been stalking me. Alone with the man who had kidnapped me. Masked, tall, muscly, scary, haunting, smelly, and murderous.

My body stilled and I fell to my knees on the carpet, like I had liquified. My chest started to pant heavily. I held my hand at my chest as if it would help catch my breath again, but it didn't.

Am I about to have another panic attack? Please don't let me black out. I braced myself for his approach, but the murderous bastard just stood there. He sported a wicked pair of black shredded jeans, hanging a little too tightly against the V of his hips. Every inch of his flesh was painted black, except for the pale skin peeking under the shreds of the jeans. He blended into the wall. *Like a shadow.* Except the green glow of his amulet shone against his remarkably toned physique. He was shirtless again.

My lips separated, but a breath failed to draw in. With heavy eyes, I trailed them across his torso—*his rock-solid torso*—studying him with a creased brow and wandering eyes. I shuddered from the cold shiver that ripped down my spine, like I had been cloaked by spider webs. He took a step toward me, and I forced myself off my knees, scampering backward with the sheet scrunched firmly in a death grip in my hand.

"No! Stay away. Stay the fuck away, you freak!" I croaked in a terrorized screech between my sobs. I tried to sound at least a little less weak, like I could fight him if he tried something on me, but it was no different to a little mouse squeak. And I didn't know how to fight or throw a punch. Or yell, as it turns out. He tensed, and the speed of his chest expanding and falling quickened. The hollow note of his breath grew louder as it blew against the metal frame of his mask. *Anger? Shit.* He tilted his head.

I swallowed hard, and my brain split into the horrifying memory of him at my bedside in the dark of the night, like a bogeyman. His faceless mask had embedded a spot into my brain. He took another step, and the floor between us suddenly felt very thin, like he was stepping on ice, and I was about to fall through the crack, plummeting to my stone-cold death. My eyes widened from the sensation of the carpet clinging to the bed sheet wrapped around me, tugging as I scurried backward further, revealing a little more of my skin than he needed to see.

My gasp bounced through the air as he was suddenly standing by my side, crouching so that he was eye to eye with me on the floor, like he had done the night he took me, be it last night, or last week, or last year. I hadn't a single slither of a clue as to how long I had truly been in that time warp.

I stayed still, frozen. I could feel his eyes burning into me, though a better term would be the lack thereof. I couldn't see any eyes. The mask was designed that way, his eyes hidden completely by the thick layer of mesh behind the skeletal eye holes. It was truly terrifying. He was truly terrifying. I wondered briefly what color his eyes were, what he really looked like.

Who he was under all the façade, but the thought was quick to stray away. I had too many thoughts in my head scrummaging around to focus on just one. And that wasn't one I should have had in my mind, anyway. The silence between us was only adding to the panic and terror that hounded me.

His stoic calm sent a wave of electric sensation I couldn't quite put my finger on. Anger and loathing were the first to come to mind, but they didn't even scratch the surface as to what truly was screaming inside of this man. He was no different to a slowly ticking time bomb, waiting for the right moment to defuse. *Fucking chaos.* More than any nightmare could comprehend. And chaos I couldn't wake from. He hovered there for what felt like too long, studying me as I melted into the carpet, quivering.

Either the theatrics of being slow and antagonizing was his thing, or he was patiently figuring out what sick fucking things he wanted to do to me. I summoned all the courage I had to finally mutter something out.

"W-wh-what do you want from me?"

It came out in a gravelly, stuttered squeak. *How embarrassing.* To be fair, I was only expecting him to reply with "Your head on a stick" or "Your soul" or something obvious that a murderer would say. But he didn't respond, which only made my breath flee my body more—breath that stunk to no end, evidence of the lack of dental hygiene. I should have brushed my teeth when I'd had the chance earlier, but I was too busy roaming around the room.

I smacked my lips shut, mindlessly darting my tongue across the fur of my teeth and the dryness of my mouth. *Yuck.* Still, he didn't move. He just observed. Being so close to the mask under the lighting, and him being so still, I had enough time to really observe him. The mouth of his mask was molded shut. *Maybe he is mute?* He didn't speak, not even a whisper. *Like a shadow. I guess his mask is mouthless for a reason. Is he even real?*

Thoughtlessly, my hand drifted toward him, completely out of my control. I wanted to touch it, to feel the mask for a reason I couldn't explain. Maybe because I thought I was dreaming, or maybe because he wasn't real. I *needed* to touch it, or him—yet another intellectual default of mine, the moral compass once again parting my soul.

A deep, animalistic growl purred from his chest. His hand snatched my wrist and clamped down hard enough to leave a dull bruise. A faint shake of his head was enough to send the message. A warning. *What the fuck is wrong with me?*

CHAPTER SEVENTEEN

YOU'RE NOT SUPPOSED TO BE AROUSED BY SHADOWS

The shadow man moved quickly, somehow throwing himself over me in less than a blink of an eye. His hand wrapped around my throat, hard. The other was around both of my wrists. Somehow, I was lying down. *What in the ever-loving fuck just happened?* I shuddered. I was tiny against him; he was pure power.

He held my arms above my head, as well as the tendrils of my hair locked in his fingers from the grasp he had on my wrists. I dropped my eyes inconspicuously to the tug of my sheet, catching a glimpse that it had wriggled even further down my body. Not enough to free my breasts entirely, but I knew my nipples were teetering right at the fold of the fabric.

I gulped, loud against his hand. The sheet was also down far enough that the burn from Ruby was now very visible and, for some reason, hurting again. I drew in a sharp breath between my teeth at whatever air I could siphon through his grip, which was not quite tight enough to completely block my airway, but it was enough to send a buzzing sensation to my brain, very similar to the same feeling the night of my twenty-first birthday, drinking with Tilly.

He mirrored me, dropping his gaze to where the sheet had fallen. The mask's thick horns hovered closer to my face as he shifted his view, tilting his head slightly to my wound. The mask looked like it might be velcroed on, though I couldn't be certain, as the hood of his cape was covering the whole piece. At least I knew for sure that he *was* human. His breath picked up pace and he shifted away from my neck.

I gasped for a full chest of air and blew it all out with an embarrassingly high-pitched pant as his fingertip trailed my delicate skin, right along the jugular, as he had done in my room. Which was inevitably thumping with adrenaline... and something dark. His delicate touch shouldn't have tightened the slither of need where it did. No fucking way it should have. But it did.

He trailed further down, and his finger pressed gently onto the wound, tracing the shape of it firmly. I yelped, and my chest caved in a wince to the pain. Then he did the unthinkable. *A predatory, animalistic, purring groan.* In response to my pain and suffering. The feared flutter in my stomach triggered the tears to come out harder, and the sick motherfucker let out a singular, wry, hoarse chuckle.

He rolled his neck back, letting his Adam's apple break free from under the mask. I blinked to free the tears so I could get a clear view of his pale, unpainted, chiseled jawline. It put an immediate stop to my sobs, like I was a deer staring into headlights.

Crap. He was not in any way, shape, or form what I was expecting, what I had imagined an unidentified, silent, terrifying kidnapper to be. At the very least, I envisioned a seedy old man behind the mask, with a sick fetish to rape and kill. But he wasn't old. He was maybe in his thirties, at most. And considering he hadn't killed me yet, given the number of times he had the opportunity to, he was... different.

I think he's—dare I say it—attractive. Double crap. He was remarkable. More than attractive. I closed my eyes to his scent that wandered my nose, one that I knew I'd never forget, not since the first time I had smelled it. Letting the aromas of his erotic, lustful, musky cologne mixed with the metallic tang of blood, fresh pine, and damp moisture intoxicate me, I fell into memory of him at my bedside again. Only this time, I wasn't exactly against the idea of it, despite the scent of blood.

And that wasn't the most worrying part. The ache between my thighs only grew the more I let the memory raid my brain, so much so that I didn't notice that he had managed to maneuver himself between my legs. And as much as I wanted to tell him to get away from me, to let me go, or plead for my life... I didn't.

Okay, seriously, what is wrong with me? I should be screaming for my life. He just poked my wound and laughed at my pain. Why aren't I screaming?

He released my wrists, though I kept them where they were, remembering his warning. *Don't touch.* He balanced himself on one knee and planted his other between the very top of my pubic bone. I quivered. An unidentified man was hovering over me, about to do God knew what to me. But the heated liquid between my slit quickly pulled me into a mindless bliss.

The shadow man pressed his knee a little harder against me, eliciting a breathy, pitched moan and another frightful tear from my eye to fall. He splayed both his arms on either side of me as he leaned further toward my face, intensifying the scent of him. My chest hurt from panting so hard.

I didn't wriggle an inch, staying complacent as he drew in

my own scent. He groaned loudly as if I intoxicated his brain in a way. I couldn't explain it, even if I tried. Like I was the smell of something he had been missing, longing for. *Craving.* His chest tightened, and he was suddenly breathing faster. Beads of sweat glistened against the black paint on his chest. Not an ounce of hair was on it other than the trail he had from his belly button, disappearing under the strap of his jeans.

A sense of desperation filled the air as his veiny, painted hand strayed, his long finger trailing down the arc of my neck again. But this time, with a different motive, sending me into an unholy shudder, somewhere between aroused and terrified. He paused at the wound again before tugging at the sheet.

A gasp ripped from my mouth as his grip quickly yanked a heap of the fabric, pulling it entirely out from underneath me and discarding it halfway across the room. I panted heavily underneath him as he leaned back slightly to burn his gaze onto my exposed, thick frame. Tears trailed my cheeks again, falling faster along my skin.

He was quick to begin prying my thighs apart with his knee. I whimpered from the intrusion of his finger as it brushed through my parted slit. My body temperature skyrocketed again, and the climax that was on edge from earlier was right at my core, ready to explode.

I whimpered, and another animalistic growl vibrated from within his chest. Only this time, it wasn't from the unthinkable. I don't know why or what had gotten into me, but I arched my back with need. I had completely lost control of my body at that point.

His finger swirled once at the swollen area of my clit, and colors of the rainbow sparked in my brain—an unfamiliar sensation. I almost fell apart for him there and then, making me feel like Jell-O. Instinctively, I lifted my hip to meet more of his touch, but his elbow knocked it down and he growled. *Fuck. Wake up to yourself, Esme. What the fuck has gotten into you?*

Had I completely lost my fucking mind? Yes, because I arched my back again and let out a loud, panting whimper.

"Please, I... " I thoughtlessly begged for a release, but he stopped. *No! This is not right. Keep. Your. Mouth. Shut.* He pulled his fingertip from between my folds, leaving a throb in his absence. And didn't that fuck off pretty quick? The cold, jagged edge of his knife pressed against the arc of my pelvis. I gasped and pulled myself back, but he pinned me down with little effort.

"No! Please don't." I cried out. *This is it. This is the moment I die a slow, painful death. He's going to kill me.*

I huffed at his strength, though it shouldn't have come as a surprise that the man was a machine. He was not sane, and I was stupid enough to forget that. I was truly in over my head, lost in my own tormented mind fuck of sexual deprivation, curiosity, and unfamiliar desires.

I shuddered as his knife trailed along on the apex of my pussy, nausea making me want to vomit. But I hadn't eaten anything yet. The pressure of the blade was not pressed with enough force to push through my labia, nor my skin, but it was enough to remind me that there was something wrong with me. Because even though I was fucking terrified, I was still soaking wet.

The shadow man growled; he knew I was aroused. The vibration hummed at my need for him, which caused my body to instinctively lift. And I think he hated that. I think he hated that I liked it. Because he pulled the knife away.

His blade met my skin once more, right at the top of my collarbone, and somehow I didn't flinch. He trailed the silver over my skin, and I let him, hitting a part of my curiosity, recklessness, and cryptic thoughts I didn't know I had.

No longer an inch of fear in my body, I groaned from the sensation loudly. *This is so fucked up.* He hissed at my arousal, the sick fucking freak. *Or am I the sick fucking freak for liking it?* I felt a warm trickle of moisture where the jagged edge broke my skin, and a string of curses of what I should say to him ram raided my brain but wouldn't come out.

He pressed harder, and the flow of blood trickled down my collarbone, over my arm, and onto the carpet. And suddenly, like I had woken up from a nightmare with a pinch, I screamed, and every good feeling I had was gone. As was he. The room was empty and the door slammed shut. *What the fuck?*

CHAPTER EIGHTEEN

RUN, ESME. DON'T LET THEM CATCH YOU

"**G**od? Or whoever the fuck will listen. Are you up there?" I gazed out my window for the umpteenth time, praying to a God that clearly *doesn't* exist—never responding to any of my prayers nor coming to my salvation. "I can't stop thinking about him. The man in the mask. My stalker. My kidnapper. Why? What do I do? Please, help me. I need you."

What is the point? He doesn't care about me, if he did, I wouldn't be here. I sighed, watching the bright, orange, beautiful sun as it hovered above the pine tree-filled horizon, slowly dropping behind them into its slumber once more. I had needed to *try* and pray for clarity, because there were so many things wrong with me.

The man in the mask nearly gave me my first orgasm.

What I felt was nothing like what I'd experienced with Damon and Ruby. I never thought I'd say it, but I was desperate for my release, for reasons I had no business trying to understand. Why have I not stopped thinking of it? The shadow man was gambling with my life—that had been threatened one too many times.

My heart practically galloped away through the forest, finding its way back home and holding onto hope. Hope that I would someday be free. After a moment, the skin of my forehead caused a wet patch on the window; I was sweating. Even by nightfall, it was still sweltering.

"Ouch." I whimpered as the sweat puddled over the new marking I possessed over my chest, stinging the wound. *Fucking, ouch!*

Maybe I should have another cold shower. Those, and walking around naked were my only choices if I wanted any relief from the feeling of my skin burning from the outside in. Being naked had become my new norm.

If I didn't oppose the idea of being naked, the maid had given me a little black box yesterday...with a black silk robe in it. There was a little tag embossed with a singular letter on it.

H.

I assumed it was the shadow man's initial, not that he, or anyone else for that matter, would tell me. Damon had also said it to the others as they crowded me in the street before they all took me, so it *had* to be him. He had even mentioned that initial after that, but my mind was becoming foggier by the day, I couldn't place it.

"Pfft, a robe." I scoffed aloud in memory. *Well, fuck him. I'll be damned if I'm going to accept the gift, let alone wear it. Even if it is pretty. Fine, stunning. Whatever. It can stay in the back of the closet where it belongs—in a heap and invisible.*

I sighed. I was trapped in a blacked-out room, alone with my thoughts and the ability to think about nothing other than the shadow man and his three fucking henchmen. The prick made my head spin. Hate didn't do any justice for how I felt toward him. My mind was at constant war with itself. I was seemingly always thinking of him and his erotic scent that was burned into my brain.

The memory of his finger deliciously swirling around my clit, rudely interrupted by him drawing his knife into me and then disappearing again like a shadow of the night. *Gah!...*

The bastard. Yet, despite all that, why does my brain want to know what his cock feels like inside me, but also want to kill him?

I hated how time passed in my room. Only relying on the light, or lack thereof, at my window to tell me if another day had passed. I had spent three of them staring out my window, plotting my escape. But by the time the border between night and day had faded, it was always without conclusion.

Until now.

I had it worked out perfectly. My plan *couldn't* fail. It *wouldn't* fail. I had been studying the maid for three days. It had been three sunrises since I had been in that room. Three sunrises since the man of my nightmares had turned me into the butter for his bread. Three sunrises of losing my sanity. Fueling my adrenaline to my plan.

But why was I sent in here instead of back to the cage with the others, where I was originally taken? No one has been in here other than the maid.

He had hurt me. And touched me inappropriately. But he didn't kill me. Why? Damon said he was going to. So why didn't he?

A more important question would be *what do I need to do*

now to get out? Given that the door was only accessible to two people that I knew of, I needed to be smart about it. I had no chance against the shadow man if he opened the door. The maid on the other hand...*the maid will never expect it.*

I had never given her the impression I would do anything stupid. I decided I would escape, under the cover of night, because daylight was too obvious. But I at the very least needed the moonlight to light my path. A *full* moon. Running down the driveway—that I could see from my window, disappearing well into the horizon—would be a bad idea. It would be too easy for me to be found.

I needed the cover of something tall, somewhere I could hide —at least until daybreak. If I wanted *any* chance of freedom, I needed to run, fast and hard...not my strong suit, as I hated exercise...and then hide.

I needed somewhere I would be invisible. *The pine trees.*

I mentally noted that the maid came into my room three times a day. Breakfast, lunch and dinner. I'd needed her at her most vulnerable, and I could only attempt it once, for who knew what consequence I'd face if I was caught? But that wasn't something I needed to nest in my head at the moment.

She would come in with the trolley of food, refreshments, and fresh towels. And in the mornings, she made the bed and fluffed around cleaning, which I couldn't wrap my head around. I was a prisoner.

Why would a hostage have the bed made, be given a nice room with a stunning view, home-cooked delicious meals that brought the color back into my face? Freshly made juice, coffee, clean sheets, a bath with a freaking rainfall tap from the ceiling, and a big-ass shower. Yet my room had locked doors and windows, no furniture, and no activities. The whole thing was a head fuck.

Would I complain? No, plus, all of that food would give me the energy to flee. I was getting out. I had paid attention to her routine, learning it never once altered. And she was *never* late. The very second the sun had darkened the horizon, the door would click open.

At night, when she brought my evening meals, she would leave the door ajar by letting the door lean against the trolley. She never set foot into the room at meal times—except for mornings. She would push the trays of food and bottle of water off the trolley and onto the floor before closing the door. I couldn't understand why, but that was the way she did it.

My conclusion? Dinner time was the only time to get the fuck out of hell. *Wait, I'm naked. I can't do this naked.* I rolled my eyes and darted off to fetch it from the closet and put it on, tying a double knot across my stomach. *Right, now I'm ready. She will be here soon.*

I turned the tap in the bathroom on, not that I was planning on bathing. Running water was my decoy—when the maid come in to bring dinner, she would think I was in the bathroom—but I wouldn't be.

"You got this." I boosted myself up in the mirror before leaving. The sunset had well and truly dwindled past the pine trees, and the door hadn't budged. *Where is she?* For the first time ever, she was late.

I sat on the bed, waiting, when something dropped to the floor from under the bed. A pencil. My brows furrowed, I stuck my hand under the bed frame to feel for anything else that might have been lodged there. I felt tape where the pencil was strapped to, and my mouth dried, finding a piece of paper.

A note. It was covered with dried, old blood, smeared by fingertips. I read it with a narrow throat.

*If you are reading this, then you too are held prisoner here. I hope this message gets to you. You are not safe here. They will hurt you. They will make your body do unspeakable things. Strip you of your dignity, worth, and body. They will have their way with you. And when they are finished, he will **kill** you.*
Run.
Don't let them catch you.

Tears poured down my face. My heart thumped hard in my chest. I needed to get out. *STAT. Where the fuck is this fucking maid?*

I flinched as the door began churning its mechanical noises by her on the other side. I leaped off the bed, wiping my tears, and stood on the other side of the door, where she wouldn't expect me. *I was in the shower, according to her.*

As she opened the door, running only on adrenaline, I slid the pencil that fell from my bed along the floor up against the skirting board with my foot. She pushed the tray into the room and walked away without so much as a second glance and the door closed against the pencil—leaving it ajar.

It worked.

In the crack, I watched the maid wander off down the barely lit hallway and disappear. I let out a relieved sigh after holding my breath for what felt like far too many minutes. *If I leave now, and regret my decisions, there is no coming back...my door will stay locked.*

Fuck it.

I left, bringing the pencil with me as a carry-on weapon. I tip-toed my way through the hallway in the opposite direction of the maid. The place was a maze with doors everywhere—ones I couldn't open. I remembered some parts of the mansion from my limited time out of my room, but not enough to know my way out.

There was an elevator. I remember that one. But that was too loud, the ding would be enough to send alarm bells. Besides, I wouldn't be able to see who would be waiting on the other side of the door from inside the elevator.

I opted for the staircase instead. Blindly sneaking my way around, hiding behind corners, weird museum-type objects, and furniture that was clearly overpriced. I stilled, listening to my surroundings. The soft melody of a piano caught my attention. *Crap.*

It was a similar melody to the old children's lullaby 'Hush, little baby', and much like the one Eminem had redone. The tune was beautiful. Tugging at my heart, it was so...sad? *Come on, Esme, focus.*

I moved further, through a few open-planned rooms as the sounds of the lullaby's closed the distance. I froze when I could see a way out, but there was a door agape beside it...right where the melodies and a dim light were coming from. One I'd have to walk past to get to the doors I needed to get out from.

I took a big breath in and made haste closer to the door, not letting my breath shatter. I gulped hard and my feet froze, again —like concrete setting on the floor. *Why can I hear...crying?* I listened, confirming that what I heard from within the room, was indeed a man weeping.

Curiosity took over my brain and I stood beside the door, completely entranced by the melody and his tears. For some reason, a sympathetic tear fell from my eye. This *is pure pain.*

Foolishly, I peered my head from the corner of the door frame to get a better chance of hearing or seeing what *should* have stayed behind closed doors, and what *should* have stayed out of my train of thought.

My heart skipped a beat, or two, maybe three. It was the silhouette of the shadow man, the dimly lit candle on the other side of him casting darkness. He sat at the piano with his black cape draped over him entirely. I frowned. He really did look like the Grim Reaper, only he was human.

I bit my tongue to stop my gasp, seeing what I could only assume was a photograph on the piano, he was looking directly at is as he played. I could just make out that the paint on his hands wasn't all there, like it normally was. Some of it was smudged on the keys of the piano, giving the impression that he played it a lot. My stomach fluttered, knocking at something I couldn't put my finger on. I squinted to get a better look, but it was no use. It was too dark.

He was completely lost in his own world, tapping away at the black and white keys, rocking back and forth in his melody between the sobs. The depressive tune and sounds of his weeps continued to twist at my heart the more I lingered. I wiped the tear from my cheek, scrunching my face in disapproval.

I shouldn't have felt what I did for this man. He was a killer. But I did. I knew I shouldn't be there, I should have been running for my life. But as it so happens, my feet were concreted to the ground.

Listening. Watching. He was hurting, hard. And whatever pain he was feeling, radiated through me, just as hard. I hated being an empath. It was evident that the man was a beautiful disaster. *A musical murderer.*

He stopped playing, and his head turned slightly, pausing his breathing in concentration. My mouth dried, and I threw my body back behind the wall.

Shit.

Shit, shit, shit.

My hand darted to my chest, coaxing it from falling out of my rib cage and I melted, a bead of sweat pooling and trailing down my nose. I froze, waiting for him to come and slit my throat for spying, for attempting to escape. But he didn't. *Maybe he didn't notice.* A travailed sigh blew past his lips and he continued to play the same melody again, lulling my quickened heart.

For God's sake woman, pull your head in. I was getting sick and tired of my moral compass not being where it should be. I was making a habit of putting my nose where it didn't belong, like a cat to a laser. I needed to get out before he found me.

CHAPTER NINETEEN

SHADOWS IN THE FOREST

My heart pounded out of my chest and before I knew it, I was out of the glass terrace doors and my legs were taking me faster than they ever had. I was somewhat thankful for the food I had blessed in my stomach from the last three days, building my energy for the moment.

I ran. Ran fucking hard. *I am doing it, I am really doing it.* Tears streamed down my face as my feet pummeled the clean-cut grass as I neared the bushland. It was so far out from where I was coming from, that it didn't look like I was making any progress at all.

The scent of pine grew stronger and stronger. I had tunnel vision for the forest I'd seen from my window, where I would hide until daybreak and figure the rest out later. There was a thick layer of fog that had closed around, and in it. I would get Tilly out—somehow. Not on my own, though. I needed backup. *I'll come back for you, Tilly. I promise.*

My path was well lit by the moon above me, and if I were

able to, I think I'd just about be able to throw a rope around it and pull it in closer to touch it. That's how big it was shining.

"Shit," I panted over my shoulder, taking one last glance at the mansion before it disappeared into nothingness. "Ha, fuck you!"

I laughed for some strange reason. Not that I found it funny. Running barefoot in nothing else but a robe wasn't exactly a comfortable sport, but my options were thinner than air. I didn't care anymore. I was free-*ish*...

I huffed through tears of laughter and fear, and whatever breath my lungs could draw in, fueled entirely by adrenaline and my imagination of the future. *I have to move somewhere else. He knows where I lived. I'd have to change colleges since he knows where I go. He knows where I worked. He knows my every move.*

And now that I think of it, I know it was him who took my fucking drawings. I just knew it.

I couldn't move in with my parents. I wouldn't risk their lives with the psychopathic lunatic who'd kidnapped me. *Fuck him. Fuck him and his stupid piano. Fuck him and his stupid peace offering, or whatever giving me this stupid robe was for.*

Without the money Tilly was earning from stripping at Jesse's club and taking home strange men for a bit of extra cash, I had no hope of surviving on my own unless I lived in even more of a slum than I already did. I'd need another job. Two. Probably three.

God I hoped Tilly and the other hostages would be okay until I filed a police report. I really did. The thought curled my stomach as I continued my journey, tiring by the minute. My thighs burned to the friction, picking up the pace a little more. So close.

The scent of rich pine and mist ripped horror through my

brain, an unwelcome scent as it came in full force. It smelt like *him.*

A stray sound juddered my ear from somewhere behind me, and panic kicked in. My head pounded a likewise pattern to my heart, but at least I had made it into the woodland. *Run, hide.* The moisture of the mist chilled my lungs with each breath, and the overgrown branches clawed at my body as I ran between them, drawing blood, which evidently was slowing my pace.

Heavy footsteps threatened as they neared. *Fuck.* Someone was coming, and fast. I bolted harder, panting, sobbing, ignoring the pelting stings at the soles of my feet.

My breath hitched and my soul parted my body as a deep, tormenting masculine laugh echoed from somewhere behind me. The echo enveloped my chest like I had been stepped on, which only charged my terror. Tears rolled down my face as I kept running to the ends of the earth, not looking back. Just running. The solid footsteps on crunching leaves and sticks inched closer and closer behind me. *I am being chased.*

"You can't hide, pet. This is *my* playground," a deep, husky, unfamiliar voice called from somewhere in the darkness. I couldn't make out if it was in front, behind, or to my sides.

I rushed my head back, barely noticing the trees flashing past my eyes. But no one was behind me, and the sound of footfalls suddenly fell quiet. My life was hanging by a thread. I had to run faster. I had to get out.

The pain of my bare feet that were repetitively getting pierced by sharp fallen branches and shrubbery slowed me. There were no trails. I had to make my own. Panic and downright terror sent me even further into the forest. *Silence.* How far I had been running was anyone's guess. The full moon that had been shining as bright as day when I left was gone. I had run into blackness.

Which was equally relieving as it was terrifying.

The darkness would give me shelter, an opportunity to hide. But fuck, it was haunting. I shuddered. The trees were starting to thin, becoming taller. I stopped to hide behind one of the thicker trees to catch my breath before I passed out. I seemed to have a habit of doing that—the forest was not the time or place for such a thing.

My head spun in dizzy spells as I sunk my back against the trunk of the tree, the silk robe clinging to my waist by the double knot. Actually, it was barely clinging; the branches had torn the stupid thing to near shreds. The sides of my belly, thighs, and arms were covered in little pink grazes from the branches.

I blew out a liberated breath. No sounds were nearby other than the thumps of my heart in my brain. Proof that I was a long way from where I ran from. And even further away from where I was going. North, South, East or West—it didn't matter, I was lost. Terrified, alone and—

Bleeding.

I clung to the tree for a long while, and my eyes adjusted to the darkness just enough to see my hand in front of me and the silhouettes of gloomy trees, and the shadows of fog between them. The thumps in my brain finally faded, and I could make sense of the acoustics around me, only hearing the odd hoot from an owl, a faint breeze howling in the branches, and a croak from a frog. I frowned. *Where there are frogs, there is water.*

I listened again, tucking some stray hair behind my ear. I turned in a circle, spinning around to see my surroundings, squinting my eyes at the distant thinning of trees. It was a lake.

Chills ran through my body, making me shudder; the same

chill that ran through my core whenever *he* was near. A distant noise caught my attention, static and muffled, like a drone. A whisper in the distance, like the ones you hear in a scary movie.

My heart skipped a beat as I focused on the words it was calling, realizing it was a feminine voice coming from the lake. *There is no way.* It was slow and washed out, a breath between each word.

"*Give.*"

"*Her.*"

"*To.*"

"*Me.*"

My throat narrowed again, and a stick somewhere near me snapped. My breath fell from my lips, and my heart practically sunk into the ground. Choking on my own breath as I pushed myself harder against the tree, my eyes darted left to right to find a shadow or change of scenery moving across my line of sight. But I couldn't see anything.

A crack of leaves sounded behind me, followed by another, but somewhere in front of me. Either *he* moved quickly, or there was more than one person looking for me. I held my hand over my mouth to mute the sounds of my pants and sobs, tears rolling down my cheeks relentlessly.

I was undeniably paralyzed in fear. How I had not passed out by then was anyone's guess, including my own.

My brain ran like a horror film. *I am going to die, like the others did. Like the note said. Like Damon said.* Shivering hard against the tree, I regretted escaping. I held no doubt that my death would be slow and painful as punishment.

I blinked to clear my clouded vision from the tears and I screamed, loud, and it echoed far beyond the eye could see—the shadow man was standing stoic between the trees, right in front of me, enveloped by a mass of fog.

The theatrics he possessed were no less than the fucking Grim Reaper, a carbon copy, just without the scythe and skeletal body. I fell into heavy sobs, but he didn't move. He just stood there, glaring at me.

I wanted to run, but my feet wouldn't budge. All I could do was stare back. He tilted his head, like he often did. And then, suddenly, a separate pair of arms banded around me from my side.

I cried out again, gibberish falling from my mouth. Granted, they were not words. I didn't have the capacity to form them, but I beat the arms that strung around me and screamed so loud, my chest hurt, earning nothing in response.

"Leave. Me. ALO—" I managed to expel from my jittering mouth, but in seconds, his hand was over my face, muting me. I felt snot bubbling from my nose against his hand as I hyperventilated against it.

If you could feel smiles, I was feeling one—burning like the sun on me—though I couldn't see his face, I knew the shadow man was beaming a hideous grin.

"Shut the fuck up." The man holding me in a death grip hounded. I knew the voice—it was the buff guy.

All too quickly, a heavy weight collided with my head—a fist, maybe—and I was out like a light. Pitch black consuming my mind in an instant.

I was captured.

Again.

CHAPTER TWENTY

MIRROR, MIRROR ON THE... FEET

Have you ever experienced asking your brain if you were dead or just dreaming? Because that was what I'd been asking since the stench of stale cigarette smoke, wet iron, feces, and urine ripped through my nose moments ago. Like a distant memory, coming back to haunt me.

My head throbbed and I had tender muscles from my cardio encounter. I had been dumped back in the cage I was thrown in when I'd first arrived. It was cold, damp, and dark.

The sound of water continued to drip onto the concrete floor from somewhere, though it sounded a little too thick to be water. Who was I kidding? It was blood, without a doubt in my mind.

My half-naked body ached as I laid on the ground, curled into a ball, sobbing. How long had I been unconscious? I rubbed at my head with a groan, a fresh lump where the old one was from the bar. *I can't blame my two left feet for this one.*

I heard the door squeaking open, followed by two, maybe three sets of footsteps and deep, whispered voices—voices I recognized. A dimly lit candle followed the booted footsteps before stopping at the gate of my cage. I sobbed a little harder as the big man who'd carried me from the forest appeared at my cage.

He looped his fingers around one of the rusty cast iron bars, wearing the same black fabric mask as he had the time before. *What is it with these masks?*

"Ahh, she's awake." His muffled voice echoed against the chilling concrete walls of my cell. *Okay, clearly I've been knocked out for a long while.*

"Mmmm. Finally, I was getting bored. Any longer and I was going to have to fuc—" another voice called. *Going to...what? Have my body? Unconscious?* I knew that wiseass voice anywhere. It was Damon.

"You know he can hear you right?" The bigger one cut him off. *He's here.*

"You guys are fucking boring. Why is *she* any different to the others? Why do we gotta do what *he* says anyway?" *He who? The shadow man? I knew it, he is the one in charge.* I frowned, why was I being treated differently?

"Shut the fuck up, man. Go get the tools." *Wait, tools?* My mouth dried. *Punishment.*

The buff guy veered off, taking the candle with him, along with my visibility. And another pair of boots stopped at the opening. At first, I assumed it was Damon, because the silhouette was tall, but it wasn't. Looking further up his body, it was the shadow man.

Fuck. The whole gang was there. Minus Caine and Ruby.

I had to squint to see, but he opened the door and stepped toward me. I attempted to shuffle back, but I was hard-pressed against the concrete. There was no more room to push away.

"No! No-no-no," I stuttered in a cry.

The buff guy returned again and put a new candle on the other side of my cage, and they both stepped closer. They studied my body with something akin to hunger and anger. I squirmed under their greed, the robe only just covering my breasts. I tucked the fabric between my legs so my womanhood was not revealed.

The shadow man leaned forward to touch me. I flinched from his rushed movement, and he retracted his hand. Almost giving the impression of *I-wasn't-really-going-to-hurt-you*, but without reading his facial expression that was hiding behind his haunting façade, I couldn't be certain.

I had forgotten how small he made me feel, even when he had touched me in *that* way—in the room. I pushed aside my stupid thoughts. It was not the time or place to be having those. In a mindless panic, I crawled to my left to try to get away from him. It was foolish, I know. I only got a foot or two before he stood on my hair and anchored me to the ground.

"Don't do that, little one, it won't work," the muscular one threatened with a laugh, his voice playful and deep. *They like doing this to people. It's a game.* I should have remembered, resisting only fuels their fire.

"Please, why are you doing this?" I muttered, but my question was left ignored. "Let me go!" I pleaded again.

"Let you go? *Let you go?*" he growled. "Are you out of your mind? You tried to run. Big mistake. Why would we let you go now?"

"Oh, God." I threw my head in my palms, curling into a ball on my knees. Muscles huffed a laugh.

"You don't belong to *God* anymore, little one." His ocean blue eyes shone from the grin under his mask, the candle making it twinkle with desire. *Little one? Fuck off.* "You belong to us."

"Get up," Damon hissed, the demand momentarily paralyzing me. His vindictive, croaky snicker hit a nerve in me that I didn't like, like I was voiceless, powerless.

I imagined that he was my pillow, punching him until I made that stupid fucking smile disappear. Until and my knuckles bled and bruised. But something inside me knew that me hitting him would only excite him, and I curled my lip at the thought.

"GET THE FUCK UP, BITCH!" he hollered again, and I scurried to my knees in an attempt to get up without letting my private areas pop out anywhere from the robe. I stayed silent, unable to use my words, the lump in my throat choking my breath.

The three of them burned their stupid eyes into me. The buff guy grabbed my arm and dragged me to a wooden chair at the other end of the room. The girls around us were silent. There were less than the last time I was there. Which meant one thing, based on that note I found: they'd been *killed*.

I wriggled violently, and the grip of his hand bruised my skin instantaneously.

"No, please!" I whimpered as he turned me around to face him, shoving me at the shoulders. I winced and collapsed onto the chair, and then Damon dropped the duffle bag beside me.

"Keep your mouth shut. We're going to teach you a lesson. Make you pay for running that sweet little cunt away from us."

I fitted into a sob and shivered. If I valued my life, whatever was left of it, I had to do what I was told. Not that I had a choice, since the odds were three to one. He pulled my arms back and tightened some rope firmly so that my wrists twisted into each other, and my shoulder blades felt like they were about to pull from their sockets.

I instinctively cried out and kicked again from the torment.

Tears burned my face, the saltiness hitting my lips. Damon grabbed a roll of duct tape from the bag and ripped a section off with his teeth, slapping it over my mouth. I was tied, half-naked, and forced to keep silent.

"Fuck, I like this." Damon moaned. I quivered underneath his bane. My legs were the only moveable limbs, but they were almost too weak to do so—they ached from running. My body was tired, and my feet still stung.

"Now...there are punishments for naughty girls who think they can escape our game." Damon breathed as the shadow man paced around my chair silently, twisting his knife in his hand.

"H here," Damon pointed at him before continuing. "Wouldn't be too pleased if I let one of his offerings get out, now, would he?" *So, the shadow man is H.* Briefly, I wondered what his real name was, but the thought was gone as quickly as it appeared. His words tormented me.

Offerings?

Offerings to who, or what? It didn't make any sense.

I muttered under the tape, inaudible sounds as the shadow man's fingers brushed the base of my knee. His touch sent an electric shiver up my thigh. Mindlessly, I kicked my legs out to shoo him away.

Oh, shit. He growled deeply, the same animalistic growl he'd made when he was in the room the other day. *Fuck.* He moved in a flash. I flinched as he grabbed my leg and secured my ankle to the leg of the chair with a cable tie from the bag.

He pulled my other foot, lifting it to his knee. I winced from the burn behind my thigh as it stretched. He held his other arm out to one of the men, as if to wait for something to be placed into his hand.

"Glass, Eli," Damon hissed from beside me, speaking for the

shadow man. Eli was the muscular man. *Eli Whitlock. Damon Whitlock. H...Whitlock.*

The shadow man's breath howled against his mask, loud and unnerving as Eli pulled out a little box from the duffle bag. Whatever was inside of it...was sliding around like broken glass as he pried it open. Eli held it out for the shadow man, and he pulled out a piece of shattered mirror.

Holy fucking shit. What the fuck?

I squirmed hard beneath my bonds, but I didn't budge. More tears came crashing down, mimicking the muted screams that I pelted against the tape. He adjusted his grip around my ankle and planted the glass against the arch of my foot.

Fuck.

CHAPTER TWENTY-ONE

BUTCHERED MEAT

F ire-like heat ripped through me, and stars circled my head. A burning pain unlike anything before crowded me. I felt nothing else, I saw nothing else. I tasted blood, the sharp tang of metallic flavors pooling under my tongue with my saliva. Then I smelled it, thick in the air... or was it coming from my nose? I didn't know for certain, but I did know that I was about to be butchered meat.

A blood-curdling scream thundered from my chest and up against the tape with each descension of the glass into my skin. He was pressing the pieces in such a way that it would purposefully leave shards buried deep in my flesh. Damon and Eli watched eagerly while the shadow man demolished my foot. Hot blood trickled like a river down the calf of my leg, running toward my thigh.

His pace was slow and antagonizing, letting minutes pass with each drag of the glass and replacing it with another when it shattered beneath the pressure. I couldn't see his eyes. They were simply voids in the mask where they should be, but I knew he could see me. Watching every tear that fell from my eyes, watching tentatively for my body's reactions and soaking each one in like a drug... *like his life depends on it.*

If I wasn't mistaken, it was like he was looking for certain reactions, documenting them and bookmarking them for a later day. *Is he studying me?*

His breath was rough, rigid and unsteady. Sounds of crumbled glass ricocheting on concrete echoed until it was almost a faded muffle in my mind. I was becoming more aware of the sound of my heartbeat, my head pounding the same beat. And feeling heavy in my body. Saliva pooled around my lips under the tape, and I struggled to swallow.

I don't know how long I was staring, but the more I tried to make sense of *him*, the more my vision became blurry, and I almost didn't notice that he'd stopped. *Come on, Esme, focus. Why did he stop? Is it over? Why is he just standing there?*

Just let me go.

He finally—mercifully—threw my foot down and tied my ankle to the chair before untying the other.

No. I mumbled the word, but it didn't sound. It was a mere croak. He was going to repeat the same process on my other foot. My maimed foot tingled in a pool of blood. It felt thick as it oozed from my wounds. *That must have been what the dripping sound was earlier—someone's blood. They already fucked someone else up, and now it's my turn.*

My chest contracted into another fit of tears which only made my head thump. Moving was useless. I was no match for the monsters that surrounded me. I was done for.

He pressed hard into my skin once more, and I barely had the strength to wriggle. Time began to blur in my brain. *Have I been here for a few minutes? Hours?* I didn't know exactly, but I knew that I had stopped screaming. I had no choice but to let my body fade into darkness. I was barely holding onto consciousness.

My skin was covered in beads of sweat and goosebumps from the shock. Surrounding sounds were nothing more than a dull drone, other than hollow moans from Damon, who got a pleasurable thrill from others' pain. *The sick freak.*

I summoned all I had to look at the three masked men again. Eli was compliant, his arms crossed, his breathing slow. The shadow man was lost in his world of torture. *Does he get off on this?* Maybe so, but I couldn't dismiss the feeling that he was set up to do this. A bet, perhaps. I couldn't be certain, but he was nothing like Damon, who was wearing a sadistic grin. And hard-pressed against his jeans was his fucking erection. *Sick, sick, sick.*

The shadow man strayed from my foot and drew into the skin of my knees with a fresh fragment of glass, like it was a canvas to paint on. I didn't make a sound. *Blood. So much fucking blood.* Eventually, walking behind me to the palms of my hands, he placed a piece of glass in my palm and caressed it gently. His hand was unexpectedly warm, sending a chill under my skin. There was a sensation there that I couldn't explain.

He paused for a moment, with a sharp inhale before scrunching my hand in his into a fist. I gasped, shattering the glass and almost my bones with his strength. The pain was excruciating, but the tape muted my bellows. My chest worked hard to resemble a scream. Unable to let the sound out entirely. He panted, groaned, and threw the last piece of glass on the floor to shatter before stepping aside, satisfied with his macabre design. I took a breath in, but no matter how hard I tried, it wasn't enough to fill my lungs.

"Now you can't run away, little one. *All destroyed.* Class

dismissed. You've learned your lesson," Eli growled as the shadow man circled me like a vulture again. I batted my heavy eyelids as their voices fell in and out. "You're *ours* now. And now that he's finally found you, he *can't* lose you."

My head fell back, and the darkness enveloped me. I let the weightlessness pull me, falling into whatever mess my head wanted to spit at me in my dreams.

I was an object. A desired item.

Like a diamond.

An offering.

His offering.

Esme, wake up. Wake up. Wake. Up. A gentle, sweeping movement of something on my head slowly tugged me away from oblivion. A sensation of what I could only assume was someone brushing my forehead with their soft hand. I stirred, but my body was firm, limp. I drifted again.

I came to my senses again as a familiar smell warmed my nose: fruity hints of spices and aromatics with an earthy tone, and whiskey. *Caine.* I tried to flinch or open my eyes—at least move away from his touch, or run, or something—but it was like my brain was dislodged from my body, a total system malfunction. *Come on, Esme, open your eyes.*

I mustered up all my strength to peer through blurry vision, but I couldn't open my eyes all the way. Unable to fight them, they fell heavy again. I drifted straight back into my state of darkness, letting his soft, somehow comforting tone of his voice lull me.

"Esme, I got you."

"You're safe with me."

"My little diamond."

As I floated, I imagined the sound of the shadow man playing the piano again, the heavenly symphony adding to my stillness. The pain that man held inside him tugged at my heart, right where it shouldn't. *Why am I feeling sorry for him? Why me?* Suddenly, vivid memories of him touching me in my sleep... finding me in the street... tearing my feet apart and chasing me in the forest split through my brain. *He's a monster.*

I jolted upright in an instant, drawing an astronomical amount of air into my lungs before crashing into a tremor of tears.

"Please don't hurt me. Please! No, no!" I cried out in a tearful shriek, melting myself into the hard surface of what was behind me, slowly coming to the realization that it was a bedhead. It took me two blinks of my eyes to note that I was back in *that* room... *again.* An immediate blow of pain warped from my feet and other places. I was hurting all over.

Pain radiated my core like I had been hit by a truck. I squinted my eyes again to the brightness of the light, a lamp perched on a bedside table. *That wasn't there before.* I tucked my knees into my chest for comfort, pulling the sheet along with me, and I winced. *Fucking hell, ouch. Why did that hurt so much?*

"I'm not going to," Caine assured me softly. His word was genuine, I think, given his tone. That and his hands were gestured up in defeat. He kept his distance sitting on the chair next to the bed I was in and an enigmatic smile turned the corners of his mouth. I darted my eyes between his soft blue ones before finally convincing myself that he wasn't going to hurt me. *If he wanted to, he would have already.*

I swallowed, dropping my gaze from his to where I felt pain. I gasped at the sight of my hands. They were wrapped in a blood-stained sheet. Startled, I looked back at him and he ran his hand through his hair with a perturbed glint in his eyes. *How long has been in the room with me? How long have I been here?* A tingling sensation formed under the surface of the bandages, and then my knees. It was there, and then I came to my senses with the amount of pain I was in.

"What did you do?" he muttered, throwing his fingers between his ashy hair again. I had almost forgotten how handsome he was, given my illicit distractions. *Me? What did I do? I am not at fault here.*

"I didn't *do* anything!" I hissed. Rage started to boil through my veins. *This is all his fault. No thanks to Mr. Fairytale jackass over here. I wouldn't have been punished for escaping if I hadn't been kidnapped in the first fucking place.* Sadness was quick to knock over the rage. I crumbled like fucking pastry and collapsed my head into my aching knees, binding my arms around me into a cocoon. I fitted into a pitiful sob.

"Sorry." he spoke through clenched teeth, like he was guilty —sympathetic, even. Instinctively, I peered down at where the worst of the pain was radiating from.

My feet.

His lip curled as his eyes followed where mine landed. He knew of what I only imagined was carnage under the bedding. Dread uneased me. The heat from the bottoms of my feet was throbbing up my leg, painfully hard to dismiss.

"I'm not the one to fear, Esme."

"Aren't you? Really? You want to go there?" I snapped. He was the reason I was there in the first place.

"I haven't hurt you yet, have I?" Caine tilted his head back knowingly.

"N-no," I stuttered truthfully. But I still didn't trust him.

"You're only in here because I managed to bat my eyelids to bring you up here."

What? I rolled my eyes. "Oh, how nice of you to spare me."

"Be shitty with me all you want, but I thought it would be nice to lay here instead of on cold concrete," he snapped, growling at me. "Don't you think?"

"Do you really expect me to thank you?" I scowled.

"No." His jaw clenched and he broke eye contact with a sigh.

"So then why are you doing this?"

He didn't answer. Instead, he leaned back in his chair and drew his perfectly manicured fingernails through his hair again, lifting it off his face. He took in a big breath before looking at me again, his tight-fitting vest struggling against the seams. He was wearing another smart outfit, just as tight-fitting as the last. It was a darker blue, with oak brown, pointed leather shoes. His shirt was a pale blue, with rolled-up sleeves, buttoned all the way up and rigid across his neck.

Fucking hell, his neck. I gulped. I shouldn't be cursing so much. *I shouldn't be perving so much.* I hated myself for admitting that he was gorgeous, but the more I looked at him the less my heart pounded. Curiosity burned inside me.

"How long have I—"

"Three months," he cut me off. *What?* An impish grin pulled at his mouth, right as mine dried.

"THREE MONTHS?!" I sputtered in shock. *There's no way.*

"Okay, okay, okay. I'm kidding, sorry." He chuckled with his hands up before continuing. "It's nightfall. You've been out for the whole day."

I creased my brow and pursed my lips. *The fucker.* "You think this is funny? You think this is a joke? Look at me," I hissed, weeping through the pain.

"I am," he said in a low tone, flaring his eyes over me. *Why did he say it like that?* A moment of silence passed and I squirmed. He sighed, grabbing an unlabeled medicine bottle from the pocket of his suit pants. The tablets rattled inside, and his watch made a similar sound around his wrist.

Fucking hell, even his wrist is sexy. All veiny and defined. His hands were pristine, like he went to the salon three times a day for a clean. He was too clean to be involved in the blood-shedding sport the other three were.

Okay, new plan. One: stop staring, for a start. Two: stop swearing. Three: stop staring. Okay, but why can't I stop staring at him?

CHAPTER TWENTY-TWO

PILLS. TAKE THE PILLS, ESME

"Here... take these. It'll help with the pain." Caine held the bottle out, leaning forward with his other arm resting on his knee. I gave him a perplexed look after staring at the unknown medicine. *Like hell am I going to take whatever it is that he is dishing out from that bottle. Who knows what could be in there.*

He sighed again and looked away, biting down in anger, guilt or something, revealing the bulged tension of his immaculate jawline. I scoffed at myself, choosing to look anywhere but him. *I really need to stop looking at him.*

"Look, I know you're pissed. You have every right to be." His tone softened, and I turned to face him.

I imagined throwing daggers at him. *Yes, I do have the right. I just want to go home.* I grabbed the bottle and laid it beside me with a huff to shut him up. There was no way I was taking anything, I didn't care how much pain I would endure. For all I know, they could be some kind of sleep drugs so that he could rape me. Or something.

But, Caine has been with me the whole time, watching me sleep. I would know if he had, because I was a virgin. There would be some kind of pain there. I swallowed nervously and clenched my thighs together before sighing in relief. Good, no pain... *there*...

"If you won't take the pain relief, at least let me help you," he pleaded.

I stared him down. *I don't understand him. I don't understand this.* "Help me? Is that really why you're here?"

"You can't stay like this, and I know you can't do it on your own. Someone had to look after you."

I held in a breath to compose myself before I jumped out of the bed and slapped him. I didn't. But I wanted to. *Why the fudge does he want to look after me?* I've been kidnapped, sliced and diced and treated like a bug on a windshield, why now am I suddenly deserving of being looked after?

"Jesus H. Christ, what is your deal? I don't know what sick fetishes you freaks have with me, but the head fucks have to stop. One minute I'm here, the next I'm in a concrete cage. And now I'm being given painkillers like any of you actually give a damn," I scoffed. He didn't seem at all shifted by my words.

"Like I said, I haven't hurt you. Have I?" he repeated, his voice turned up a notch as if he were asserting dominance.

I hesitated. "No, but—"

"I may be involved in the things my brothers and sister do, but that doesn't mean I can't do my own thing. I'm a grown man. Besides the point, if you saw what you looked like when you slept, I think you'd be pretty glad I was here to hold your hand." I frowned, and he continued. "Whenever a nightmare ripped through that pretty little brain of yours, your body went through what looked like an exorcism." He stopped again, leaning forward and shifted his eyes to the crimson soaked cloth around my hand. "All I had to do was hold your hand, and you stopped."

What? He held my hand? Wait, was he rubbing my head? I couldn't be certain if I was hallucinating but I remember it. He was talking to me.

"So... I wasn't dreaming of someone watching me sleep then?" I asked. Someone watching me sleep was probably the least of my concerns. After all, I was used to that happening a great deal. What, with my stalker and all.

"No, you weren't."

"Stroking my forehead?"

"Nope." Caine shook his head and flexed his brows.

"You...held my hand?"

"Yes, little diamond," he remarked, adjusting himself and pushing back in the chair, slouching in *that* way.

"Oh," I croaked, swallowing the lump in my throat. I was starting to very much dislike that everything he did was making parts of me warmer than it should. I frowned again and he mirrored me.

"Look, unlike them, I have morals, okay? Is that so hard to understand? That someone actually cares about you?"

What the heck? My brain was screaming at me that it was all so fucking confusing.

"Cares about me? You fucking kidnapped me!" I snapped.

"I didn't... I mean. Well... I did, but. *Fuck*," he grunted, crossing his arms and jittering his leg. I jolted, my breath picking up the pace.

"I don't understand. Any of it," I spoke with a nervous breath.

"You never will. Fuck. I should have just left you in the basement with the others." Caine stood, throwing his hands through his hair again before sitting back down. I felt guilty, for reasons I couldn't possibly explain.

A tear made its way down my cheek, choosing to look away and keep that to myself. We sat in silence for a long while, and he never once took his eyes off me. The pained twinkle of guilt over his face only grew as time went on, which oddly gave me a sense of relief. *If he was even remotely feeling guilty for helping kidnap me, then good. Rot in it. The rat.* But I wasn't like them, I didn't want people feeling things other than happiness, even if it caused me pain.

"Thank you," I breathed honestly. I hadn't moved other than to eye the pills beside me every now and again. The pain was almost unbearable now, and I could feel the shards of glass burning, like they were moving under my skin. I would have to find a way to get them out somehow.

I contemplated taking the pills, but if I did, what would happen after that? I was certain they weren't regular Tylenol. I had a hard time focusing at the best of times, let alone with drugs in my system. Something more than that would knock me into next Tuesday, and as much as I wanted that, I didn't want to succumb to the idea of being unconscious anymore.

"It's fine," Caine said finally, rising from his chair. *Wait. Don't go.* "Wait here. I'm going to draw you a bath." *Well, that's not what I had in mind.*

My lips parted, about to respond with a *"no way, Jose"*, but by the time I had the ability for words to come out of my mouth water had already begun pouring from the ceiling tap in the bathroom. *"Wait here," he says—well, where else am I going?*

I leaned over to see him floating around in the bathroom in the gaps of the door. *Gah.* He really was an outstanding looking man. I hated that. Actually, I loathed the fact that I found *any* of them attractive.

Caine returned moments later. "I won't hurt you. I give you my word." He offered me his hand, and an inkling of a feeling set in my body that I could trust him. *But what is his word to me? Nothing.* Even so, it was still better than any of the others. The want and need for a bath ran higher than my doubt for Caine's word anyway.

I took his hand in mine, the other tucking the sheet under my arm and he pinched the bottom of the sheet up so that I could move freely. I winced from the pain of the glass aggravating my wounds as I got to my feet.

"Ow," I yelped as a tear fell down my cheek.

"I got you." Caine held me in a way that did not hurt me. I looked down, seeing exactly what I feared. I shouldn't have looked, but I did. I had been absolutely, entirely, fucking *massacred.* "Jesus... christ," he grimaced.

I was covered in dirt, blood, cuts, and bruises. My upper legs were coated in dried, cracked blood. Some wounds I could pinpoint from running through the forest, and a few black welts were from firm grips. As for the rest, I had no idea where they came from. I was butchered.

My knees had welts and shards of glass through them, but the worst source of pain was my feet. They had poorly wrapped bandages around them, soaked in blood. Pain ripped through me, hard, causing the bleeding under my feet to begin again, pooling all over the carpet. My head spun.

"I can't. I can't," I cried out, throwing myself back onto the bed in defeat.

"Are you okay?" he asked. My lips curled back in a sneer.

Am I okay? Was he serious? Had he any idea what the fuck I had gone through?

"What do you think?" I huffed through a sob.

"I'm sorry, you're right. Here." Without hesitation, he changed his grip on me, scooping me and the sheet that was draped around me up. I gasped as he cradled me into his arms without taking his eyes from mine. Caine carried me to the bathroom effortlessly before lowering me *and* the sheet into the warm bath.

Maybe his word is genuine. Maybe he really won't hurt me. I mean, he hasn't before. Not really. He had the opportunity to hurt me. I was defenseless. And yet, the sheet was covering my naked body, so I was not exposed.

I winced from the sudden sting of the warm water hitting my wounds, but it was short-lived. Eventually, the water soothed away the aches and pains. I sighed in relief and drowned in it. Caine stayed completely silent, letting me lose myself to rid the pain in my own way. His eyes were so piercing under the light, not as blue as they usually were. They weren't the color of the ocean, like Eli's, or devilish, like Damon's.

Caine's were like a puppy's eyes, *soft and pure.* And they wandered over my body. For a moment, I was thankful the soaked sheet was the way it was... hugging my curves. I let him mentally undress me. I liked the sensation it gave me, the way he was looking at me. It took my pain away. I squirmed at the unfamiliar sensation. *Am I turned on?*

My lips parted and my breath staggered, my hunger mimicking his. I frowned. *Am I so deprived of a human being's touch that I am turned on by anyone who gives me attention?* I'd spent my entire life invisible. No one wanted the chubby white girl. That was obvious in college. I was the jello girl, the ugly girl, the nerd, the loser. No boys wanted me. *Until now.* Suddenly, I was the main attraction. *The diamond.*

"Why do you call me that?" I broke the silence, and seemingly the shift in the room. He cleared his throat.

"Diamond?"

"Yes," I said under a low breath.

"I told you—"

Mindlessly, I dropped my eyes to somewhere I really shouldn't have.

"Ah, sorry!" I shouted, cutting him off. His erection was bulging at the seams of his suit pants. Guilty from my perverted glare, my eyes widened, and an embarrassing noise fell from my tongue, followed by a throb between my legs. *Oh, no, not this again.* I struggled for a breath, shifting my eyes elsewhere. The disgust I had for myself looking churned my stomach. *How embarrassing.* I looked back to face him wetting his lips with his tongue. He chuckled deeply.

"Don't be sorry for something your body wants, little diamond." Caine's voice broke as he said that name again. He paused, offering me a reassuring gaze. I gulped hard, and he darted his tongue over his lips again, intensifying the pulsating sensation between my legs. "It would appear that I want the same thing."

I said nothing. I couldn't... my brain had no ability to do such a craft of speech. I watched his chest rise and fall as he stood next to the bath, not touching, just looking. I mentally begged him to touch me in the spot that had been aching to be touched for far too long, but I was too scared to ask, and too scared to do it myself. He exhaled for what seemed like forever. Finally, he murmured.

"As tempting as you are, Esme, I can't." My heart pounded

as he began backing away from me. *He isn't going to leave me here, is he?* "Because no matter how much I want you, you don't belong to me. You never will."

"But—"

"I've overstepped. I'm sorry. I shouldn't have brought you here. I-I... " He hesitated. Before I had the chance to respond, he was gone, the door to my room slamming behind him.

I laid in the pool of blood and water. I shuddered, and tears streamed down my face. I was alone.

Again.

CHAPTER TWENTY-THREE

PARALYZED

I held my breaths between each one as the metal twangs and clunks sounded from the doorway. I'd spent the majority of last night in the bath alone, picking out whatever shards remaining in my body I could.

By the time I was done picking at my wounds to my best ability, the bath had turned stone cold, and I was left more dirty than I had been when I'd first gotten in. The water was redder than I was, if that was even possible. And I was exhausted. My feet were all the shades of purples and reds, barely resembling the color of my own skin. *What it used to be.*

The door lock clunked a final time, unlocking for the maid on the other side. What was once a dry mouth suddenly watered, saliva pooling from the aromas of freshly cooked eggs, bacon, and toast. They radiated through my nose, I had no idea how weak and famished I was. I guess pulling glass from the bottoms of my feet and my knees was a good enough excuse to become famished.

And if that wasn't bad enough, I had to actually get *out* of the bath. The pain was more bearable on my knees than it was to walk, so I crawled as far as I could, making it only as far as the chair Caine was sitting. I was mostly immobile—not paralyzed —but being mangled didn't exactly leave much ability to move comfortably. *They can't keep doing this, can they? They said they were going to kill me, and yet here I am. Breathing.* Fortunately, the bottle of pills was still there to save the day.

It didn't take long after fumbling myself back to bed that I caved and took two, going into a slumber the moment my head hit the pillow. Falling into a disengaged sleep, I dreamed of my new personal hell of the last couple of days, or weeks—however long I'd been there. If the kind of bullshit they imposed on me was going to keep happening, I was going to need a doctor. *Who am I kidding? They don't do doctors. They're monsters.*

Food.

I need food.

Or do I make a run for it? Those were my only two options.

Food or flight.

I sat wrapped in a towel on the chair, waiting for the maid. Despite the mess I'd made on the floor beneath me and on the seat, it still smelled like Caine. It shouldn't have made the flutter in my stomach dance, but it did. But there was something about his kindness that clung to me, giving me that hint of hope that I clearly needed. *Am I delusional, or just hungry?*

Caine didn't seem like the others. And if I was being honest, having watched a few movies in my life, murderers and crazy kidnapping freaks simply did not just hand over medication to relieve the pain of their victims. Nor do they give them a somewhat nice cozy room that wasn't a rotting cage.

I shouldn't complain. It could be worse. Besides, I did get to watch the morning sunlight kiss the sky, and see the shadows of the forest I was running through a mere twenty-four hours earlier dwindle away—that was nice—better than the view of a concrete wall. Or at least that was what I thought I was staring at.

Whatever pills Caine had brought in were strong. There were at least another five days of them left in the bottle so I'd need to ration them out. *Caine waltzed out in a huff last night for whatever reason, so God only knows how long I'll be here alone, without access to a refill.* I rolled my eyes to the use of the word God. *God. Pshh. To hell with him.*

Gah! That reminds me of something Eli said. "You don't belong to that God anymore." Whatever the fuck that means. The fuckers, all of them. Toying with my head with their fucked up game they're playing. Wow... *who am I right now? I* really *need to stop swearing so much.*

Breaking me from my mental case, the maid walked in. I frowned, unease stirring at the pit of my stomach. It seemed that every time that door opened, something bad happened. Her body language was not weak, like normal.

Perhaps this is a new maid. Come think of it, they probably sacked the last one for letting me escape.

Sacked? Killed, more like it.

I involuntarily imagined Eli's hand around her throat. It wouldn't take much. He was a monster of a human. One tight squeeze, and her head would pop off her shoulders like a ping pong ball. *There is something about Eli that I can't quite put my finger on. He is loyal to the shadow man, no matter the cost. But why?* Given what he said to me—something about me being an offering and whatever I was here for—seemed to have only just begun.

The maid wheeled a trolley of food and fresh linens into my room—or at least, I thought she was the maid—followed by a second person. *Shit.* It was Ruby *and* Damon. They were two faces I'd like to never see again, but there I was, looking right at them. Damon offered his signature self-satisfied smirk, and Ruby creased a brow at the blood all over the carpet. I shuddered. It was everywhere. No doubt it was also through the hallway and the stairs from Eli carrying me from the warehouse... however long ago that was. The room was like a scene from a fucking horror movie.

Ruby ran her eyes up and down my body, pausing briefly at my feet that were entwined in the sheet I'd torn up and used as fresh bandages, before peering back at the bed where the sheet *was* with a perplexed look on her face. Damon sauntered across the room toward me. My breath hitched, and I mindlessly sank into my chair, dreading where he was going to go. I couldn't survive another attack. Another torture session. I had learned my lesson: don't run. I summoned whatever bravery I had in me to not cry or show weakness, but it wasn't much.

"There's my favorite toy," Damon mocked.

"Get away from me!" I snarled in pure fear, but it was far from a threat. It was more antagonizing to them than anything. Tears pooled in my eyes but didn't fall. I managed to lock them in somehow. *All I do in this place is cry... tears equal fuel... stop, Esmeralda.*

Damon chuckled, stepping closer and kneeling in front of my feet. The illicit thought of me dragging glass over his pretty little baby face ran deliciously through my head. I frowned. *Get a grip woman.* He was so young, sporting peach fuzz stubble. Hardly a man. Couldn't grow a beard, even if he wanted to.

"No!" I exclaimed again, lifting my feet away from him. My words hanging in the air, very much ignored. He began untwirling the wraps on my feet, and I instinctively kicked, causing me to gasp in an instant. Clearly, I didn't learn my lesson the first time. He growled and I drew my hand over my mouth, panting into it.

"Do that again, and you'll lose these pretty little fucking legs. Haven't you learned your lesson yet?" His tone was empty, barely a whisper, and disgustingly playful.

I didn't want to go through that again, or anything like it, so I softened and loosened my body, submitting to his intrusive hands. If I valued my life at all, I was to obey him, even if the thought made my lip curl. *This fucker will get his way no matter the cost. If things don't come willingly, he will take them.*

"That's what I thought."

He caressed my feet, tormenting me gently with insincere praise. *Nice* wasn't Damon's thing. He was as much of a condescending pain in the ass as he was evil. And he looked good doing it too. I hated that. But it was true, nonetheless.

I said nothing as I observed him running his hands gently around the painful wounds on my feet, regretting that I hadn't taken my chance earlier in the morning to pop more of those pills.

His lips parted, and an enticing glint in his eyes formed, making the lump in my throat choke me and the tear free from my eye. I had done well to keep it at bay until then.

"Mmmm. He did good. That's what naughty girls get for running." He craned his neck toward Ruby. "Hey, Kit Kat, let's take her to the ball." *Does everyone have nicknames in this hellhole?*

"Ha, are you trying to get castrated?" Ruby scoffed, crossing her arms. She seemed annoyed yet amused by his outburst.

A ball?

A frolic-around-in-fancy-dresses ball?

Absolutely not. How about you just let me go? I vaguely remember Jesse mentioning them at the club. Something about an uncle and charity events. My mind wandered. *Why would he get castrated?* I frowned. Damon waved her off, poking his tongue out. He was up to no good. Stirring the pot, perhaps.

"He's not here. He will never know," Damon added.

"Your funeral." Ruby shrugged. They bickered on for a bit like I wasn't there, though Damon still had a hold of my leg. I stayed silent, wincing occasionally to his abrupt movement as he spoke with his hands.

When he removed the last of the wrap around my feet, he looked up at me through his long, pretty eyelashes. I swallowed, paralyzed in the chair in his presence. He danced his brows with a grin only a mother would love. The schmuck freak of nature.

"Come on, piggy, let's go. We've got shit to do," he mocked.

"Piggy?" I mirrored without realizing, before squirming from the sting of the word. He smiled with a purr, leaning in close to me. I shifted a little further into my chair and gulped again, loudly.

"Piggy," he whispered through his teeth before continuing, "because you bet that sweet fucking ass we're gonna play that game. *Piggy*... in... the... middle."

I released the breath I had hostage in my chest. *Fuck.* Panic and curiosity marrying each other... not the best combination.

"Now get up."

"What? I can't. Look at me," I grunted. *Is he bloody blind?* He tutted with a laugh.

"That? That was just a scratch. There's much worse to come. Surely, you've worked that out by now?" Damon dragged the last part of that sentence in a way that painfully etched into my soul as he tapped his finger at my head, alluding to the idea that I wasn't smart. *I can assure you that I have a higher IQ than all of you put together.*

He really was an antagonizing asshole. I pinched my eyes, throwing daggers at him like I had been practicing. *Fucker.*

"Don't threaten me with a good time."

"I didn't say anything," I muttered. He cocked a brow, and a smolder crinkled his face.

"You didn't have to. I can see it in your eyes."

"See... what?"

"How much you wanna fuck me," he said without hesitation.

"I don't-I-" I stuttered, shaking my head, but the words were mostly inaudible and crackled.

"For fuck's sake, hurry up," Ruby shouted. Damon clearly didn't register her, as he flared his eyes down to the area between my thighs like I was his next meal. *I'd believe that.* I gulped, hard.

"I'd destroy that little cunt in two seconds flat."

"Oh, God," I whimpered under a breath, turning my head away from his stare. Guilt and impish thoughts stapled me. Granted, he wasn't wrong. That was what made everything in my body squirm like my skin was crawling. *What is wrong with me?*

"Come." Damon pinched the side of my neck, and I flinched. I had no choice but to move and follow directions.

"At least warm her up, jerk," Ruby added. *What?* Damon laughed, tossing his head up at her. I kept my head down, cringing and panting heavily through each step.

"Good one, sis."

Sister...I still can't wrap that around my head, they look nothing alike. The pain radiated so hard that my legs were tingling with pins and needles as Damon and Ruby led me down the hallway, his grip on the nape of my neck firm. I was somewhat thankful for the wall that I held myself against for balance and strength.

Breaks or pauses weren't permitted. I had to keep walking.

To wherever it is they are leading me.

CHAPTER TWENTY-FOUR

A SEX ROOM

*W*homp.

I yelped from the sound of Damon's studded paddle across a hostage's ass, drawing blood.

"Ah," she howled, but it seemed it wasn't *just* a howl of pain.

Whomp.

"Ooh."

Whomp.

Dramatic inhale... and a... *moan?* Given the trickle running down her leg, she was aroused by it. I watched from where I was told to sit—next to Eli—as Damon caressed the area he'd hit, an action I assumed that would soften the blow.

"That's a good little *whore*. Take it! You're no use for anything else, are you?" Damon hissed, but the girl didn't answer. Only a mere whimper left her lips as if she enjoyed the viscous words he spat at her. He shifted, putting his hand firmly at her chin and pinching tight. "Are you?" His tone was laced with aggression and temptation. *The hell... what is wrong with these people?*

"No," she weeped. It wasn't a weep of sadness or detraction, though. He looked rather pleased with himself and his punishment, if that was what it was. I couldn't tell. It reminded me of my heated moment with the shadow man. *The bastard.* The marriage of pain and pleasure when it swarmed my body, his knife trailing along on the apex of my private area. The memory had been scorched into my mind, and to be fair... it was a memory I wouldn't mind staying.

Ruby and Damon continued to take turns messing with the hostages, *hitting* them, *beating* them, *kissing* them, and touching them in ways that I never expected to see. They were in great amounts of pain, and downright terrified, but they were enjoying it. And as much as I hated to admit it, I was, too. My forbidden area was thumping with heat from the illicit visuals of Damon and Ruby against the other girls. *What the fuck is wrong with me?*

I was enjoying it—watching them. Forced to sit there and watch. Though, I wasn't exactly sure if "forced" was the right word. We were there until nightfall. I barely even noticed that Eli was still next to me. When they were done with one, they'd pull out another, like they had done with me when I first got there.

The girls waited in their cages, spent, battered, bruised, and breathless. But those girls didn't get the same treatment as me. *Why? Why am I different?* Squeezing my legs shut wasn't a cure for the pulse that beat between them. It only made *it* worse. I was certain that if I saw another orgasm, I was going to have one myself. And that was everything wrong in one sentence.

Damon had two sides to him. He was either the one putting girls on their knees to have them devour his length until they were foaming at the mouth, like I had. Tears ran down their faces as they choked on his ridiculously sized cock. But he didn't climax. No, he saved himself for Ruby, showing his other side.

It was like no one else was in the room. He got to his knees and begged her for his release. She teased at his arousal with her fingers in *his* forbidden area. I remember Tilly mentioning it once or twice.

Anal.

Damon's creamy liquid had spiraled fast and hard from his erection, and as sick and twisted as it was, I never once moved my eyes away. I wanted to look away, I really did.

The evening continued to boom in all kinds of kinks and shambles. Scarlett and another girl came in. Violet, too. They came of their own free will. Not hostages... and *not* tortured. The place turned into a whore house. They were only happy to be upfront, spread like a buffet for Damon and Eli to munch on. And Ruby. A fucking sex dungeon.

How long does this sex stuff even go for, anyway? I had not a single clue, but for many hours, I managed to get only a few words out of Eli. We had a few drinks together, and occasionally I even earned a smile from him. The scotch was bitter at first, but it helped with the pain, so I didn't dare turn down the second.

Eli was much older than me, almost thirty-four. I didn't know why he did—the alcohol, probably—but he told me that Caine had an important role for me and the hostages. That blond masterpiece that I had stupidly called Mr. Fairytale was the lure, *the bait.* Because of his baby sweet eyes and kindness, it was easy to rope the girls in. *Of course. Easy trap. Pssh, Mr. Fairytale, my backside.*

I learned that Eli was the muscle of the operation—typical—big, tough, and scary. Even so, he seemed genuine and truthful, but I still didn't understand it all. None of it made sense.

Actually, the more I found out, the more lost and confused I became. And the likelihood of ever getting out of... wherever *there* was... became more distant.

I listened, tuned out and completely numb as they talked around me as if I wasn't there. As if my life didn't matter. By my fifth drink, I was seeing stars, and was almost completely free of pain. Just frozen in the same spot I'd been sitting for far too many hours.

The sex eventually subsided, and I overheard a man's name being mentioned a few times. Soren. He was the wealth behind the mansion, the face of the Whitlock family, and everything else in between, give or take. There was a lot of missing information. Either I stopped listening or words became scrambled in my head, but I knew that whatever was going on in that family was more shady than fifty shades of grey... not grey... *black*. But where was so-called Soren?

Why me?

Why any of us? I was always asking *why*, but it was always left unanswered.

I wasn't certain if I should be eavesdropping... I figured they would probably kill me anyway, so it didn't matter if I knew their secrets. Above all else—which surprised me the most—I learned that I was the only one who had been given a room of my own.

And a toilet, a bath.

A shower.

A toothbrush.

But no matter how many times I questioned, poked and prodded—why they wanted me dead, why I wasn't already—Eli wouldn't tell me.

Damn that night.

The night I was plucked away callously. The night I lost sight of Esmeralda Pierce. *The night my life changed forever.* I was a hostage with a death wish I had never asked for. I was an offering, but for what? I hated the fucking bastard... *H.* The shadow man. Whatever—*whoever*—he god damn went by. No amount of alcohol could drown the hate I had for him, and the sick, twisted game he had.

Eli said something to me about Soren, but I didn't respond. I nodded and gave him my empty stare. He waffled on about something to do with the shadow man being on the hunt for someone for six years. It was mostly untranslatable. By then, the alcohol and sexual haze had messed with my head entirely. *Does he mean me?*

"—in the lake, one, two, ten, twenty, thirty... now you," Eli's words were clear, a laugh at the end. My heart pounded, the words pulling me from my trance. *How am I so calm right now?* The shadow man was a murderer.

A cold, hard murderer.

And I was his prey.

"Are you bragging about our lifestyle or gossiping, brother?" Damon hissed, pulling himself back into his jeans as he stumbled over. Had he had more sex? Or had time messed with me?

"What I say and do with our little prisoner is my decision, and you'd do well to remember that," Eli scoffed back. His tone had a possessive twang to it. As if he were guarding me, for some reason. But then he continued. "He's going to kill her anyway, so no harm in telling her about the Whitlock brothers."

Damon rolled his eyes and tutted, "Fucking softy. She's weakened you already. Look at you."

"Look at me? No, look at her. She's been a good girl, nice and quiet sitting there, listening to me tell my stories. She gives *sitting pretty* a whole new meaning." Eli slouched back with his arms behind him, slung over the couch. His demeanor changed from top dog to jackass in a split second.

I struggled to hold down the bile in my throat, the feeling of everyone's eyes burning on me causing the unease to rise. What good feeling I had sweltering between my legs earlier in the night was long gone. *Get your mind out of the gutter. You fucking idiot, Esme.* The shadow man was a sick freak. *And to think this man has been near me on multiple occasions...* God, it made me wish I wasn't breathing.

"Mhmm, such a pretty thing," Damon added, stepping a little closer but keeping his distance. Eli stood to grab another drink from the bar, and I sat still, the air smelling of sex and static charge.

"All those girls done and dusted and you still want more? Is there any cum left in you? You'd be a flour dispenser by now, surely," Ruby chimed in. An involuntary chuckle snorted from my nose, and I pinched my lips together. *Good one, now I'm definitely the center of attention. Great—not.*

"I hear you're coming to the ball?" Eli slurred, loud enough so that Damon could hear, though he was talking directly to me.

"What?" I responded numbly, not really focusing anymore. *I didn't think Damon was serious when he said it earlier. Why in the fucking hell would I be invited to a ball?* Of course, I was their little toy to play with. That was why there was a stupid ball. I was a rat in a cage to poke and prod. I dreaded the idea of it, but did I really have a choice? *No.*

When you know death's going to be knocking on your door, but you don't know when, you just want it to be over. But only he knows when he is going to pay you a visit. He wants you weak, when you least expect it. He already haunted my dreams, and I was already weak. *Why wait? Why make me go through all this? And how the heck would that be possible?* Last time I checked, I was useless. It's not like I could do the fucking waltz —not with my feet.

"Yes. Tomorrow night. Oh, this should be good." Eli clapped his hands, rubbing them together like he had just won a pot of gold. He and Damon both fixed their gaze on me with devilish grins. I shrunk into my seat.

Eli slapped the back of his hand against Ruby's arm, who was neck-deep in a bottle of whiskey. "If *he* finds out, whooo-ee, Damon's a goner."

She snapped her neck to face him with tightened eyes, her hand quick to her knife at her thigh, ready and waiting to clock him. But she didn't. She huffed and rolled her eyes, like she was the sister in charge, watching sibling rivalry unfold. Like they were the mischief makers, naughty little boys up to no good, and she was the one responsible for their messes.

"Ahh, fuck. Come on. He won't find out. As long as someone doesn't *loud mouth*." Damon waved him off.

"I'm not keeping my mouth shut for you. You know I'll be the first to tell him you're sneaking around with his prized possessions," Eli grumbled.

"I supposed he's too occupied down at the lake, anyway."

It was then that my heart sank again. The lake. *The murders.* My unsteady breath echoed throughout the room, but they bantered between each other like I wasn't there. Like the threat of death was no different than turning a pot of water for a coffee, like every other day. *Do they really care so little about the lives of those they take? Gah.*

"Don't I get a say?" I vomited the words before even realizing.

"It's a date, then," Eli said, not looking at me. Silence filled the room for a moment before he continued. "So, that leaves us with the burning question... whose date is she gonna be?" His grin spread from ear to ear, and his shiny white teeth popped from his lips.

As handsome as he was, he was amused in a way that made my head race. My mouth dried. *These people are insane.* Damon's lips parted, about to speak, but another voice called from the doorway and cut him off, startling me.

"Mine."

My heart skipped a few beats before returning to its normal pace again. The voice turned Damon's lips. *Is he jealous?*

"I'm taking her," the crisp melody chimed again. It was Caine.

CHAPTER TWENTY-FIVE

A HOSTAGE AND A BALL

The beautiful summer sun glistened on my skin, a surreal sense of warmth I didn't know I needed. *Do I pray? Here... now?* I considered it, but then I didn't. The heat of the UV rays had the power to draw out all the trauma, harm, and pain from my body instead.

After coming back into my room last night following that eventful, kinky, whatever sex show I was made to watch—okay, fine, *wanted to watch*—I dived straight into the pills. They clearly didn't mix well with all the drinks I was fed, because I couldn't remember falling asleep. And when I finally woke up I had to ask myself what year it was. *2023, Esme. Remember?*

For the first time since I'd been taken, I finally felt at peace. Ruby had taken me downstairs after breakfast, and if the bizarrely offered joy of being let out of my room unbound and ungagged wasn't enough, it didn't end there. I was gifted yet another robe, along with a notebook and pen. *And* fresh panties with a matching bra.

Then all I received was, "See you a little later," followed by her humming Victorian-style music and splaying her arms out with an invisible dance partner, scooting around the room... and then she left. I was alone, left to my own thoughts and devices... again.

The ball.

The stupid ball.

Granted, I had hesitated for a long while, pondering if I should put the darned things on or not. I wanted to throw them into the toilet and flush them away—they were something Tilly would wear, slutty and far too revealing—but truth be told, a little part of me wanted to wear them without so much as a glimmer of give-a-crap on my face.

The matching set hung perfectly on my curves, like it was custom-designed for me and my body shape. It was the first time a bra had ever fit me without pinching. The stupid things were expensive, and made me feel so, too.

I squirmed in the daybed I was perched on, feeling the emerald green, silk-like fabric kiss my skin... in places that were a little too comfortable being... the silk running between my thighs and covering my lady area, following straight through the crack of my bottom. The pieces were smoother than a baby's skin, delicately enveloped by a layer of lace that rested at the arc of my breasts, along with a pretty tassel dangling from the center.

The wire was strong underneath, holding my girls up to the nines, nearly to my neck. I looked like one of those goddamn strippers from the clubs. *Who even am I?* At least I was given a robe, the absolute bare minimum to cover the monstrosity underneath.

Is the price of paying to look like a whore worth my

temporary freedom out here? Probably not. But damn, this feels nice.

I wasn't exactly ecstatic to be a ball attendee—nor to be Caine's *date*—but I didn't have a choice. I was going to have to suck it up. Based on the conversations last night, the shadow man won't be at that ball. *Good.* Maybe, just *maybe*, I could enjoy myself.

Yeah, right! Isn't that a farfetched theory? I was a toy. I wasn't there for my own fun. *Maybe I should try and run for it again? No one could stop me. There isn't anyone around. No. We've been through this.*

I wasted no time taking pencils to paper, losing myself in drawing my surroundings. The terrace had 180-degree views of the property. Even sitting at ground level, I could see beyond the horizon. There was no fencing. If I didn't have butchered feet, it was prime potential to run, but I had learned my lesson. The property went for miles and miles, inevitably out in the middle of nowhere. I should have been smarter with my escape last time, because going anywhere on foot wasn't really an option. The only way *in* or *out* was by motor.

There were even landscapers sculpting the place that had been there since before I came downstairs. Drawing gave me a sense of feeling like I was at home, though I knew I wasn't. It was… nice. The birds chirped in the background as I sat in serenity, my pencil sketching out a swarm of Emerald Swallowtail butterflies fading away from a black shadow over the horizon. I was the butterfly, and the shadow the shadow man. I was flying away, right the hell out of there. To freedom.

I jolted, catching sight of a small feminine figure moving swiftly in the corner of my eye. It was the new maid, waltzing into the terrace. Bringing a tray of biscuits and a teapot with two cups and sitting them on the coffee table beside me. *Two? Is she joining me?* The woman stared directly into my eyes, scanning me for whatever reason, like a silent interrogation. It was long enough to make me squirm.

"Sorry, I didn't mean to—"

"It's alright," I interrupted her. She seemed genuine in her tone. I went to thank her, but she had already returned inside before I had the chance, pressing her finger on the pad beside another door and disappearing behind it. *The kitchen, perhaps?* She was not as petite or weak as the other one.

I put the paper and pencils down and went to pour myself a cup of tea before realizing I wasn't alone. Ruby was back, watching my every move as she twiddled her little pocket-knife between her fingers. I hadn't a single clue how long she had been there. *Two cups.* I flipped the other cup the correct way, straining hers first. She glared at my drawings as I poured.

"Thank you." She nodded softly. I didn't respond to her other than a crinkled smile, confused that she even had the morals to thank someone. Something shifted. Her body language softened, somehow. *Have I gotten her completely wrong? Maybe she isn't as bad as the others. Caine wasn't.*

She sat beside me, dropping her boot on the table and crossing her ankle over the other. She stopped to look at me, and then the artwork that was under her shoe before moving them off the table. I frowned at the gesture. She reminded me of Tilly with the *tough girl* act. *I mean... she was raised in a family of boys. Of course she would have a wall up...* not that Eli gave much else away on that subject. She gave me no reason to fear her.

So I didn't. I decided I wouldn't let fear get to me. *Not even about this stupid ball I'm supposed to go to. Nope. No siree.*

I let the heat of the rich, earthy smoothness of tea tickle my lips before sliding down my throat. A comforting sensation, one that made me know I was still alive. For the moment. I thoughtlessly admired her tight physique in her typical attire: black latex skintight pants, studded bulky boots, and black lace crop tee, showing off her aesthetically fit midsection even when sitting down.

She was the male version of Damon, but less of an asshole. Her sharp black hair framed her face, and the winged eyeliner really pulled her look together. She was beautiful. *The ultimate bad bitch. The fuck-around-and-find-out bitch.* I found myself squeezing my thighs together to rid the sensation of admiration. *Oh, God... not again.* I needed a distraction, stat.

"You don't look like someone who would drink tea." *What? Did I say that?* Yes, I did, and with a little too much awkwardness. I checked the knot of my robe that I had tied three times, it was still tight and nothing was showing. She laughed, flexing a brow.

"Humor me."

"Well, it's just that you're—"

"You know people that aren't like *you* can drink tea, right?" she cut me off, perplexed and with a snappy tone. *Great, brain to mouth malfunction. I've pissed her off.*

"Sorry. I'll... just... " I trailed off, picking up the pencil again, tucking my knees into my chest and dropping my head back into sketching.

She watched me as time went by, humming a lullaby of some kind as she twirled her blade again. Between peering occasionally above my knees to use the pine trees as inspiration for the backdrop, I was glancing at Ruby. She must have been doing that *thing* with the knife for a very long time; she had calluses on the tip of her index finger, where she was twirling it.

I wondered about her upbringing, and what would possess a woman to get into the type of place she was in, curiosity taking charge once more.

"How did you get that?" I asked, referring to her finger. She flicked her eyes to where I was looking, and for a moment it looked as if she was reliving her past, her expression sad and empty. Then she smiled.

"If you repeat the same torture for a period of time, eventually, it stops hurting," Ruby answered truthfully, and I knew for sure that her words had more meaning than just her finger.

"Oh. Were you—"

"Tortured?"

"Y-yes." I nodded hesitantly. My heart pounded in my chest, not knowing what reaction I would receive from her.

Ruby paused for a long while and then shifted in her seat, turning her head to the side and pulling her hair up off her neck. There was a tattoo behind her ear. The number 115 with the hash symbol before it. My mind ran a million miles a second, thinking of what it could possibly mean, only coming to the conclusion that she wasn't the only one with the number.

I said nothing, only a gasp falling from my lips. I let myself get lost in the paper again until the border between day and evening faded, completely losing sight of the night's proposed ambitious activities and all the memories that haunted me.

"Come. Soren is waiting for us," Ruby muttered, turning her phone back into her pocket and walking to the terrace doors. *She has a phone?* A perplexing grin turned the corners of her pretty mouth, crinkling the black lipstick. My stomach fluttered with nerves. I stood, unsteady on my feet but somewhat able to tolerate the pain. Though for how long I could, I didn't know.

"Ruby?"

"What?"

"Will I stop hurting?" I asked, balancing myself using the edge of the couch. She looked away for a second, then spun on her heels, waving me off entirely.

"Let's go."

CHAPTER TWENTY-SIX

A BUTTERFLY, FOR MY BUTTERFLY

"He's got his work cut out for him." Ruby cocked a brow, trailing her eyes over the scabbed wounds on my knees before hovering them at my feet for a while, then bringing her gaze to my eyes again and rolling hers.

The weightless suspension curled my stomach, the uncertainty of what was going to happen to me letting my head run wild. The room we had walked into—behind the doors of the fingerprint entry—was open spaced. There was a fireplace, lounge chairs, a bar, and raked ceilings. It gave the design a little character. The mansion was almost cathedral looking, but modern.

More fancy chandeliers hung above us, and a handful of fancy art spread on the walls. I'd need at least three business days to tour the place. It was huge. Whoever designed the building had good taste.

The maid from earlier was there, and she brought us a tray of champagne flutes. I took one and downed it, frowning at myself for not letting it even settle on my taste buds before swallowing.

I sighed and took a second to get myself together before plucking up the will to respond to her.

"Is anyone going to hurt me?"

She hesitated a while, then a devilish smile flipped across her lips before finally speaking.

"Not around the people that will be here tonight. *Unless* you misbehave." Her voice was stern, and her eyes were dark... playful. My eyes widened, gulping hard at the thought of their twisted version of punishment from last night.

"O-kay," I stuttered, and then froze as Ruby's hand approached my cheek, slowly brushing it and then tucking some stray hairs behind my ear. I swallowed as the thoughts of sin hit me. My legs quivered, sending shockwaves between them from her touch. And there it was—*the need*—tugging at me.

She flared her eyes between mine and my lips, causing my breath to scatter. I hadn't touched myself before. I'd never had the need or want to. But since I've been a prisoner, it was all I thought about. *Maybe I should try it? Having an orgasm.*

Wait... no, I can't. The shadow man was a stalker, he probably had my room laced with cameras. There was no way I was going to give myself my first orgasm for him to see. Someone else should do it. *Maybe Ruby can?* She laughed, pulling me from my unwanted thoughts.

"Come on, you need to get ready for tonight's masquerade. Soren will fix... " she sighed, a rueful look on her face appearing before she stepped back to gesture to all of me. "Well, *this.*"

I cleared my throat, lulling the sexual tension that threatened to take charge of my mind.

"I've never been to a masquerade ball." *Or any ball, for that matter. Up until the night of my twenty-first birthday, I had never even worn a dress before. I'll probably be made to wear heels.*

However am I going to manage that? I'll need to take at least four pills if I am expected to stand for longer than five minutes.

I don't even have four pills.

"Don't tell Caine that." She smirked. My brow furrowed.

"Why?"

"It'll make his head swell. He's a giver, in more ways than one. If he finds out he's giving you your first fairytale ball gown, dance-the-night-away experience, his head will probably implode."

Fairytale. The word stirred a part inside of me, like a trauma response or something. I remembered something they said about the shadow man killing whoever brought me to the ball. *They are his family? He wouldn't kill them over a woman, would he?* If I was going to be honest, the whole thing was almost like a spiteful dig at *him*—to get caught. I didn't know, but I needed to find out.

"Will that man really kill him?" I croaked, barely a whisper. To think I valued Caine's life made my stomach turn. But no one deserved to die, and certainly not for me. Unless it was Damon. Screw that guy.

"I think I like you. You're... *interesting*. It's refreshing," she uttered and pointed to a step stool on the other side of the room, completely dismissing my question. "Stand up there."

A little woman in a dress suit stood next to it, fiddling nervously with the needles on her little apple-shaped pincushion that hugged her wrist. *A seamstress.* Terror was written all over her face, but she kept herself looking at the floor. My mind wondered that maybe the poor woman was held there at gunpoint or something for her services. I pushed the thought aside, complying with Ruby's instruction.

"Francis here is going to take your measurements for your

dress. And then, Soren," she pointed to a very well-dressed man at the other end of the room, "Will do your hair, nails, and makeup." *Huh? When did he get here?*

I looked at the man that was sitting on one of the sofa chairs with his leg over his knee and a glass of whiskey in the palm of his hand. His presence screamed wealth and power. Soren's hair was salt and peppered, but he certainly didn't look old. I mentally rolled my eyes at myself, because I was about to internally say it again. *He is attractive.*

His skin was European-toned, olive and rich, not a wrinkle in sight. Clean cut stubble was that of a mature man. I'd be guessing he was in his mid fifties, with a fit physique and a sculptured face.

I squirmed because he was staring directly at me like I had been served to him on a silver platter. *Soren. What a name.* I plunged my eyes to my robe, noticing the green lace of my bra poking out from underneath. I adjusted the fabric, covering myself a little more from his intense gaze, unsettled slightly, because he was old enough to be my father.

Soren had barely twitched his fingers, and the maid was already rushing to the bottle of champagne sitting on ice. He didn't take his eyes from mine as she poured the glass of champagne beside me. She passed it to me as I stood on the stool, trying to get a hold on the nerves that were stewing in my gut.

It was like he knew I needed that second drink more than water. I threw it back, and the immediate buzz gave me the ability to swallow the nerves, and some of the pain to a degree. An involuntary sigh of relief parted my lips as the welcoming heat hit my belly.

"Hello, Miss... ?" Soren questioned.

"Umm. Pierce. Esmeralda Pierce, sir." *Sir? Why did I say that?*

"To whom do I owe the pleasure of you in attendance to my ball tonight, Miss Pierce?" he asked. I couldn't be certain if he was messing with me or genuinely curious about my reasoning of being there. *His ball? Now everything Jesse had said in the club is making sense.* I went to answer him, but Ruby spoke first.

"Your boys are up to mischief with this one. You can only take one guess at who to thank."

"I wasn't talking to you," he growled at Ruby, then frowned for a response from me.

"D-Damon, sir," I stuttered.

"I highly doubt that."

Ruby laughed, taking a sip of her champagne before responding. "It seems as though there was a bit of a discrepancy as to who was paired with her."

"Interesting." Soren did not seem the slightest bit interested in Ruby or what she had to say. There was so much to him that gave me chills, like he knew everything and revealed nothing. "Anyway, Francis?" He clicked his fingers, and the woman began in a flash, measuring me up before scurrying away.

The sewing machine buzzed aggressively every now and again in the other room as I was being pampered by Soren. A man of few words, other than randomly questioning what I knew about the Whitlock family. I answered him with my whole truth, not that I remembered much of that night in *that* room with Eli and the others.

The only thing he offered me was the tedious, perverted look on his face. I couldn't count how many glasses of champagne I had while I was being dolled up to the nines. I was whirring. .

I couldn't believe that I was getting my own dress. A custom-fitted dress, at that. I hadn't seen it yet, but I imagined it would be nothing less than spectacular. I hadn't been pampered since Tilly had done it the night we celebrated my birthday. I frowned at my coherent thoughts. It all felt like a distant memory. *I promised if I found a way out, I would come back for her and the others.*

But I didn't see that through, did I?

Enough. Let's just get through each day.

It was well and truly into the night by the time Soren had finished turning me into whatever princess I was deemed to look like. I was somewhat thankful for the numbing feeling the alcohol gave my body. Thanks to the buzz of the champagne, the ache in my feet had faded to near nothing, but not enough to stay standing, much less dancing. *Dancing. Will I dance?*

My lips parted, eliciting a gasp as the seamstress waltzed around the corner with an emerald green silk satin gown draped over her arms, the color and fabric identical to my undergarments. My stomach churned, unable to knock down the thought of the shadow man having something to do with it, even though he wasn't around. *First, the matching lingerie. Now this? Gah!*

"Robe," Ruby growled playfully, eyeing me up and down.

"Robe?" I mirrored her nervously and drew in a harsh breath, then darted my eyes to Soren.

"Yes, robe."

I didn't want to strip before him. His expression darkened, and he clenched his jaw, shifting in his seat slightly. An enticing grin broke across his face. I swallowed hard. I didn't have a choice in the matter, as Ruby was already prying at the knot around my belly. I closed my eyes and let her tug it off, leaving me standing in nothing but my bra and panties. *That went easier than I had anticipated.* Expecting shame and guilt to riddle me, but it didn't.

Thank you, alcohol.

I stepped into the dress, and it enveloped my body as she fed the zip up along my spine. I instinctively arched my back and let a shallow breath out at the sensation. She huffed a slight laugh, noticing how reactive I was. *How embarrassing. It just never ends.* Ruby placed the two silver heels at my feet and I stepped into them.

The two stared at me as I stood before them on the pedestal. The A-line shape dress hugged my curves so tight that my midsection was cinched like an hourglass, a slit down the thigh. The satin fabric caressed my skin just like my bra and panties did. It was almost too tight, restricting my ribcage slightly. *Am I going to be able to breathe in this thing?*

"Well, shit." Ruby couldn't find the words. *Well, shit is right.* I was a princess. A fairytale princess. The woman who fitted my dress brought out a gift box with a white ribbon around it, similar to the ones the robes had come in. She handed it to Ruby before disappearing again.

"This is for you."

"Me?"

"Mhmm," she mumbled, handing it to me. I opened it, revealing a green and gold glitter lace masquerade eye mask tucked neatly inside. *I almost forgot that this was a masquerade ball.* One side was delicately crafted with a very large butterfly wing.

A butterfly wing. Of fucking course. The other half was elegantly laced with golden swirls and patterns. When I pulled it out of the box, my breath split, seeing the embossed label signed underneath.

A butterfly, for my butterfly.
H.

Fuck.

They *were* all playing tricks on me. I shuddered, but Ruby paid no attention to my woe. She tied the mask at the back of my head with the ribbon, securing it in place. When I faced the mirror on the wall, I barely recognized myself. *Wow.* The holes in the mask for my eyes made my green eyes even greener. I was speechless.

My makeup was sultry, a scandalous glow to my once tired and pale skin, with shimmers of gold sprinkled over my entire body, matching the glitter on my mask. My cheeks—what you could see around the mask—were peachy and snatched. I didn't think my doe eyes could get any bigger, but with a little white highlight in the corners and on my waterline, they were like a cartoon drawing, polished with golds and greens on my lids and a false wet look lash.

Soren had finished the look with a vibrant red lipstick in matte finish. My mind wandered, a desperate *need* for Caine to smudge it with his lips filling my thoughts, like Tilly had mentioned in the bathroom that night. I vaguely became aware of the hums of engines roaring outside before falling quiet again.

"They're going to enjoy this one... while it lasts." Soren's voice was deep, and sounded like it should be the opening of movie trailers. There was an accent somewhere, too, but I couldn't quite predict exactly where from. Croatia, maybe. He definitely wasn't American. Neither was Ruby. *While it lasts... you mean while I last?*

"Mmmm. Yes they are," Ruby muttered back, her tone a little too devious. *And cue the dark thoughts. Great.*

He tsked. "It won't come without consequences, though. They should know better than to ruffle his feathers."

"Yep." Ruby's response was delighted, with a smirk as she stared playfully at me. I squirmed at the thought of what my night would let out. It didn't make sense. She said I wouldn't be hurt—if I behaved. And by *behave*, they meant *follow their rules.*

I wanted to believe her, I really did. But going anywhere with the Whitlock family would most definitely mean that I would be inflicted with pain. *Including Ruby...* only then did I recall her putting her lighter to my skin.

It took far too long to realize that I was not only dolled up to be put on a silver platter for *him*, the shadow man... I was destined to be served up to *all* of them. Terror quickly made its way through my veins.

Piggy in the middle.

CHAPTER TWENTY-SEVEN

WHAT IN THE UNHOLY FUCK?

R uby pulled her cell from the pocket of her dress and tapped on it a few times before dropping it back in and zipping it closed again. A young man in a black tailored suit filled the void of the door, behind where Soren was sitting earlier.

Subtle hints of soft lulling, classical Victorian-style melodies chimed from further within the mansion's halls. *Ball music.* My heart fluttered. *If I wasn't so terrified this would be more exciting.*

"Enjoy. I'll see you out there later. Don't bid away too much money," Soren winked, almost insincerely. I assumed he'd freshen up before he joined us. *Bidding...* I wondered what charity the ball was for. Jesse had mentioned that there were fundraisers.

"This way please, ladies." The young steward offered his arm out to me. My feet were concreted to the floor, scared to take a step. God only knew how much pain it would radiate—the alcohol was wearing thin, and it had been hours since my last pill. I stretched to reach his arm, but Ruby yanked it back with a tedious cocked brow.

"Remember... *behave*. I won't warn you twice," she demanded, radiating complete seriousness. I gulped hard, and she spun my wrist so that my palm was open.

My eyes widened as she dropped three painkillers into it—the same ones Caine had given me. She must have grabbed the bottle from my room. Or maybe there was more? My mouth turned a genuine smile, grateful that she considered my pain enough to give me relief.

"T-thanks, Ruby," I stuttered. There were no liquids around, so I deposited them into my bra. I hadn't a chance in hell in swallowing three without a drink of some sort.

I took the young man's arm and let him guide me to wherever it was we were going. Ruby followed, and my heart pounded, not knowing what my night would bring. At least I had painkillers on my side, and I assumed more alcohol. As we walked, my mind flipped and spun with the uncertainty of what those men would do to me, trying to hold onto a sliver of hope that they wouldn't hurt me again.

The steward led us through a room mostly empty with a few chairs scattered around it, like a formal sitting or waiting room, then into another, and another, and another. *How many rooms can this place possibly have?* My eyes widened again, taking it all in.

"This place is huge."

"Soren gifted it to... well, you know who." Ruby chuckled at her own remark. My mouth dried. *Him...*

"This is his place?"

"Yep."

"So, your uncle knows about... all the stuff that happens?" I strung my sentence out, regret on the tip of my tongue but I hadn't the ability to stop.

"Who do you think covers everything for us?"

I scoffed with an eye roll, loathing on my tongue, and a tight fist. *Damn him. Damn them. Damn this entire family.* Ruby's hand was over my ass before I had the chance to consider my next choice of words. *I'm being smacked like a schoolgirl. A warning. Behave.*

We kept walking in silence. *Good, I don't need any more of a reason to learn more about these sick people.* I drew my attention toward the sound of vehement voices as we moved further into the mansion. It sounded like a lot of people were there for the event.

We finally reached a pair of floor-to-ceiling arched double doors that led into a grand room behind them. An involuntary gasp fell from my lips, and the alcohol suddenly felt like it was in full swing—though it had been a while since I had any—making me dizzy as I admired the elegance. I felt like royalty.

It reminded me of standing in line at that club, when the guard let us in even though we were at the back of the line, and again when the waitress led us to the VIP booth. The feeling of royalty didn't last long. Suddenly, I felt very small and out of place. Especially without Tilly. I instinctively drew my hand to my chest. *It will be okay. Tilly, please be okay.*

Another young gentleman appeared with a tray of four champagne flutes, two pink and two white. *Good, now I can take my pills.* Not to mention needing to drown the complete shit show of emotions I had raging through my brain. I grabbed myself a glass of the pink champagne with a strawberry in it, swallowing the entire contents in seconds, along with the pills from my bra. Then Ruby and I strolled inside the grand room.

My jaw dropped to the floor, seeing the twenty feet or more high ceilings, two white marble staircases with iron railing on each side of the room, a balcony above overlooking the grand entrance, and a huge hanging crystal chandelier in the middle.

The whole place was covered in marble; the floor, the walls. The ceiling was stone with insanely detailed gypsum patterns with gold finishings. The place was stunning. It was like we had walked into a different mansion, one half modern and dark, the other Victorian and bright. A whole new world.

"Shit," I muttered, my mouth agape as I took it all in. In complete disbelief that it was my reality. The young man led us between the two staircases through the open double door, where the gathering was being held.

It was loud. Ruby stepped in first, and I was able to catch a better sight of her figure in her dress. A sight to see. I had only seen her in black and gothic attire until then. Her red lace gown fell from her waist easily. She suited that color very well. *It's nice to see her in red lipstick instead of black, showing the feminine side I got a glimpse of earlier today. But... where is my date, Caine? Shouldn't he be bringing me here instead of Ruby?*

Everyone was mingling and being served more bubbly champagne and little appetizers by men in long black tailed suits, black masks, and white gloves. Laughter and joy filled the room. Once I had picked my jaw up off the floor, I smiled ear to ear, finally spotting where the beautiful sound was coming from; a woman dressed in white, playing an exquisite harp at the other end of the room.

The women present were dressed very well, and *very* expensively, and the men looked sharp and wealthy—royal, even. The golden masks gave that extra elegance appeal. I wondered briefly if they knew any of these people were killers, kidnappers, criminals, and drug dealers—and whatever else I could mention. They were trouble from the get go, and I was smack bang right in the middle of it.

I clenched my teeth. Something in the pit of my stomach made me want to scream and thrash for help, yell that I had been kidnapped and I was going to be murdered. But I didn't. *Behave, remember?* I found a nearby table instead and sat down at, letting the mild tingle leave my feet. Come on drugs… hit me. *I probably shouldn't have taken all three. Ah, I think that is the least of my worries.* My eyes roamed over the vibrant people around me, full of life and smiles. *Fun.* I creased a brow, noticing my name perched on the top of a little card on another table.

I moved and sat at that chair when a very tall man in a suit and golden, half-faced mask made a grand entrance like he owned the place, jumping around like an idiot to the beat of his own drum, playing the air guitar and grabbing random ladies and spinning them in a circle before grabbing the next, clearly drunk. I scoffed, and then an involuntary smile tickled the edges of my lips as the crowd hyped him up with their claps.

It took me way too long to realize it was Damon. *The fucking idiot.* My breath hitched when he spotted me, and an impish grin split his mouth. The dimples in his cheeks hollowed in a way that only made me squirm *in that way.*

Crap.

I pieced together every scrap of courage I could to stay calm, remembering that Ruby said I wasn't going to be hurt if I behaved—*obeyed.* My mind wandered again. *Will there be sexual things? Go away! Stupid brain.*

I gasped from the abrupt band of his arms as he drunkenly wrapped them around me, smothering me against his suit before leaning back against the chair. But it was not the time or place to gouge his eyes out with my freshly painted fingernails Soren crafted on me.

"I should have guessed it was you," I snarled without meaning to. *Behave!*

Granted, it was hard to choke down the nerves in my voice, but I was thankful for the buzz the champagne had given me... a confidence buzz. Besides, if I showed any weaknesses, Damon would play with them like a puppet on a string. Like a *toy*.

The smug fool started rolling a toothpick between his teeth. I imagined him choking on it. *Let him choke to death while I watch on.* I scolded myself from the intrusive thought as his crisp blue eyes burned into me—well, my perfectly plump breasts—lingering. I rolled my eyes, mad at myself for admiring him while he admired me. If looks could kill. He whistled around the toothpick.

"*H* picked a good dress," he muttered out with a flirt. I rolled my eyes again, and he laughed before continuing, "I like your tits."

"Jesus, Damon," I scoffed at his lack of charm. He really was an asshole. *A hot asshole.*

Ruby finally shuffled away from whoever she was chatting to, and sat at the opposite side of the table to me. But still, no Caine. He was my date, so where in the heck could he be?

"Ah!" I yelped from the sudden intrusion of yet another arm that reached around from behind me. My heart nearly pounded out of my chest, but it lulled quickly. Given the width of the arm and the tattoos, I knew it was Eli.

He grabbed my hand and gave it a small kiss, his genuine smile peeking through the shiny gold mask. And those beautiful ocean eyes. *What the unholy fuck? What is it with these men? Give a girl a break. Aren't I a prisoner?* It didn't feel like it.

My heart stilled as I lost myself in his gaze. There was something about Eli that was just... delicious. Though there was something about *all* of them that was just... delicious.

Each one was different from the other, each tugged at different parts of my oddity than I'd care to admit. But nonetheless, those feelings were there. And I hated it. Not because it was happening, but because I liked it.

CHAPTER TWENTY-EIGHT

FALLING FOR THREE

The pain killers had well and truly settled into my system. So much so that I felt almost ditsy… a little airy fairy in the brain department. *I really should not have taken three.* The night played on and the waiters and waitresses brought out delicious meals and more champagne than I could poke a stick at. I didn't engage in any of their chit-chat. There were far too many opportunities of food to be engorged by. Who knew when I'd eat next. The voids of my stomach had filled so much that I didn't think I could manage another bite at least for another week.

"Let's go dance," Damon challenged Eli. *Yes, go over there, somewhere. Leave me be.* He pushed aside his last plate of food, and then both of them turned to look at me. I swallowed down the strawberry that I held hostage in my mouth from my last glass of champagne. *Oh, shit. They mean with me.*

I shook my head, throwing my hands up in refusal and they both smirked a little too eagerly. "I don't da—" a mere whimper fell from my lips, but I was interrupted before I had the chance to object.

"It wasn't a question, *piggy*." Damon's eyes narrowed with demand. A daring, sinister darkness puddled where the blues were. *I don't dance. I can't dance. Not like this. What about my feet?* I dreaded the thought and shook my head again, but before I knew it, I was being yanked against my will by the two of them.

The ballroom was silent for a moment, with everyone waiting with their partners for the cue of the next song to play. "The Blue Danube Waltz Op. 314" by Strauss began to echo through the room. I knew it because I spent most of my studying time listening to classical music.

Eli adjusted himself behind me, pressing his hip into the small of my back and curling his fingers into the arc of my waist. I gasped from the touch, sending an elicit shiver down my spine. And between my legs. *Shit.* Damon towered over me to my right with a lustful look on his face.

Oh, crap.

Crap, crap, crap.

He leaned in closer, and Eli nudged me into him. My body was hard pressed against Damon's lean torso, and my backside against Eli's. I felt so small between them. *The piggy in the middle.* Damon was well over one and a half feet above me— *and I had heels on.* Eli wasn't as tall, but his muscles enveloped my body without hesitation, making me look small.

Damon turned his arms behind me with a groan as the tops of his hands brushed against Eli's belt and he planted them just above my ass. My cheeks flushed, and the flutter between my legs only beat even harder than a mere moment ago. *Shit.* Their breaths split down my neck from both front and back.

"We're going to have fun playing with our new toy." Eli's voice vibrated in his ribcage, and it ricocheted against me, making my spine shudder with an unfamiliar excitement.

"Mmm. Such fun," Damon echoed, brushing a coiled tendril of hairs away from my face before hovering at my ear. "How are your *poor* feet? Do you need a nice cock to lean on? You *poor* thing," he teased. He didn't care that I was in pain. I knew that for a fact. Rather, he *enjoyed* it.

An embarrassing, breathy squeak slipped from my lips from the sudden sensation. *Is that... ? No, it couldn't be.* But it was— *a cock*—pressed up against the arc of my ass. Only the fabric of Eli's pants stopping *it* from going any further. My breath hitched and I snapped my head up, darting my eyes around as I came to my senses. *Is anyone watching us?* No one seemed to care.

"Jesus," I muttered, not knowing what to do or say. *What will they do to me?* Damon laughed, taking charge in where our bodies swayed over the dance floor. I didn't know how I was moving so well, but I didn't have a moment to spare to consider my pain.

As I scanned the room, something familiar caught my eye. In a tight-fitting suit at the other end of the ballroom floor, looking like melted butter and gawking at me with an intimate glint in his eyes, was Caine.

He wore a solid gold mask that covered the top half of his face. My body flushed beneath his glare, my cheeks included, thankful they were covered by my own mask. He was so fucking handsome. The butterflies in my belly tripled and thundered, as did my pussy. *For fuck's sake. I really have to stop swearing.*

He was standing next to Soren, who was adamantly admiring his work. I couldn't blame them, I looked... edible. *Ironic.* I mean, Tilly had done an amazing job on my makeup, but Soren? Well, he was something else.

Damon released his hold on me and trotted off to stand next to Caine and Soren, turning to look at why they were so fixated on with me. He towered over them both as all three of them gawked. I stiffened in my spot as Eli adjusted his grip to my breasts, whispering heavily in my ear.

"You have no fucking clue how much we want you, little one." Damon smirked, as though he could lip read what Eli said. I shuddered, and my legs went a little weak. *Oh, my. I am stuck in some very unfamiliar waters.*

"Why are you doing this?"

"For fun. Why else?" he asked as he squeezed my breast firmly. He made no sense. *I thought he was the loyal one. He always seemed as such. God, my head.*

"You're all insane," I muttered weakly, trying to muster as much loath as I could instead of sounding like I was enjoying his touch. It seemed as though I wasn't as convincing as I thought… the three of them looked like they were short-circuiting. Their eyes continued to follow us as we strummed around the floor to the beat of the music.

Eli glared between my eyes and F cup breasts that were on full display, spilling from the cups as the V-shaped bust ran down the mid of my cleavage, stopping at the grove of my ribcage. The gown draped over my waist and collected in a puddle at my feet. He toyed with the straps that fell off my shoulders, sitting firm around my biceps.

A penny wasn't spared on the dress, and the little woman who worked effortlessly had made it fit *perfectly*. The shadow man inevitably had taste, even if the thought of him made me

curl my lip in disgust. I was *ravishing*. On purpose. For them…
for him.

My breath weakened as Eli shifted his hands down, finding
the slit of my dress that ran up my thigh, leaving the palm of his
hand there and the other around my waist as we continued to
maneuver. I mindlessly gnawed at my bottom lip as they walked
over, Caine included.

"Hello, diamond," he flirted, his eyes practically peeling the
clothes from my body. I squirmed under his intrusion, but let him
continue. I was becoming more aware of the sensation of my
silk-green panties collecting moisture. *What is wrong with me?* I
wanted to say hello, but as usual, I wasn't given the chance.
Damon swiftly took me away from Eli, and suddenly I was chest
to chest with him after performing some ridiculous pirouette.

"Oof," I uttered.

"You should really be more careful, dancing like that. Your
feet, remember?"

What do I say? I don't think I have any words in my vocabulary.

"I'm fine." *There.* That might shut him up. Caine stood back
with his arms crossed, admiring the way Damon stood over me
with hunger. I tilted my neck back as far as it could go, just so I
could get a glimpse of the dimples from Damon's grin beneath
his mask. I drowned in the denial of the desire I had for him.

"Ready? Ready? Watch this." Damon pushed back from me
and charged his body into a rhythmic dancing pattern—to
classical music—dancing about like an idiot to the beat of his
own drum. A smile stretched ear to ear on his face, and the
others'. An involuntary smile cracked my face. He was a fucking
idiot. *The buffoon… a hot buffoon.*

Caine had his eyes locked onto me the entire time, biting his lip, waiting for his chance to strike, letting his brothers have their turn with me first. *Brothers—I'd do well to remember that. Why doesn't that deter me, by the way?* I was only happy to let them stare. I liked it. It made me think less of the man who had me wear the dress in the first place.

The music soon changed to a steamier melody, a different waltz. Damon moved behind me, his arms wrapped around my waist, pulling me closer against him once more.

"This is more like it. Something a little more your pace," Damon said with a low tone. I squeezed my thighs together, but the throb at my pussy only intensified.

I mindlessly let my neck drop back against his chest, pushing my chest out slightly. He had a full view of my breasts from his height. He groaned, and Eli found his way back into the steamy triangle, to my front. An illicit moan threatened to break from my lips as the intrusion of Eli's hips pressed against mine. His leg parted my thighs, leaving me no choice but to squat over his leg.

"Good girl, put your weight on me. That's it. Rest those pretty little feet," Eli breathed. My cheeks burned crimson, feeling the moisture between my legs flow a little more than earlier, sending a shiver up my spine.

The sensation of Damon poking the back of my ribcage made me gasp, loudly. There was no hiding the impressive erection pressed against me. Eli chuckled deep in the back of his throat. *He knows what's going on.* Granted, it was all over my face. *Need.*

"Do you like his cock against you, little one?" Eli purred, and I mindlessly nodded. *Wait, did I just say yes? No! No, no, no.*

Yes, yes, yes.

Damon squeezed my waist. I moaned, throwing my hand over my mouth to mute my impulsion.

"Good answer," Eli deadpanned. We were in front of a crowd of people. How could I be that careless? Damon dragged his hands lower, teasing the bare skin of my thigh that was draped over Eli's leg. He pried my legs further open using his knee.

My hips rolled into the arc of his erection from the angle, and my heart thumped hard against my chest. I lost a beat for a second, flushing cerise to the delicious spell the Whitlock boys had me in. I glanced around, embarrassed of my encounter. Caine was very pleased with what he was glaring at: two ridiculously hot, masked kidnappers in suits, sandwiching a virgin hostage. Both with solid, throbbing erections.

I looked down over Caine's spectacular, short frame, and right below his belt, tucked to one side, was a bulge. *Fuck. That makes three.* A sound darted from my mouth again, and my pussy clenched.

"Jesus. Fucking hell," I whimpered, not certain what come over me. Three men had wild, beating cocks. *For me.* Right out in the open, none of them having a care in the world. I had to admit, Caine's bulge was impressive, and I found myself absently staring. And if that wasn't bad enough, he adjusted himself so that I could see more of it. *Holy shit.* From what I could see, Caine was *thick.*

I battled with my brain about which of the boys I'd let ravish me until I was spent. My moral compass was nowhere to be seen. I muttered an inaudible, defeated, breathy moan as two hands wandered up my frame. Damon's staggered breath raced down my spine as Eli's fell over my chest. Damon squeezed one breast, and Eli the other.

"I'm going to cum on these tits one day. Right here," Damon

hissed, and he squeezed, hard. A bestial growl hummed from his chest, and *that* enticement was all I needed to arch for more. I panted heavily as their forced swaddle pulled at something inside of me to the point where I felt like I was going to come undone for them right there in the middle of the crowd. *A climax? Is that what is pressing me?*

"Yes, brother. Me, too," Eli added.

Brothers. Didn't that just unlock something buried in the dark?

Brothers. Fuck.

I was turned on by it.

CHAPTER TWENTY-NINE

PIGGY IN THE MIDDLE

"We could take her right here, right now. What do you think, Damon?" Eli hissed. *Oh, God. Please, no. Please do.*

Shit. What is happening?

I sucked in my lips to mute the intrusive moan that threatened to escape. I couldn't bear it anymore. My breathing was eradicated, and getting louder and louder. Not that they were fazed.

"In f-front of all these p-people?" I squeaked, barely a whisper. Eli's eyes darkened, and his tongue found my neck. I gasped, and Damon whispered into my ear as I arched to Eli's touch.

"You think these people give a shit? Look around, pop tart. If anyone so much as blinks an eye at you, I will put a fucking bullet between their eyes. You're *ours* to play with."

I mindlessly rolled my hips so that more of my core pressed against Eli's leg. I don't know how or why, but the sensation tugged at me somewhere it shouldn't. It really fucking shouldn't have, but it did. Something was very, very wrong with me. *Wait? A gun?*

"*Oh.* Say it again, D. She likes it," Eli growled, his voice laced with desire. *No, don't say it again.* Damon's core temperature shot up a notch, and it warmed my back, a nervous bead of sweat trickling down my spine. *I should be terrified right now.* The nut job just mentioned a weapon and some innocent's life, like it was no less than a dollar on a horse race punt.

Damon was fueled by Eli, giving off the impression that they had done... *that* before. He purred and shifted himself slightly, pushing my needy, wet area against Eli's leg—*and cock*—a little more. Holy shit.

"Ah!" I jolted from the sensation of something solid and firm at the small of my back. The cold metal cooled my body, chilling my core. I shuddered, and suddenly, the thing was between the slit of my dress and resting on the soft skin of my upper thigh. I didn't know why, but I moaned, an overstimulating explosion of unfamiliar pleasure striking through my blood. *That's definitely a weapon. Proof that he isn't messing around.*

"Do you like this? My gun?" Damon sneered.

What in the actual fuck?

I had a fucking gun between my legs, two hard cocks against my body, and a third watching in anticipation. Not to mention my thumping pussy that was threatening the spiral of an orgasm. *No, I can't be like this. People who get kidnapped aren't supposed to like this.* But I so desperately wanted to understand what everyone spoke about. To feel it.

The climax.

My first orgasm. But I was absolutely not going to let myself fold with a weapon against me. It was wrong. Very wrong. But as I tormented myself in denial, the barrel of it shifted further up my leg, stopping at my labia.

"Mmh." *Oh, no. What the hell was that sound?* I wanted to say no, or go away, or please stop—anything—but the humiliating whimper was all I could slip through my lips. The sound turned the edges of Eli's mouth into a deadly smirk.

"Fuck. I knew this one would be a little twisted, but I didn't think this much," he teased.

"You sick, little, *bitch*," Damon added, the words stinging my chest.

"No, I—" *Please stop. This is too much.*

"She's desperate for it, no matter who is at her dispersal," Eli cut me off and the panic began to rise and take over the stupid sensations that I had—*shouldn't have had.*

"Or what with, it seems. Desperate little slut," Damon mocked.

Just as my body wanted to crumble underneath me, Eli's fingers brushed over the pistol's barrel, then to my lace G-string, sending a shockwave of pleasure over the bud. His eyes sprung wide open, as did mine. My cheeks burned crimson. He groaned deeply, and pushed the fabric aside, revealing the wet area that was my pussy. *Just kill me now. Fuck.*

Fuck-damn-shit-hell.

Shitting hell-fuck-shit... fucking hell... God damnit.

"Jesus Christ. D, she's soaked." Eli's finger found my clit without warning, and I yelped at the intrusion, and then sighed, shaking my head profusely. If he did that again, I was going to come undone. "Damn, we gotta make sure *H* doesn't kill her just yet. I want her too much. We've not had one like this." His voice was taunting as it rippled over me.

There was that word again. *Kill.* I shivered, and like a bucket of ice-cold water was dropped over me, reminding me that my death was right around the corner. Tears filled my eyes. I scrunched my face inward, choking the waterworks down as best I could. *Don't show weakness. Weakness is fuel.* But all that brought me was dizziness.

"Me too, brother," Damon hissed, a darker edge to his voice than before, then a wash of black shadows like thick smog filled my brain. My body felt heavy, imagining the shadow man's black-painted hand band around my throat as he watched my life slowly fade. The scent of pine, blood, and moisture filled my nose like an etched memory, like he was there.

In an instant, Eli's hand was snatched away, and I became aware that there was another presence beside me. My heart pounded heavily and I closed my eyes, everything inside of me freezing over.

"Me three," the voice threatened with a jealous fringe, asserting his dominance. That he wanted his fair share of me too. I sighed, relieved that the voice didn't belong to the shadow man. It was Caine's.

Damon and Eli shuffled somewhat, and Caine threaded his fingers between my hair and then to my cheek. His hard erection throbbed against my left hip. *Three men... I am sandwiched between three pounding cocks.* I was sick of saying and hearing the words, but I was indeed the piggy in the middle.

"How does it feel?" Caine whispered, pressing his finger under my chin and his thumb over my red lip. For a moment, I could not even think of my name, let alone have the ability to respond to him.

I was butter... brainless, from his smell, his eyes that devoured me behind *that* mask, his grin. His touch. *If only Tilly was here to see this.* My mind, body, and soul were somewhere else. Somewhere in the shallow throes of imaginary death and pleasure.

"How does w-what feel?" I mumbled. He smirked.

"Three men just dying for a taste of your..." he paused, and looked down where Eli's had been earlier before locking contact with me again, "what I can only imagine... is a delicious pussy."

I drew in a rapid breath through my teeth, letting out a breathy moan as I attempted to clench my thighs together. More moisture pooled between my slit.

"I... " I murmured, but couldn't get the rest of it out. I panted heavily against the trio, and they were ravishing every torment they dished out for me, like a game. My arousal was their weapon to use against me. And I was letting them.

Caine leaned forward and his warm breath shot down my neck, eliciting *another* moan, only louder. I was using every inch of my body to choke down the building pressure in my private area, my skin crawling with heat.

"I... " I tried again. It was useless. It was too much.

"I... I what, little diamond? You want *us*, don't you? We can smell it on you. We know you're dripping for us." He drew in my scent, clearly intoxicating him as he groaned.

"*Us?*" I squeaked. *Does he mean... all three? At once?*

"Yes," Eli and Caine groaned the word in unison.

"N-no," I muttered, shaking my head, but that was a lie. *Wrong answer.* Damon jolted my body into Eli's cock a little more. The top of my clit pressed against his erection. I shuddered and groaned, throwing my head back against Damon. "Please, stop this."

"Don't lie to us, little one," Eli croaked.

"Please, stop!" I shouted, panting hard and then pursed my

lips to slow my breath. Pushing the sexual tension away again. I was seeing stars and colors I'd never seen.

"Does she need a reminder of what happens in our room?" Damon added. *No, no way. No. I mean, yes… I do want them all. All at once. But why?*

"Come on, little liar, out with it," Caine teased playfully. My throat tightened, and I summoned whatever I had left in me to reply, truthfully.

"Okay, fine. Yes."

"Yes what?" Caine demanded an answer.

"I-I want… all of you." Shame riddled me, everything screaming at me that what I wanted was so terribly wrong. But there was a gun on my leg, did I really have a choice? Would I have said yes even if there wasn't one?

Caine pulled my knee against his hip, forcing my legs to open wider than they already were. His erection made contact with the side of my leg, and the sensation drew out my heavy panting again. Having nowhere to go and nothing in me to fight them, I let them tease me. Sandwiched between the three of them like a can of sardines, I couldn't be certain if I was going to burst into tears or climax.

Eli's sharp blue eyes burned into me as Caine's finger trailed from my scabbed knee, up the sensitive area of my thigh, and paused at the arc of my pelvis.

I shuddered, not knowing how much longer I could hold out. Something had been teetering on the edge—*down there*—for so long that I was aching on the inside. I rolled my neck back and Damon's warm, staggered breath channeled down my chest. Caine's touch left me breathless. He was gentle, unlike the other two.

"Don't cum," Damon whispered in my ear. *Don't… what?*

"What?" I panted. *What makes him think I am going to—* "Fuck!" I bellowed, my body jolting into an arch against the sensation of Caine's thumb making contact with my clit with greater pressure than Eli had before. I was a coiled spring on the edge of an explosion. Damon's hand curled around my mouth as he pulled me further against him.

"I said, don't cum," Damon's threat hissed through his teeth like a snake in my ear, and I moaned against his hand. This man has a gun, and yet it was the furthest thought in my mind. *Shit.* I was well and truly in over my head.

"So fucking wet for us," Caine groaned as he inspected his wet, glossy fingers, the glisten in his eyes displaying the same level of hunger and need as mine. My needy breath pounded against Damon's hand and Eli chuckled. *Fuck.* I chomped down on my lip, I needed to get a grip.

I didn't speak. I didn't need to. My words were written all over his fingers in liquid form. *I am in liquid form.*

"What's he going to do when he finds out you're here with us… and not in your cage, hmm?" Damon tormented. *Shit.* I had forgotten about *him*—the shadow man. *Wait, that makes no sense. Didn't he know I was here?* The mask I was wearing had his name on the tag.

"I mean, I couldn't care any less about what he thinks right now. I've spent too long watching her face beg to be fucked to give a shit what he thinks." Damon's already hard cock hardened more, if that was even possible. Perhaps he was excited by the thrill of pissing the shadow man off.

"I don't know. I do know one thing for certain, though," Caine hovered his lips to my neck and Damon tilted it back for him, so he had more area to find. The heat of his breath made every throb between my thighs pump so loud, I could hear it in my head.

"He's not here for her right now, so... " Caine paused, cocking a brow and nudging a response from me. "Little diamond?"

"Yes?" I breathed, and almost plummeted into ecstasy as his tongue glided up my neck and pulled back.

"You... "

"Belong... " Damon chimed in, licking over the wet patch.

Desperation and humiliation washed my face, and then Eli planted his tongue and slithered it over where Caine *and* Damon had marked.

"To... " Eli mouthed.

Suddenly, without warning, a cold chill hovered through the air and over me, barely noticeable, but enough that Caine frowned. *Did he feel that, too?* He darted his head toward the crowd beside us, and Eli and Damon followed in unison. Caine's jaw clenched hard and the space in the room thinned, cracking with tension. Everyone's body stilled and the enigmatic stare that washed over Eli's face churned my stomach. Something wasn't right.

Is he *here?*

"Ah, *shit.* We have company," Damon sighed, unable to hide the vex in his voice. He grumbled before continuing under his breath. "Fuck. It was just starting to get good." *Shit. Fuck.* It was happening. He'd come for me, mad that I wasn't in my cage... mad that I was with his brothers.

Caine pinched my neck and forced my gaze to the shadow man, who was standing on the other side of the grand entrance, stoic and unreal. Not moving... staring. No one noticed he was there, or if they did they didn't care. Caine pointed at the black figure staring at me and whispered in my ear.

"*Him.*"

Him? Him, what?

"You belong to him," he finished, his tone almost weak and somewhat jealous. My heart pounded out of my chest and the tears fell heavy down my cheek. The heat of them cooled my flushed cheeks as I collected my head into my hands. My head felt like it was going to implode. Nothing was making sense.

"You boys better fuck off, quick. I'll deal with him," Caine snapped. All of them released me from their grip, and I wobbled to catch my balance again, my feet throbbing as they took my weight once more. I frowned, trying to scan the room for the shadow man, involuntary smelling for his scent. But it was unfulfilled. He was gone.

I stood there adrift for a while. Snot and tears demolishing my makeup. My head thumping, my feet throbbing, all traces of a buzz of alcohol and painkillers were long gone.

"It's just you and me now, little diamond," Caine's voice purred into my chest as he pulled me against his rock-solid body.

"No," I whimpered, smacking at his pectoral muscles... not that it did anything.

"Yes."

Revolt ran through my veins, and my lip curled in disgust. My moral compass was back in full form. And didn't that just make me heavy?

I belong *to the shadow man.*

CHAPTER THIRTY

DID YOU FORGET WHO THEY WERE?

He's not here. It's okay. You'll be fine, I tried to coax myself, even though my heart still pounded. It hadn't settled since I saw the shadow man. *How long has it been? Minutes? Hours?*

I'd been stewing in my intrusive thoughts the entire time the bidding took place in another room of the mansion. I was an absent mess, not because for most of the night I had spent it being sandwiched by three brothers, but because I was *owned* by someone. My masked kidnapper. My stalker. My nominated *killer.*

My brain was fucking fried. I was their toy to torment, and they had certainly done just that. The puddle between my thighs was clear evidence of that. I hated that I was still there. I hated how Damon was right, and just how desperate I had been. How desperate I *still* was. I hated how I liked the feeling of his cold gun on my skin—a fucking weapon, one that could have easily killed me.

Who was I truly fooling? I *wanted* to hate it all, but I didn't. I just hated what was happening to me. Maybe I did deserve to die, for acting on sins. Because it wasn't like I was screaming out for help with a rape whistle. But that was the problem; I wanted more.

Heaven wouldn't dare let me in now. I want to get the fuck out of here. Even if it means that I'll be locked away in my dark room, I'll let the blackness envelope me.

I could squirm all I liked, but Caine had a firm grip on my arm. He hadn't said a single word, other than muttering when he made an expensive bid on something. Every change I had to glare at him, his expression conveyed nothing other than regret and—remorse?

I was locked beside him by his strength, patiently waiting for the bidding war to end. Soren was hosting the charity ball, and the Whitlock brothers had donated the items to auction off. The fuckers. The lot of them were obviously rolling in cash, and people had come from near and far just to be there.

The more I thought about the shadow man, the more I was hit with nerves about who was around me. *Do they know who he is? Is he one of them among us? Unmasked?* The uncertainty chewed away at my head for far too long.

When the bidding came to an end, the crowd roared into cheers before shuffling out into the garden, where we were informed the celebratory fireworks would take place. The lighting in the estate was dimmed, only wicker lanterns illuminating the area. The music was loud, not a single voice could be heard over it... not even if I screamed.

"Ow," I whimpered as Caine suddenly grabbed my arm a little harder. *What's happening now?* A concerned, possessive frown grew over his face as he peered down at me through his eyelashes. I gulped, but stayed quiet, panning my surroundings.

Everyone was cheerful, either dancing or watching the sky, waiting for the colored light show to crack.

Even though his grip wasn't hard enough to hurt me, it was enough for me to mimic his concern. He was perturbed by something. I couldn't put the name to it. I shuddered, and his arm banded around me. I drew in a rapid breath as his arm locked over my chest, pulling me backwards against his broad torso. Like he was shielding me from something—or someone.

I felt a cold chill race through my spine, like ice was being injected straight into it. My breath staggered before I held it in instinctively, because I knew for sure that I'd smell *him* if I breathed normally. But I couldn't hold my breath forever, so I drew in with my lips parted. *Nothing.*

"Caine?" I squeaked, and lifted my head up to glance at him. He sighed, shifting slightly, but didn't answer. After a while, I tried again. "Is he going to kill me?"

He stirred again, but he wasn't giving away anything. Caine's eyes scanned the garden deeper than the last, confirming that he definitely was looking for someone in particular. His grip tightened again before a snort sputtered from his nose. He was furious about something. Regretful like I had suspected and something else I couldn't put the name to.

"Sorry, little diamond," he whispered. *Sorry? For what? What the fuck is going on?* His tone was sincere, wounded even. And then the first set of fireworks blew off, crackling in the sky, startling me.

I winced as his hold around me tightened once more, causing a raspy cough to sputter from my mouth. His thumb caressed my collarbone, but his grip didn't soften and it wasn't going to stop me from trying to break free. Fear was taking charge of everything in my being, so I kicked out.

I wriggled, and tugged, pushed, and heaved. First to my left, then to my right. *Nothing.* I didn't have a clue how to perform self-defense. I continued to pry Caine's grip as the fear intensified, the smell of pine grew stronger and stronger.

"Shh," Cain lulled, but it did nothing other than make me fight more. It was no use. He was too strong. Tears flooded down my cheeks, and my heart felt like it was being squeezed internally. As I began to give up, energy wearing thin, the smell of moisture and musky, earthy tones filled my lungs, and the metallic twang of blood loomed under my nose. *It's happening. Ruby lied. It's happening.*

Then the second set of fireworks powered into the sky, louder, and bigger than the last.

"Caine," I pleaded through whatever oxygen I could take in through terrorized panting. No one could hear my cries.

"Stay still." His voice was shallow, filled with melancholy. A hoarse growl vibrated from behind us. *The shadow man.*

"Hel—" I cried out again, but Caine's knee collided with my lower back, and I dropped to the ground like a sack of potatoes. I could have sworn I heard him say "sorry" under his breath as he knocked me down, but the thought disappeared quickly.

I gasped at the opportunity for air as I began to crawl away, coughing and splattering. My eyes stung from the tears, causing my makeup to run more than it already had.

There was resistance; someone was standing on the train of my dress, putting a stop to my escape. A hollow, muffled laugh broke from... *him,* lifeless and menacing.

Run!

Fucking RUN!

I thrashed and wriggled in terror, trying to pull free from the tension. The dress pulled tighter against my arms, and then it tore, busting the slit of my gown beyond the dip of my pelvis, my green G-string on full show. *The green G-string* he *gave me.*

And then, the tops of two black shoes stepped before me, right under my face.

He was there. For me.

The fucking shadow man.

CHAPTER THIRTY-ONE

DELUSIONAL GOOSEBUMPS

My heart pounded harder as he crouched next to me, and I gasped as the serrated edge of his knife met my chin. Instantly throwing me into a frenzy of Deja Vu. *Again.*

I crumbled like pastry into a fit of sobs. His black cape draped over him, and pooled around his body like the other times I'd seen him. *Like the Grim Reaper.*

"Please! Let me go," I gargled my plea, muffled from the snot that had trailed to my mouth.

The shadow man put pressure under my chin. I winced from the sharp friction on my skin. He shook his head, slowly, shifting his knife away, depositing it somewhere in his jeans, but I kept my gaze.

His bright green, glowing amulet dangled from the chain around his neck, as well as another necklace with a thick, black key. The large tears in his jeans at his knees conveyed hints of pale tones of his skin, reminding me that he was real—he was human—and I wasn't in a nightmare again.

I shuddered. *Why do I have the habit of forgetting that he is real?* As if being his butchered prisoner wasn't enough of a reason. He shifted backward, appearing amused at my glare. His fit, black-painted chest rose and fell. That man seemed too calm to be a murderer. The sensation was strange, something I couldn't identify. He was so... mysterious.

I was not the best at reading people, but the way he was looking down at me was not only that of revolt, but also curiosity. It gave me the impression that maybe there was a reason he hadn't killed me yet. *They said he was going to, so why hasn't he?*

I didn't know why, but that thought made me stumble on another from my past. *"Don't play with your food, Esme."* Something my father always used to crack at me for.

I was the food on the shadow man's plate.

He was playing with me.

My heart rate danced as the shadow man stood, shifting to stand taller. I drew in an enormous breath of air, allowing me to take him in more. Another firework routine sounded, and sparked the sky to life. As each one expanded, they beamed off enough light to see the shadow man's entire figure. The thick horns curved out of his mask and curled above his head, like a ram's would.

I jolted from his sudden movement and frowned in disbelief. He was holding his hand out for mine. My heart stopped momentarily before finding a rhythm again. I couldn't get a grip of him. He was all over the place, and it made my head spin.

I had seen him cry. I had seen him shred my feet to pieces. He had chased me through the deepest, darkest parts of the woods. He had stalked me, and kidnapped me. He had given me peace offerings of clothing like I was a fucking servant from

Harry Potter or some shit. *Dobby is a free elf, or whatever.* He was inevitably fucked in the head.

My mind wandered. *Maybe he has two brains. One that's a normal human one, and the other that's disfigured, pulled right from the viscera of the devil.* That made logical sense in my head, but it was far from reality. Those sorts of things didn't exist.

My eyes darted back and forth between his veiny, black hand that was out for mine, and the empty holes of his mask. A flutter in my stomach grew as I summoned whatever courage that was left in my body to take his hand, but hesitated.

He twisted his head to the side in a provoking yet playful way. He was clearly enjoying fucking with my mind. I was going to implode there and then. He looked down at his hand, and clenched it into a fist with an animalistic growl, bellowing from his nose. A clear message: hurry up and grab it. I complied with great difficulty and my palm collided with his.

"Ah," I jolted from the intrusion. An electric shock, like I had clasped my fist around an electric fence, split right through my entire body. He pulled his hand back in an instant. Stars spun around me, and white flashed across my eyes. *What the fuck was that?*

My mouth dried, and I tried to swallow. Images and waves of sexual tension, mixed with torturous nightmares of drowning and thick black darkness… fog? They swam through my head like a vision—*death*. His breath escalated, suddenly angered. *He must have a short temper.*

He ushered his hand forward again with a threatening growl, as though it was my fault for the electric twang. I didn't hesitate, I grabbed his hand and he pulled me to my feet, a little too hard. The sensation hit me again, but he saw it through.

Oof.

I had planted the flat of my hand against his chest to break the collision of his tug. My breath shattered, as did his. He stilled, looking down at me pressed against his chest with his hand at the small of my back.

I didn't know or understand why, but I liked the feeling of his long, gentle fingers there, curling into my dress.

Goosebumps.

I glanced at my hand. I considered moving it, but I didn't. Neither did he. If anything, I think he liked it too. *More* than I liked it. I shouldn't have felt what I did. I really should not have. But there was something I couldn't put into words. A chemistry, or whatever. The butterflies in my stomach swirled.

This is impossible. I'm fucking crazy. I'm delusional.

A dim stimulating growl vibrated at the pit of his chest, rumbling through every cell in my body. I couldn't tell if he wanted to fuck me there and then, or kill me. His body's expression was that of a vicious cycle of revolt and arousal. I sighed, pulling myself together.

"What are you going to do to me?" I whimpered, trying to break the eerie silence, but he didn't respond. *As per usual. Was I really expecting anything more?*

For what felt like a lifetime of him holding me there, neither of us moving, he let out a painstaking sigh. And even though his breath was cloaked by his mask, a wisp of it ran over me like needles. Sharp, intrusive, and *pleasurable.*

I couldn't push aside the thought that something was biting at him, from the way he looked at me through the voids of his eyes. I couldn't pinpoint the ambiance, it was like he was suddenly looking at the pot of gold at the end of the rainbow that he had been seeking for centuries.

Like a diamond.

It made no sense, but my moral compass was knocking on my door, and the sadness of reality hit me like a tonne of bricks, right in my chest. He was going to kill me.

Without warning, his hand grasped around my neck. I threw my body into a fit of kicks, squirming in defense. It achieved nothing. I felt like my head was about to separate from my spinal cord. I gasped and gargled as my feet dangled above the ground, the shadow man holding me at arm's length.

Caine didn't offer a sliver of help. *Why would he? They're killers. How could you forget that, Esme?* I wrapped both my hands over his, trying to pry them from my neck as I fought for air. But all it did was give into his sadistic challenge. *His game.*

His chest exhaled with a brutal grunt, and he squeezed even tighter. My brain throbbed in my skull, and I felt the water in my eyes fall into the sockets, and the snot squeezed from my nose like a toothpaste tube.

He was no stranger to this. He adjusted his grip, allowing me to take a breath as he lowered me to the ground. I could feel him smiling as he squeezed just his thumb and index finger into my neck, right at my artery.

He was *not* trying to kill me at that very moment, because if he were, his grip would have stayed around my airway. Granted, I could hardly breathe as it was because his grip was so tight, but it was clear that my demise wasn't his plan—*yet*—he wanted me to pass the fuck out.

I sobbed heavily between whatever I had left before the oxygen to my brain depleted. He tilted head again, in *that* way that only unsettles my stomach, my blood pumping hard against his grip.

I could feel him in all his power, for what he truly was. *A monster.*

I didn't *have* to know his name to know he was a monster. I didn't *have* to know what he looked like under his mask to know he was a monster. I didn't *have* to know the reason he had watched me to know he was a monster. I didn't *have* to know the reason he took me to know he was a monster. I didn't *have* to know why he wanted to kill me to know he was a monster.

I didn't *have* to know a damn fucking thing to know a monster was a monster.

But I *wanted* to.

And I think I *needed* to.

The shadow man's head tilted again but in the other direction, and I felt the darkness nearing. I gulped as hard as I could manage under his grip and closed my eyes, accepting defeat. My body sank into weakness, but he held my weight entirely.

I succumbed to his cold, dark shadow and let it envelope me.

I jolted, throwing myself awake with an almighty gulp of air. *Is every time I wake up going to be like this?* The sound of a blood-curdling scream ripped through my ears, echoing through my bones.

I shuddered, and goosebumps wreaked havoc over my skin. *What the fuck?* I blinked my eyes a few times, but they didn't focus. It was pitch black. I crooked out my neck left and right to make sense of where I was, but I winced from the dull ache around my throat, mindlessly moving my arm to rub at it, but tension stopped me. *Wait, why can't I move my arm down?*

I was bound by something. I tugged again, realizing that my arms were hanging high above me, holding my weight. I was on my tiptoes. I wriggled at the pressure, feeling a pair of rusty old iron cuffs clamped tight around my wrists, the shackles clanked against the walls that closed me in.

The scream from somewhere nearby hit me again, and terror washed over me like ice-cold water. By the chilling concrete radiating up my spine and the stench, it was obvious where I was. I was in the fucking cells. *Again.*

"Ffffuck," I scoffed, yanking at the chains. *Fucking hell.* "If you're going to kill me, can you just get it over with?" The sentence came out in a yell-cry. I was getting sick of the merry-go-round.

"Shhhhh," a whisper of a mousy voice echoed from within the walls, the voice of another hostage.

CHAPTER THIRTY-TWO

I AM 'THE DIFFERENT'

There was someone in the cells with me. I frowned. *Huh? I could have sworn that the place was empty last time I was here—or as close to. Maybe she and I are the last ones left?*

"Who's there?" I asked quietly.

"Umm, Emma." The girl's voice was sweet, perhaps even a little too calm, given the circumstances.

"What's going on? Why is there screaming?"

She didn't reply, and as if on cue, another scream bellowed, shaking me to my core. But the dialect was different from the last, it sounded... pleasurable. *What the?*

It was coming from another section of the cells, maybe even the same corner that they had taken me to, where the chair was. Another sound echoed, a woman... moaning. A weird tingle ran a course through my veins, fluttering between my thighs.

I frowned at my intrusive thoughts. It soon became clear that they weren't just pleas and screams for help. They were erotic calls. And they were getting louder as they ricocheted from the walls. Her sobs and agonized screams melded with her pleasure. Begging, pleading, crying. I shivered. Suddenly, it went still. Those people were fucking sick.

"What the fuck is going on?" I repeated. *Is she having an orgasm or dying?* It sounded like both.

"Shhh. Keep your voice down, or you'll be next."

"Next to wha—" I pried, but she cut me off.

"The freak dragged one of the other girls over there after bringing you here. So shut your mouth!"

"You mean the one with the horns?" I had to clarify.

"Yes," she whispered back, her voice holding onto horror that I couldn't possibly miss. I scoffed mentally. *Or you'll be next. Pfft. This fucker has had plenty of opportunities to kill me, and still hasn't. He had a prime opportunity in the garden, but he didn't take it.* I still didn't understand why.

"Did you go to the ball?" I opted for a different conversation, not interested in staying silenced. *Damn that fucking ball.* I winced to an ache that I hadn't noticed until then. God, my feet ached. I wanted so desperately to rub them.

"What? No. Wait, you went to a ball?"

"Yes. His brothers made me go. They teased and tormented me in front of all those people… then I woke up here. Again."

"Wait, so you've seen him *outside?* Other t-than in h-h-here?" she stammered, her words tumbling over each other in a frenzy. It was like I had been given some kind of special fucking treatment. My stomach dropped as the thought of what Damon had said hit me. "*Why is* she *any different to the others?*" It was clear that whatever was happening with those girls, was very different from what had happened to me.

Unease pounded through my veins. *Silence.*

I opened my mouth to reply to the girl, but a flicker of light emitted from the other end of the cellar—*basement?*—where the sounds had come from. The sound of my heart pounding drowned out almost all thoughts and feelings. Someone was dragging something—or someone—along the concrete floor.

Step by step, it closed the distance to where I was bound. It was the shadow man, holding a candle in one hand. Bile surfaced to my mouth, seeing what I saw.

He was pulling a body behind him with his other hand. *A dead body.*

The visual forced tears from my eyes and down my cheeks, my chest struggling for a breath. He walked slowly, with a predatory gait. Between each footfall along the concrete had to have been two painful seconds. It was utterly haunting, wicked. And all I wanted to do was hide under a bed from him like scared little children did in movies.

But I am nowhere near a bed to hide under, and this isn't a movie.

His breath was rigid against his mask, as though he had just ran a marathon. He stilled before tilting his head toward me for a moment. *Why does he always do that?* I blinked my tears away so I could get a clear view of the carnage, seeing that his fist was tangled in a loop around the woman's hair. He continued dragging her lifeless carcass behind him, a thick trail of blood following.

And just like the eerie shadow that followed him, the shadow man was gone in the darkness once more. Instinctively, I tried to cradle myself for comfort, but the only thing that straddled me was a torn-up, silky green dress and cuffs.

Eventually, time had passed for long enough that the tears

felt like razors shredding from my eyes. The silence was so loud that all I could hear was white noise. I sighed.

"Where will he take her?" I whispered, though I wasn't sure exactly to whom, and I didn't really *need* to ask. I already knew.

The lake.

But clarity was better than curiosity.

"The lake," a different voice called, tinged with a hollow sadness, as if they were resigned to their fate by now. "But he's never done it here. Not all the way. Something is different."

Me... I'm the difference. I let the words sink into my head for a moment before asking another question.

"How long have you been down here?" I asked, not entirely wanting to know the answer. She sighed. Her breath sounded fractured, and laced with fear, like I could almost hear her reliving the exact moment she had been kidnapped, and brought here.

"I-I don't know, I'm sorry."

"Oh," I breathed. After a moment, she shuffled before continuing.

"It's hard to tell time when every second of the day is black, and the only sounds you hear are screams or cries, whether you're the one screaming or not." *Jesus. How many people are they killing—have they killed? Is this a one-man operation?*

"From what I can gather, they get bored quickly, so rotation is key. Obviously. They get their fix, he gets his." *Fuck.* My immediate thought was Tilly. *Has he killed her, too?*

"Tilly?" I yelled out without thinking. "Are you in here?" My throat thickened in anticipation, waiting for her reply. But the silence was the only response. My stomach churned, nausea taking hold at the thought of what they may have done to her.

"Sorry," the girl spoke softly. Her voice seemed genuine and sympathetic. I cried again, hard.

A squeak of the door pulled me from my limp, teary gloom after God knew how long. The mutters of terrified women peaked in unison, just as they always did when that damned door opened.

I had the gut-churning thought that I would be next. My eyes widened, and I peered around hurriedly. But the darkness was still all that filled them, other than a hint of a glow. A green glow. The shadow man was back from wherever he went—the lake, more than likely.

His sluggish footsteps neared, his green luminance bouncing off the walls. My heart pounded, catching sight of him as he stepped into my peripheral vision, stopping at the gate of my cage.

His flawless metal mask and the horns were the first to greet my glare, then a fluorescent light, trapped in a little glass charm that shadowed his broad, athletic chest. It was shining brighter than I'd seen before, and it made me tingle all over my skin.

A tingle that *should* have been resentment. *Is what I am feeling... excitement?* I shouldn't have been feeling it. But I was. He was a fucking killer, and my brain still couldn't let that bit sink in. *What the fuck is wrong with me?*

He was breathing heavily again. *I mean, I guess dragging a dead body to the lake, through the middle of a forest and back is a marathon.*

My lips parted and I drew in a sharp breath, letting the smell of *him* ignite the flame that had laced my flesh. I observed the shadow man as he stood at the gate of my enclosure, almost like a mannequin. He tilted his head, and for some reason... I mimicked him.

The paint on his body had faded slightly and had drip-dried down his torso, the faded trail leading to the V of his hips. From sweat, or from being in water, I guessed. I would have said from kinky, criminal, man-whore business, but I couldn't let my mind wander more than it needed to. I already had a hard enough time stopping my eyes from gawking at him.

I squirmed, trying to lull the butterflies that were dancing through my veins. *Shit. Not again. Come on, Esme, get a fucking grip.*

I shook my head with a mumble as he grabbed the key around his neck and began turning it in the lock at my enclosure. I was certain that he was smiling at my terror. Tormenting me by moving slowly and quietly, not speaking a word, or even a slither of a threat.

Nothing.

He unlocked my cage, and my heart skipped a beat. I wriggled under my restraints as much as I could manage, with nowhere to go.

Don't show weakness. He wants you to be weak. I sighed, and it was there and then I decided not to fight him. I gulped, and went utterly still as he stopped before me. I wouldn't give into his game. I wouldn't give him the satisfaction of begging for my life. He liked me weak, so I'd give him the opposite.

Wrong.

I gasped from the electric twang that flowed through my veins as he grabbed my waist and pulled me against him, my arms taut above me. That stupid charged touch. I was sure he felt it too—no, I knew he did. My arms tingled at a full stretch, pulling at their sockets, and I bit my mouth shut.

I closed my eyes to block the pinch of pain. But still, I didn't shriek or struggle. Though, the pain there was nothing compared to the swelling ache of my feet. *I don't think sprinting through a forest with lots of sticks, branches and butchered feet was the best idea.* He lowered his gaze down at the split up my thigh from where the dress had ripped further, no thanks to him. And I let him. I let him work me out. I willingly accepted him to decipher me, as I was doing to him.

I wondered just how much he could see out of that mask, whether he could see the green of my panties that poked out from the dress's tear. The shape of my nails that Soren had styled or the freckles on my face. Or if he could see just how much he both *terrified* and *aroused me.*

He groaned, and his finger trailed along where my flesh was exposed, burning a trail of heat along with it. I sucked in my lips, muting my sounds, for I only knew they were going to be illicit. *Well, that answers that question. Clearly, he can see very well.*

The longer I studied him—which was a long time, by the way—the more he became a head fuck. But one thing was clear, darkness was his ally. And no matter how dark it was, it was clear this hell was his haven. He liked the dark, and the dark liked him, taking victims one by one for his own fantasies.

It was *his* game, and the forest was *his* playground. I was merely his token... ready to use in his game, at his dispersal.

He sighed, seemingly withholding anger or some kind of frustration, and released his grip from my waist. He stretched above me, prying at my cuffs. I held my glare at his chest, trailing up to his exposed neck, and... jawline. A sharp jawline. *This is ridiculous.* There was no way I was going to admit that my kidnapper, come torturer, come impending murderer had a very high chance of being sexy under that mask. *There is no way!*

A breathy sound flew from my nose *and* chest that I had no control over. Did I just fucking giggle? *What the hell, Esme?*

I just giggled.

CHAPTER THIRTY-THREE

FIFTY SHADES OF GREY ELEVATORS

Giggled? Really, Esme? The shadow man didn't acknowledge what I had done, thankfully. If he did, he hid it well. Instead, he continued attending my straps until the metal clunked and freed my wrists. Instant relief hit me as my arms fell to my sides, and my feet took my weight fully once more—even in heels. Pins and needles shot through me as the blood returned to my arms, and oddly numbed my feet.

I held my composure as he wrapped his veiny hand around my wrist, squeezing hard as he pulled me beside him. I complied without a murmur or protest, letting the thump of my heart echo in my ears.

I had barely gotten a step forward before he pushed me, not enough for me to stumble but enough to wobble in my heels. Ouch, *very* ouch.

"Wait," I pleaded desperately. I needed to take these fucking shoes off, the pain was now almost unbearable. He paused, surprising me, and gripped my arm tighter, vexed by my distraction.

"Can I at least take my shoes off?" I asked—or begged, I wasn't sure. *My feet hurt because of you, fucker.* "Please."

He hesitated but finally sighed, dropping his gaze to my feet. I was quick to hover on one leg to grab at the shoe and rip the darn thing off. He let me pull the first off but I winced as I went for the second.

"Ow!" I cried out as he squeezed around my arm harder and growled. A warning to either stop what I was doing or to hurry up. *Well, I can't walk around with one shoe. Fucking idiot.* I wished I had the courage to say that.

I cocked my brows in disbelief as he dropped to his knee, and his now warm hand cupped my thigh. I shuddered as it trailed down my leg to my ankle. It took everything I had to keep my mouth shut. He tapped at my ankle, and I lifted my leg in compliance, planting my hand on his shoulder for balance.

The shadow man inhaled deeply, and his muscles tensed to stone, a quiet growl forming in his chest but he was quick to lull it. I stiffened in unison, but I didn't dare move. He finally continued, and pried my heel off with ease, discarding it somewhere on the concrete behind me.

My head raced a million miles a millisecond. *Is this... kindness? Or part of his twisted game? To mess with my head?* If that was his intention, he was succeeding.

"T-th... " I began to thank him, but I stopped, remembering that my moral compass did exist, *somewhere* in my body, and that this man was a fucking psychopath. He did not deserve a thank you or sliver of kindness from me—at all.

Like nothing had happened, he shoved me forward again. Ouch. The three painkillers Ruby had given me and the alcohol I had consumed had long since worn off.

The door closed behind us, and I couldn't see a thing other

than the shadows of whatever reflected from the glow of his amulet, and subtle reflections of us on the polished cars we walked by. I felt the cold, polished concrete floor on my feet. The smoothness was oddly soothing against my welts. We were in the garage, I remembered being there before—with Ruby.

A light flickered on from inside an elevator, the other end of the insanely large garage. I could see the cars clearly, and Damon's bike. There were so many modern expensive cars, though, that I couldn't make out what they were other than their logos. BMW, Mercedes Benz, and Porsche. I couldn't make out the others.

We continued to walk past them swiftly, not at the shadow man's usually slow and tantalizing pace. But seeing all those snazzy cars, I knew for sure I could get away. *If I only had the key to one.* I imagined disappearing into the horizon before my eyes had a chance to blink. My stomach fluttered from the thought of escaping again. *Yeah, because that worked out so well for you last time, idiot.*

The consequences I was walking on should have warranted an immediate stop to my thoughts. But it didn't. I pushed them aside and kept walking, purposefully slowing my pace to gawk at the shiny cars a little longer, and plot my next escape.

They were all in a row, tidy, and clean. Except one. I remembered seeing it when Eli pulled me out of the trunk, and again when Ruby took me to that godforsaken room. I frowned and unintentionally stopped, craning my neck to get a better look.

It looked like an old car, like one you would buy as your first car for a few hundred dollars. It was shoved in the furthest corner of the garage, where as little light as possible could reflect against it. *Why would anyone keep that?*

It was nothing but a pile of twisted, crumpled, shattered steel with rust, and wheels. I could make out at the very least it was the remnants of an accident of some sort.

The shadow man pushed me again, growling in that way of his with loathe and revolt, as though whatever that car was meant something to him. He sure as heck didn't want me gawking at it.

The elevator was bright, and I struggled to focus my eyes after being in the dark for so long. I could remember Ruby taking me through it, but I didn't remember it being so bright. I kept my eyes on my bare feet. *Don't look up at him. Don't do it. Don't do it, Esme.* But I knew I couldn't keep my curiosity from rearing its ugly head. In that light, I *had* to take a look at him.

Oh God, elevators. Why now is my only thought, the ridiculous cliché elevator scene, in that ridiculous fucking movie that Tilly had made me watch? Fifty shades of goddamn grey. The I-won't-kiss-you-but-did-it-anyway 'cause "*fuck the paperwork*" scene.

Screw that scene. Screw that guy. And *screw this guy*. This was no movie, and the shadow man was certainly no Christian Grey.

Though, I have to admit, now that I think of it, I do feel a lot like Anastasia: lured in, and entirely captivated by a total freakin' monster of a man.

I peered up at the shadow man through my eyelashes and watched his muscles contract and release as he did the most human thing possible: *breathe.* His breath was hollow and strained, his chest expanding with each draw of breath was quickly becoming an addiction.

I had only really glimpsed at him in the darkness until then, other than flashes of fireworks. It seemed almost illegal to look at him under a bright light. A hell of a lot less scary. But I still couldn't see past the mesh of the mask's eye holes.

I swallowed over the lump in my throat and drifted my eyes further up, having forgotten just how tall he was—*no, I haven't. Shut up.*

I gasped, throwing my head back down to my feet. *Busted.* He was looking straight down at me. A mocking blow of air escaped his nose, amused. Another pinpoint to him being human. *How long is this freaking elevator, anyway?*

He adjusted the grip around my arm and I stupidly peered up again, glaring at the veins that trailed up his. They were thick. The black paint had faded enough to see many thick colossal scars on both arms. I winced, imagining how they got there. They were old, but they would have had to have been painfully deep to have caused that much damage to the flesh.

I darted my eyes around his bare chest, finding more and more scars over his body. He was *covered* in them. My heart rate rose, as did my temperature. I couldn't help but sympathize with whatever pain he had been through, and I hated that. Why did I not feel scared at that moment?

He really wasn't as terrifying under this light. My mind trailed off. *I want to know how he got those scars. Did he have a car accident? That would explain the car in the garage. Why doesn't he talk? Why does he wear a mask?*

I gulped, and he copied the action, only louder, as though he was processing my curiosity.

The elevator stopped. My already palpitating heart was under enough stress, it didn't need any more, but I couldn't help but assume the worst; that we would end up in another type of rape dungeon.

Esme, stop your nonsense. This is NOT Fifty Shades of Grey!

I flinched as the doors slid open, what I feared we would arrive at and what was reality were two very different things.

It's a stunning room. I think it is… his room.

CHAPTER THIRTY-FOUR

HIS GAME

ow. I took a moment to adjust myself. The room the shadow man took me was everything like how you would imagine it to be, becoming more obvious it was his room.

Every inch of the room was either black or dark velvety ruby red—his true style—blood and shadows. It was gloomy, but also not, somehow. The ceilings were made entirely of mirrors. Like the club, PUSS. But it dawned on me that maybe they were for *other* reasons. I shuddered at the thought.

One spot of the ceiling in the middle of the room had an open space, the barrier of the space was framed by a metal structure, and laced with beautifully crafted pentagram diagrams and yellow micro-LED lights twinkling through them. *Huh. Well, that's weird.* I craned my neck further, widening my eyes at how big his room was.

"Woah," I whispered in awe, barely paying attention to the fact that I had spoken my disbelief aloud.

Crap.

I spun around to look at him, realizing that I no longer had a firm grip around me. He was leaning on the frame of the elevator door with his arms crossed, and his head tilted. *Why does he do that?* I could tell that he had a self-satisfied smirk across his face, not that I could see it.

And I assumed that it wasn't just because I spoke aloud, but because I had walked halfway into his room—out of arm's reach without noticing. He was just standing there, watching in enjoyment. *Double crap.* But he didn't growl or wrap his hand around my throat like it was a necklace, he just stood there.

I took another step in, away from the shadow man, and my eyes found the bed. *Holy ever-loving fuck.* A black, king-sized, four-poster bed, dressed with black silk sheets and European pillows.

Can this man get any more original? Black, black, black. Dark, dark, dark. Spooky, spooky, spooky. Okay, I get it.

My stomach dropped, and a gasp fell from my mouth when I realized there was a cage next to the bed. I twisted around quickly again to give him a side-eye, and I jumped out of my skin. He was right behind me.

"Shit," I exclaimed. But again, he just stood there, all enigmatic and stoic. A huff escaped his nose, leaving everything to the imagination. I rolled my eyes with a frown. The little amulet he had around his neck was no longer illuminated, it looked empty. *Why would he carry an empty glass amulet? This man just gets weirder and weirder.* But he didn't seem at all concerned that I was glaring at him and his weirdness.

Beautiful, but weird. I shouldn't admire someone I didn't know the name of, or the look of. I shouldn't admire murderers *period.* But I did, and I was getting sick to death of admitting it to myself. Denial was a fucking bitch. And so was the fucking cage I *knew* he was going to put me in. Like a fucking pet.

I ignored it and glanced elsewhere. The floor-to-ceiling windows that lined the entire room were draped with black velvet curtains. Outside, the view was electric, *those fucking pine trees*. As much as I hated the haunting darkness that I knew lurked in there, it was beautiful. Granted, that thrilling darkness was in the same room as me.

Why did he bring me to his room? It was the exact same view from the room that I was typically held hostage in, only another floor higher, at a guess. When I had escaped the first time, I had counted three levels in the mansion, and I knew Ruby had taken me up at least one flight in the elevator. So, we were up high.

My feet kissed the warm black tiles that were elegantly coated with reds, golds, and white marbled swirls, and the furniture fittings were finished with polished gold touches. It was still dark out, much like the rooms I had walked through to attend that stupid ball, but entirely opposite in color.

Something caught my eye out the window, moving closer to see a few cars disappearing into the horizon. Then, more, and more. *Wait, were they the guests from the ball? Has time really slowed that much?* My head spun as I revisited my day.

I went from drawing butterflies under the sun, to being in a steamy three way love triangle at a ball, to being strangled until I was unconscious in the garden under crackling fireworks, to waking up to a woman's carcass being dragged out by the scruff, before finally ending up here in a room with a cage by a psychopath's bed that looked like no other than a dog crate— for me.

Will this night ever end?

Before I knew it, I was being thrown into the cage like a naughty puppy that had just peed on the carpet. He locked me in with a padlock in one swift movement. *Fuck.* It was cramped in there, half my size, leaving me no choice but to tuck my knees up into my chest. The little green lace from my underwear peeked from the tears of the dress.

I didn't know what had happened, or why, but the mood seemed to have shifted. The revulsion he had for me was back in full force, and it made the hairs on my arms stick up. The shadow man's moods were unpredictable. I hadn't done a damn fucking thing wrong, and yet he was rolling in loathing, fuming with mildly knocked-back rage. Why he gave off the impression he hated me so much, I'd never know. He didn't speak.

His breath sped up and he clenched his fists. I swallowed in angst as his faceless, empty stare burned into my body, like my skin was about to ignite. I jolted as he threw the back of his hand against the cage, and the piercing sound of his metal rings droned into my ear.

I sobbed, freeing all the tears from my eyes. He sputtered a sadistic growl with an almost angered weep and stormed off, the elevator door closing behind him, and the lights turning off in his absence.

I rolled myself into a cocoon, imagining that I was home, safe in the comfort of my own bed, with Tilly and my favorite pillow that smelled of my shampoo. And *no* fucking shadow man.

I lulled myself into an uneasy sleep and let the night consume me.

Bright light. Why is there a bright light? I fluttered my eyes open to the sunlight beaming warm through the window on the other side of his room. Not wanting to wake up and face the day, I held myself for another moment, stewing in my numb body. *Wow, that hurts.* My spinal cord felt like it had rearranged in five different places, and my body ached with pins and needles.

Curling into a ball in a tiny cage half your size wasn't all that comfortable, and I wished the asshat had dragged me back to the *other* room—my room—iInstead of beside his bed. Even the cold concrete in the cell was more tolerable.

I huffed and wondered whether he had watched me sleep like he used to, but then I remembered he had left. I was alone.

"Grr!" I grumbled out loud, clenching my fists. The bastard. It made no sense. It really didn't. The man was a cold-hearted killer, and yet he cried like a wounded lamb when he played the piano. *And took off my fucking shoe, the same way a gentleman would.*

Maybe he has a heart buried deep down somewhere... pfft. Yeah, right. Only a sick, twisted one. My stomach churned and I grimaced. I was starving, already. Granted, I ate three times my bodyweight last night, but the food was too good to not eat. And who knew when I would eat again?

I huffed aloud again, and an involuntary laugh fell out of my mouth. You know when you're that fucked up, you laugh, but it isn't funny? Yeah, I'd gone that kind of mad.

I cleared my throat and rolled over trying to limber up some of my aches and pains. Sure enough, there he was.

"Oh, for f—" I said petulantly, choosing to bite my tongue for the rest of the sentence and curl back into a ball with my hands covering my face. *This guy again.* He sat on the armchair next to the bed with both legs pried apart, slouched, and staring at me.

A smirk burned against his mask. I couldn't see it. I didn't need to. I could tell it was there. I could feel it. No doubt having a laugh at my outburst of commentary and scoffs to myself, he'd probably thought I was delusional.

You would think I would have at least gasped at the sight of him, as the freak had been staring at me sleeping for God only knew how long. But I had nothing to offer him. Well, other than the puddle of saliva that had pooled under my tongue that I was dying to spit at him. I didn't, but I wanted to. Very unlike me, but I guess he was bringing all that out of me, wasn't he? When you push someone into the corner far enough, they'll bite back.

I frowned at myself. At least, given all I had been through, I still had my virginity to hold onto. *Mine.* Not theirs. Not his. *Mine.* My mind wandered again. Part of me felt sad about that, where I shouldn't feel sadness. What if I died without experiencing sex? That should be the last thing on my mind, but the last few days had been a ticking time bomb of this fucking built-up sexual tension.

Gah!

The tears in his jeans teased me with the pale tones of his unpainted skin, and I shuddered. *Why? It's just skin.* His fingers drummed along the arms of the chair like he was waiting for something, maybe annoyed that I was staring, again.

"What do you want?" I snapped impatiently. I was getting sick of the burning sensation of his stalkerish stares. Frustration and anger took charge of my normally squeaky but kind voice, but the fucker had me thrown in a cage without many things, including my dignity, but more importantly without access to a toilet. I was in desperate need of a pee, given the amount of alcohol I had consumed the night before.

He adjusted slightly in the chair, merely blowing a hint of a laugh through his nose, which only aggravated me more. I trailed off, I dare say my period was only around the bend. I was in a foul mood, and I was damn pissed that this fucker couldn't, *wouldn't* speak. It was so infuriating. He was so infuriating.

"What? Cat got your tongue?" I offered another smart remark, I didn't care if he wanted to kill me there and then or laugh. I'd at least be put out of my misery of being in that hellhole once and for all.

But to my surprise, he did nothing, not even daggers through the beady little eye holes that hit me. Or a kick to the cage, a spit. *Nothing.* He just sat there, staring. *Comfortably.*

Too comfortable, too quiet. His calm annoyed me. I had to look away before I did something that I regretted. I grumbled and rolled back over, and then tucked my knees into my chest. Out of sight, out of mind, if that was possible with him.

Solitude comforted me for another hour or two at a guess, until the maid showed up with a ridiculous selection of food. She placed it on the bed and glared at me before scurrying off again, the elevator silently closing behind her. The scent of eggs, bacon, pastries, and coffee intoxicated my every thought, to the point where I was choking on my own saliva. I hoped the prick would let me eat, but it looked like there was only enough food for one.

I half rolled over to face the bed again, and peered at the food, trying my best not to look desperate. He mockingly held his arm out, gesturing toward the food like an invitation to come eat. *Prick.* Anger came racing into my veins like a welcome gift pack. I gritted my teeth but my heart sank, sadness quickly taking charge. The sadistic asshole chuckled, rolling his head back at my deprivation.

That was his game.

CHAPTER THIRTY-FIVE

SWALLOWTAIL

I spun over in my cage again, arguing with myself and the tears that threatened to fall from my eyes. Damn it. I fucking hated it. I didn't want him to keep seeing me weak, knowing that it was what he craved.

It wasn't long before the shadow man stood at my cage. The freak of nature sure did have a way of moving around without so much as making a single sound. I didn't look. I kept myself rolled in a ball like a cold kitten.

My brow turned at the sound of a soft crunch. *What is this spooky fucker up to now?* Then, tuffs of pastry fell past my eyes and onto the floor of my cage, falling from between the bars up high. He was holding a croissant above me, rubbing it between his fingers. His torment made my lips purse together so hard they hurt, creating a white ring around them. He repeated the gesture again until the croissant was gone.

I scoffed with an eye roll. If that point in time I had a blanket, I would have drawn it over my face and hidden. *What is he, two?*

I flinched from the cold hit of freshly squeezed orange juice as he poured it over me, the antagonizing piece of crud. The sticky, sugary residue clung to my skin and dress like candle wax. I tried to hold myself together.

I felt like I was being bullied in high school all over again. It was humiliating. Every emotion hit me: anger, fear, dread, lust, hunger, regret, sadness, pain, humiliation, numbness. It was impossible to channel them all out. But the floodgates finally opened, and a sob wrenched free.

A rumble sounded. Not only was I beyond starving, but my bladder was screaming at me louder than my gut. As much as I didn't want to, I needed to ask him to let me out. Otherwise, I was going to pee there and then, and that was the last thing I wanted to do. *I think the fuck not. No. I won't let him humiliate me like* that.

I pulled back my tears to the best of my ability and turned to look at him. The shadow man stood tall above me, a little too proudly. It made me furious, but I choked it down, anger wasn't going to get me to a toilet.

"I need... I need to use the bathroom," I pleaded, but I received nothing in return. He just stood there, growled and crossed his arms. Tapping his fingers on his forearm. I sighed, in defeat. "Please." I pushed as much fake sincerity into the word as I could muster.

He squatted and teased the key between his insanely long fingers hanging from the chain around his neck. Dread unfurled within me. *Is he really going to let me pee myself in here?* His breath fell heavily against the metal of his mask. He was hesitating, that much was clear.

I drew in an involuntary inhale through my nose, expecting

his scent to drown me. But it didn't. He didn't smell like his normal self. Not even a little.

The hints of blood and pine were gone, the musky earthy tone of his cologne marrying the hints of the body paint. He smelled… nice. *Normal.* I frowned, glaring at him in all his glory, crouching before me.

It was strange, seeing him in broad daylight, seeing new features of him that I hadn't seen in the elevator. I'd never seen a man with jewelry before, he had two silver rings on his right hand, one round topped one with markings I couldn't make out, written in runes or tongue.

I frowned at the rectangle one, engraved with the word "HUNTED" and a lighter engraving like a reflection under it saying "HUNTER". His other hand had two very similar rings, but they were more chunky. They were bespoke, adding to his mysterious apparel. *The weirdo.*

He was more human-looking and less Grim Reaper during the day. Less terrifying. His amulet—the one that glowed at night, was empty, nothing other than a spec of stone, like a crystal. And because I was always having a brain-to-mouth malfunction, I spoke.

"What does the amulet mean?" My throat narrowed from my impulsion of asking about him. *I don't need to know… do I?* He squirmed, making the hairs stick up on my arm. He didn't offer a response. *Of course he didn't. What was I expecting?* He never spoke, his main language was a growl, huff or a deep breath.

He took a small step back to let me out. I didn't hesitate, the tugging of my bladder won me over. I winced, taking a good moment for my body to let me stand upright after being cramped for so long. A hollow puff fell from my lips. *Ouch.* My feet tingled.

"Th-thanks," I stuttered, walking backward toward the bathroom door, keeping my eyes on him. Each time I stood a step, he took a step closer.

Oh, hell no. If he thinks he is going to come into the bathroom with me while I take care of my business, that is just adding to a whole new level of freaky. I frowned and gestured my hands up, so he didn't follow me.

By the time I reached the toilet, he was already leaning against the bathroom door frame with his arms crossed and his head tilted again. His breath remained calm. I rolled my eyes, but the dull ache at my bladder was stronger than the need to punch him in the face. If I could even get to it. The metal on his mask was thick, I'd never hurt him no matter how hard I tried.

I shimmied my mangled dress in a way that the slit in it worked in my favor, pulling the length of it into my thigh and tugging my panties down without my private area on display. I took care of my business. An instant hit of relief, no thanks to all that champagne I had.

My mind wandered as the endless flow of pee sprouted from between my thighs. *Shit.* My panties had blood on them. My period had arrived. *Fuck. Well, that explains my desire to spit at him, and punch his lights out.* My heart pounded and my cheeks flushed. *What now?* I wanted to ask him about sanitary items, but I knew I wasn't going to get anything from the fucker. I swallowed hard and shoved the thought aside. Luckily my periods were light anyway, I could probably manage using the fabric from my dress if I needed to.

I washed my hands, and the refreshing water soothed me slightly. I wanted a shower so bad, to stand in there for hours like I had done in my room the next level down, and let the sins of thinking of the Whitlock boys in illicit ways drain away. *Brothers.* I shuddered. *Shut up, Esme.*

I wanted to ask him a question, but I hesitated, and I knew I'd regret it. I just *had* to know more about him, and why he was... the way he was. It would be like annoying a guard out the front of the queen's castle, but I had a habit of never knowing when to shut my mouth.

"That song... what was it that you were playing the other night? I didn't recognize it."

He knew what I was talking about straight away, for his Adam's apple bobbed and his body stilled. I had caught him crying, clearly at his most vulnerable. *Wait. Did he just... squirm? Is he shy? Embarrassed?*

I snickered. *Bingo. A weakness.* Then, suddenly the mood shifted again, with loathing rearing its ugly head once more. His chest rapidly began to rise and fall, and it was a warning in a don't-test-me way. But I didn't care. I wanted the fucker to speak. Now that I knew where his big red button was, I figured I'd push it to see where it got me.

Because, after all... I was still alive.

"I saw you cr—" But he was quick to cut me off. His hand wrapped around my neck faster than the speed of light. That deep primal growl purred in his chest, the vibration shooting up his arm and against my jugular. I probably should have held my tongue; I'd clearly hit a nerve.

I wanted to see what would happen, and test my boundaries. He was going to kill me anyway, so they said. The shadow man's grip was tight, but I could still breathe—he knew where my pressure point was—if he wanted to press it, and make me pass out.

I could feel his heartbeat pumping through his veins against my throat. He wanted me scared, and I was. But I couldn't shake the feeling that he was reserved, perplexed... *curious?*

"Do it," I hissed. "You have the chance to kill me, so do it," I grumbled with whatever breath I had.

I didn't pry at his hand for my release, I held my stare heavy into the mesh of his mask's eye holes, hoping that somehow I was staring into his own. Part of me wanted to believe that his face was as ugly as his soul, but the tug in the other part of my brain said that wasn't entirely true.

Maybe he thinks he is ugly. Maybe all the scars on his body travel to his face. Maybe all of this leads to a form of self punishment, or sabotage.

Humans aren't born monsters. It's learned... provoked.

I knew he could take my life in an instant, but he didn't. I was done playing his games. If he wanted me dead, then the asshole needed to get it over with. But his breath shallowed, and he let his grip loosen completely. He gulped hard. I didn't give him the satisfaction of seeing me rub the ache that he left around my throat.

A moment passed before he grabbed my arm, pulling me to his side before throwing me back into the cage.

"You can't keep me here forever, you know. I'm not a fucking pet," I muttered, unable to choke down my disappointment and heartache. I knew I wouldn't get a reply but that didn't stop me from hoping that he would.

The fact that he couldn't strangle me to death was my proof that something deep down, was telling him not to. *But why?*

It was there and then that I knew for certain that there was more to him than met the eye. I needed to work him out, somehow. In seconds, he locked my cage and hovered at the gate with his fingers coiled around the bars, looking straight into my soul.

Our breaths synced, and shattered together in ways of tension unexplainable. It was static. I squirmed at the very tension between us and he breathed in heavily, holding it in before—

"You are my pet. My little *swallowtail*."

He.

Spoke.

CHAPTER THIRTY-SIX

A KILLER'S PET

A groan rumbled in the back of the shadow man's throat in response to my submission: I was on my knees at his feet. It had happened before I even had the mental capacity to acknowledge what I had mindlessly done. *Obey.* Like a pet. *His* pet.

There is something about this feeling that felt nice—another defect of mine, I guess.

My stomach rumbled, I was starving. But what even was my life? I'd gone from being threatened that my life was going to end to being on my knees for the man who was *supposed* to be doing the killing. I couldn't believe what was happening—and I had done it all too easy.

My heart fluttered and my stomach swirled. He hadn't said another word since he said his first... however many days ago it was. He had spoken. I heard him. Hearing his voice made me feel another thing more than I didn't need to. It was deep, *really* deep. And hoarse.

It was strong, and powerful, and it had made my core hum,

273

no—it still did. Yet I was certain that his tone was also married with sadness. Likewise to his scent and presence, I would never forget his voice. It has been etched into my mind in a way I could not explain.

Little swallowtail.

My favorite butterfly.

I knew it was him who had taken my drawings from my room when he was stalking me. Not to mention the green dress at the ball... and lingerie... that just so happened to have matched the color of the butterfly, and my eyes. The butterfly mask too, it all linked together. That was all him. Indeed, there was so much more to the shadow man that met the eye.

I squirmed from his touch as he stroked my head, like a dog. I caught a whiff of my scent, realizing I stunk an unholy amount. *Holy shit.* I hadn't showered in more days than I'd not eaten.

Only blessed with the subtle touch of hygiene each time I washed my hands after using the toilet. Which was weird, being granted access to the toilet—I was a prisoner. The other girls certainly didn't get that treatment. Thankfully, my period was light. I had managed to wipe up some of the blood that had leaked in between toilet breaks with my dress.

He only came into his room to let me out of my cage to release my bodily fluids and left when he threw me back in again. It was getting easier to walk without throbs shooting up my nerves from my feet. *Funny how spending days without standing helps to heal wounds.* I'd never walk normally again though. My body was healing over the shards still in my feet, I didn't know how an infection hadn't run through my system.

He planted his index finger under my chin, pulling it up slightly to meet his gaze for a moment before releasing it. I had a tear threatening to leave my eye, blurring my vision slightly, but it stayed complacent. I think he took in the pity I was, in a heap under him on my knees. Dirty, weak, vulnerable, sore, starving. Though, I was sure that was just how he liked seeing me.

Confusion suddenly slapped me in the face. My freakishly tall, psychopathic, masked, *lunatic* kidnapper... was drawing a bath. I gulped hard. *What is my fate?* I didn't know if he was going to kill me in it, bathe me, or bathe himself in front of me as another form of torment.

The shadow man moved to stand behind me. I squirmed and muttered a whimper to the unusual sensation of his fingers as they ran through my knotted hair, brushing the knots before letting the tendrils fall again. His finger followed my spine, trailing down to the zipper of my dress, the feeling a little too intimate. He fiddled at the zipper teasingly, and a breathy moan freed from my lips. *Oh, no.* The suspense ripped havoc in my veins, leading right to my... *Oh, for fuck's sake.*

I opened my mouth to object, but he was quick to move, his index finger pressing against my lips. He wanted my silence. Through an unsteady breath, I complied, sucking my lips into my mouth and swallowing over the lump in my throat. I flinched and then tensed from the cold shock of his knife sliding over my upper arm. *Not this again.*

He was trailing it over my skin blunt side down as if not to hurt me. He lodged it under the sleeve of my dress and sliced through the fabric with ease. It wasn't the first time his knife had kissed my skin, but it shook me all the same. The flutters of excitement between my thighs stirred, and I arched from the sensation. *Why?* Something about him scaring me and not hurting me relished me to my core.

Though there was no pain, the pressure of the knife left

behind a white line against my skin. He repeated the movement to the other side of my dress when...

"Mm," another involuntary breathy moan fell again over the streams of water flowing into the bath beside me. *I have no control.* I squeezed my thighs together to relieve the throb as he entwined his fingers in my hair. He pulled my head back to look at him standing tall above me and held his index finger over the mask, somewhere where his lips would be, shushing me.

He growled in his signature *don't-challenge-me* way. But I wanted to. I wanted him to speak again. *Come on, say something. Do something.* But he didn't. He gestured with his ebony hand for me to get up, and I did as he asked with a grimace. My feet still hurt terribly, but I was getting better at hiding that it did.

He is going to take my dress off.

He is definitely going to give me a bath.

My skin felt like it was about to melt, and a bead of sweat trickled down my neck. His knife met the small of my back at the bottom of the zipper. I bit down on my lip, hard, trying to mute the moan that was threatening to blurt out. *What the fuck is wrong with me?*

He carefully dug the knife into the fabric upside down so as not to cut me. The throbbing intensified from the touch. And in one swift movement, he dragged the knife in an upward motion along the side of the zipper. My body jolted forward from the pressure of him pushing into me, eliciting the moan that I *was* trying to keep down. *Crap.*

The soiled, crimson dress separated like cracking an egg and pooled at my feet, leaving me in just my bare skin, and the stunning green matching lingerie set he had given me. Exposed to him for his appeasement.

A hungry tormenting groan escaped his lips. *Arousal.* In shame and flushed cheeks I instinctively drew my hands to cover myself, but he was quick to pull them back to my sides. His breaths quickened from behind me.

I wondered if it was hard to breathe with the mask on, especially at that moment, as we were *both* clearly enveloped by sexual heat.

His fingers twiddled and tormented the flesh under the clips of my bra and goosebumps rose on my skin. Even though I was scalding on the inside. I arched from his touch once more, he was slow with it, letting me adjust to the newness. I didn't understand anything that was happening, but I wasn't straying from the idea either.

This was uncharted territory. *Dangerous territory.*

He gradually unhooked the clasps of my bra. One, two, three and then the fourth. I gasped as it sprung open and fell to the floor. Nerves tingled me. I was *almost* naked. He grabbed my shoulder and hesitated for a moment.

I craned my neck to look at his hand, and he squeezed it slightly before spinning me to face him in an instant. My heart skipped a beat before finding a steady rhythm again, and I gulped down the lump in my throat. Nerves riddling my bated breath.

His finger dipped into the pocket between my belly fold and under my panty line. His warm touch sent me into overdrive. I moaned, hard and loud and he retreated. Tilting his head. *Fucking hell what is happening? Just kill me now, please.*

The sensation of... something... built heavy into a tight pressure. Just like it had last time, only far more intense. But the jagged edge of his blade brought me back into the here and now. He nudged it firmly against the arc of my pelvis, just like last time. I shuddered, pushing the stars in my brain away. I didn't make sense of it, but the temptation to not rip off his mask and kiss him was hard to choke at.

He dropped to his knee, not letting the knife move an inch as he *very* slowly pried at my panties with his other hand. The curled horns had lowered to my nipple level, inches away from brushing them and the desire to touch them won me over. I trailed my fingers over one horn, enough so that he didn't notice. It was ribbed, and it felt like they were made with a thin type of material, like from a 3D printer.

He pulled his head up to look at me, then shifted his hand to my backside, nudging me even closer to him. *Oh, wow.* The horn touched me, my nipple reacting and tightening at the sensation. I chewed at my lips, silencing myself as that electric wave hit me again like it had in the garden after the ball, the night I grabbed his hand. He groaned deeply, confirming that he had felt it, too.

I gasped as he forcefully pushed his hand between the slit of my thighs, leaving me no choice but to pry them open for him. I was only happy to comply, until the tug of shame washed over me. Remembering I still had my period. *Oh, God, how embarrassing.* I clamped my legs together in protest, but he growled, shaking his head once and held them open.

I rolled my head back, looking at the ceiling before closing my eyes—out of sight, out of mind. He tugged at my panties for the umpteenth time, and something made contact with my clit, both of us reacting, realizing that I was soaked, and not from blood.

Whiplash hit me hard and fast from the sensation, and a sound I didn't warrant intrusively escaped my mouth, *another loud moan.* He drew in a rapid breath through his teeth as he let the fabric fall to my feet. He was crashing in waves under me like he was staring at the gates of heaven.

He was weak. Vulnerable. Purring.

Shit. I am his weakness.

"Fuck," he muttered breathlessly. I couldn't hold back. I panted heavily under him, and he swirled the little bud again. A *need* for my killer pounded within me. I had no control over my mouth, mind, or my body.

I shook my head as though I was trying to tell myself that I wasn't enjoying what he was doing to me, but that was a lie. I looked down at him as he stared at my exposed, glistening, and crimson pussy, not at all bothered by my hair there. The shadow man was longing for me, and I only returned the same desire. I wanted him to take my virginity right there and then. And didn't that just fuck my head a little more? I wanted to fuck a killer.

My killer.

Fuck.

CHAPTER THIRTY-SEVEN

THIEVES VS. THE SHADOW MAN

I *want his kiss against me. No, I* need *his kiss against me. So fucking bad. Why? Why does he make me feel this way?* Am I desperate, or just stupid? He swirled my swollen knot again and I shuddered. I almost came undone for him there and then, but he stilled.

"No. Please," I moaned without thinking. I didn't *want* to say that. I didn't *mean* to say that. But I wanted all of it so much, I wanted a release. I needed a climax.

"You're pretty when you beg," he mocked after far too long. Shit, I was... *begging*. Like a fucking dog for a treat. *A pet.*

The shadow man stood, leaving me panting and hungry. I flung my eyes wide open and my jaw dropped; his erection was hard pressed against his jeans, pumping like my own heartbeat. I frowned at the many raised bumps along the swelling length. Piercings?

He tapped at the screen for the bath—like the one I had in my room—and the water lulled. The bath was filled to the brim. He nudged his head, and I followed his order, climbing into the bath. The heat of the water soaked into my aching body, like a sponge. *Heaven.*

And as though he just couldn't stray from touching me, the shadow man's hand dropped into the water and trailed up the peak of my breast. I rose to meet his touch and dipped my head over the edge of the bath, absorbing every inch of pleasure that he undeniably gave me.

"I want you clean. Understood?" He grated out, his tone controlled and demanding.

I nodded... I think, and his hand moved away. I wriggled with a whimper in his absence, taking a moment to gather myself again and closing my eyes, but when I opened them, he was gone.

What the? What is with these people randomly walking out while I am in the bath?

Fucking periods. I hated them. *That's what happens when you skip a pill, or two, or however many I'd missed.*

I rummaged around in the shadow man's bathroom for a sanitary item at the very least, but all I could find was a foam sponge in a bowl with bars of soap on the bench. A foam ball. Not ideal, but it was all I could find to soak up my period blood without snooping more than I should.

I took the little sponge and quickly gave it a rinse under the tap before stowing the thing up in my *cave of wonders*, an awkward pinch but manageable. It was no tampon, but it was better than being dirty. I really didn't fancy using my dress as a wipe anymore. *Oh, crap. My dress.* I still couldn't comprehend that I had just enjoyed a decent soak in the tub. *His tub.*

I stood naked in front of the mirror, drying my hair with the dryer I had found in the drawer. And if he owned a dryer... he couldn't be bald. I took a good look at my weathered body. Despite my refreshing, cleansing soak, I truly was a walking wreck. Still, who knew a murderer would have so many hygiene products? And expensive ones at that. He was a sucker for quality. I couldn't help but dote on him for it.

He obviously looked after himself in that aspect. Then again, he'd probably spend hours in there getting the paint off before reapplying it again. There were moisturizers, aftershaves, cologne, cleansers, face masks, and all kinds of skincare. Some of them specifically to help with scarring. My mind trailed off and my heart sank, wondering how he got the scars that he was riddled in.

He still hadn't returned, and I'd been in here a few hours since. *I want you clean. Pfft. Yes, boss. Goddamn! Get out of my head.* I sighed at my reflection. My hair was so frail, but at least it was clean. And my skin was deathly pale. I needed food, stat, or my death was going to meet me before the shadow man had the chance to take me out himself.

I ran my fingers over the traces of nicks and faint bruises that covered my skin from running in the forest, then the semi-healed burn wound, then the pink laceration on my chest, and whatever else in between then and now. I hated who looked back at me. Empty, void of everything that had once made me... me.

I scribbled on the fogged-up mirror, for no reason other than because I felt like it. Giving me a confidence boost and words of encouragement to make it through another day in hell. *"You'll be okay."* I finished the doodle with a heart underneath.

Without warning, a tear slipped from my eye as I grieved my old self, all traces of her long gone. I slapped my cheek, hopefully, to knock some sense back into myself. With a huff, I stopped crying and spritzed myself with his cologne. I ought to brush my teeth, they felt gross. I did, using a brush that I had found earlier.

His masculine earthy cologne soaked into my core. It was... *nice.* It didn't take long for the intoxicating smell to make my downstairs area throb for him. Seeing as I now had no clothes, I opted for the towel, I wasn't going to spend my days in tiny prison cells naked. I ventured back into his room for a look around. As I walked, I felt the ache down low, my desire and need for him still knocking away at me.

I didn't touch myself in the bath. As much as I wanted to, I couldn't. It was a sin. All of it was, but something in my core wanted *him* to do it. I wanted *him* to be the first person to give me my orgasm. As deranged as that sounded, I couldn't fight myself on it.

I brushed my intrusive sexually deprived thoughts aside and craned my neck around the room, making sure the shadow man wasn't there. He wasn't, but there was a freshly cooked meal on his bed. I groaned from the smell of the piping hot meal as it ripped through my nose. My stomach screamed at me, and my mouth salivated.

I couldn't hold myself back. I dived straight for the bed, gulping the freshly squeezed orange juice before tucking into the meal. Crunchy roasted potato chunks, beef bites, lamb chops, gravy, a buttered bread roll, and an assortment of fruits and ice cream.

Barely breathing between each swallow, I was a wild, untamed beast. A swine. *God, I'll need a shower to wash off the mess I've made. Ah, crap.* Food was everywhere. All over my face, breasts, and the bed. I gasped, twisting my neck left and right to find the damn towel. *Shit.* It was sitting on the floor in a heap halfway between the bathroom and the bed. I leaped off the bed to grab it when the elevator door suddenly opened.

The shadow man filled the void. I gulped hard at the bread roll I had swirling in my mouth, hiding the evidence of what I had in my hand behind my back. *Yeah, like that's going to work.*

He had no cape on. Just his black ripped jeans, and the mask. *That fucking mask.*

I was in so much trouble.

"Sorry, I, I was... " I trailed off, backing up slowly toward the bed with my arm covering my private areas, my cheeks flushing bright red. He dropped his head to look at the mess before lifting it back up again, and strolling into the room. The shadow man took a brief glance at the bathroom before peering at me again.

He muttered a sound, like a rapid *hmm*, but didn't seem mad. At least, I didn't think so.

I sighed. "I was hungry." As if that would make things better. He tilted his head, then slipped his hand behind his neck, pulling slightly. I frowned. Maybe he was sore, or perhaps delaying his punishment, pondering what to do with me. I mindlessly ran my tongue along my lips, lapping up the leftover butter that was smeared on them... and my face.

I watched his stomach muscles stretch and contract tightly against his deep, rapid breaths. I took another step back closer to the bed so I could grab the sheet in an attempt to cover my indecency. *Yeah, he has seen me naked, but Jesus Christ this has to stop.* He took another step closer, and my stomach fluttered.

"Little pet, thieving?" He tsked, his voice muffled against the mask. "After I've shown kindness and let you bathe yourself?" He took another step closer. The tone of his voice wasn't menacing in the slightest. Rather, it was playful, catching me off-guard.

I took another step back, and another, and the back of my knees contacted the bed frame. I lowered myself onto the mattress, scooting under the sheet. He came even closer, and I pushed back against the headboard with my knees tucked against my chest. I wasn't thieving. Well... fine, I was.

"I wasn't... " I whispered, but he was too quick. *Did I expect anything less?* His body weight pushed me hard against the headboard as he threw his body over mine, digging his thumb and middle finger against my jugular with haste—a *need*. Holy hell, the sensation was incredible.

His scent was all over his bed and bedsheets, but it wasn't the cologne he had recently used. The smell intoxicated my nose. An involuntary breath parted my lips. As if I couldn't get any more obvious about how much I enjoyed smelling him, even though it was the very smell that haunted my every thought. He groaned in response to my breathy sigh.

The sudden intrusion of that goddamn fucking static charge ran its course in my veins again, and my pussy thumped to its rhythm again. The sensation still aching from our little rendezvous earlier.

The shadow man let loose an intimate growl as his body hovered over mine, making me feel like Jell-O. The room spun, and I felt dizzy. I wanted to feel more of the electric heat. I bit down on my cheek as the temptation to not touch him made my skin crawl.

"Am I... in trouble for eating?" I whispered under his grip, but he ignored me. He yanked the bed sheet off me in one swift movement, tossed it onto the floor. He was good at doing that. I panted the vision back to my eyes again from the release of his grip. He drew in a large breath through his nose, filling himself with his cologne that wafted from my body, and his shampoo in my hair.

"Hmmm," a deeper noise vibrated from his chest. I tried to squeeze my thighs together, but his knee was firm between them. His body language was screaming a million mixed messages, and it was exhausting just trying to read them.

"Do you know what happens to little thieves?" The muffled tone of his voice wasn't helping the flutter between my legs. I swallowed, struggling to shake my head around his grip on my throat.

"I'm sorry." As I squeaked the words, he removed his grip, moving his hand to my belly.

"You didn't answer my question," he demanded. His tone lowered, shifting once more. *Wait... what was the question again?* I wriggled under his weight as he pushed harder against my full stomach. *Ow!* A small punishment for my greed.

A moment passed and he pressed harder for my response, immense pain thumping my core. Suddenly my moral compass stormed in and the memory of him slashing my feet washed over me, and I remembered there and then just how much of a monster he was. Tears stung my eyes.

"I'm sorry. Please. I... I don't want the glass again. Please," I sputtered. He purred intimately. He liked me weak.

I gasped, in total shock. He was wiping the tears that were trickling down my cheek with his thumb. I sobbed harder, and my body trembled like I was having a seizure. He chuckled darkly.

"I love it when you beg for me. I almost considered not

hurting you, but... I'm going to have to teach you a lesson, aren't I, pet?"

I shook my head, but before I knew it, he threw himself off me. My heart pounded from his rapid movement. He pulled a remote from the bedside drawer. I sighed loudly, in relief that it wasn't a knife. But that relief was short-lived.

CHAPTER THIRTY-EIGHT

ROPES AND CHAINS

The shadow man tapped a button on a remote, and the mechanical sounds of clunking woke to life from the ceiling. It was coming from the area with the steel frame and twinkling lights. Unease settled at my sore belly, seeing a square frame lowering from the ceiling. *Fuck.* I gritted my teeth, dreading what in the fuck was about to happen. The metal frame lowered midway from the ceiling before locking itself into place. *What in the Mary St. Joseph is this contraption?*

The center of the frame had a large steel hoop. I kept darting my eyes between the shadow man and the frame, seeing that he was enigmatic, as usual. He maneuvered to the other side of the room. I panted in panic on the bed as I watched, the whites of my eyes on full display as he pressed another button on the remote. More mechanical noises chimed. I gasped, completely breathless as the entire wall behind where he was standing lifted up into the ceiling.

The whole thing. Like the garage door had done when I first got there. The shadow man was uncloaking an entire wall of black, red, and gold ropes, perfectly bunched in a row. My breath picked up the pace the more I looked. Many black and silver chains, ones of varying thickness and length. *Chains, so many chains.* All hanging neatly under red LED lights.

Nerves laced me as he grabbed several rolls of the black-colored rope before pressing the button again, and the wall lowered back down to its original state. It was like a secret torture wall, only there were no torture devices. He ushered me to stand, and I hesitated.

My breath quivered as he pointed to the ground in front of him. Hesitantly, I pulled the sheet up with me and stood, about to take a step forward when he growled. He shook his head. *Sheet off. Come on, you can do this. He's already seen you naked. Even though that was true, I wasn't as scared then as I am now.*

I blew a sigh from my lips, letting it exit my chest completely before allowing the sheet to drop in a puddle around my feet. He drew in a sharp inhale through his teeth, and instant arousal blossomed in his jeans. He stood there a moment, stoic.

Taking in all of me, his head lowering slowly. His gaze hovered for a long time at my pubic hair, I gulped and my cheeks burned. I couldn't see them, but his eyes were hungry, happily devouring me again.

He was careful with his movements, entwining the rope around my arms in rhythmic patterns. Each interlace was carefully placed around my arm, not a single gap between each row of the smooth black rope. I jolted in a whimper as he yanked the ropes, testing the strength and tightening them in place.

Tug. *And again.* Thread. Tug. Repeating the pattern.

I arched from the rough, unfamiliar sensation and the

uncertainty. I could feel my arousal coming back again, not that it had gone far. I studied him as he grabbed another piece of rope and held a section to my stomach.

"Press." His sultry deep voice tickled my pussy.

Obeying, I pressed my hand at the rope on my belly, and he paced around me like a vulture. The torment of him doing the same movement in the cellar before he maimed my feet hit my mind, and my lower lip trembled. He carefully threaded the rope around my midsection line by line, and it dug into my rolls as he tugged. Being so exposed to him made me ache in more ways than one.

But the longer I stood there for him, the more I was only happy to do so. My excitement and arousal married my fear and panic. I didn't know what was up from down, left from right. His game was twisted and confusing. He was dangerous. Lethal and vile for the things he had done—*no, will do*. And yet, he made me feel comfortable in my skin, somehow.

Because even though I had shame written all over my body, he still had an impressive hard-on. I gulped at the size of his bulge, noticing that it had a wet patch around it. If I had the capacity to turn him on, maybe, just maybe, I wasn't as ugly as I thought I was.

But he was a psychotic killer who had more than likely killed my best friend. *So why am I feeling this way? And why do I have to keep repeating that damn fucking question?*

"What is all of this for?" I drew in a quick breath as he tugged the ropes tight into a knot, securing my arms behind me. He didn't answer. He moved lower and threaded a pattern of ropes around my thigh, and my pussy throbbed beneath his tender hand that brushed a little too closely to the swollen area.

He continued the same pattern on the other thigh, and I stood in front of him tied up like a pork loin. Then he twirled his faded black finger in a 360-degree motion, gesturing for me to spin around. I did as he instructed, and his hands ran through my damp hair, brushing his fingers through the knots.

Unintentionally, I let a taut-lipped moan free. I didn't know what magic he had at his fingertips, but it made me melt like butter and was impossible to deny or hide. He followed my hair down to my ass, separating it into three sections. I swallowed hard. He was plaiting my hair—*with rope.*

"Mmmm," he purred, before returning to the side table, pulling out a hair tie and... lipstick. "Head up."

He cupped the back curve of my neck, holding the weight of my head in his hand. I felt as though my legs were giving way. God, he made me feel so weak. He pulled his other hand up to my mouth, and slid his thumb across my bottom lip before letting it flop back against my teeth. I panted again and he chuckled. My cheeks flushed in an instant.

"So sensitive, pet." His breathing quickened, and he glided the vibrant red lipstick across my lips, not once smudging it over my lip line, showing his gentle side once more.

Yes, that's me. Sensitive and goddamn ready to explode. I could not cope with the edging anymore. I just wanted a release. I was absolutely disgusted with myself for wanting the man who had, and was still destroying me.

He threaded the loose end of my ropes through the metal ring in the middle of the steel frame and pressed a button on the remote. My heart pounded as the ropes started to shift under me as the frame lifted slowly. He pressed the button again when my feet lifted off the ground, and I was merely tip-toeing.

I whimpered from the unfamiliar position my body was in. There was pressure, but no pain.

He threaded a section of the rope that was secured in the plait of my hair, around my foot. He tugged at it and my foot lifted toward my head, pulling my hair, and leaving me no choice but to stretch my neck back from the pressure. I was airborne.

He secured it in place, and repeated the same on the other side, only threading the rope from my foot to the knot at my back. I was a pretzel. A naked pretzel. I looked like I was doing a ballet performance from The Swan Lake. Actually... I looked like a puppet.

I was thankful for the sponge inside my body, preventing blood from oozing everywhere, not that there was much.

He stood there like a mannequin, admiring all of me before him, and dangling like a fucked-up chandelier. A dull ache at my shoulder blades niggled, letting me know that my tendons were taut to their max. My body spun for a moment before finally slowing, finding a spot to stay in... if I didn't move.

"Hmmm. Pink nails look nice on you. And the red lipstick? Fucking perfection," he mused. I croaked, but no words left my lips. He chuckled at my undeniable arousal for him. "Awh, my little puppet queen."

I panted at the sound of a belt unbuckling. *What?* He adjusted me so that I was level with the buckle of his jeans.

"Bite," he demanded. My mouth trembled before finally pulling myself together and opening my mouth, letting my teeth chomp down on the buckle. I was sure he would have been uncomfortable, his erection was hard pressed against his jeans. *His very tight jeans.*

The little bumps of what I had assumed were piercings outlined through the fabric. *He outlined the fabric.* And wholly heck, wasn't it impressive? Not that I knew... I'd only seen one once. He pulled back, letting the belt slide through the tabs and then I spat it onto the floor. I held the air in my chest, biting my lips as I watched him free himself. His cock stood proud at attention.

I was right. His cock had *nine* piercings up the shaft of it, like a fucking ladder. I gasped, wriggling against the ropes, and in true shadow man style, he huffed under his nose. *He's amused?* He had more metal through him, but that was the one that took my attention first.

The other two piercings were placed evenly on the top through the perfectly smooth head. Mindlessly, I licked my lips. *Fuck.*

This freak was giving me more reasons to want him more than I did. And more than I cared to admit. *Why are his piercings turning me on?*

"Open," he ordered, his voice infused with heady desire.

I didn't hesitate and his cock rammed to the back of my throat, violating my jaw as it widened to take his impressive girth. The hit of his cock and his arousal of it in my mouth tugged at my forever lingering orgasm.

"Ffffuck," he groaned, and I whimpered instinctively. His piercings bumped along my bottom lip as he pumped in and out, some hitting the tips of my teeth. I moved my tongue over my teeth so he didn't run his cock over them or hurt himself.

I took him all, and happily. My only option to breathe was through my nose as he swelled thicker inside my mouth. *He's really enjoying this, as am I.*

I kept my breath hollow, trying hard to ignore the throbbing of my pussy and the threatening orgasm. But the more his rhythm picked up the pace, the more I ached for him. My hair pulled at the scalp from the pressure of my foot and ropes pulling against it, but fuck it felt good.

I gasped for air as he removed his length from my mouth, spinning my body so that I was facing the other way... blind to his touch. I saw stars momentarily as his thumb found my clit. I almost folded for him there and then but the intrusion of my period stopped me.

Between sobs of pleasure and panic, I cried out as he inserted a finger where my sponge had been lodged. I yelped as the sensation brought me closer to my orgasm but also a string of stinging pain. My cheeks flamed.

"WAIT. I.-I-" I stuttered, embarrassed to bring up the sponge that was crammed in there. He paused, waiting for me to find myself again.

"Use your words, pet."

I moaned from the use of his pet name for me. *Fucking hell, think Esme.* It was hard to use my words, given that my heartbeat was pounding at my pussy. I had been aching for days for my release. And every time I squirmed, it pulled my hair, and I liked it. Really fucking liked it.

"I... I have something... *in there.*"

"You're about to," he growled.

"No. Wait," I squealed, and without warning he suddenly shoved *two* fingers into my pussy. I cried out from the unfamiliar pain. And then, he twirled and pinched at the sponge before pulling it out, the blood-covered DIY tampon now in his grasp.

"You mean this thing?" he toyed, throwing it on the floor.

"Yes," I muttered mousily, a tear flowing down my face from shame. *How embarrassing.*

"I see... "

I shuddered. *Is he not bothered?* Obviously not, for he continued his sexual torment against my clit, rolling a rhythmic pattern. *Slow, stop, slow, stop.*

"Oh, Jesus H Christ. Please," I begged, mindlessly through taut lips. My release was so close, the need for him was too strong that I couldn't deny it anymore. I didn't care about the glass, the stalking, the kidnapping, the starving. *Nothing.* I didn't care about anything. I just wanted *him.* Whoever *he* was. It was so twisted.

The throbbing was getting heavier where he swirled, yet somehow lighter. And my throat was thickening to the sensation. I panted against his touch, unable to deny how good his rhythm felt, he was gentle, soft, caressing. *He is still a murderer. Yes. But right now, he isn't one.*

And he was clearly not a stray to blood, or the female monthly visitations... periods. He steadied, letting my orgasm subside. I panted hard, so hard my chest felt dry. *Swirl, stop, swirl, stop.*

"Fuck, you sound too good for a virgin." His voice was as breathless as mine, but he paused, leaving me desperate as he spun me around again to face his veiny cock once more. Pre-cum dripped from the pumping head. It was thick and sticky-looking.

Instinctively, I licked my lips and opened my mouth for him, letting my tongue lap up his wetness until it was down my throat. *I want more.* He rolled his head back and curled his fingers around the nape of my neck, muttering something to himself as he thrust hungrily into the back of my throat. It was all kinds of fucked up, but I fucking loved it. *Ecstasy.* I was only happy to accommodate him.

"Fucking hell, swallowtail. I put you up here to teach you a lesson," he scoffed as he dove into me again, then paused to continue. "But I'm only teaching myself one."

My saliva poured out of my mouth as I reveled in his enjoyment, lubricating each thrust. I could feel his orgasm building. He growled and grunted, moaning with each pump. He hissed through his teeth and let my body swing on the ropes against gravity, only making his cock reach further down my throat. The paint on his chest began to strip away from sweat as his orgasm was building more, and more.

I frowned at a stray sound, pulling me back to reality. His pants vibrated, and a ringtone followed. He growled aggressively, and the heat from his body thinned to nothing as he pulled his length from my mouth. Leaving it feeling hollow in his absence. Someone was calling him.

"WHAT?!" he roared through the phone in rage. He holstered his throbbing, pierced, impressive length back into his jeans before walking somewhere distant in the room, perhaps the closet as his voice fell nearly silent. I panted in his absence. The throb in my pussy echoed in my head. I slowed my breath to reduce my heart rate, and licked the saliva and his taste from my lips.

I thought he said I was going to be punished for taking his food. This is hardly punishment. This is pleasure. Only God knew what he was thinking.

Only a few moments passed and he stormed back, I imagined steam sprouting from his ears. I swallowed hard at his sudden shift in mood. Everything was cold and I had again lost sight of who he was.

A killer. My killer. God, I am fucking delusional.

He lowered me down so that my knees touched the ground, his knife once more digging into my skin. He abruptly sliced the ropes from my body.

"We will finish this later," he hissed. I should have been a little more scared than I was, but the sensation only added to the sexual tension I had between my legs. He chuckled, pulling my hair so that my ear was at the cool metal touch of his mask. I moaned from the illicit movement.

"Hmm. Does my horny little pet like that?" he gritted between his teeth into my ear.

The heat from under his mask sent a shiver down my spine, eliciting another moan that almost mirrored a desperate sob. He growled for my response. I offered a nod, it was all I could let out.

"Hmm, well this just won't do. I was *supposed* to be punishing you for stealing." He sounded disappointed, in a way.

"Why string it out?" I breathed, curious as ever.

"I wasn't planning on it. But, now I know how much I fucking love that you're my defenseless, weak little puppet. I think I might just wait a little longer... or not."

I couldn't help the sadness that struck me as he put me back into my cage again, naked, and still very much hungry. Granted, it wasn't a hunger for food. He stood tall above me, only mimicking my sadness. *I think*. All traces of anger had long gone.

"I don't understand." I sniffled as I gazed at him through the metal bars. He sighed and reached into his pocket. I couldn't believe my eyes; he was passing me a singular tampon. I grabbed it, but his touch was cold. Too cold. Unease swam over me, pushing aside the desire I had for him. Like my moral compass had come back, swinging a fist.

"If you did you'd only make it harder for me."

"Harder to what?" I didn't want to know the answer, not really. But before I knew it, he was in the elevator and holding his hand against the door to stop them from closing behind him.

"To show you that I cannot wait to watch your life drain away for me."

He rolled his head back, releasing a sadistic chuckle. My lips curled in disgust, and the food in my stomach threatened to release. The echo from his laugh made me shudder as it faded down the channel of the elevator. It was haunting.

Tears fell and I screamed in anger.

What the ever-loving fuck?

CHAPTER THIRTY-NINE

SINNING UNDER TABLES

I *cannot wait to watch your life drain away for me.* The shadow man's words repeated over and over in my brain, and I think I had counted every shadow on the wall. Hours had passed and my heart still hadn't lulled. My eyes stung. My chest hurt. My pussy ached... *why did it have to ache?*

He was a killer.

Why did I have to remind myself of that so often? Why did I give him the satisfaction of knowing that I enjoyed his delicious antics? Even as fucked up as they were. And what made it worse was that the fucker gave me a tampon. A fucking tampon. Did he feel... empathy? I didn't put it in, I didn't want it. I was having no more of his stupid gifts.

I tossed and turned in an attempt to escape my intrusive thoughts, and my ass bumped the side of my cage. It wobbled more than it should have. *Huh, that's weird...*

I did it again, and realization dawned on me like a bolt of lightning. I gasped and jolted around.

"Oh... shit," I whispered. The padlock wasn't secured. Did he forget or was he stupid? Adrenaline flowed through my veins.

Could this be my chance again? I could make it to the garage... if only I had a key for one of the cars. Maybe I could run for it? But not down that forest again.

My head raced with ideas. I knew I shouldn't attempt what I had done once before and was heavily punished for.

Butchered. Absolutely butchered.

But me being me, I acted on impulse and pushed my finger at the open lock, letting it slide through the bars and fall to the floor. *Freedom.* I leaped out of my cage and made haste toward the elevator door. Glancing briefly at his closet, I found a few capes hanging up and took one. I'd have been stupid to try escaping completely naked.

The thick, heavy fabric enveloped me. It was ten times too big, but it did the job to cover my indecency. It smelled like him —*his real smell*—not the cologne he'd recently tried to cover up with. I was both revolted and intoxicated.

I pressed the button for the second floor, as I remembered my way from there, having done it before. The hallway was dark when I reached it, but there was a room further down with the door left a-jar, and a light beaming on the other side of it, flickering. Like a TV did.

No! Not again. Nope. I'm not going to stop.

I drew in a big breath to mute my staggered breathing and tip-toed my way. Stopping at the edge of the door. I listened for someone on the other side, checking whether the coast was clear. But the only sound I heard was the hum of electronic devices, like a bunch of computer noises.

Esme, are you listening to your moral compass?

I blew out a sigh and stuck my head around the crack of the

door. But the sight before me made me sick to my stomach. The entire wall at the back of the room was one big lit-up screen of security camera footage. Every square inch of the screen displayed different footage of me.

All me.

I had truly underestimated just how much he had been stalking me before he took me. At home. At the clubs. At college. At the café. With Tilly. On the bus home. Me in the cage in the cellar. Me in that other room. The one time I fell asleep naked on the bed on that really hot night, legs sprawled. I could see *everything.*

There was me, Damon, Ruby, and Tilly in the room where I was first taken, along with the other hostages. Me spying on him when I caught him playing piano. Me running out of the terrace into the forest. Me putting on my formal gown. And earlier, dangling for him by his fucking ropes.

With his cock sliding in and out of my mouth.

And right at the bottom left corner was his room, and my cage. *Empty.* Then there was live footage of me, standing at the doorway in the hallway dressed in his cape as I stood at that moment. He had been watching my *every* move. Fear swam through my veins, threatening to swallow me whole. *Fuck.* I couldn't hide. He was everywhere.

I shrank into myself, gasping as the sound of footsteps from the bottom of the stairs neared. *Shit, shit, shit.* I panicked and bolted into the room, spinning my head to look for somewhere to hide. I ran to the other side of the room, where it had the least amount of light reflecting from the screen, finding a low bench that I could hide under.

I ducked under it, using the cape and its hood to envelope me and my pale skin. With his slow, unrushed shuffles, the shadow man walked in, closing the door behind him... and locked it. He looked exhausted, vexed even, hunched over and seeming somewhat defeated. Far from the anger and loathing hours before.

He walked straight to the marble bench in front of the screen and poured a scotch into a glass before sitting on the singular sofa with his back and side to me. I drew my hand over my mouth to silence my bated breath as he pulled his mask off and plonked it on the bench before him, taking in his drink in one gulp.

I couldn't see his face, but I could see the shadowed glow of his profile, his jawline, and his impressive Adam's apple. The lighting hit him differently, if I was further in front I'd have been able to see him entirely, but then, he would have seen me too. He pulled his phone from his pocket and tapped a few buttons. Thankful he hadn't yet noticed I was gone.

I watched silently in awe as he unzipped his jeans, prying them down to his knees. *Oh, holy... shit.* The screen changed to a single view of me in the ropes earlier, dangling from the ceiling. He rewound the footage to the start and set it on a loop. The footage of us began to play, *volume included.*

Moisture, his groans, my moans... the sounds of them shot pleasure immediately to my pussy. I sucked in my lips to mute what I knew was threatening to come out, a fucking moan. *Oh, no.* He began to stroke himself over the footage of us. His hand banded his cock with a firm grip, not at all fazed by the piercings down his shaft. The metal-on-metal sounds of them twanging against his rings between each stroke sent an erotic shiver down my spine.

This feels illegal to watch. Heat pooled between my legs, and a sense of desperation hit me.

Acting entirely on impulse, I shuffled my back against the wall with one hand cupping my mouth and the other at my pussy. I placed my finger over the sensitive little bud between the slit. Right where the shadow man was not too long ago.

I had never done it before—touch myself—but I wasn't going to let that stop me. Whatever I had been feeling recently was enough to trigger the curiosity. *Fuck the rules. Fuck the sin. The Whitlocks have had me on edge for too long. I* need *this release.*

The sensation of my sensual touch made it hard not to fold right there and then. But I figured that if I could maintain my rhythm, I could climax at the same time as he did. Is that weird? *This is so wrong, but this feels... So. Fucking. Good.*

I swirled at my clit and found a rhythm that almost matched his, focusing on all of my core and body. When he sped up, I sped up in unison. When he slowed, I slowed. He built up his orgasm, and in turn mine. Granted, I was probably closer than him, given that I was sweating.

I panted heavily for him, scrunching my face to mute my moans. *This is harder than I anticipated.* He had no idea I was there.

His grunts and groans hit a new level of volume, and he shuddered. I felt pressure, somewhere in my core and lower down, like I was seconds away from exploding. He stilled, and then spiraled. Silky white liquid spouted from his cock like a fire hydrant. I began seeing stars, and fireworks crackling in my brain. Colors of the rainbow shot through my mind like I was having a stroke or something.

"Oh, fuck. Oh, fffuck!" I panted without realizing. I instinctively rolled my eyes back into my head and dived into oblivion, ecstasy hitting me in full force. And suddenly, I shuddered from the sensation of peeing myself. The warmth gushing between my thighs hit me as I faded in and out of my orgasm.

I trembled and rolled between shattered breaths and darkness. I started to come back to the here and now, still trembling as I regained awareness of my surroundings. I peered at the pool of juices left around me, as though I had just had a shower. *Wait... did I... pee myself?*

My hand glistened with the shimmering liquid between my fingers. It wasn't my blood—it was clear. And had an unfamiliar sweet smell. It couldn't have been pee. My cheeks flushed crimson as his cape that I was wearing was soaked. *What is happening to me?*

Before I had the chance to come around more and make sense of what the fuck just happened, the silhouette of *his* legs stood before me. I swallowed hard, peering up under the top of the desk I was hiding under. Beads of sweat ran down his chest over his sculpted torso, washing away more lines of his black paint, exposing more of him. His scars included.

He had pulled his jeans back up and thrown his mask back on. *That fucking mask.* Shit. All I could do was sit here in shame and fear as he puzzled me.

"Did you just... ?" he breathed, trailing off as though he couldn't believe what had happened. *Yes, I did. I did.*

CHAPTER FORTY

PIGGY IN THE MIDDLE...AGAIN

I *did just have an orgasm—my first orgasm—over a man who is going to kill me, while watching him watch me give him a blowjob.* I was sick. Sick, sick, sick. But why the in the ever-living fuck did I want to do it again? Why did I want *more*?

I muttered something in a pant, but I had no idea what. My brain was short-circuiting. I thought he would have been mad because I was out of my enclosure, but he was the complete opposite. He did not have a slither of anger or revolt in him. *I wish I could see his face.*

Both his arms tugged at the nape of his neck, as if in astonishment.

"Fuck, swallowtail," he grunted breathlessly and that static charge filled the air between us once more.

I glanced at my glistening hand, mentally scolding myself as the shadow man held his pale, thickly veined hand out for mine. I was nothing but an errant fool. His hand without paint from wiping his seed off.

Not only had I given myself an orgasm, I had to have gone

and done it to my psychopathic kidnapper, who said he was going to kill me. And I did it without a second thought. *There is something very wrong with me. Don't bother looking for me, Jesus. Just hand me over to Satan.*

I am a sinner.

And what's worse was that the fucking ass hat was *still* holding out his hand, and I didn't have anything dry to wipe mine with. The cape that enveloped me was soaked. Hell, I was soaked, and the carpet was soaked. My brain was still short-circuiting.

My first orgasm… at twenty-one years of age.

Without warning, an impish grin turned my lips. Something about doing wrong tugged a little too nicely at where my moral compass should be. *If I even have one anymore.* I felt *too* good… different.

He yanked me to my feet, wet cape included and a nervous giggle slipped from my lips. *Jesus Christ, pull yourself together, girl.* I forgot entirely that the man had said only hours ago that he could not wait to watch my life drain away. *Fuck.* I really had lost my fucking head.

Like someone had snapped a finger, the terror ran back through my veins. Funny, clearing out my orgasm must have given me some clarity. It all made sense: no wonder the college boys failed at school, because their constant need to blow a fitful orgasm got in the way of their brains' ability to function. And the girls: prowling around with their hiked up skirts for a bit of a clit twirl, no matter who by so they can get their fix… *I can finally understand why.*

As it was exactly what had been happening to me, but I was so blindsided by my sexual fantasies that I forgot the very thing that the shadow man had given me nightmares over. *To stalk me, and kill me.* And even after all that, I didn't care—I wanted *more.* I actually felt like I had only been given a crumb for dinner yet the meal was sitting right in front of me.

The shadow man took my cape off and wrapped the one he was wearing around me, before walking me down the hallway. I dove my nose into the hood to satisfy my cravings, the smell of him intoxicated me, tormenting the hunger that was still between my legs. It reeked of blood. *Fresh blood.* He'd been in the forest, I was certain. That would explain why he was a little sluggish. Had he been killing more women?

How many? Am I next? My stomach curled, the mixed messages making my head hurt. Those poor girls, and Tilly. *And m*e. *Where is my Tilly? And why the hell do I go so long without questioning her whereabouts?* I hesitated, but I needed to know.

"Umm... can I ask you something?" I squeaked, not entirely sure where I stood at the moment with him. Where his body language was. He seemed disgruntled by my question, but responded anyway.

"You just did."

His hand pressed firmly against the small of my back the entire time we walked, keeping me rooted to the present. *Where are we going anyway?*

"No, I mean another one. Umm. Okay... I'll just ask anyway... " I paused, taking a breath before continuing, "Where is Ti—"

"She's not what I want, pet," he grumbled, cutting me off. He knew exactly who I meant.

"That didn't answer my question," I hissed. He said nothing and we reached the door to the room where all the heat happened. *The sex, the lighter burn, the punishments.*

Three pairs of eyes burned into my skin as we opened the door.

"Ah, so you did keep her. Where have you been hiding her?" Damon's taunting voice growled. Maybe that was why the shadow man had taken me to his room in the first place, so he could hide me from those horny fuckers and keep me all to himself. I frowned, seeing everyone was there, all accounted for. *Limbs and all.*

Including Caine. *Who has been who knows where until now. The fucking bastard.*

I trailed off, seeing that no one had bags of frozen peas on their junk—a clear sign no one had been castrated. The shadow man hadn't killed Caine—or anyone else, for that matter—for taking me to the ball.

I gulped at the burning of their beady eyes lighting up at the sight of me, like I was a singular fry and they were a flock of birds. I'll admit, wearing his cape did make me feel... *something.* Like I was special. Maybe more so than the other hostages.

I was flustered and dripping in my own bodily fluids. And now I smelled of blood. Not mine, not his. It was positively wicked, and repulsive. I think Caine's jaw was on the ground. He couldn't stop trailing his eyes over me. Damon was sitting on the same chair as last time, with a leg over his knee, his arm draped over the side of the chair and a glass of scotch dangling from his hand. *Is he trying to be like his Uncle?* His little black fabric pullover mask had two eye holes, and the bottom of it was curled up, allowing access for his drink.

That fucking jawline. Seriously, who birthed these men? They were ridiculous. Chiseled and sharp, sticking out so aggressively that if he wasn't careful, it would kill someone. I found that strange, because none of the Whitlocks looked alike—at all.

I couldn't identify what was playing around us exactly, but it was rock. Maybe metal.

"Brother." Eli, the buff one, was the first to stand up off the couch, throwing off the girl who was on his lap. He was built much bigger than the others, and he seemed close-gated, but I had a feeling he had a sweet side somewhere. He put her back into one of the empty cages as if she weighed less than a feather, and fetched the shadow man a bottle of alcohol from the bar, tossing it across the room.

But Damon jumped up and caught it like he was in a football match, cradling it at his chest. He opened the bottle and filled his glass before tossing it to the shadow man. He took a few gulps from the bottle and pushed it against my chest, then found himself a seat on one of the chairs opposite Caine.

Damon scooted in next to him. I stood at the doorway, my feet cemented to the floor, unable to map out my next move. *Fuck it.* I brought the bottle to my lips and took a decent gulp, fire immediately radiated around my lips. I coughed from the severity of its strength, and Damon chuckled in response to whatever whispers Caine said to him.

I knew it was something about me, given that their eyes hadn't shifted from me. They sat there like little schoolgirls, giggling in class when they gossiped about boys. The sight of them chuckling oddly warmed my heart a little. I rolled my eyes at their immaturity, which Eli noticed and offered me a tsk. He was like an old gentleman, the father of them, the one to pull them all in line.

Eli grabbed the small of my back and ushered me further into the room to stand directly before the shadow man. Their voices fell quiet, and they all looked at the shadow man. Damon nudged Caine on the arm with his elbow, as if humored by something. *What happened at the ball?*

"So, pet. Which one do you want?" the shadow man provoked. My breath hitched and my eyes widened in complete disbelief. *What?*

"What?" I whispered, my throat thick and almost inaudible. He gestured his arm out, first to Damon, then Caine, then Eli. I craned my neck to glance at them all. My heart pounded. The memories of being sandwiched between those three men, and our heated antics washed over my brain. Damon's gun at my skin, *and* their erections. *"We could take her right here, right now." "So fucking wet for us." "She's desperate for it, no matter who by, or what with. Desperate little slut." "Little diamond? You want us, don't you?"*

My pussy pulsated at the memory, and I squirmed from the delicious sensation. I was outnumbered again, and something ached for them all to be against my body once more. I was already wet from my orgasm, and there was more trickling from me. Those men made me sweltering hot. I hated it, and I hated myself for liking it.

"Who do you want?" the shadow man repeated, startling me from my train of thought. There was a dark, dominant edge to his voice. I swallowed, stammering. Time froze for too long.

"But. I—"

"Take off the cape. Maybe that will help you decide," he ordered, muffled and sexy-scary-like.

Oh, fuck. "What?" I gasped, barely a squeak.

"It's very obvious that you want to. Even knowing who we are, you still can't help yourself. But if you can't decide who you want, then you'll have all of us."

"Piggy in the middle," Damon called out.

"The robe, pet."

I drew in a rapid breath, and my jaw fell to the floor. *Piggy in the middle? All of us? No. No, no.*

Yes.

My heart pounded hard against my rib cage. I didn't hesitate a second time. I shrugged the wet, heavy fabric off and it pooled at my feet, leaving a thump as it hit the ground. *Is that obvious?*

Four sharp inhales split through the room simultaneously. The shadow man wriggled in his chair, adjusting yet another proud erection despite his release just moments before. I stood breathless for a moment and collected my thoughts, biting my lip to mute my sinful agreement that was screaming to come out of my mouth.

Whatever they had planned for me, *I wanted it*. I wanted it more than the air at that point. Maybe because I knew it was a sex plan, not a murderous one. Or maybe because I was just insane. I didn't know, but if you handed me a mirror I'd not for a singular second recognize who I was.

The shadow man's hands band around my thighs, pulling me closer to him. Before I had the chance to redeem my balance, his hand was cupping my pussy, eliciting a breathy moan at his intrusion. Ecstasy threatened to take over there and then.

He groaned as he found a rhythm against my clit. On instinct, I rolled my hip up to meet his touch and arched my neck back. He was so gentle with it, yet so hungry and forceful. Another sensation split over me, Eli's chest melding against my back. I could barely focus on his touch, but I made sense of him tucking his arms under mine. He lifted me with ease and moved me to the couch.

The shadow man followed, perching a position in the middle,

Damon and Caine followed. The shadow man shuffled back into a reclined position, jolting his neck back to Eli in a signal of some kind. His erection pressed hard against his jeans, and the outlines of his piercings were evident once more. He was throbbing again. *For me.* My hungry gaze prompted him to pull at his jeans, freeing his erection. I moaned. *Shit.*

My eyes widened. Damon, Eli, and Caine followed suit, removing their pants. *Holy fuck.* Four men stood with their cocks standing at attention, leaving me no choice but to admire them. And as much as I very much disliked Caine, I was staring at *his*, too.

CHAPTER FORTY-ONE

HOLY GUACAM— NO! HOLY FUCKING MOLY!

I fell into a heavy panting rhythm of arousal. Damon's was by far the biggest of the four; it was very long, and the little ring at the tip glistened in the lighting.

I think at that moment, I was grateful for Tilly's forced rendezvous, even though I hated it; watching *Fifty Shades of Grey*. Anastasia was a virgin, like me. If she could do it, so could I.

Eli's cock throbbed aggressively at the small of my back. His thick length had a little ring pierced through the top, along with two at his balls. I had to admit, it was hard to focus on four men at once. Especially when you were using every inch of your core to focus on breathing.

Caine's cock was the cleanest, with not a single piercing or slither of hair. I gasped when the shadow man's hand met my pussy once more. I darted my eyes back to his eye holes in the mask before dropping them to his length, and his piercings. I could only imagine what it would feel like inside my pussy. And

I had the feeling I was going to find out soon. *Fuck. Doesn't that just make my head spin circles?*

"You look like you're going to faint, little diamond," Caine's voice was so breathless. It was hot. The asshat, but how could I be mad at that moment? I fell for his stupid charm at the club, I fell for it again when he was in *that* room, and at the ball. Yet there I was, naked before him.

Eli held my balance, and I let my head fall back against him. His warm breath sent a shiver down my spine. I cried out as the shadow man inserted a finger into my pussy. It hurt, but it was more of a shock than pain. It didn't hurt as much when he had ripped out the sponge.

He drew in a sharp pull of air before finding a rhythm in a "come here" motion with his finger. Hitting a spot I'd not yet felt before. It was deep and heavy, pulling my orgasm closer. I moaned with a shudder against Eli, who was only happy to take my weight.

His hands cupped my breasts, and the cool air burned my chest as I panted heavily. His tongue slid up the arc of my neck, drawing my mouth into an O. Through my faded vision, I could see Damon and Caine watching hungrily.

What the? My heart skipped a few beats, seeing Caine's hand wrapping around Damon... *stroking.* I stilled, and moaned harder, my pussy tightening around the shadow man's finger to the pleasure and the visual.

"How does she feel?" Damon whimpered, pumping with Caine's hand.

"Like a fucking river," the shadow man growled breathlessly, slowing his movement slightly so I could catch my breath. I sighed as he pulled back my climax.

It took every fiber in my being to not explode for him, but he knew exactly what he was doing with me, seemingly understanding how my body worked, and where my limits were. I wanted it to last forever. *I don't want to die. I want* this.

He pulled his glossy-coated finger out of my pussy, leaving me in a state of desperation. Then, he held it out for Damon. *Fuck.* Without hesitation, Damon opened his mouth. His tongue caressed the shadow man's finger and slurped up the liquid from my pussy, but he didn't swallow.

I was so grateful that in this moment my periods were light. My mind trailed off somewhere it didn't need to, realizing they were brothers. *Brothers.* But maybe that wasn't true, because none of them looked alike at all. It wasn't meant the same way as college; when the boys would call each other "bro". *Oh, hell, what is that? Fuck!*

I was pulled quickly from the delirium as the shadow man dove *two* fingers back inside me that time, breaking my hymen. I felt it *all* to my core with both pleasure and pain, intoxicating my entire thought process in the moment.

But the burning heat only lasted a moment before I mindlessly lifted a leg onto the couch to open wider for him, accommodating, and welcoming his slow tormenting thrusts of his fingers. He was stretching me. He was aiding the course to his destruction.

He is going to take my virginity. And I will let him, without a shadow of a doubt.

I shouldn't be excited about losing my virginity, let alone to my killer. But nonetheless, in the position I was in, I wasn't about to put up a fight, and to be quite honest... I was damn fucking tired of going to war with my mind about it.

Damon and Caine scooted off the couch to stand, and he dropped to his knees before him. Damon tenderly grabbed the sides of his head and pulled his gaze up. Caine was *begging* for something. I couldn't be sure what.

But it soon became clear, because Caine opened his mouth, and Damon deposited my fluid mixed with his saliva directly into his mouth, sealing their galluptious behavior with many tongue-devouring kisses. *Fuck.* Eli chuckled, amused by my uncharted, confused arousal.

"Mmmm. Diamond is so sweet." Caine licked his lips while his eyes were on mine. *Sweet? Am I... that?*

My pussy clenched tightly with the pleasure, feeling every curve of the shadow man's long fingers, bringing my climax closer. The shadow man pushed further into me until I squirmed and then inserted another finger. I yelped once more, and a tear freed my eyes from the sharp sting my body was ringing through me. I didn't mean to cry. At least, I didn't think so. I certainly didn't want him to stop.

I relished the pain through the pleasure as he tore through what was left of my hymen. I was *his*. He was claiming me at that moment, and I was only happy to let him. It was far from saving myself for marriage, and that was supposed to be for only *one* person. *This was with four.*

He swirled and twisted his fingers, with his thumb against my clit as he stimulated me deeply, softly, then slowing again, letting my orgasm build and fall. I could no longer take it.

"Please," I begged. Without thinking, I reached behind me, finding Eli's cock. I gasped when I finally made contact. I was running off desperation, adrenaline, and nerves, yet somehow completely in control of what I was capable of.

He adjusted himself so that he was properly in my hand. I could barely wrap my fingers around him. Leaning hard up against him, he took my weight as I began to stroke him, in the same rhythmic speed the shadow man was performing on me. *Am I doing this right?* Up, down, up, down, gentle yet firm.

"Good girl. You know what you're doing. That's it, stroke me like that," he moaned. A surreal experience. I guess that answered my question. I closed my eyes in awe of the pleasure rippling through me. There was no way on heaven or earth that I could offer a reply. I knew my words wouldn't word.

Something hard but soft tapped me on my left cheek. Damon's cock. The asshat was slapping me with his dick. I tugged away my pleasure for a moment to purse my lips at him with a fuck-you-ass-hat side-eye. But I'd come so far, and I wasn't about to say no and fuck up my own pleasures.

My position gave me the opportunity to turn my head and allow him to enter my mouth. Without a second to spare, he made himself comfortable inside my jaws, my throat swelling to accommodate all of him as he thrust intently, muting my moans with the fullness.

Caine scooted to my right, and I blindly offered my other hand to him. Landing in the palm of my hand was his wet cock, the tip soaked with his sticky residue. It throbbed, and I began to stroke it the same way as Eli's.

"That's it, little one. Find your pace," Eli purred again, down my neck. Ecstasy swam through my pussy, teasing me on the edge of my climax, but not enough to tip me over entirely. I mumbled something, or tried to beg, but Damon was too big, and I could barely breathe.

"Fuck I've missed your throat," Damon hissed, the feeling of pleasure enveloping his tone.

I arched my pelvis for more. I wanted the shadow man deeper, I wanted me fuller. Suddenly, he squeezed my thigh with a growl. *Another warning.* He was controlling everyone's stimulation and climaxes. He stilled for a moment, and all four of them maneuvered in unison. *What's happening?*

Eli began to lower me, and I gasped, feeling the soft wet tip of the shadow man's cock at my entrance. I flinched, and my eyes fluttered in panic. *Fuck, what do I do? This was finally happening.* The shadow man cleared his throat, and then Damon pulled his cock from my mouth.

I took a deep breath. They were letting me take a moment of thought to recenter myself and adjust to the fact that my virginity was about to be taken from me. I wondered... *seeing as the shadow man is the one controlling us, is this showing me kindness, allowing me a breather?*

He tugged my waist, pulling my entrance a little closer. Eli continued lowering me, until the shadow man's cock was just past my entrance. *HOLY GUACAM—*

NO! HOLY FUCKING MOLY!

A sting hit my core, heavy and intense. Then a flash of light hit my head.

"Fuck," I cried out, and tears streamed down my face as he practically split me in two.

The electric thunder between us threw my body into oblivion. Stars, fireworks, rainbows, and ecstasy hit me like a freight train. I clenched around his cock and into a fitful, shattering climax. I descended into a realm only in existence to those who had the pleasure of an orgasm such as that one.

CHAPTER FORTY-TWO

LOST OR GIVEN?

The shadow man was possessed by my swollen pussy. He groaned and drew in a rapid blow of air through his teeth as he melted himself deep into me.

"Fffu—" I couldn't get my words out. Relentlessly, Damon pulled my head and forced himself into my mouth once more with a vigorous growl. I glared at his dark eyes, almost black with lust—the same pair of eyes that had helped the shadow man gut my feet with the glass.

My breath hitched, and my feet tingled from the distant memory. *So much has happened between then and now.* I breathed heavily and blinked my eyes to focus on the pleasures, lulling aside the traumatizing memories.

Caine winced from my grip around him. Unintentionally, I was crushing it. I released my hold and broke free from Damon to apologize.

"S-sorry," I breathed, and went back to what I was doing, accepting Damon's wetness in my mouth once more and stroking Caine—without the death grip.

The pleasurable sensation from the shadow man's piercings rippled against my inner lining, the dull ache building to a throbbing heat as I clenched harder around him.

I had the attention of four men: two in the palm of my hands, one in my pussy, and one in my mouth. *What the actual fuck is wrong with me?* What I was doing was long past the line of sin, I was going to go straight to the gates of hell. *Did I have regrets? No... but ask me again when this is over. I'd probably have a different answer.*

Without warning, I recoiled again, hard. Pleasure swallowed me more than the last, only this time the pulsation of my orgasm gripped around a cock, giving an entirely new sensation to an orgasm.

Thrust.

Clench.

Thrust.

Clench.

Thrust.

Clench, eye roll, body quiver, pressure everywhere, pleasure explosion, what is this heaven?

The hit of the shadow man's abrupt thrusts took my breath away. He groaned, so loud for me as if he forgot to breathe. *I* almost forgot to breathe, and I was breathing hard enough, considering the snot bubbling at my nose from the pressure of Damon in my throat.

Acting on mindless impulse and instinct, I maintained my rhythm for Caine and Eli despite my lack of oxygen. I kept building their climaxes and another of my own.

"Good girl, you're taking it so well for us," Eli praised in a dominant whisper as he caressed my breasts, eliciting a fitful subdued moan. *Fuck.*

"Little diamond loves to please us," Caine purred.

Yes I do.

I murmured a moan through spit and bubbles around Damon. It was too good. I rolled my hips against the shadow man, finding that delicious deep spot his fingers were before. Greeted with more pressure the more I pressed the crown of my cave against him. The temperature was rising.

I mirrored my momentum the shadow man did on me, onto the other brothers. Molding a perfectly steamy, erotic fuck-fest-twisted-love-triangle... if you counted a triangle as having five corners, and not three.

Alas, I am the piggy in the middle once more.

Beads of sweat poured down Damon's rugged youthful core, the saltiness seeping into my lips. Eli's hot breath hounded down my core. He took all of my weight—*something that I don't have the ability to*—against his broad, stubbled chest. The tingles of his growth radiated up my spine.

I was in fucking heaven with the alterations of sensations.

When I said I wanted more, I wasn't expecting this. Granted, I wouldn't take it back for the world.

Not even if it meant my freedom.

I was in a state of wonderland, and I didn't want to ever leave it. Had I completely lost my fucking mind? *Yes.* Those brothers were psychopaths. And I cared nonetheless.

"My pet. Make my brothers cum," the shadow man demanded from beneath me. *Goddamn. Am I ever going to get used to hearing his voice?*

I shivered at the pleasure of his tone and like a loyal servant, I obeyed with great pleasure, picking up the pace. I moaned and hardened my grip on Caine. He groaned loudly in response, his hand planted at a spot on my ribcage.

Eli moved his hand off my right breast, and Caine cradled it. Too big for his hand, he pinched at my nipple. I arched my back more from the rush of delicious, new sensation... pain, and invited it in. My head was going to explode with all of the sensations I'd never met with, suddenly bombarding me.

"That's it. They're so close," the shadow man cooed, continuing his relentless pace. I shifted my pelvis and dug the shadow man even deeper into me, and I whimpered from pleasure.

He hissed and pounded harder, grabbing the bundles of flesh at my ass with both hands. He lifted, tilted, and lowered me against his thrusts, repeating the deep, slow, intense motions before speeding up. He dug his fingers into my body like he was kneading dough.

"Fffucking hell, swallowtail." He pumped rigidly with more haste. He was so close to his climax, I could feel it. I accepted his wrath with open arms and began to pick up the pace on the two brothers, letting the third claim my mouth the way he wanted. My neck was cramping to no end, but I held myself together somehow.

My mind split in four places at once, a heavenly torment. Caine shifted again and found my clit, sending me near to oblivion once more. I don't know how many more times I could orgasm, exhaustion was starting to take charge.

The shadow man throbbed as Caine twirled at my little sensitive spot. "Oh—" I muttered whimpering moans between whatever gaps I could find around Damon. My pussy clenching around the shadow man hungrily, earning more groans.

"You are so fucking twisted," Damon hissed mockingly with a grimace of humor on his tongue. He snagged a fistful of my hair and yanked it, the tendon on my neck strained from the pressure. I flinched but accepted him.

"Our little slut," Eli mirrored his tone, squeezing my left breast harder, bruising the skin with his grip. I moaned from my ruthless pet name and the twisted pain, succumbing to the fact that it brought great pleasure.

The wet sounds of kissing grabbed my attention, Damon and Eli were entwining tongues, sending Damon over the edge.

"I'm going to fill this whore's mouth with my cum. Fuck." Damon clenched his body to stone, and his heat thumped into the back of my throat hard and fast, breathless from his orgasm. I choked and sputtered the concoction of saliva and his seed, but his liquid wasn't stopping.

"Open more, and swallow him, pet. He's not done yet," the shadow man ordered.

I swallowed, *again*, and again, so that he could deposit more of himself. And just when I thought he didn't have more to give, he pumped his hips again, letting more fluid flow from him. Tears and more snot trailed down my cheeks from the pressure.

Then Caine's body reacted and stilled. He coiled like a snake into a forceful orgasm, his warm liquid shooting over my hand, belly, and the floor. The shadow man took over, his thumb caressing my clit in similar patterns to his thrusts. My orgasm was at its peak, but he didn't let the ecstasy take me.

He slowed, then picked up the pace before slowing again. I finished swallowing all of Damon's seed and adjusted myself as his length finally left my mouth. I looked straight at the shadow man, and my heart pounded in excitement from the sight of him, seeing that his legs and stomach were soaked.

I gasped. He was completely coated in my fluid, and his sweat, and blood. *Oh, fuck.* The black glistening paint swirled around his pale skin. He seemed to enjoy me admiring him, as his grip on my body tightened.

"Eli's turn to cum, pet," he growled in another command.

"Oh, god," I pleaded, trembling my body against the two men. I couldn't put my finger on why the way he demanded and gave orders made me feel that way. It just did. I picked up my pace, putting my all into Eli, letting his breath penetrate my ear and rip through my spine.

"Fuck. Good girl, " Eli muttered, then shuddered underneath me. His warm liquid pooled into my other hand and my over ass, somehow he continued to hold me without batting an eye.

"Woah," I gasped as the shadow man yanked my arm, pulling me closer. All too quickly I was sitting on him entirely, so that my breasts were at his mask. I panted a deep breath, taking in the new position. He was deep, *really* deep, like his cock was in my core. He didn't thrust, he was still, again letting me adjust to him.

It was just me, and him. He reached behind me and pressed his grip at the small of my back, then curled his fingers in my hair with the other hand, and with great force pulled my neck back. My body arched in response and he groaned as my hip tilted for him. The static charge hounded through us with all the colors of the rainbow as he pushed his all into me.

His body stilled with mine, and his hot liquid filled me, claiming me with each pump of his seed. The heavy sensation sent me into a wave of fireworks as our molecules fused. I pulsated my climax around him, joining his.

The ecstasy was like he and I were the only beings on the planet. I wondered if sex was always like that. *This good, this depraved, this perfectly matched.* I was spent, dizzy, bleeding, panting, and trying to bring myself back to earth... back to the moment.

I couldn't shake the feeling, like we had bonded there and then. And that was only half the problem, wasn't it? I didn't even know his name. I didn't even know what he looked like.

My killer.

My mind started to race, quickly returning itself to my reality. I mentally scolded myself for my sins. *I knew I would regret this. What the fuck is wrong with me? This man said he was going to kill me, and yet, I just fucked him without once objecting to it.*

And I just lost, no—gave—my virginity, to not just one man, but to four!

But no matter how much I admonished myself, I suspected that none of their sick games were over yet. *And that this... is just the beginning.*

CHAPTER FORTY-THREE

BATHED IN BLOOD AND A KISS

"Y ou look like you need this." Eli handed me a glass of red wine as I remained on the lap of the shadow man, stuck and gasping for a breath. I winced from my brain thumping in my skull. I was so hungry, or was it thirsty? I didn't know what was what.

"Th-thanks," I muttered coyly. I needed food, not dicks. *Get a grip, Esme. Fuck.*

I took the glass and let the rich bitterness roll down my throat. The entire glass was gone in a flash, comprehending what in the holy grail, gang bang, kinky fuckery just happened. *You got railed! That's what.* Crap.

Eli cleared his throat as if he was surprised I'd drunk the fruity beverage so fast.

"Uhm, maybe not then. Here." He handed me the bottle, and I didn't hesitate. I grabbed the damn thing, holding it up to let its contents wet my tongue and drown me. It quenched the thirst I didn't know needed quenching. It tasted so good, far better than the whiskey they had given me the last time I was in the room.

My mind wandered, barely noticing the shadow man scooping me off him, and the juices that were dribbling from my pussy. *Fuck. Wait... juices, and not just mine. His seed was inside me.*

I shifted onto the couch, noticing an uncomfortable ache between my legs, like a bruise. I had completely lost sight of who I was, and the more I started to come around the more I realized what the fuck was happening. My body started going into shock, shivering and entirely thoughtless.

I shuddered and tears began to pour down my cheeks. I was under no obligation to stop them. I started seeing stars from the pressure in my head. The shadow man stood, tucked himself away and then collected my numb body up off the couch. He cradled me like a wounded baby into his body and I couldn't fight the feeling of succumbing to the darkness.

I let it close in around me, and my past nightmares along with it. The same words rolled around in my brain, over and over again.

I cannot wait to watch your life drain away for me.

Drip.

Silence.

Water? Am I... dead?

I blinked a few times as the sounds of water falling stirred me, but they faded just as fast as I did, drifting in and out of consciousness.

Esme, wake up!! WAKE UP!

Drip.

Silence.

I heard the water again, and I jolted upright, my eyes immediately finding the shadow man's mask. *That fucking mask.* I was just dreaming—there was no water. He was standing beside me, staring at me like a vulture. The same way he did in my apartment.

I soon realized that I was in *his* bed, cradled in his sheets, *and* his cape. I inhaled his scent, it intoxicated my brain in an instant. *Why did it have to do that?* I gulped, the sensation suddenly tugging between my legs again at the memory of him inside me. The ache in my body was dull, I was hurting, all over.

"How long have I been out?" I squeaked, pushing up against the headboard with a grimace. *Ouch.* I was sore, very sore.

"A day. Come, pet. I drew another bath," he answered like a robot on autopilot. I squirmed. Something was different about him, his mood was something I couldn't quite make sense of. Maybe he was vexed by something?

We shuffled to the bathroom and I took a quick glance at the beam I was suspended from the other day... night? I frowned at the memory, *puppet queen.* I then turned to peer out the window, seeing that it was just going on dusk, it looked gloomy outside.

We finally reached the bathroom and he stood there with his head tilted, gesturing with his hand that I take off the robe. Him and his demands... *this man.*

I could barely stand, and despite being unconscious for a day I was so exhausted. My brain hurt just as much as my body did. I *needed* food, I was surely perishable by now. I trailed off, admiring him in all his haunting, confusing beauty. How could a psychopathic murderer be this fucking beautiful? I didn't even know what he looked like, but I couldn't shake the fact that there was a pull that he had on me. I hated it.

I trailed my eyes over every scar on his skin that flared under the black paint. My stomach fell in thought again from how they got there, there were so many of them. I hurt for some reason—my stupid sympathy was at it again.

I mindlessly drew my finger to the now crusted burn that Ruby had given me, then trailed to the cut on my collarbone from him. Though they were nothing compared to what he had, *he* was leftover carnage. He squirmed slightly. I gulped around the golf ball-sized lump in my throat, hitched by how wounded he was.

"Did they hurt?" I whispered with furrowed brows. He growled under a breath, clamping his fist. A warning to butt the fuck out of it.

He offered me nothing other than silence, and a second prompt to disrobe. I didn't push. I didn't want to hit a nerve that I had no business poking around. I dropped the cape over my shoulders, not having a care in the world of my nakedness. He clearly wasn't fazed by my weight—not that I should care what he thought—I was a hostage after all.

I couldn't stop my eyes from trailing him up and down, his glorious height, and frame. And his jeans that hung from the v of his hips... his torn jeans, and a worn-out brown leather belt. *Gah!* He was fucking beautiful.

His skin showed where the paint had run from his sweat. He clearly hadn't showered since our heated antics or put fresh paint on. I bit my lip at the sight of his pubic hair on his stomach, trailing in a perfect line before hiding under his jeans. He was breathtaking. I knew he was a monster, but under all the façade, I think maybe... he was a beautiful, wounded soul.

Begging for love. *Somewhere*. He tensed, and for some reason I cowered.

"Don't pity me," he scowled, a perplexed hiss in his muffled tone, as though he was choking back a layer of anger. A moment went by and he sighed, brushing my hair behind my ear and gripping my head with his hand. "I can hear your head running a million miles an hour, swallowtail."

The shadow man was right, it was doing exactly that. I couldn't lie, I felt like I was living a real-life version of Sleeping Beauty. He told me he was going to watch my life drain away for him, and yet I *almost* didn't care. Princess Aurora knew of her impending death. She was told specifically *not* to touch the spinning wheel, or she would die. But she did it anyway, cast under a spell she could not resist it, pulled to it by a siren.

No different to the one the shadow man was doing on me. Why couldn't I resist him? Why did I want more of him? The man barely spoke a word but when he did it drowned me and every thought I had in my head. Like a power. Manipulation. Mind control. And when he showed a sliver of kindness, his genuineness of showing it in the first place consumed me in whole.

"Sorry. I just... " I admitted. But his hand moved and lifted my chin, pulling my eyes to the emptiness of his mask's eye holes. Somewhere I was aching to gaze, his real eyes. My mind trailed off, what color were they? Were they big or small? Were they electric or haunting? I filled in my curiosity and just believed that they were probably black, and empty.

"Get in," he demanded, not cold but not overly kind either. He was reserved.

I followed his order and lowered my toes into the water. *HOLY CRAP!* I gasped, and spun my head around to glare at him with an enraged frown. He chuckled. The water was freezing, and only the cold tap had filled the bath. What the fuck was his deal?

"In... pet," he said carelessly.

I winced, then breathed through the unkind hit of the cold water as it rippled through my body. I could almost feel my core temperature drop in response. My breath picked up the pace from the shock and the shadow man stood back to watch me suffer, amused somewhat.

"I like this," he exclaimed dryly.

"What, making me suffer?" I snapped back. My eyes followed him as he moved behind me. His hand found my throat and I froze expecting him to squeeze, but he didn't. His mood seemed like it was all over the place, unpredictable. Especially when he was like *this*: blank, emotionless, *confused?*

"Yes," he whispered, hesitantly.

I frowned, realizing that his behavior was a pattern, as though he drifted in states of disorientation before nightfall. Because that was always when he acted out like he did, I was certain of that. Like a wolf to the moon.

I shuddered from the chill as he strummed his fingers over the arc of my neck and chin softly, before trailing his fingertip slowly down to my chest, teasing at the crusted pink skin from Ruby's burn of her lighter.

A whimper slipped from my lips, realizing there and then that I was getting that feeling again... arousal. I rose my body from the cold water to meet his touch and we collided again. He groaned, as is fighting off his own arousal before grabbing my breast, hard. He showed it no mercy as he massaged it, and it was turning red from his kneading. I grimaced, but I didn't pull away or break contact.

"Why?" I blew the words from my chest, but he didn't respond. He shifted further forward and his warm breath fled from under his mask, hounding straight onto my skin. I shuddered from the combination of sensations. Cold meets warm.

He moved his attention to my other breast, echoing the same hungry massage, eliciting a moan. I didn't know how I had more to give, but my orgasm was building from his touch alone, and I was struggling to keep it at bay. The wicked furor of cold water was no longer my first thought.

It was like he was a professional at mind control, the shadow man was my only focus. And as though he could predict my inner thoughts of struggling to keep my climax roaring so soon, he demanded sternly.

"No, swallowtail. Not yet."

I jolted and squirmed from his touch as he squeezed harder as a threat to not climax, but it only made me fall closer to the edge. I'd had a taste of sex and pleasure, and I wanted more. More of him and his electric touch.

He grunted from the pit of his chest, purring at his sexual torment on me. I shuddered. He pulled the knife from his pocket, and brought it to my neck. I stilled, and then my heart ricocheted in my chest from the cold jagged edge that was pressed firmly at my skin.

Was this his punishment for building an orgasm when he had said no? Did he think this was going to stop it? *Because he was very wrong.* I had lost my fucking mind, adrenaline was quickly becoming my drug, making me lose control of my own thoughts.

"Mmmm," I moaned without realizing. That sound should have been something very much the opposite of a cry from pleasure. A knife could take my life away. *It could drain it.*

Easily. But I was only happy to pull my neck further back for him, exposing my pumping jugular.

"Fuck... " he panted through gritted teeth.

Not what he was expecting.

He was transfixed, and I registered there and then that I clearly had the man in a chokehold. I knew that he wanted to scare the living fuck out of me, and he did. But he wanted me in ways he didn't understand or have control over, and I soon learned I wanted *everything* he had.

He groaned, trailing the cool metal of his knife harder against my thin flesh. The shadow man drew a cascade of blood as he split my skin diagonally across my throat. Not enough to kill me, and not enough to cause significant damage, but enough so that it would not take long before my blood clotted to stop the flow.

I moaned to the seduction of pain, and I closed my eyes to mentally scold myself, only seeing stars when I did. It took every bone in my body to not unfold for him yet, I wanted it to last. But by the sound of his breathing, he was holding himself back too. I should be fucking terrified of this man, but I wasn't. *Why?* I should have been crying for mercy, because he had a knife to my throat. Even after telling me that he would kill me. But I wasn't.

"Please." I begged for my release that lurked at my clit... if only he would touch it. He whimpered and pulled his mask up slightly.

I gasped, because he caught me off guard. He didn't push it far, only revealing his pale hairless chin, chiseled jawline, and the lips of a fucking God. I bit my lip in anticipation, realizing how desperately I wanted his kiss. His lips were smooth, soft pink, and plump.

Suddenly, I winced with my eyes widened, catching sight of

a scar peeking from an area of his face I couldn't see. The moment was short-lived, and I drew my attention back to his lips, moaning thoughtlessly to the thought of them on my pussy. The shadow man drew his tongue out to wet his lips, and shook his head.

"No, pet," he growled with an impish grin. His voice was clear without his mask, sending a wave of desire between my legs. His teeth were glowing white, this man... was Godsend.

I shivered, falling into a heavier trance of breathing. Even his tongue was fucking beautiful, a perfect blend of pinks and purples. He started chewing, licking, and growling like a primal fucking animal. And then suddenly, his mouth was at my neck, his tongue lapping up every drop of my blood that he had drawn from his knife.

I cried out, and he nipped the arc of my neck with his teeth, eliciting a deep coarse groan to bubble from his chest. He glided his tongue over the tender area, and my pussy pulsated at the twisted pained pleasure "Oh, my... G—"

"Pet!" The shadow man was quick to mute me with a stern hiss.

Has he swallowed my blood? Why do I like the idea? The bath was turning crimson... I was laying in my own pool of blood. He tugged his mask back to where it was and I frowned. His hands ventured down my body, one finding the base of my pussy, and the other at my breast again. I squirmed to meet his touch, and he dived between my fold, caressing my clit hungrily.

"You want this?" His muffled deep voice crawled under my skin.

"Mhmm." A mindless plea was all I could offer him.

"I want you to beg, when I tell you to," he added teasingly, with a hint of anger.

"I. I... " I couldn't mutter out the rest. My brain was short-circuiting from the rhythms of his finger, and I was feeling dizzy from the loss of blood, and his lips on my skin. He was making me dive into desperation and messing with my mind. And the more my sexual ache thumped harder for him, the more the blood on my neck seeped out. He stopped his movements over my clit.

"Am I understood, pet?" his tone was laced with more anger than the last, panic once again taking charge, something wasn't right.

"Yes, okay." I nodded with my eyes wide.

"Good," he praised. He pulled his finger from my swollen clit before cramming two of them into my mouth. There was a sweet flavor as he swirled his fingers over my tongue, learning that the sweetness... was me. He purred, tugging my bottom jaw down, and leaving my mouth in an O position.

"Keep this open," the shadow man demanded dryly. I did as he told me, and he tugged his mask up again. "I want to... try... someth—" he paused between each word, stopping mid sentence to lean over my chest.

He lapped up my blood that was trickling down my neck and over my chest. He took in a mouthful before shifting, and hovering over my lips. *Oh, shit. This is so fucking wrong.* He was no vampire, nor was I. But it was so fucking good. Deranged. Hot.

Suddenly, his lips found mine and he drove his kiss straight into me as he deposited my metallic warm crimson liquid into my mouth, mixed with his saliva. *Holy fucking, fuckity, fuck, fuck.* The static charge punched me directly in my soul, and in my pussy. I moaned from the sensation of two warm metal bars that were impaled through his tongue. *Tongue piercings.*

I imagined what they would feel like on my clit, I shuddered. They swirled against my tongue and my climax was on the edge, like I could see the cum fairies in my brain again, ready to bless me with more pleasure. Could he get any better? Damnit. I moaned in disbelief, he was kissing me.

No... he was fucking me with his mouth. Without warning, he pulled his kiss from mine, and my blood, and saliva drooled from his lips, trailing down his neck.

"Beg, pet," he commanded.

"Please," I panted for him in desperation.

"Again," he hissed. I begged again, pained with ache.

"Please," I whispered breathlessly. He smirked, and then his tongue slid around his lips. The piercing twanged against his wickedly straight teeth, covered in *my* blood. He swallowed.

"Hmm, swallowtail?" the shadow man groaned, a daring edge to his tone.

"Yes?" I wept, barely holding myself together.

"I want you to cum for me."

And with that, his warm unfiltered, unmasked breath crawled under my skin, and I fell off the edge of the earth for him, hard and heavy.

I fitted into my climax, and another, letting the stars race around my head, and the colors of fireworks cloud my vision. And just when I thought that maybe he was not a monster, everything in my body came to a raging stop.

He shoved my body underwater, and I inhaled a gulp of it. Coughing bubbles in an instant. I couldn't fight against his strength as he held me submerged.

The pleasure from my orgasms washed into my fear of death.

I thrashed and screamed, but he held me down with a shaky arm. Water spilled from the edges of the bath onto the floor.

Suddenly, he pulled me up for a breath by the nape of my neck, and I drew in a rapid blow of air. I yelped a terrorized plea for help, but he dropped me in again.

His crimson covered teeth carved with a satanic grin was the last thing I saw.

CHAPTER FORTY-FOUR

WARNING SIGNS

"Help! Somebody, please... . help!" I cried out. I tried to scream louder as I tossed my body in and out of the water. Helpless against the weight of fate. I gasped for my life, and with every ounce in my body was fighting against the black-painted hand that held me under.

The shadow man.

The bubbles and faded screams surrounded me, and the blood and water continued to envelop me, trying to take me to the place of the dead.

"Give."

"Her."

"To."

"Me."

The luring, static, radio-like voice ricocheted my brain as I twisted my body more than the last, and thrashed like an alligator would when attacking its prey. I heaved and pried at his grip, but what was the use? He was too strong for me.

I could feel it... my life was draining away to nothing.

My death was a virtue.

He said he would, and he is delivering.

My heart slowed, and swirls of his black paint diminished through the water. I could see a black smoky haze surrounding me. I could see his face. His mask was gone, and blood trailed from his mouth like an animal. The shadow man was revealing his true self.

A monster. He was rabid.

It seemed as though he was consumed by whatever darkness had a hold of him. Like how it happened in my nightmares. I faded to nothing, pumping the last beat of my heart as he let go of my body.

I slowly descended away from him, sinking into the nothingness of the water. The viscera of death—the water's belly—just as he desired.

I cannot wait to watch your life drain away for me.

The shadow took my life.

Suddenly, I jolted upright with an almighty gasp. Darting my eyes around to find my surroundings, tears streaming from my eyes and trembling down my face. Sweat beaded down my body, I was soaked—but I wasn't in water. Panting and shaking heavily with my hand against my chest, my heart pounding to breech from my rib cage.

My heart.

It was still beating. I was the remnants of a trembling, haunted mess. *What the fuck happened? Where am I? How am I alive?*

I pursed my lips and caught my breath, coming back to the here and now. Tuning in, I could hear familiar whispering male voices, and music. It wasn't bright, so I was able to gather my surroundings without squinting. I looked down, seeing that I was naked, and chained by the ankle—very much *NOT* in a bath where I last was.

Murder attempt number... how many is that now?

Fuck.

I knew in an instant that I was in one of the cages... in that damn sex room, or whatever it was called. I must have had a nightmare. *Why did that feel so real?* It must have been real, I was sure of it, because I remembered my last memory of the shadow man holding my head underwater. *So how the fuck did I get here?*

"Yeah, I guess." I heard Eli's voice speak.

I could see that he was with Caine, they were facing the other way and clearly transfixed on a girl who was stripping her clothes off for them, and another crawling to them with a small bottle of rum in her teeth. They continued to mutter between each other, so I wriggled down slightly so that I could still see them. The music was quiet enough that I could hear them, but only just.

"What the fuck is up with him, anyway? He's got a bad case of fucking sundowning since *she's* been here." I could make out Caine's voice.

"It's a pity, really. He hesitated on her last night. He's a fucking mess," Eli responded. I lifted my head slightly, seeing him taking a swig of the rum the girl had before continuing. "She's the one... he said so himself. But he's never hesitated."

Caine snatched the bottle and skulled a few sips himself. He swallowed with a sigh, then grumbled another vexed reply.

"Well, she is different. Maybe it's not as it seems anymore?"

"Yeah but how long does this go on for? She knows too much already."

"That's true, and he would be stupid to fuck this all up now, for his sake. We've come this far. Six years too long," Caine remarked. Eli scratched his head in frustration. *Huh? Six years?*

"I know, brother. I'm getting tired, and I didn't sign up for fucking babysitting duties, either." Eli slapped one of the girls on the ass hard, and laughed. "Good girls. Now, leave us," he scolded, and she scurried off back to her cage, shutting it behind her.

Tears flowed down her flushed cheeks, she glared at me with a solacing frown before curling herself into a ball. The other girl followed, closing the door behind her, then looked me up and down with a furrowed brow. I rubbed my throbbing head, and my mind wandered.

What the fuck happened in the shadow man's bath? What do they mean by she's the one? What did they mean by he hesitated?

Has he hesitated to kill me? And what was six years too long?

FUCK! Why the hell do I never know anything?

Rage took charge, making me grit my teeth. And I had the fucking audacity to of doted on him and his stupid scars, his stupid piano playing, his sad whimpers and sobs. *Fuck, that... that... fucking swine!* I scoffed out loud, and their voices fell quiet. *Crap.* I had done that out loud.

"Ahh, the diamond has awoken," Caine said softly. Eli scooted off one of the sofa chairs and scurried toward me with a devilish grin. I squirmed from the intrusion of his gaze as he stared at me. *Why does he have to be so attractive, especially under this lighting?*

The LEDs at the bar had been turned low and on red, kind of how I imagined a *"mans crib"* would be lit, with some kind of sport in the background on a TV. Or like a bar... strip club even.

Fuck that guy and his handsomeness. Luring me into his gentleman nature at that club. *Son of a b—*

The flutters in my belly started to charge between my thighs. *Shit.* Not again. Not now.

"Look at you. Even after he tried to kill you, you're *still* hungry and desperate." Eli tutted and shook his head in disapproval.

Damnit, Esme!

Guilt rippled through my veins, and I flushed, shaking my head in denial. *Is my desperation really that obvious?* These men *all* took my virginity, and all I wanted was more. I couldn't control what my body wanted. I trailed off, remembering an article I had read once, about bonding to the person you lost your virginity to.

I curled my lip in disgust from the thought of being "bonded" to the shadow man. *Is that why we had that electric current between us?* I was certain that when I had read it, that it also mentioned to truly bond and connect, the *other* person must feel the same way, or the connection was broken... void. Because a bond isn't one sided—*it is dual.* Eli pulled me from my musing.

"Are you hungry, little one?" Albeit his tone was riddled with seduction, but I wasn't falling for it. I shook my head again, because I knew that he didn't mean for food.

He pried at the buckle of his belt, and I drew my eyes to it unintentionally. *Fucking hell.* Someone had tried to kill me, you would think that it would have been enough to keep away my depraved sexual thoughts... but it wasn't. Eli tutted again.

"Be a good girl, and answer me truthfully." I gulped and shook again. He stepped closer, pressing for an answer.

"No," I snapped. *Liar.* I was starving—for food. Real food.

Eli laughed mockingly. He could see right through me.

Unease swam through my veins as Caine strutted over with a key. I wasn't scared of him exactly, but he had proved enough that he was an untrustworthy bag of crap.

He unlatched the padlock of the chain wrapped around one of the iron bar's of my cage, which was connected around my ankle. He gawked at me with a wicked smirk and then opened my enclosure. Caine waited for me to exit, but I refused.

I didn't trust him a single inch, and as handsome as he was, he was a slimy pig, like the rest of them. His blue doe eyes tugged at my heartstrings, forcing a tear to shed from my eye without warning. *This is all* his *fault.* I shuffled backward with pinched brows.

"Stay away from me!" I hissed. But his hand banded around my arm and I was yanked out, shoved forward, dragging my chain along the ground behind me and then pushed onto the sofa. "Ow! Bastard."

I scrunched my legs up sideways to cover my pussy, in an attempt to keep some dignity. My head spun in circles just from walking over here. I had no idea how much blood I lost in the bath. Not enough to die obviously, but enough to know that I was very frail, and starved.

I hadn't eaten in… days? Not since the shadow man caught me eating his meal. I trailed off, sobbing to the head fuck in my brain. My eyes widened as Caine noticed my woe: he was dropping to his knees before me, and planting his perfectly manicured hand over my thigh.

The sympathetic glint in his eyes was genuine, and it threw me off guard. I needed answers then and there. *No more distractions… ask for answers.* Eli smirked and scooted next to me and I gasped as Caine moved from my legs to the other side of the sofa.

What are they up to? I squirmed, and that feeling of not having a voice started to wash through me. I felt small, worthless, and empty. My heart started pulsating again.

I gritted my teeth as Eli began to stroke my head like a lost puppy, his crystal blue eyes burning down on me, as though he was waiting for a reaction from me. He chuckled, before curling his hand around the nape of my neck, pulling me into his frame.

"What is your angle?" I snapped.

"No angle. Just a pretty little toy for us. Ain't that right, brother?"

I flinched when his grip forced my head to face Caine. I trembled into a fit of tears. The feeling of weakness hurt, and was almost unbearable. I was too tired, too weak, and too hungry for whatever fiasco they had planned for me.

"Mhmm," Caine muttered in reply and licked his lips. I clenched my jaw in frustration, keeping my eyes anywhere else but him or Eli. I just wanted to go home, or be dead, anything but *there.*

He held me with a tight clasp, and his tongue slid along the burning cries that were trailing down my cheek. Eli was tasting my sad, defenseless, saltiness, and I shuddered, then revolt kicked up a notch and cracked through me like a spark of lightning. He swallowed.

"I love it when they cry." Eli hummed and I jolted my head away.

"Don't touch me!" I snarled, crossing my arms. Caine grabbed my chin softly, and a genuine, apologetic glint burned into my eyes.

"Trust us, little diamond. Relax... we aren't the ones trying to kill you," Caine comforted warmly. *Really? Warmly? That isn't warm nor is it comforting, that's just blunt.* He brushed the side of my cheek with his hand, caressing his thumb along the area Eli had rolled his tongue over.

"We just want a little more of you, before—"

Caine danced his brows, pausing his words and dove into my mouth with his tongue, leaving me no choice but to lose myself. I exhaled breathlessly as our connection broke, and the flutter in my stomach returned. A little spark lightened my core. The sensation of craving, wanting more, and hunger began to boil. *For fuck's sake.* I really had no fucking control.

Wait... before what?

CHAPTER FORTY-FIVE

NAIVE

I jumped from Eli's big hand abruptly prying my thighs apart with force. He shifted, tugging at his loose sweatpants, and freeing his impressive cock and then teased the sensitive flesh around the arc of my pelvis.

I moaned, but Caine's tongue muted me, keeping me calm... to a degree. Eli's index finger found my clit, and swirled a delicious momentum. My cheeks glowed in a bashful crimson. I was wet, much to my disgust.

"Of course she's dripping for us. Well, for you, I think, Caine." Eli purred against my ear. *What? What is he insinuating? That I, for one second, even remotely like this guy? Bulldust.*

Caine scooted off the couch and knelt on the floor before me once more, then planted both his hands on my knees. Without warning, he pried them apart and plummeted his mouth between my slit. I cried out from the immense amount of pleasure that hit me, but Eli hurried his mouth against mine. I entwined tongues with him as I melted like butter to Caine's twirls of his tongue on my clit.

I listened to Caine lapping up all of my secretions, and my body made more for him faster than he could swallow. *Is this normal? Or am I just a sinful slut?*

"Fuck... ing, hell. Our little toy has delicious diamonds, Eli," Caine groaned in disbelief. I tore my lips from Eli's to let out a back-arching moan. There was no way that I could kiss someone *and* have my pussy licked at the same time. I needed to catch my breath.

"Is that so?" Eli replied. I pursed my lips to focus on a breath, catching sight of the hostages at the other end of the room, watching us. "Eyes on me, little one. Don't worry about *them*." He finished the last part of that sentence like those girls were just a number... nobodies.

His breath shredded through my mouth again with such desperation, and I became limp to his forceful kiss. He was a passionate kisser, as far as kisses go. Caine's tongue found my sensitive little bud again, and his rhythm fastened. I rose my pelvis for more, panting under the heavenly sensations crashing through me.

"Oh my god!" I whimpered. The two worked together to build my orgasm, bringing it high before dropping it again, exactly like the shadow man had done. Eli broke away for a moment and cleared his throat, then finally a wicked grin burned his face. I gulped. *This can't be good.*

He shifted slightly, and Caine's hand reached up over my thigh and made contact with Eli's cock. He gripped it firmly, the piercing shining above Caine's hand as he began to stroke it. He took his tongue away and tugged at his pants before gathering his own cock into his palm, and repeated the same pace on his as he was on Eli's. *Fuck.* Eli's hand moved to find my wet bud, rolling his fingers around in circles over it.

"Mhhm," I squeaked as my climax was at its peak. *Just a little bit more.*

"You like this, diamond?" Caine muttered under a raspy breath. But I couldn't reply with anything other than another, "*Mhmm*". He built both of their orgasms as Eli's built mine and I found myself somehow even more turned on than before. The heat was becoming intense, but I was still not granted an orgasm, no matter how close to the edge I was.

I didn't know how long in *pleasure town* it had been, but they both adjusted themselves, moving to another position. Eli turned to face me fully and scooped me up so that I was facing Caine, his face was drowned in hot, steamy, and hungry sweats.

My back was to Eli, he began to lower me over him with ease and as he did I mindlessly tried tucking my legs behind me but my chain snagged on something. Caine freed it, and then I felt Eli's wet tip hover at my entrance. I didn't know how he was holding me like that, but he was, and then he lowered me a little further.

Suddenly, I was impaled. Filled. I cried out, wincing from his girth as he claimed my still-wounded pussy from the shadow man. Fuck, it hurt, but I rolled my hip further into the pleasure and pain, letting it consume me.

Caine leaned forwards and dived hungrily into my mouth as Eli thrust into me, hard. He tasted heavenly. *I tasted heavenly.* He was a fantastic kisser, though. *How could I forget how consuming he is? Caine was my first kiss.*

I trailed off, thinking about the night it had all begun, and why the shadow man didn't kill me, *again*, among other things but it was hard to focus. It made no sense, none of it did. He had so many fucking chances to take my life, but he didn't.

Damnit. The fucking question was overpowering my want to

orgasm, I needed to get my answers, otherwise, I was never going to enjoy... *this*. I pulled away from Caine, and sighed.

"Wait. Please," I begged quickly. Eli stopped hesitantly and knotted his fingers in my hair, then tugged hard. I gasped from the force of my back landing against his sweaty chest. He pulled my hair so that my head tilted, and his mouth was at my ear.

"This better be good, little one. What is it?" he roared, sending an illicit shiver down my spine. I grimaced, sitting like this pushed his cock further into my pussy, right on that sweet spot. I blew a rapid breath to compose myself before finally responding.

"I need to know. Please. I'm desperate for an answer."

"Need to know what?" Caine asked.

"Why me?"

Eli let out a wry chuckle. "If you're a good girl, we will tell you after you've finished."

"Finished... what exactly?" I muttered with a frown. Eli dug his grip around my waist, pulling me in tighter against him. The dull ache of his cock hounded my core, the sensation reminding me of gagging bile. He swirled my clit, and pumped into me hard, eliciting a breathy moan.

"Us."

Caine chuckled at Eli's bluntness. I hesitated, then nodded my head in agreement.

"Good girl. Now, open up for Caine," Eli commanded. Caine stood, and I opened my mouth wide into an O shape. I rolled my eyes as he lingered his impressively clean, tidy length at my lips with an eager gaze. But he didn't push into my mouth like I was expecting. It was almost as though he was waiting for my permission.

I raised a brow at him, an immediate prompt for him to shove straight in. I had the motive to get the fuck over and done with it, so I could find out why the fuck I was in their hell. I was getting sick of arousal getting in the way of answers. Despite my coherent thoughts, I couldn't deny that I was enjoying Caine and Eli's pleasures.

I swirled my tongue around Caine's cock, letting it poke and prod the furthest area of my mouth. I had been told that not having a gag reflex was a good thing, but I didn't know that it would have been *that* good. I also didn't realize that I was taking charge, swaying my hips a little faster, and deeper. Eli stirred with a blow of air.

"Little one, clenching hard on my cock like that will only make me cum," he breathed, and then tilted his head to face Caine before continuing. "She obviously likes your dick in her mouth," He added, but I tuned out, pulling my focus on Caine. He was so clean and smooth, not a single hair or piercing.

"I can't wait to fill that mouth of yours," Caine whispered, and then Eli pushed deeper inside me. I shuddered from the bitter-sweet pressure. Eli was nothing compared to how the shadow man fucked me. Nothing would be close to it.

He drew in sharply through his teeth, pulling his head back as he pushed all of himself into my throat and pulling back all the way out again, slowly repeating the momentum. Each time Caine hit the back of my throat, Eli hit the tender spot of my pussy. I moaned as Caine threaded his fingers through my hair, controlling the pumps a little easier.

A stray flicker of light broke my attention, but I pushed it away, pulling my thoughts back onto the brothers. *Brothers.* The word tickled that part of my brain again. *You know this is wrong... very wrong, Esme.* And yet, I gladly pushed down with each thrust, and my climax finally peaked. Caine pulled out slightly, and I cried out.

"Oh, my... fuck... I'm going to—" I howled, and ecstasy flooded my veins. I lost myself in the moment.

Eli shivered, and groaned loudly. My juices poured around Eli's cock as my pussy pulsated tight around him from my climax.

"*Fuck*. That's it, good little slut." He hissed the words down my spine, and then slowed his pace, allowing me to come back to reality. I shuddered, trying to pull myself into the here and now, but then Caine shoved back between my teeth.

I moaned at another climax stirring behind the last, but I tore my attention to an unfamiliar sound. I blinked, and then jolted. The shadow man was sitting on the chair in front of us. He seemed cool, calm and collected with his legs pried apart. He slouched back, swirling whatever nails he had over the tip of the chair's fabric.

I gasped and in an instant my chin tremored. I wriggled, trying to break away, but Eli pinned me firmly in place and chuckled with exhilaration. My heart started to pulsate erratically.

"Don't worry about him, little one. He can have you later." His tone was provoking. I winced. *Fuck, how long has he been there?* I fell into a sob, and a rush of emotions ran over me. Terror was most highlightable as it rippled through my veins with great force.

I had been so very naive to say that the man didn't scare me, because he certainly did. All the good feelings that I had were *long* gone. The shadow man shifted in his seat, enough to adjust his cock that was straining at the seams of those damn fucking ripped jeans.

"Let's put on a show for him then. On your knees." Caine startled me, pulling me off Eli. I stood, and then he guided me back onto the couch. I pivoted to my knees, and he pinned my hands onto the sofa's arm. "Stay," he demanded.

Another sex position... how great. And in front of the shadow man? Why did that feel like a sin in itself? Eli sauntered to the other side and faced me. Without hesitating he shoved into my mouth. I coughed at his brute force and a lone tear escaped my eye. Eli turned a heinous grin toward Caine.

"Your turn, brother," he coaxed, with another pump into my mouth. Caine followed his demand, moving behind me and onto his knees.

I kept the shadow man in my line of sight, watching him strum his fingers at the edges of the armchair, his expression seemed only ambiguous. His body reacted to mine as I winced at Caine's grip around my waist. His cracked ebony painted chest chest rising and falling deeply, as if to calm himself.

Caine swiveled my hips into position, and his wet tip pressed my swollen entrance. He dug his fingers into the arc of my pelvis even further, and I clamped my tongue against the base of Eli's cock in response. I didn't understand why, but the shadow man's glare fueled my impulse to push back for Caine.

Three seconds. That was how long I counted after my grin kinked under my eye and pushed my ass back as hard as I could. The impalement of Caine made me lose my mouth's pressure around Eli in an instant. He hissed in pleasure as I let him dive into my pussy.

I moaned, and eagerly watched the shadow man's every breath. He didn't move an inch, other than the drum of his fingers, and his chest rising and falling, heavily—*then heavier, and heavier.* Thankfully, he was staying put on that chair, the hell away from me, but that wasn't stopping me from needing to piss him off. It was clearly working.

Caine was thicker than Eli, so he made it harder to concentrate as he needed to push a little harder to thrust through my clenches. But the more the shadow man watched, the more I clamped down and was turned on. *Fuck.*

"God fucking damn. She's tiiight," Caine groaned, and pounded with force. I cried out, blowing a rapid breath to ease the dull ache. The shadow man puffed his chest.

"*My* little swallowtail. Filthy is a good look on you, and so are my brothers," he claimed, arousal lacing his voice. *Filthy?* I shuddered, letting the word darken my core. *Filthy. Brothers... shit. This is so fucking wrong. Well, no fucking shit, Esme. Why can't I get that through my head?*

Well, so much for that plan. What I was doing hadn't conjured a thing to him. What made me think for a second that I would make that man jealous? I mean, really? *I've become that delusional.* And what was with the way he said "*my*" by the way? I didn't know, but his tone lingered in my thoughts like a droplet of venom. It stung, leaving a sour taste in my mouth.

I didn't belong to that fucking psychopathic killer. I was not *his* fucking pet, though I had the uneasy feeling that he had said it that way as a stern warning that I was in fact *his* toy, and not theirs.

Revolt curled my lip but was suddenly abruptly interrupted, Caine banded his arm around me, and found my clit. He didn't hesitate, swirling with anticipation, and his warm breath sent a shiver down my spine, directly to my pussy. I couldn't help but feel as though he too was trying to show some kind of ownership over me. H e always had that strange connection with me. I couldn't quite put my tongue on it.

As much as I forced my body to block out the way he satisfied me, I couldn't. I muttered my moan around Eli's cock as they were bringing my orgasm up once again. My head was all over the place, stuck in a timeless loop between a horror movie and a porno.

A single tear trickled down my face, pooling at my lip that was white and curled over Eli, the sensation of hopelessness hitting me as my body jolted aggressively from their thrusts. I was as turned on as much as I was demoralized. It was debilitating. But Eli had said that if I kept at it, he would answer my question, and that was all I needed to keep me going.

Another stray noise broke my attention again. I pulled my full attention away from the slippery wet sounds coming from both of my ends, hearing the soft irregular breaths from somewhere behind me. Only now just remembering there were five pairs of eyes burning into me: the three Whitlock brothers, and two other girls.

The thought tugged my climax closer, it wasn't far away. I knew that meant I was defective; being turned on by someone else watching. I could live with that. What I couldn't live with was the fact that I have had hot, sweaty, ten out of ten sex with no other than the man from my nightmares... my proposed and ever continuing threatened killer.

Eli held the back of my head as he pushed me into his thrusts, right to the back of my throat. The more Eli pushed, the more I pressed back into Caine. They both dove into me with a primal, competitive hunger. After a moment, Eli pulled himself together, slowing and then removing himself. He grabbed my cheeks with his thumb and index finger and turned my head to look at the shadow man.

"Little one? I want you to cum. Cum for *him*," he

commanded in a growl before shoving himself back into my mouth again. And as if his words were like fucking magic, he pushed my orgasm over the edge. I thundered into an intense climax, clenching around Caine as I kept both eyes on the shadow man. The strength of my orgasm almost pushed him out of my pussy entirely.

"Oh, fuck, diamond," Caine groaned, pulling his length from me only slightly, and in seconds his hot liquid spouted all around the outer lips of my pussy, and on my ass. Then, Eli rolled his eyes back, and let go in unison. I choked down his saltiness as it pumped through my throat. We panted heavily, our bodies dripping in every bodily fluid possible.

Stars floated around in my brain, and both Eli and Caine tucked themselves back into their pants, leaving me spent on the couch, hollow and dizzy. I rubbed my forehead, trying to rid the confusion. Disgusted in myself to no end. I jolted, suddenly seeing the shadow man standing before me. His breath had picked up the pace.

Wait, is he... mad? I gulped.

"Filthy little pet," he snarled under his mask, rage embedded in his tone.

Without warning, he jerked me up off the couch to my feet and I squealed. Terror galloped through my veins as he tugged me away by the arm. I stomped my feet, and dropped myself as dead weight in protest, but it did nothing. *Has he come back for me to finish the job?*

"No! Get off me!" I yelped as the tears sprouted down my face, but nothing came of it.

"Oh, H? One more thing, before you take your... *little pet*," Eli called out wryly.

The shadow man planted his feet vexingly into the floor like concrete. He waited, and then Eli scooted beside him. I flinched from his speed. Eli's bright blue eyes shaded to a murderous black in a trice, and then glowered at the shadow man.

"Pay the debt, will ya?" Eli said sparingly, as though withholding disappointment or disapproval. *Huh? What debt? I thought this whole family is rich?* I couldn't be sure exactly what was going on, but it made me shudder. The shadow man rattled a hum in his chest, annoyed at whatever Eli meant.

"You can't keep going on like this. You know she's the one," Eli added again as he threw his hands up in defeat. With one last tug of my arm, we were out the door. "Get it done, brother!" he called out again.

The rattles of my chain around my ankle echoed through the hallway with each step. *What debt? I'm the one… to what? And what needs to be done?*

Wait. Is it… my death?

CHAPTER FORTY-SIX

THE GAME

I fidgeted nervously and kept my eyes on the floor, feeling shamed by the intrusion of the shadow man's signature terrorizing stare. I meddled at the chain around my wrists that were bound tightly behind my back.

The chain trailed from around my neck, down along my spine, and then linked to the other chain wrapped around my ankle, the other end was grasped in the palm of the shadow man. I looked and felt like a max security prisoner. But the only person that needed a max, was him. I swallowed the fear that was very clearly taking charge of my body, dreading what was to come.

"Look at me," he hissed, his voice stern with control. I sobbed, not wanting to look at him, or speak. I was not a fucking pet. I flinched. His long painted arm grabbed my chin, and he nudged my head to meet his mask with force. He may have been able to lift my head, but I was holding my eyes to the corners away from his gaze. *Fuck him.*

He held me there for a moment. His breath wrenched through

his chest, noticeably getting angrier by the second. *Is disobeying his orders pissing him off?* I smiled internally, taking comfort in the idea of vexing him. *He can rot in hell for all I care.* And as much as I tried, I couldn't push away the terror enough for a hint of strength to stand against him. He left me no choice but to clamp my eyes shut, and tremor.

Snot and tears streamed down my face, fitting into the reality of just how fucked I was. I was a mess. I'd not eaten in so long, and I was so tired—no, exhausted. So fucking drained. I had been fucked, fucked again, drowned, and starved.

"Please. I-I can't do this anymore," I whimpered and fitted into a heavier sob. The shadow man gritted his teeth, and squeezed harder.

"Look at me, pet," he said. I finally opened my eyes, and the burn of my tears clouded my vision. I blinked, before finding his mask's eye holes, and then just by looking at him, my stomach churned from hopelessness once more. He sighed, turning his head away for a moment.

"Not like that," he scowled. I couldn't quite put my finger on it, but it almost sounded as though he was asking, not demanding.

I gulped, thinking of my words carefully.

"I don't know what you want."

"I told you. I want to... *need* to kill you, Esme," he admitted, as though his life was dependent on it. Making me feel worthless in his presence. "I need to watch your life drain away."

I hesitated, sniffing the snot back up my nose from my persistent crying before taking a breath.

"Then why didn't you?" I deadpanned. He paused, like I had bewildered him with my question, but he didn't answer.

He toyed with the chain I was tied to, letting the weight of it run through his hands. The sound of his rings clunking along the shackles sent a haunting shiver through my core.

It triggered a distant memory of when he had been in my room, stalking me, and toying with my hairbrush. I remembered the sound of his rings clearly, twanging against the handle as he twiddled it in circles in his palm... *when I thought he was just a nightmare.*

He finally shifted, before groaning as he unlinked it. The grip loosened and he unraveled it to free my hands, and then my ankle. They tumbled to the floor in a heap.

"I like you in chains. Bound for me," he admitted softly, before picking one of the chains back up. He looped it around my neck, locking the links together loosely so it dangled over my chest. He held the other end of the shackles in his hand.

"Why?" I whimpered.

"Because... " He sighed, holding onto his words. "I like exotic pets, Esmeralda Pierce. And now that I've found you, I... " He paused again, tilting his head to the side and then backwards as if in frustration.

"Fucking hell. Don't look at me like that, please." The shadow man spoke the last part of that sentence with a saddened edge. *Am I looking at him a certain way? Other than the one with tears pouring from my eyes? He told me to look at him, so I am.* I squirmed.

"I don't understand," I whimpered again. As if I couldn't get any more panicked, he had used my full name. How in the bloody hell did he know that? *Because he was a freaking psychopath. A stalker. A kidnapper. A killer. That's why.* He tapped his fingertips aggressively on the side of his mask, somewhere where his temples would be.

"Don't *try* to understand me, pet. I'm a twisted sociopath, and I'm on a revenge mission," he derided with disgust, very clearly toward me. I shook my head in confusion and fear, and my hands trembled. The shadow man continued. "The moment you showed up in my head was the very moment you agreed to play our game. "

"What game?" I cried. I still didn't understand.

He tittered, as though annoyed I didn't know what he meant. "It doesn't matter now. You'll learn soon enough, Esme."

Fear took charge, I stomped my foot and raised my hands up.

"NO! I've had enough. I am fucking done with whatever sick fucking bullshit you've got going on in your head. I want nothing to do with it, or your brothers." I gasped for air before mindlessly shouting again. "I want this over with. Do you hear me? So if you're going to kill me, get it the fuck over with. You spineless cunt! Or—" I winced, the back of his hand was quick to meet my cheek, jolting my head to the side and cutting me off. The sting burning my skin.

"Or what?" he grumbled.

"Or... just let me g-go," I breathed the words, barely audible under my tears. He laughed dryly, before slapping the other cheek. I cried out, dropping to the floor on my knees. The sting was twice as hard as the last, and the pink welts tingled my face. He towered above me, and then he banded his hand around my neck with a tight squeeze.

"You must be out of your damn fucking mind if you think I'm going to give you up, pet. You are *mine*. Nothing but a pawn before the king," he hissed. Revolt and utter disgust riddled through his body and voice. *He is making no sense.*

"You're a monster," I trembled my response. It was a mere squeak through his tight grip. I pried at his hand for a breath but accomplished nothing, I gulped once more. Suddenly, just when I thought his hold couldn't get any tighter he adjusted his grip, and curled his thumb and index finger, pressing slightly into my auricular nerve. I weeped at the strain of the pressure and an unfamiliar loud ringing in my ear.

"You haven't seen *monster,*" he purred.

I had hit a nerve, a big fucking nerve. *A pawn? What in the fuck did that mean? What did anything mean?* I heaved, hearing the sound of my heartbeat pounding in my throat. Finally, he released his grip before storming off to his bedside table. I panted the air back into my lungs. Barely able to focus as he fiddled with the button on a remote.

The wall opened for him, startling me, but I stayed where I was; concreted to the floor. *The ropes... fuck, not again.* He pulled some of the red ropes down off the hooks, and sauntered back. My heart pounded, he looked like he was engulfed in flames. *Fuming even.* I have never seen him like that before.

He began threading the ropes around my limbs much like the last time. And in such a way that each row was evenly placed, as though to not cut off my circulation entirely, but to cause an intense throbbing sensation. But if you were to be held in them for long enough, only God knew what would happen.

"Please, stop this," I muttered. But he ignored me. He was in his own world.

He tethered them around my waist, knees and thighs, and a new section of rope around my wrists. I swallowed down the lump in my throat that was thickening by the second. He began suspending me from the ceiling like he had done before, stopping just as my feet had lifted from the ground.

"Ah!" I shrieked as he tightened the first lot of rope that was up my legs from my feet, and connected to the ties around my waist, pulling it tight. *Too tight.* My quad muscles strained under pressure as my feet were pulled toward my ass as the framework suspended me. I was hanging by my wrists, and knees. My belly facing the ceiling.

He was careful with his placement, it was like an art in itself, all the ropework. Each rope had a pressure point over my body, and he knew exactly where they were. There was a reason he had me that way—and I knew for certain that it wasn't going to be anything hot and steamy. No, he was too livid for that.

I was a defeated mess, in sobs of fear, and torment. My back faced the floor, and my hair dangled down with the chain that was still around me. I sobbed over the heavy ache at my shoulders, wriggly slightly to relieve the pain but it was no use. My arms felt like they were pulling out of their sockets. I blinked heavily from the sensation of blood rushing to my head, only adding to the dizzy spell I was already in from starvation and exhaustion.

Time passed by slowly, I would guess I hung for an hour or two, crying and left ignored. I couldn't be sure, but everything was numb by the time my tears had finally rested. He had stayed grounded, standing there staring at me, and admiring his artifact. He hadn't spoken a single word, nor had I. I was hung like a museum ornament, a puppet.

My little puppet queen.

"Ahh, my pet. You look good hanging up there for me. Quiet. Weak. Defenseless," he uttered with arousal, filling the silence in the room that had been stagnant for too long.

He finally moved, leaning down and trailed his fingers along the crusted scars on my feet. I gasped, and tried to wriggle away, but again I was met with hopelessness. Accepting defeat again, I sobbed.

"You're a freak," I sputtered the words in a panic, but he stayed silent.

He bent toward my front and yanked at the chain around my neck, I yelped from the intrusion. He moaned, pulling the knife from his pocket. I whimpered as he hovered it at my lips, the cold jagged edge resting on them. The tip under my nose, and the handle at my chin. He shushed me.

"I know. Now... quiet." He tugged the chain further down so that I couldn't move or breathe clearly. In turn, my body strained from pressure, the top half of my body wanting to go one way, and my lower half the other.

He held me there for a moment, and then he pressed his knife down over my lips, slowly. Pain engulfed me in a hurry, putting my body back into a panic reaction. I was feeling the same thing I had felt with the mirror shards at my feet, but on my lips. I cried out, but the sound only rumbled in my throat.

With a twist of his wrist, the knife shifted and was the opposite direction. He glided it down the corner of my cheek and mouth, penetrating the skin as he ran it down to my other. The blade juddering over my teeth in the process.

He repeated the same action to my other cheek. At that point I was screaming silence, held tight by the chain. I accepted the torture, for if I moved and thrashed around the carnage and pain would be worse. All I could do was let my adrenaline take charge, making me shiver with fear.

I could feel his eyes burning against his mask at me, as though he were fueled by hatred and revenge. Like I was held responsible for something. *Payback? Why do I have that suspicion?* Finally, he let go. Then the sensation of blood trailing over my nose hit me. Some trickled into my nostril, and some pooling in the corners of my eyes and entwining with my burning tears before reaching my forehead, and dripping onto the carpet.

"You're a f-fucking mons-ster," I grouched as my body shook uncontrollably. I spat out the blood from my mouth and he tilted his head and chuckled.

"Just you wait until I take you down to the lake, pet. See how spineless I am then. I know that you know what happens down there, and I know that you love being fucking terrified of me. Don't you?" His voice was somehow even lower than it already was, threatening and aroused.

I ignored him, the freak. *A monster. How many people has he killed? WHY* ME*?!* He wrapped a white cloth over my mouth, much like the one he had shoved in there the night he took me. I winced as he pulled at the wounds.

"Don't you?" he repeated viciously. I muffled a cry and a small shake of my head, not knowing what else to say or do. It was all I could manage.

He secured the cloth behind my head, and then disappeared briefly before bringing back a tin bucket. My heart pounded as he strategically placed it under me. He crept around slowly, and my mind trailed off. I didn't know what was worse, the anticipation of his torture, or him moving around so slowly.

If you didn't know any better you would say that he *was* the Grim Reaper. The shadow man had taken a leaf from his book, because he walked like him, dressed like him, talked like him. He painted himself black, dressed in a cape, killed people, and wore a fucking skulled mask. That fucking mask. I mean, *was he* any different?

I jolted, suddenly being pulled from my delirium. Pain buried me like a lightning bolt had hit me. I screeched out a muffled, blood-curdling scream. My skin was being torn open by his knife along the midst of my thigh. He was pressing it deeper as he skated it further along my body between the ropes. I trembled to the agonizing pain, the cloth holding onto my tears and cries.

I could taste the blood in my mouth, only just realizing that was why he smelled of blood, all the time. *This is him, and this is his game, I think.* He had clearly been holding back for some reason, but his true colors were coming out now. I was fucked. And I was *going* to end up in the bottom of that fucking lake.

Just like everyone else.

The bucket under me collected my blood that was dripping from me. I was pouring thick crimson trails from everywhere. I shuddered from the sound of droplets hitting the bottom of the bucket, and the bile surfaced my throat. Every emotion hounded my very core, and it tapped at a part of my soul I never knew existed.

My chest was aching from crying, and the fucker was loving

it. I could sense the relief pouring from his body with ecstasy during each drag of his knife as it soared across my skin.

Like it was setting him free. The shadow man didn't stop, he pursued butchering until there were no more blank areas of my skin left. Like he was painting a canvas. Some deeper than others, some more painful, unless I was acclimatizing to the trauma.

I started to fade with the blood loss, everything finally going numb. I drifted into a state of fog, fractured between reality and visions. I dazed into a distant memory of the shadow man at the piano, the melodies ricocheting in my brain.

I squirmed, pulling myself back to the here and now. My eyes were heavy, but I realized that he had stopped hurting me. I was grasping onto the fact that I was hearing muffled whimpers, and sobs.

They weren't mine.

I struggled to focus on him, but blinked unconsciousness away. Seeing that he was indeed crying. Why? I breathed in, rapidly catching sight of a tear trickling under his mask. He stood tall, panting before finally calming his breath to the same state as my own. Slow, almost non-existent. He sniffled his tears as he held my weakened head up, looking straight into my soul through my teary emerald eyes.

I couldn't fight the darkness anymore. It finally cloaked me, and my body fell heavy against the ropes.

Blurred visions of him, and a red coated, dripping knife was the last thing I saw.

CHAPTER FORTY-SEVEN

I DESERVE TO DIE FOR MY SINS

Moisture tickled my senses, something was trickling over my forehead. The soft sensation was the first thing to tug me into consciousness. *It's probably my blood still.*

I listened, hearing sounds of gentle splashes of water. The droplets fell on my head again, pulling me away from my drift a little more. I tried, but couldn't move, realizing my body was heavy and weak. The more I succumbed into reality, the more the pain radiated through my entire body.

My eyes wouldn't open, no matter how hard I tried. I breathed slowly to the sounds of my surroundings. A weightlessness suspension warmed me, like I was floating. I wondered if what I was hearing was condensation dripping over water, it relaxed me. My brows furrowed to the frogs croaking, and an owl hooting afar. Tree trunks and branches squeaked softly in the distance to a slight breeze.

I drew in a deep breath through my nose, inhaling the breeze that drifted over my face, and my heart pounded. *Holy fucking shit. We're in the lake.*

I jolted upright and tore my eyes open, realizing there and then where I was. The smells of mist, pine, and rotting flesh intoxicated my brain. Bile surfaced in my mouth and I gagged, the stench of a rotting carcass—or in my feared thought, *carcasses*—rippled through my core.

The shadow man was cradling me in the water that was tucked in the middle of the forest a *long* way from anywhere, or anyone. I had come close to the lake when I had escaped last time, but it didn't smell like... *this*.

His grasp was soft, and light. He must have been dripping water on my head to wake me. My breath hitched and I shuddered from the thought of being in rotting human-flesh-filled water. I blinked away the clouded vision, seeing the soulless mask looking back at me. I tried to say something, but a croak was all that rattled my chest. My tears and cries were still muffled by the cloth over my mouth.

I flinched as he tugged it down, the icy cool wisp of air burned my teeth as I drew in a breath. I trembled, shaking my head.

"W-why me?" I breathed weakly, desperate for answers. He didn't respond, he just stared. *What the fuck is happening to me? Why am I here? Why didn't he kill me? Will he now?* I frowned, the memory of his tears washed over me.

"Why are you doing this?" I repeated, realizing just how much pain I was in.

I could feel every welt on my skin throbbing. He didn't answer, he just sighed. His mood was the total opposite of what he was in his room. Whatever traces of evil I had seen earlier... however long ago that was, were gone and he had dwindled back into his soft lulled state. No monster in sight. I grimaced and shivered again, eliciting a gulp from his throat. With each passing second the pain was becoming harder to ignore.

"You wouldn't understand," he muttered finally, his voice was a low and mellow tone, perhaps regret?

I squinted my eyes in confusion, my head thumped from his mind fuck, he was up and down like a yoyo. *One minute he's tying me up and slicing through me like I was Thanksgiving dinner. The next he seems concerned about my lacerations, and very much* not *killing me.* Unless he anticipated letting me die slowly.

It made no fucking sense. I knew for sure he didn't give the same treatment with the other hostages as he had done with me. I wouldn't be surrounded by the smell of rotting flesh if he did. So why me?

I broke contact, seeing that the blood hadn't stopped flowing from me, it was entwined with his black paint in the water around us. It was nightfall, but the sky was illuminated enough to make sense of what was what. I summoned all I had to speak.

"We're where you do the fucking bloodshed, so just do it. Get it over and done with," I coughed before adding my desperation, "Please." I would rather be dead than experience another second in his arms. I never thought I'd beg for my death. But there I was.

He composed himself and drew in a sharp breath, it seemed as though he had so many emotions flowing from within him. It was exhausting just trying to understand just *one* of them.

I sensed maybe grief, trauma of some kind, there was darkness for sure... revenge, and lust maybe? Definitely pain, and for sure love and loss... betrayal? But what the fuck did I have to do with it? Killers always had motives, people don't just go around killing people for fun, there was *always* a back story. So what was his?

I sighed, he was no different from the way he had been at the piano, and after carving my body to pieces. Why did he change so much? He stilled at my vanquishment, as if hesitating to speak.

"I… am going to kill you, Esme. But… " He paused with a loud gulp, and his breath quickened. Uncertainty of his next move sent a shiver down my spine. His breath panted under his mask. "Fuck," he breathed in desperation. *But what?*

BUT WHAT, YOU MOTHER F—

Suddenly, he pulled his mask up to his nose, and without warning, his lips drove into mine. I juddered from the sting, but the static wave of electricity split through me harder than it did the first time we touched, and any other time it had happened after. His kiss shoved every hint of pain away, but my senses came to me when I needed them. My moral compass uniting with me once more and I squirmed away from his kiss. He broke away and carried me to the edge of the lake, the cool air stinging my skin as it lifted from the water.

"But what?" I pushed, spitting out the taste of his saliva. If he wasn't going to kill me, what the hell was he going to do? He pulled his mask back to its original state, and laid me down on the ground against the water's edge, and then stood above me. His height and body expression made me feel small and worthless, yet he had some kind of sadness. He tilted his head sideways and sighed.

"But. What?! God damnit!" I shouted, pausing between each word.

I shuffled backward a foot or two, whimpering from the aches. Then suddenly he launched forward, grabbing my ankle.

His hand pressed against one of the cuts, eliciting a blood curdling scream from my chest, and then he pulled me back to the spot I was before.

I stuttered something I couldn't make sense of, and he stood back to take a long look at my weakened, defenseless body. I was wet, covered in blood, leaves, dirt, bruises, and welts. He grumbled softly, as if to gather every ounce in his body to speak.

"But. It seems as though... I have somehow discovered a taste for you." *Huh?* His voice was melodramatic and confused. He lowered himself between my legs, parting them with his now white hands. He hovered there, contemplating his next move, which only rattled me more.

I couldn't tell if he was going to hurt me again, leave me here to die, or fuck me all the way to oblivion or Satan's door.

"And I want... *need*—" His hand met the top of my pussy, and I gasped. He groaned before continuing. "This."

He hissed and twirled his fingers at my entrance before pulling away. I gasped, biting down my own want for him, even though the thought made me sick. I was a mangled mess, and yet I still had that fucking *cum fairy* tapping away in my stupid head. *Fucking... fuck!*

How can I still want this man? How can I still crave this man, after what he has done?

I was too scared to speak, because whatever I was thinking of saying, and what would actually come out of my mouth, would be two very different things. The words *fuck off* came to mind, but I knew I would only fuck that up... I knew for sure that I would splutter *fuck me* instead.

I studied him, only feeling the sense of being bewildered. I could feel his hunger deepening as he hovered between my legs. His breath fastened, anger and being withheld from something at his dispersal once more. I flinched as he stood up with great speed.

"Fuuuuuck!" he shouted loudly in frustration with his hands behind his head, much like you would when you lost all your money on a bet in a horse race. It echoed through the forest, ricocheting off every tree and shadow that haunted the place. A sense of rage had expelled from his body, and then as if he forgot I was even there he stormed off into the water.

I watched with my brows furrowed, what the fuck? He walked a long way out, until he was belly deep, maybe a little further. He was looking up at the waxing moon that had lifted higher than earlier, shining between the trees and giving a little more light to the forest. Fog began to rise from the ground, thickening slowly.

My breath paused as he tugged the hood of his cape backward, and then pulled his mask off, the horns following it back. His hand knotted his beautiful wavy hair and I swallowed in anticipation, unable to pull my eyes away. I was looking at him like I had never seen him before. I had every chance of making a run for it. Had he assumed I wouldn't try?

I remembered the last time I was in the forest, his voice had echoed through the trees, haunting me. *This is my playground.*

I wanted him to *haunt me...*

I wanted him to *hate me...*

I wanted him to *fuck me...*

He was right about what he said earlier—I did love that he terrified me. And I hated that. I scoffed at myself mentally, I was a broken coo-coo clock.

My heart pounded, seeing a thick black smoke fall over the lake. Adrenaline sparked me, and I got to my feet pushing through the pain to make a run for it. Only realizing sooner that instead of running away from him, I was somehow walking toward him.

For fuck's sake, Esme!

He seemed to have found peace there, in the water. *This is his forest. This is his haven. The darkness is his ally.* Maybe he was a relative of Pocahontas, listening to nature, or whatever. That was what he looked like he was doing. *Wait, is he... talking?* He was definitely saying something—and not to me—but what I didn't know. He was too far to hear.

What the fuck is this man doing to me? Even after all was said and done, I still found myself stuck in his dark lure. I couldn't fight the urge. I just... needed him. I shuddered with each step I took into the water, breathing through the pain. I tried to swallow the lump in my throat, only I couldn't. How could I? I was walking directly to my butcher.

I finally came to a stop behind him. He would know for sure I was there because I was breathing so heavily. I prayed mentally, *please be ugly... please be ugly.* Maybe that would make it easier to hate him. But he didn't turn, he just stared at the stars, clasping the amulet in his hand.

The black fog finally closed in, sending a chill down my spine. An identical sensation to the one he had on me before he would appear in my nightmares. I think at that point I was only one more unbalanced beat of my heart before I would have a stroke. I was only holding on by a thread—*his thread.* Like a puppet.

His puppet queen... Fuck.

He shifted, pulling his horned mask back on and drawing his hood over his head. I held my breath as he turned fully to face me.

"You just can't stay away from me can you, pet?" he

groaned, but by the time he had finished the sentence he was hard-pressed against me, and ignited the spark once more. I inhaled vigorously, summoning all that I had to answer him truthfully.

"No," I croaked, knocking down the pain that hit me while speaking. The shadow man sniggered as if taking great enjoyment from my denial.

"And I thought I was the shadow," he muttered breathlessly, and then cloaked his arms around me, tucking under my ass. *What?* He scooped me up into his embrace and I instinctively wrapped my legs around him, and then drew my arms behind his neck. *Why am I doing this?*

My brain was screaming at me, telling me no, but it was as though he controlled my mind and body all at once. Not a soul on this earth could miss the electric wave of sexual, lustful suspense that split through us through the fog, and I suspect that he couldn't explain why either.

"You are," I admitted mindlessly. "You've been my shadow for so long, I don't even know what my own looks like."

"Are you not scared of me, swallowtail?" he asked. *Why?*

He for some fucked up reason seemed to have a mission to kill me, and yet there I was. Still breathing, tangled in his embrace. Everything he did, and every way he touched me sent shivers down my spine, and tightened my core with excitement.

"I—"

I didn't get to answer, he pulled up his mask to his nose and our lips met again. I didn't have an ounce of regret that I was kissing a stone cold killer. I was terrified, yes. But not of him killing me. I was terrified that I was falling in love with a man I had no business with. I could feel every one of his molecules entwining with mine, like two worlds were colliding. I didn't even know his name, or what he looked like... well, not entirely, anyway.

I pulled back to peer at him, losing myself in what I could see of his lower face, and then thoughtlessly planted my hand at his exposed cheek, my thumb brushing right where his scar was.

"You can feel it, too?" I asked. He winced. I couldn't believe I was touching his face. His skin was smooth, and freshly shaved. My heart was fluttering out of control, touching him that way.

His body tensed and then he growled. I jolted my hand back but he was quick to grab my wrist. My breath stopped, expecting a punishment of some sort, but I frowned instead: he was pulling my hand back to his face.

"Yes," he admitted, truthfully, I was certain of that. "Touch me," he whimpered his demand weakly, like a wounded baby bird. I did, planting both hands on his cheeks. His shoulders dropped as if my touch was dissolving his inner demons... his shadows. He moaned, the feeling that it was his ecstasy.

"Why?" he breathed, nudging into my hand and pushing the back of it against his shoulder.

"Why what?" I muttered nervously. He drew his hand over my other one and I melted, all traces of pain were gone, as was his.

"Why can't I kill you?" he asked with desperation as if I held the answer.

"Why do you wa—" I started to speak again, but he shoved his lips against mine once more.

Why do you want to kill me? Why am I so different?

Suddenly, his arm moved down between us, prying at his jeans and releasing his cock. Our seal didn't break, and I didn't hesitate. I swayed my hips quickly for him, letting him find my entrance. Without any mercy or delay, he submerged into me.

Ecstasy hit me far away from the moment and the second the head of his cock hit the knot in my belly, I plummeted into an orgasm. Every crack of lighting struck me as I collapsed for the man, and I did so without a slither of regret or guilt.

I deserve to die for my sins. He is my every sin.

CHAPTER FORTY-EIGHT

I WON'T DIE FOR A MONSTER

"Ah," I cooed in pleasure and pain, catching my breath. My head pounded from my release. The shadow man hissed through his teeth as I clamped down around him, coming back to the here and now, letting myself expand to all of him and his piercings as they rippled through me.

I rolled my head back in euphoria, and my hair floated over the water. He held the small of my back and the both of us became entwined in a heated trance in the lake, and I let him lift and lower me at his discretion over his cock.

I couldn't shake the feeling that he drove into me with needy, hungry thrusts like someone was watching. I pushed the thought aside to stay in the moment with him, but a static drone drummed in my ear, piercing my head.

"Ow." I winced as the motionless hum of a female voice rang. *What the fuck was that?* It resembled something like a scary movie; static and eerie. I couldn't make out the words as my head was in other places.

"Fuck," the shadow man growled, and slipped his hand

between us again, finding my swollen clit. He swirled the delicate bud as he pounded into me, the two sensations together pushing another orgasm closer to the edge.

"Oh, God!" I cried out. He chuckled sadistically.

"No, Esme. That's not my name," he growled between his teeth with a vicious edge to his voice. *There it was... that change.* The dislocated darkness hitting him once more like it did every fucking time the night comes to its full peak.

The pattern.

"I... I don't know your—" I froze, and the voice circled again, hearing her much clearer this time.

"Bring her to me," her voice was slow, and mysterious. Magical, even. I shuddered and my eyes widened. *Why has it come back?*

"Please tell me that you heard that?" I screeched. The shadow man chuckled in response, he seemed in no way, shape, or form concerned by it... her? Maybe I was hallucinating. Maybe my body was imploding or something.

"Your debt." Her voice was louder that time... closer? I craned my neck left, and right. Nothing in my peripheral vision other than what was already there.

"W-what is that?" I pushed. But he didn't respond. He brought his hand to my throat, eliciting another moan from his.

"Mine," the distorted woman's voice echoed again, closer again but on the other side of me. Her tone was possessive. *Does she mean me?*

I panted against the shadow man's grip, freeing a tear from my eye. The rush of white noise was identical to the one before my nightmares, it would go from one ear and then to the other. Like something was circling me.

"Ignore her. I'm not done with you, pet," he muttered bluntly. *Ignore WHO?!* I tried to ask that, but I was silenced by his grip.

He swirled my clit once more, and as though his fingers possessed magic the world stilled again, and I squeezed around him. There was something about where he was squeezing around my neck that made me feel intense pleasure, and dizziness. He turned my brain to mush. *What is with that?*

I didn't hear the voice anymore after he said to ignore her. I didn't know if that was because he told me to, or because the voice didn't actually speak again. He thrust into me, and squeezed my neck harder, building his orgasm. The shadow man was clearly coaxed by his mental separation. It was like he was becoming a whole other person, dislocated.

He pulled himself from me and started carrying me to the water's edge again. His erection was on full show, hard, and throbbing. His jeans hung firmly around his thighs, and yet he managed to walk without tripping.

I glanced over his body, seeing that his skin was without a trace of black paint, it had washed off in the water. I swallowed, remembering that he was human and not a figment of my imagination. The sight of him that way only made me want him more, regardless of what was going to happen to me.

Without warning, he pinned me against one of the pine trees, instantly making me feel like Jell-O, which wasn't hard, I was terribly weak. *How much blood had I lost? How much will I lose?* The bark from the tree stung at the lacerations on my back as he pinned me tighter. I grimaced at the pain but focused my attention on his cock before me.

"Mmm," I muttered nothing. My stomach was tangled in hunger for him.

I admitted to myself at that moment that I would never tire of the man until I was dead. And that was so fucked up. How could you truly feel this way for someone without knowing their name or what they looked like? Much less knowing that he was a cold hard murderer who had already tried to kill you a handful of times—and not succeeded—*on purpose?* It made no sense, I knew that, but nonetheless it was real and very much happening to me... *us?*

"I want you to give yourself to me, Esme," he groaned, and pressed his grip on my ass, insisting that I lift a leg for him. I did without hesitation and he slammed his cock back into me, claiming me once more.

"I-I'm, I'm. Oh, fuck." The strength of his thrusts pushed me harder against the tree, letting me shatter around him into yet another fitful orgasm, it was short lived but just as powerful. I panted, pulling myself together.

"Swallowtail?"

"I am... *I am.* Can't you see that? I've given you everything. There is nothing left of me," I squeaked truthfully. Because I was truly giving him every inch of my mind, body, and soul for him to devour, was I not?

"*Mine,*" the voice whispered again, but I shoved it aside and then the shadow man's body reacted to it... er, that time.

"No!" he roared. I gulped, because I knew he wasn't talking to me, he was responding to the haunting voice. *Is it a person? Maybe he drugged me, and I am hallucinating?*

My heart pounded and I looked at him with an alarmed glare. He ignored me, and became spiteful with each thrust. I had no ability to reject or deny him, even if I wanted to. *What am I doing? This man is and will continue to destroy me.* But I was only happy to let him.

I was becoming trapped under the surface of my own words,

those supernatural whispers showing me that there was more to him than I anticipated.

"*Your debt, my love. Give her to me,*" the voice coaxed again, like a siren. He growled back at the strange static with an animalistic flare, possessive. Like a wolf protecting its pack. I moaned and clenched from the sensation of him being this primal. He groaned in response.

"Do you like that, swallowtail?" He drew in a breath sharply before tangling his fingers through my wet hair, pulling it back to reveal my neck for him.

"Yes," I whimpered truthfully. He drew in my scent and his cool exhale ripped down my spine, sending a delicious shiver down it.

"You like being watched?" he asked teasingly.

"Who? What? Oh my God... what is wrong with me?" I howled through my orgasmic tears, my brain splitting into two directions. One side was as sick and depraved as he was hearing a wandering voice, and letting him fuck me to oblivion after carving into my body, almost killing me. And then the other side was my moral compass, fighting me to my core that this was so very wrong.

"Everything," he deadpanned, and then his tongue glided along my neck. I gasped as his bite sunk into my neck, drawing blood. He pinned me harder, the sensation of his cock pushing further into me and illicitly lapping up all the blood he could, making me shiver. His lips met mine and he deposited my blood with his saliva through his kiss, and then he broke away, licking the last of my flavor from his lips.

"Fuck, that mouth is so very dangerous," he admitted. He pulled out of me, taking a moment to catch his breath, and then pulled my hair back, hard. Suggesting that I get to my knees.

"Oh, god," I whimpered. I winced through the tingles of pain and kneeled, looking up at him through wet lashes. I looked like a desperate, weak mess at his feet. I knew what he wanted, and I wanted it just as much... if not *more* than him.

I opened my mouth for him, and he gave my head a soft stroke before knotting his fingers at the base of my neck. I rolled my tongue over my bottom teeth so that his piercings didn't tear from his cock, and he pushed himself in. He pumped a few times before pulling my head backward by a bundle of hair and my gaze onto him, seeing the dimples on his chin in full form.

"What is my name, pet?" he commanded. *What? Not this again.* I shook my head in confusion. *I don't know his name.* "Come onnn, say it," he pushed again with a playful snort.

"I don't... I don't know your name?" I admitted truthfully, in question.

He laughed loudly. "You keep calling me by the name in your sleep. You always have, and I fucking love it. Now, say it." His grin was ear to ear. It was fucking ecstatic, but I still had no fucking clue what his name was.

"Please. I don't know," I sobbed under his grip.

I wished I did know, because I'd call for it, loudly. I only knew of the name I had given him, was that what he meant? *Wait... had I been saying it out loud?* I hesitated.

"Uhm, the... shadow man?" I muttered weakly, barely able to scramble the words before he pinned his pierced cock back into my mouth with need. He moaned and his body reacted, his muscles tensed, and he rolled his head back, letting his seed flow down my throat.

"Fffuck. Yes, pet." He shuddered, and I took all of him as his heat filled me.

He caught his breath and quickly pulled me up so that I stood before him, and then he wrapped his hand around my neck once more. His shift appeared stronger. I swallowed his bitterness and waited for his next reaction. I couldn't shake the feeling that his grip on me was different to the last, it wasn't sexual in the slightest.

What side of him would I see now that *pleasure* had passed? Was his darkness going to come for me once more? *Will he hurt me here, kill me now?* Would he tell me about the voices? So much was left unspoken. I squirmed, seeing the hatred he had for me return.

"Are you going to kill me now?" I asked hesitantly, panic bolting through my core again. And the pain over my body started pounding once more.

"Don't look at me like that." He squeezed harder so that I coughed against his grip, both my hands meeting his trying to pry him but my strength against his was second to none.

"But I can't *not* look at you," I coughed. And I think at that moment, I tried to cry, but I had none left to give. His chest rose and fell hard, as though he was vexed, angered, and feared all in one.

"You are making this very hard for me, pet."

Without warning, he softened again, and his thumb brushed my bottom lip before moving his hand to my cheek. Once more tugging at his heavy, steel mask—revealing a wet patch on both sides of his face. *Tears?* Maybe it was just water, or sweat. His emotions were incredibly unpredictable and exhausting.

Up.

Down.

Up.

Down.

"How?" I sobbed dryly and he curled his fingertips into the base of my neck, pulling me to his lips once more.

I pushed on the tips of my toes, stretching as far as I could, ignoring the pain that radiated up my carnage thighs. He bent a little for me and if I wasn't not mistaken, it felt like an apology, my lustful confusion for him only adding to the concoction of this sick twisted ordeal. His kiss was deep.

I trailed off, imagining what the rest of his face would look like under the mask. An angelic face, soft eyes, and a gentle heart. Or would it be the total opposite? It couldn't be—seeing the jawline that I was seeing, that would be the furthest from the truth—he was fucking gorgeous.

But the fact that there was a dark shadow that followed his very existence, and a strange voice, the shadow man made it very clear that he was not the man that I needed, nor was I to be feeling the way that I did. He was a lost soul caught in the middle of a very bad nightmare.

He broke our seal, putting my mental drift into a pause and held me at arm's length, his gaze scrolling up and down, and taking in my carnage.

"Because you're dangerous. And yes, I will... I will kill you. I promise. I *need* you to die for me. But damn that fucking mouth, Esmeralda."

His words were entirely truthful as though his life depended on that fact. He shook his head in disbelief and kissed me again with a greater passion, as if my lips held all of the answers he was looking for, but disappointment pitied him when they were not there. Making my mind wander once again.

Why do I need *to die for him? Where was the voice in all of this? Why did the voice go away after I touched him?*

Was I his... cure? His rain, and his nemesis all in one?

"To me, my love." The static voice broke again, not as close as the time before, but enough to hear her.

"I don't understand," I sobbed. He swallowed, and dropped his mask, throwing the hood back over his head. The dislocation of anger swarmed over him again, and the black fog thickened.

My senses came in again in full swing, terror throbbed everywhere it should in order to get me to wake the fuck up. He wanted to kill me. He wanted to destroy me. *He needed to kill me.*

And I *needed* to get the fuck away from him, because I didn't deserve to die for a monster.

CHAPTER FORTY-NINE

RUNNING HOT

Confusion, and mind fuck was all that was spinning in my head. I had been awake for too long. I sat on his bed under the sheets with my knees tucked up against my chest, chained to the bed, exhausted—but couldn't sleep, mentally drained, confused, and staring at the black empty walls for what... comfort?

I was covered in dirt, sweat, welts and bruises. My wounds had started to heat up and swell. They were incredibly red, and weeping. I knew for sure I was days, or even hours away from a debilitating infection. And I now had the endless cycle of the same questions repeating over and over again in my brain.

Why did he cut me? Why did he make me bleed into the bucket? Why did he take me to the forest? Who was the voice that spoke, and he responded to? Why did he promise to end my life, but not do it the first million times? Only to bring me back here again.

Everything ached. I was weak. My head thumped. Goosebumps flared my skin... though I was warm to the touch.

But at least I was fed... well fed. I mean, a shower would be great. I had never eaten at the speed of which I did. I hadn't eaten in days. And water. Oh my God, water. I wanted more but *he* didn't allow it.

Dawn was about to peak, and I hadn't even had the thought to shut my eyes, my head was still engulfed in flames from our heated, twisted, hateful, lustful, electrical what-the-fuckery in the forest, and the god-damn fucking shit show before that: hanging from the fucking ceiling like a puppet being drained of my blood. Why? *Why!?*

I could feel the shadow man's eyes burning into me. He had been sitting on that chair beside the bed since we returned hours ago. He had carried me over his shoulder the entire way back to the mansion, and hadn't offered a single word or a solace of conversation since telling me that *I*—of all people—was dangerous.

Pfft. What a conundrum.

I suspected it probably wouldn't be long before I would pass out from exhaustion sooner or later. But for now, I was destroying my mind for the umpteenth time. Fighting with myself that I really was *not* falling in love with that man. I wasn't... I absolutely was not. So why couldn't I stop looking at him? No. The man was a killer, he did not deserve me, or my life.

I knitted my brows, he was the remains of a drunken mess, swallowing gulp after gulp of the liquor down his throat, and occasionally taking his eyes off me to scribble in a notebook. I learned that the dissociation seemed to pass the more he drank, *and* the more daylight reared.

He drowned himself in alcohol, burying the hatchet that was eating him. I yawned, it would be sunrise soon, so I laid the other way in the hopes I would fall into a decent sleep, despite the pain that riddled me.

But a loud singular thump sound caught my attention. I craned my neck to see what it was. It was the shadow man. He had passed out into a drunken coma, hitting the back of his head against the wall. I guess that was no thanks to the entire bottle of booze in his gut, and he still had a hold of the empty bottle in his hand.

The vision of a glass bottle only spun me into a pained memory, one of shattered mirror. Replaying the scene of him gutting my feet with it for his enjoyment. And if that wasn't enough, the fucker upped it a notch and needed a good go at mincing the rest of my body.

Suddenly, without any signal, I felt anger boil as it rippled through me. *Good.* I needed the motive to get the fuck away from him. I needed to remember that he was a fucking sadist murderer. A psychopathic, blood-shedding, soul-crushing monster.

I need to remember that. I need to. My life depends on it... remember? Gah!

Tears threatened to fall. I didn't want to cry again. I had cried so damned much and I was too exhausted to let it keep happening. I studied him for some time, seeing that his breath was slow, and peaceful. Like his mind was finally at rest from his wars. I stared at the key dangling on the chain around his neck, illuminated by the glow of his amulet underneath it. It was the very key that would unlock the padlock on my chain.

The very padlock that he had forgotten to secure around my cage the last time I escaped. *Not that it got me far.* I tutted, succumbing to the realization of just how much I wanted that key. How much I *needed* that key. I needed to get the fuck out I wasn't going to let myself wander from the path *again*. And I certainly wasn't going to run into the forest.

I would find another way. Maybe flee to Mexico. Get out of Sayville for good, and start a new life. Somewhere where he wouldn't find me. Fuck. I sounded delusional. I puffed a heavy sigh, and it blew off the bead of sweat at my lip. The building temperature was getting to my head. I shuddered.

A moment of time passed before I summoned everything in my being to do something about it, then inclination got the better of me. I pushed myself off the bed, and as light as I could tip-toed toward him, biting my lip in anticipation. Oddly enough the sensation of a different type of pain helped keep me awake, and gave me the ability to put more attention into not letting my chain twang on the floor and wake him.

I reached the end of my tether, extending the furthest my body could go to reach the key. I was only a fingertip away from grabbing the necklace, but the chain was straining at my ankle and on the bedpost I was tied to. There was no way on God's green earth that I would balance on one leg to unlock the chain. No. I wasn't going anywhere... not without taking his necklace off. My mind trailed off again. Watching him sleep in his drunken state put me in a prime position to do so.

Escape? Sure. Cut his dick off? Sure. Unmask him? Sure. Dagger his heart? Sure. But I wouldn't. Focus, Esme. I pushed my intrusive thoughts aside, to hell with those thoughts.

I rubbed my clammy forehead from the doubts in my plan, swallowing the lump in my throat. I needed to pull back the hood of his cape so that I could free the necklace. My stomach tangled and knotted with fear of being caught again, next time I wouldn't be so lucky. I blew through pursed lips and moved my hand gently past the curved horns, and then slowly rolled the hood of his cape backward.

His breath remained slow, still in a state of comatose. Good. I frowned, confused in thought. His thick, mousy brown hair had sprung up in response to the hood coming off, feeling that it was so soft and velvety. I could see the straps of his mask, it was secured tightly around his head, and I couldn't imagine it would be very comfortable. The thing was made entirely of metal, and the horns must weigh a tonne.

His skin was mostly pale, only some of the black pain remained around his shoulders and neck, some down his arm but was smudged. And his jeans were no longer wet. Suddenly the bottle slipped from his hand and crashed onto the floor. I gasped and stilled in a panic.

Shit.

The thud didn't wake him, but he stirred and his head separated from the wall and then dropped heavily against his chest. I stayed grounded for a moment, letting my pounding heart slow back to a somewhat regular rhythm again. I pulled myself together, swallowing the lump in my throat again, and pried at the chain around his neck. Beads of sweat poured from my body. *I really need to get the fuck out of this place. To a hospital!*

Clink.

The padlock opened for me and I returned his necklace back to the way it was. I turned on my feet slightly, yielding to glance at the shadow man just one more time. I wanted so desperately to see what was under that mask but I lulled the thought. I quickly grabbed one of the capes hanging up in his closet and threw it on. My heart rate spiked as I stood at the elevator door, praying that he wouldn't hear me leaving.

The doors were quick to open and I flew into the cube, pressing the button that would lead me to the garage door. All traces of him disappeared through the slit of the elevator door, and I was gone. *It's finally happening. My freedom! No distractions.* Adrenaline was taking charge over the building infection.

It was so dark in the garage, I could only see faint glints of the cars from their glossy paint. I scurried further into the garage, relying on only my memory of where things were, and then I jumped out of my skin. The lights in the garage boomed to life. *Shit. Fuck, fuck, fuck.* I scrambled, checking my surroundings, seeing no one. It must have been that sensor again. I caught my breath before continuing my mission.

I could see the same bike from the time before and the unmarked SUVs, as well as the fancy sports cars, and finally the little crushed-up car at the back corner. All of the vehicles were cleaned, waxed, and exactly as they were last time, maybe slightly off-mark. I paid no attention to the door that led to the cells. Which was no doubt still overflowing with abducted girls. Tilly's face washed over me.

Fucking damn it. Tilly. What has he done with you? Why am I only now just thinking of her? I'm a terrible friend. I really had lost it. *Remember, Esme. No distractions.* I stood at the door of a black Mercedes A-45, staring at my reflection in the black tinted windows. I frowned, not really believing what was looking back at me... *me.* I think. I was whiter than paper, covered in bruises, blood, deep flesh wounds, and hopelessness. Fuck, my head ached and throbbed.

I swallowed, seeing myself as carnaged as I was only hurt my heart more... *good...* it was fuel for me to run. *Keys, where are the keys?* I fumbled with places in the car I'd likely find one with trembling hands, finally finding two of them in the flap of the visor.

"Fuck, okay." I stared at the keys in my hand that was ready and waiting for my demand and blew out a rapid blow of air. I had no idea how to drive a car, let alone a sports car. My ride was the local bus or a cab, and there were so many buttons in the thing. *I just need the go go pedal so I can haul ass, and that's it!*

The scent of new leather ripped through my nose. *Has this thing even been driven?* I put the keys in the cup holder, my hands trembled as they gripped the steering wheel in nerves, or was it a fever? *Holy shit.* My escape was so close. *How do I turn this thing on?* I found a button that read START. The engine roared to life at my fingertip, it was fucking loud.

"Shit," I grimaced.

Running on adrenaline I hit a button on the remote and the garage panel door opened, letting in the light of the sunrise. I squinted from the bright intrusion, taking a second to focus my eyesight again. The crumpled little car in the corner glimmered under the beams of sunlight. I was staring right down the barrel of my freedom, and it was so close I could taste it.

All I had to do was put my foot flat to the floor and leave the dust behind me. And just as I went to send it, *someone* stood in front of the car, startling me.

Blocking my way, and blocking my freedom.

Was Caine.

CHAPTER FIFTY

REVOLVING DOORS

"W here in the *fuck* do you think you're going?" Caine howled as he slammed his hands against the bonnet of the car.

He scrunched up his face in fury before charging toward the door and hauled it open. His facial expression was quick to diminish, disquieted by the sweat pouring from me. His mouth opened, taking in the mess I was.

The bruises, the dirt, the sweat dripping from me, the variation of dried, clotted, and weeping blood from near infected wounds. No doubt being immersed in a lake full of dead bodies had only made things worse. Nonetheless, Caine seemed upset by it. Guilty? Pained? I shivered. Heaviness tugged at me now that the adrenaline was wearing off. He shook his head.

"Fuck's sake, come here," he said softly, and then pulled me from the car. He held me against him tightly before holding me at arm's length, eyeing me up and down. He tutted with a woeful expression, as though he was taking pity in me.

I frowned, not expecting to see him like that. The Whitlock

brothers were fucking serial killers. Serial killers don't have morals. Besides, it was his fault I was taken in the first place. He turned us on our feet but I scrambled free.

"No. *No!*" I cried, scurrying back to the car. But he grabbed my arm—thankfully, not where a throbbing wound was—and pried at my hand for the garage key that I'd grabbed from the cup holder.

"Give it, Esme," he warned. I hesitated, then finally opened my hand and he took the remote, pressing the button.

The garage door sounded as it closed, and I fitted into a sob. The darkness locked me in again like the prisoner that I was, I had lost my chance. I shuddered again, the sensation of hot and cold sparking through my veins, the adrenaline had kept it at bay, but the chills came in hot and heavy.

"Let me look at you," he tutted before continuing. "He's gone haywire on you. Fucking haywire," he grumbled.

Caine threw my arm up over his shoulder, and pulled out his phone. He tapped at the screen, pulling it to his ear. I leaned into him to relieve some of the throbbing, noticing that he was happy to take my weight.

"You're gonna wanna look at this... garage... I don't give a fuck, Eli, get in here... now!" he roared through the phone and shoved it back into his pocket.

I couldn't tell how long we stood there, swaying, but Eli was quick to barge through a doorway from a stairwell. Why not the elevator? He glowered in response to seeing me half conscious against Caine, almost as though he was surprised that I was still alive.

"Ahh, fuck." Eli ran his hands through his short hair and scurried over quickly, scooping me up like a small child. Caine cleared his throat and rubbed the back of his neck for clarity.

"What do you want to do with her? She is supposed to be fucking dead. We can't take her to the hospital. She's seen too much, and I don't have access to his files for a fake ID," Eli muttered to Caine as if I wasn't there. He sounded pissed.

I summoned enough energy to mentally throw daggers at him for saying that I should be fucking dead. *The fucking ass hat. Can't take me to a hospital?* But I needed medical attention, stat. Frustration boiled inside me, there was a reason the shadow man didn't kill me, and whatever it was had his brothers stumped.

Caine rolled his neck around, relieving the tension. "Fuck. I dunno man. But I won't leave her like this. Fucking... Bloody Mary of hell, dammit. He fucked up again. She's the one, Eli. That was the deal. That was *his* fucking plan, ever since... ." Caine swore and chanted, cutting himself off at the last bit. Again, it was like I wasn't even there.

Uh hello, I'm still here fuckers! Those words again, *she's the one. Fuck them.* I rolled my eyes and accepted that I was basically invisible.

Eli turned on his feet, and I caught a glimpse of sadness tickling his face as he looked at the car and then turned to Caine. *I had always suspected that the car had something to do with the shadow man, and given Eli's face, and Caine's words, this just confirms I was right.* But what did that have to do with me?

"I know, brother, I know. But it's gone way too far now. I'll just do it myse—"

"You can't, it can only be done by him, you know that," Caine cut him off, his tone vexed, yet tinged with another I couldn't put my finger on.

"So what then?" Eli asked.

Someone just take me to a hospital, please? Caine sighed with a genuine, worried look on his face.

"Bring her to my room. I'll sort it out," Caine offered softly.

"Wait," I slurred, barely able to form the words, I wasn't far from passing out. The pair turned their full attention toward me, and Eli raised a brow, prompting a response. I wanted to ask about the car in the corner, but all I could manage was my finger pointing in the general direction.

That car could have been my answer to the shadow man.

What if that car was the reason why I am here, and why anyone is here? Why he does what he does? Why they do what they do?

I was going to find out. Because I wasn't dead, and he *won't* kill me. I'd at least die trying.

My arm was quick to lower weakly and I fell heavy in Eli's arms, and then darkness closed in over me hard and fast.

CHAPTER FIFTY-ONE

INVISIBLE ANGUISH

"T he moment you showed up in my head was the very moment you agreed to play our game."

"I like playing with you."

"You must be out of your damn fucking mind if you think I'm going to give up this game."

"I need to watch your life drain away."

"I put you up here to teach you a lesson, but I'm only teaching myself one."

"You are mine. Nothing but a pawn before the King."

The sound of a drink being poured into a glass woke me from the shadow man's words that had run havoc in my nightmares, waking up periodically only to fall into the same one again. He had killed me over, and over, and over again. Stuck in a time loop.

I batted my heavy eyelashes, pulling myself into the here and now. Foggy, groggy, but somehow no longer aching all over my body. *What the? Why do I feel... drunk?* I was staring at a white ceiling, covered by a nice warm blanket, in a nice warm bed, and no chains, ropes, or padlocks. *Where am I?*

Suddenly I remembered Caine saying in the garage, "bring her to my room." *This is his room.* I pushed myself up and shuffled my back against the headboard.

Damon was on the other side of the room pouring himself a drink, *shirtless. Of course.* I frowned, craning my neck around to investigate the newness, realizing that the room smelled of Caine. An earthy low tone with fruity hints of spices and aromatics, and whiskey.

I peered at my arms, seeing that there were little white tabs... like sticky tape, covering my wounds, and stitches on the deeper ones. *STITCHES? Who's been inside me with a freaking needle? Where? WHEN?* I started to panic, my heart tapping uncontrollably.

I lifted the covers and looked at my legs, the tabs were there too. I grabbed at my neck, it felt bruised and had raised bumps there too. I was covered. And someone had been mending me. *Why?*

"You just keep poppin' up don't ya. Piggy?" Damon's crude words and husky voice made my lip curl. His remark was that of a smart ass, full of attitude. But I swallowed his attempted insult, because it wasn't my weight that he was ridiculing; flashbacks of the ball played in my mind, it was such a distant memory. *Piggy in the middle.*

I rolled my eyes and went about with what I was doing before he interrupted. I observed my surroundings, seeing that there was a door and a few fancy ornaments on a buffet table, a bookshelf, a bathroom, and a small buffet where Damon was standing. The room was very well designed, luxury Victorian meets modern style—like the shadow man's room and the room I was held captive in, however long ago that was—but light and bright, inviting.

"Ignoring me might be a silly choice," Damon threatened, but unintentionally I continued to dismiss that he was even there, trying to put the pieces of my puzzle together.

It was dark out, and directly through the windows was a balcony, and if I squinted hard enough, I could see a faint glint of pine trees in the horizon. I scoffed. That fucking forest. *This fucking place. That fucking man.*

Gah! My mind pondered. *Does Caine live here? Do they all live here? Where is Caine? How long have I been here?* I could tell it had been long enough that my head was no longer thumping, and my body didn't feel like it was about to ignite from infection. I trailed off, retracing my steps to get some clarity.

I remember being suspended from the ceiling, and the shadow man draining my blood into a bucket. I remember waking up in the forest, barely, only bits and pieces scrummaging in my mind.

Oh, shit. I remembered that we had sex... *stupid girl.* And then, almost a blur, I remembered escaping my chain and making a run for it, only Caine stopped me. And that was all I could put together. *What happened after that?* Other than being sewn up and given some kind of medication to *not* die. *Where is the shadow man?*

I sighed, realizing that no one ever answered questions anyway, so what was the point of working myself up over them? I snuggled further into the blankets, it was nice. I laid there a while and then flicked a glance at Damon, he was tapping away on his phone, grinning impishly. *You are supposed to be ignoring him, Esme...*

He was leaning backward against the bench, looking all cool-guy, with no shirt and in his signature black jacket and black jeans. *Tight* jeans. Even from that far away he was still a giant. Like a human praying mantis. His beautiful beige skin cast a glint under the lighting.

The v on his hips protruded from his waist, making it very difficult to not look at. The guy had more than the average person needed for abs. I frowned. *Is he wearing eyeliner?* I couldn't tell, but he was wearing jewelry. Black and silver rings, a sweatband, and a black studded leather one around his wrists. And a cross necklace, that he now had in his mouth. I squirmed.

I wasn't overly keen on being left alone with him. There was something about Damon that was even more unsettling than the shadow man. Besides, it really should be illegal to be that fucking hot.

I felt like it was only a week ago I had been telling Tilly that I hadn't found anyone on the planet of the earth attractive. *I really need to stop calling these brother's anything other than monsters.* That was until I met *Mr. Fairytale...* Caine. And Damon, and Eli. And... I trailed off again.

No. We are not talking about that asshole. Fuck that asshole. He can rot six feet in the fucking ground for what he had done to me. Part of me wished he had killed me, and put me out of my misery. But the other part of me just wanted to go home and forget all of this happened. I whimpered in thought.

Home.

Oh, God, Tilly. My stomach knotted.

"She's not what I want, pet." The shadow man's words echoed in my head, when I asked about her whereabouts. What did that mean? *Was she... no—I can't think like that.* I hoped that she was safe, I didn't have it in me to pray. As much as I wanted

to pray for her, my faith was gone, *He* had failed me. Completely.

Sadness hit me like a freight train and I cried, hard. Damon took a swig of his drink before slouching himself on the chair beside me. He sat there staring at me with his leg over his knee and a self-satisfied smirk across his lips. His limbs resembled spaghetti... Damon's legs were simply put, too long, like one of those stilt acrobats at a circus. The prick was enjoying my gloom. I scoffed and pulled the duvet over me and I let the tears flow without his judgment, but that did nothing because he laughed dryly.

"Just because I can't see you doesn't mean I can't hear you," he uttered. I ignored him and cried for long enough that my chest and eyes ached.

When I finally peered my head out of the wraps Damon was still in the same spot, nibbling at the cross on his necklace. I hadn't really noticed his jewelry before. A devilish grin triggered the dimples to dent his cheeks. His eyes were dark, and his brows were creased.

I knew for sure that he was mentally fucking the shit out of me. The horny asshat. Unintentionally, I drew my tongue across my lips to wet them, as they were dry and cracked from sobbing so much... not to mention being sliced open by a goddamn knife, but by the look on his face, he had other ideas.

"Like what you see?" He adjusted himself on the chair, his muscles flaring at his will. I cleared my throat. *Fuck*, I really did need to stop staring.

"Don't flatter yourself," I scoffed, rolling my eyes at him before continuing. "My lips were dry." *Why did that sound like I was lying?*

"That's a lie, and you know it." Damon's voice was playful,

but etched with a demonic tone, like he was up to no good. He threw his head up and puckered his lips. Ugh, he really was a fucking prick. I sneered with a huff in disgust.

"Fuck off," I snapped. His lips curled and in the blink of an eye, the palm of his hand was against my cheek.

Whack.

Right along one of my cuts. I yelped at the throbbing sting. Tears trembled down my cheek again, though I think the shock hurt more than his hit.

"Watch your mouth, *cunt...* " he hissed.

I rubbed at the sting that was now flushed crimson, and bleeding again. The grin on his face split even further. He leaned over me and planted his hand on the other side of my head, locking me under his hold. I breathed rapidly, uncertain of his next move.

Suddenly, he yanked at the covers off and then trailed his hand along my leg, balancing on one arm. He tapped his hungry fingers firmly over the welts with a groan. I winced, squirmed and whimpered weakly, scooting further backward, which wasn't far. I cried out from his elbow making contact with my chest as he pinned me down hard, winding me on impact.

"If he can't do it, I will. I don't have feelings in my way," he groaned. I coughed and gasped for air but no relief came, he was putting all of him on my chest. Any harder and I'd crack a rib.

"G-get off m-me, Damon," I squeaked under a singular, pressed breath. Terror hounded through my veins.

"What's in it for me if I do, hmm?" He adjusted slightly, trailing further along my skin to the arc of my pelvis. I shuddered from his intrusive touch, even though I wasn't a stray to unwanted touches, it was different. *Very* different. "I know this pussy is a fine piece of work," he purred, his tone hinted beastly and primal.

"No. Get off me!" I pushed again with a little more force than the last. He stopped staring between my legs and snapped his dark gaze deep into my eyes, a threatening look.

"Nah, come on. You've fucked everyone else here. It's my turn now. Little slut, aren't you?"

I shook my head, fighting with all that I had, and managed to free an arm out from under him. In an instant, I struck his face. My still pink, but cracked nails made contact with his cheek. He stilled and his eyes darkened again, if that was even possible. I gulped, and regret swam over my face.

"You're going to regret that," he snarled, and I believed him. He drew his knife out, from where I didn't know, and planted it under my chin, startling me from the speed of his movements. He pressed it right against my carotid artery. I grimaced but held my composure, one move and I was game over.

"You think you scare me?" I hissed. "Are you forgetting who your brother is? You've got nothing on him." I vaunted the last part.

Granted, some of that was a lie. I was fucking terrified. But I needed to stand up to him, I suspected he wouldn't kill me anyway. Otherwise, he would have already, and he wouldn't be in Caine's room babysitting me for no reason.

"I've been playing nice until now. I don't... fucking... like you." He paused between each word before continuing. "You've made a mess of everything here. But now you're here all alone, with *me*."

CHAPTER FIFTY-TWO

BROKEN

I scoffed, offering him nothing, not even my eyes to look into. I closed them, turning my head to the side.

"And I know *very* well who he is and what he's capable of, but here is something *you* don't know,"

What? A moment went by and as much as I didn't want to, I opened my eyes to look at him again, hoping that he would continue.

"I am ten times worse than he will ever be. I *don't* hesitate. I *won't* hesitate. And he isn't my fucking brother. How have you not yet worked it out yet?"

"Worked what out?" I sniveled under the pressure of his blade. My head raced through ideas, but empty thoughts were all that filled the space in my brain.

He laughed. "Soren adopted us, you fucking moron. And the only reason we get away with half the shit we do is because he's the biggest fucking drug dealer of the entire South and East Coasts. How else do you think all those bodies in the lake don't get found? No missing persons files. Na-da. Poof—history all gone. You're dead as far as the USA is concerned. You and your friend."

So...not brothers and sisters. He dug the knife a little further, and it pinched. I couldn't make sense of why he needed to overshare his family history... validation maybe? Drug dealers and murderers. *That explains the medications I had been on, you can't just take them off the shelf. Not to mention the fact that no police have come looking for me, or Tilly.* So the Whitlock brothers weren't really the Whitlock brothers? *That's why they didn't look alike.*

"Now. Be a good whore for me, and shut the fuck up. Am I understood?" he demanded with an insincere smile. I froze, leaving me no choice but to nod him away. I did and he removed his knife. "Good. Now, I'm going to fuck you seven ways to Sunday, and you're going to take it without objection. Got it?"

He squeezed my thigh tightly, his fingers curling into one of the wounds with stitches. Immediate pain fireballed through me and bile pooled in my mouth. I cried out a bone-chilling scream but he only laughed in response.

"What the fuck is wrong with you?" I screeched, in tears.

He squeezed again and stars throbbed in my head.

"I *said*, be a good girl and fucking take it without objection. Say yes."

I nodded and squeaked, "Okay." Anything to get him to release his grip.

He moved quickly, shoving his knee against my leg to pry it open. I jolted to the intrusion of a solid leathery object shoved into my pussy with no remorse. My heart pounded, what in the ever-loving fuck was that? Knowing well and truly that it wasn't his cock I pulled my all to ask.

"Is-is that... your knife?" I stuttered in a heaving, breathy panic.

He chuckled deeply and pushed it further into my pussy. I heaved and dry retched to the sinful sensation, there was not an ounce of pleasure—*this was nothing like fucking any of them, this was downright fucking wrong.*

"I said I'd fuck you seven ways to Sunday, but I didn't say what with," he sneered, and then I started to shake uncontrollably, feeling immense pain flaring my skin and bones.

"No! Stop. Help." My tone was mono and barely in existence. What was the point? No one was around to help me.

He tutted and twisted the knife like he was digging. I squirmed in denial from the familiar knock hitting the delicate area of my G-spot. *Oh, fuck no. I am not about to be condemned for liking a goddamn fucking weapon in my pussy.*

"Hmmm, what a little whore. I think you like that. What about the other end?" he toyed with a curled lip, pulling the handle from inside me. I shook my head rapidly and yelped, loudly.

"No!" I sobbed and tried to squeeze my thighs together, or move—somewhere. But my body was as good as filled with concrete. I wasn't going *anywhere.*

His strength pulled my legs back open and the jagged edge of the blade made contact with my skin along the inside of my labia. Another blood-curdling scream howled from my lungs and he whimpered weakly from my sounds.

"Mmm, fuck, you sound good. Crying like a scared little squeaky toy trapped in the jaws of such a big, mean pitbull," he hissed. I fought for a breath of air and my tears stung from streaming. Snot and saliva spouted from my nose and mouth. I cried out once more as the sharp edge planted softly on my clit, but he took it away before I had the chance to blink. "This little cunt seems to hypnotize him. Why is that so, huh?"

"I don't know," I bellowed truthfully.

"Well... I guess he can't have it if I destroy it, can he?" Damon mocked, his tone was far too intimate. *He was right. He is worse than the shadow man.*

I think I muttered the word *"no"* a million times over through my sobs. I felt a slither of blood trickle down the arc of my labia. *He did cut me.* But I think only just. He purred and maneuvered himself, unzipping his jeans, and freeing his cock. It stood proud to attention, throbbing aggressively, and his piercings twinkled with his pre-cum under the light.

Disgusting pig. Filthy, mother-fucking-fuck! I cussed mentally, my chin trembling at my reality, knowing what was my fate. Settling over the depressing fact that I'd take a thousand deaths over... *this.*

He slammed into me, and the air in my lungs thinned from the pain of his length. I gagged on impact and saw stars. He was fucking huge. All I wanted to do was curl into a ball to ease the sensation of what I could only describe as being kicked in the belly, but only worse.

"Fuck this little cunt *is* tight. I can see why he wanted to keep you around." His thrusts filled and emptied me with no emotion, leaving me no choice but to accept him. And as I did, I felt my soul leave my body.

Damon stilled momentarily, before grinning a little too eagerly, the pale blood that I had drawn from his face trickled slightly. The door's void was now filled by the silhouettes of

Caine and Eli. I squirmed under Damon. Adrenaline taking charge.

"Help me, please!" I squawked, but neither came to my aid.

Caine's face was glum, helpless. He clenched his jaw and looked away. Eli's expression was not much better. I sunk into defeat, because I knew I wasn't going to be saved anytime soon. *This is all a trap. I'm being kept alive just enough to be used at their discretion.*

My chin trembled more and a deep wounded whimper exhaled from my chest. Damon's cock throbbed inside me, and my wounds matched a similar tempo. It was excruciating. Caine cleared his throat, hesitating. *Is he scared of Damon? Is there a hierarchy system?*

"You were supposed to be watching her, not fucking her. Jesus Christ," Caine hissed.

"Oh... well, you see... It's quite a slippery hazard down here. I just slipped." Damon gestured between my legs, humored and not at all concerned that he was fucking someone against their will.

Get this fucking monster off me.

Caine clenched his jaw again from my sorrow, the bulges protruding as he gritted his teeth. His beautiful blonde hair cloaked parts of his face. He wiped his fingers between his tendrils but they only fell back the way they were, fluffy and freshly conditioned.

"Brother... " Eli growled, as if trying to reason with Damon.

"Fine," he grouched, accepting defeat and rolled his eyes at Eli. He pulled out and tucked himself back into his jeans. "Have her then," Damon scoffed and stormed off, barging between Caine and Eli, and disappeared into the hallway.

"What's gotten into him?" Caine questioned with a frown,

looking back over his shoulder. Eli shrugged his shoulders and stormed off after Damon.

Caine looked back at me, and in an instant, I crumbled like the flakes of pastry that the shadow man had once sprinkled over me, fitting into a fit of unbreathable sobs.

CHAPTER FIFTY-THREE

THE TRUTH HURTS

"Here," Caine uttered, passing me another medicine bottle. His voice was rigid yet somehow soft, like a baby bird. The bottle was similar to the one last time.

I whimpered from the sting around my labia as I shuffled upright, leaving the bottle by my side. It had taken me far too long to stop damn crying. I was disgruntled from all this mess, because everything and everyone around me was trying to hurt me. Or kill me, and yet always kept failing to do so.

Every breath was a painful reminder that I was still alive and suffering. I didn't think I would ever feel the way I did, I actually *wanted* to die. Just to get it over and done with. *I want out of this fucking merry-go-round*, and actually manage to escape this hellhole.

Caine shuffled from beside me and fidgeted, I flinched and sobbed a little deeper, disoriented with my surroundings. *Who in their right mind would be physically able to cope with this if it kept going on?* There were only so many times a person could endure being butchered, strangled, starved, raped, and tortured.

"I'm not... I'm not going to hurt you," he comforted genuinely, his voice lower than the last. He held his arms up in protest as if to prove a point.

I blinked a few times, trying to make sense of what had happened, or what could happen next, before finally nodding at him. I didn't think he would hurt me.

He scooted into the bed, and in seconds, taking me by surprise, he cradled me into his chest and tucked my head under his chin. Even though Caine was the reason I was baited and taken in the first place... his arms were nice to be in.

He said nothing, and we just let time pass by in silence. I couldn't describe the feeling, but I felt heard. I felt... *seen*. Like I wasn't a nobody. I wasn't someone's pet. I wasn't a prisoner. I was just a broken person in the arms of another.

Caine peered at me under his lashes before finally speaking again.

"Can you take them... please? You're due again. Everything must be hurting by now." He tapped at the bottle next to my leg. I nodded and he opened the bottle.

They were a different color from the last pills. Perhaps stronger, with antibiotics at best, maybe, but I didn't ask. I didn't care.

"D-did you do these?" I squeaked, pointing to the little tabs on my skin. Some of them had come off or torn, skin included, thanks to Damon. I was bleeding again.

He nodded with a warm, self-gratified smirk.

"Do you not remember?" he asked, frowning. *Well, if I knew, I wouldn't be asking.* I shook my head, swallowing down fear of how much I clearly had no recollection of. "Yes, I did. I've been in here for the past twenty-four hours with you."

He passed me a glass of water from the bedside table. "You

were out of it when I patched you up, but you've been in and out since. You were talking, too."

"I was?" I shrugged, trying to wrack my brain for a memory, but crickets were all I could hear. I had nothing, not a sliver of a visual other than my last—*the crumpled car in the garage.* I wondered what I had said.

Caine nodded, holding a drink of water at my lips to take my tablets. Why did he do that?—*care.* At least he wasn't going to leave me in the bath again. *Wait... I think I remember something.* I was so weak and barely conscious but I remember it.

"Did you... take me to the bathroom?" I asked. If he did, that memory was foggy.

"I did that too, yes."

Okay, so he is my nanny. He's been mending my welts from the shadow man and letting me go to the toilet, giving me medicine and water. Why? I should be dead... like they said.

"I remember some of it," I admitted softly.

He furrowed his brows and shook his head in disapproval.

"I shouldn't have left Damon with you. I'm sorry."

I squeezed my thighs together instinctively, the sting hurt but I figured it could have been worse.

"What about the shadow man? Where is he?"

"The who?" He wore a perplexed frown on his face. I raised my brow. *Come on, as if you couldn't work that out.*

"Your brother," I stammered dryly.

Caine chuckled, humored by my pet name for the shadow man.

"He'll be back."

"Oh," I sighed with a great amount of sadness, twiddling my fingers for comfort. Caine's gaze was warm and content. "Why are you being nice to me?" I finished in question, still dazed by what had happened and my lack of memory. He tutted.

"Well, I'm sure you know by now, I'm not a monster. I just have fucked up brothers. Look, this wasn't part of the plan." He held his hand up in protest again, and I believed him. "*You* are not supposed to be alive right now. I'm sorry. I know that's hard to hear, I really am sorry. You don't deserve that. You don't deserve any of this. And we don't know why Hux—" suddenly, he slammed his mouth shut. *Was he just about to reveal his name?*

A moment of anticipation passed, my head exploding with endless memories and thoughts and feelings, swarming hell in my brain before Caine stopped procrastinating.

"Well... *he* has gone fucking haywire, and we're trying to work out what his deal is. You were everything he's been looking for, Esme. Dragging us along in his ride. Ever since he finally found you... " He sighed, threading his hand through his hair again like he had already said too much. I blew a rapid breath in confusion, shaking my head.

"Why me? Why had he been looking for me?" I asked. My frown of concern was desirous. Caine hesitated but continued anyway, almost giving me the feeling that needing to tell me more information helped him more than it did me.

"You're the pawn, Esme."

He said it all too easily. Like he had said it a million times. I'd heard that line before. The shadow man's words came through my mind as though it had never left, *"nothing but a pawn before the king."*

"What do you mean... pawn? Is it just me? Are the rest of the hostages that keep dying pawns also?" I hounded the questions like I was in an interrogation, I couldn't spit them out fast enough.

"Yes. Pawns… Contributions… Offerings. *Look,* I know that, to you, this is all fucked up. More fucked up than I care to admit. I didn't want any of *this*." He seemed pained by something. I scoffed. *Come on, get to the point.* "He's not right in the head Esme, I know, but he's our brother. He's *my* brother. He's been in a dark place for years, ever since… " He clenched his jaw, guilt washing over his face, but he didn't continue.

Frustration rippled through me but I held it in. "Ever since?" I prompted him.

"The accident. We do what we do for him… we would do anything for him."

I stared at him blankly. Another painful, still moment went by, waiting for him to say something else but he didn't.

"What are they—*we*—being offered or pawned off for… to? Does it have anything to do with the voices in the lake?" I asked.

"You wouldn't understand," he deadpanned. *Absolutely the fuck not, we're not doing this. We're not giving me a sample of information and then aborting ship. Out with it!* Heat rose under my skin and I finally snapped.

"Jesus fucking Christ, Caine. I've already been butchered half to death, more times than one! If anything, I deserve to fucking know!" I shrieked, startling him.

"I know… I know. I'm trying. We've not told anyone all this before. Just bear with me, okay?" he asked calmly, the glint in his eyes was that of a scalded dog. As though he would get into trouble for telling me, but needing to comfort me anyway. "You're the reason he got in this mess in the first place," he added.

NOT HELPING!

I huffed but alleviated the daggers that I was throwing at him mentally for taking so damn fucking long.

"Okay, great start, but I don't understand," I confessed. He took a moment, seemingly going into a dark place in his head.

"It happened six years ago."

I tilted my head, realizing *exactly* what he was talking about. I knew for sure.

"The accident?" I pushed.

I stared at him long enough to make him regret the decision of confessing his life stories to me. His lips pursed and a mixture of emotions washed over his expression, looking mostly of grief before finally giving in. He sighed, then nodded.

"Six years ago, almost to the day. He was driving her far away." *Her? Who's her?* Caine almost lost it there and then, a single tear formed at the base of his eye. He was pained. I swallowed, mimicking his discomfort. "It was raining. The roads were wet, we were going too fast, and... he lost control. The car spun out and smashed into the trees in the gully, rolling seven times into the ditch."

We? I waited. But nothing followed.

"Again, you're missing the part where I have anything to do with this," I retaliated.

He pinned a brow, and then nudged away the tear with a blink. Albeit, my voice was dry, but I was getting sick of waiting. *Get on with it.*

"Let me finish." He waved me off. "How do I say this right? They *both* died at the scene. He was pulled from it first and the paramedic revived him, and *only* him. He's not been the same since, not without her."

"Who?" I squirmed as I asked the question.

Caine peered over his shoulder, his movement filled with urgency. But no one else was there and the door was still closed.

"Esme, please, I've told you too much already."

I arched a brow. "Actually, you haven't told me enough. What does it have to do with me?" I pushed again, dominance taking charge of my voice. I think for the very first time in my life. Caine snuffled as if living the moment like it was yesterday in his brain. A raw memory.

"Fuck. He couldn't live without her. He couldn't live with himself. It was killing him from the inside. Until one night... something changed. I couldn't believe it myself. Whatever fantasy land he was in, it was helping him. Until it wasn't. Then it started getting worse."

"What was?" I questioned, my head only getting more twisted and clouded.

"The voices. The shadow."

"The ones at the lake?" I rubbed my forehead. It was slowly starting to make sense.

"Yes. At first, it started in the late afternoon. He lost control, blacked out, and started having hypnotic-like dreams, and nightmares. We tried everything to understand him and the things she—*it*—said. But they got worse and worse. Controlling his every thought."

"And then what?" I asked with as much patience as I could.

He sighed dramatically. "He tried to kill himself. Because the voice told him to. Because it said it would take his pain away." My heart pounded. *I knew that man was suffering from something.*

"Tried?" I breathed. *An unsuccessful suicide? This still had nothing to do with me.*

"Yes. And that's where you come in, Esme. I have a better

idea, can you stand?" he asked, a comforting smile tickling his lips.

"I... I can try. Why?" I absolutely most certainly could not stand, much less walk, unless I wanted my death then and there. But I wasn't about to let my body ruin my chances of learning why I was pulled into purgatory.

"I want to show you something. You'll understand more if I do. As much as I know I'll regret it. you're here, so you deserve to know."

I nodded, and we were out the door arm in arm, going snail's pace down the corridor.

CHAPTER FIFTY-FOUR

LOVE LETTERS

W hy did I agree to getting out of bed—*before* taking those damn pills that I'd left sitting on the bed, and very much not in my body? Well that was the problem, I didn't know. I was too busy thinking about what Caine was wanting to show me. He had led me to the garage.

"How did you know I was trying to escape, anyway?" I frowned, stumbling on the memory of him finding me in the sports car beside me.

Caine pulled his phone out, tapping a few buttons before showing me the screen. The garage was on surveillance, the screen replaying a snippet of footage. I was in clear view. *Crap.* There really was no way of escaping this place without someone watching.

Wait… what else has he seen?

I mentally punished myself, I should have known. I should have remembered that there were cameras everywhere, I had seen them in the shadow man's... office? Whatever that room was. Granted, I wasn't really thinking. I was... touching myself. My cheeks flushed.

"Oh." I smiled at the memory coyly, and he tucked his phone back with an I've-seen-everything flexed brow, dancing over his pretty face.

I paced slowly back and forth beside the beaten-up car in the garage, taking in all of its carnage and clutching the sheet from Caine's bed around my body. It had been so long since I had worn clothes, I wondered if they would even fit if I was given the pleasure to wear them again. Thankfully I had stopped bleeding, for the most part, but the sheet was covered in red. My body was hurting, really hurting.

I pried my neck around to glare at him and he gestured to look inside the car. He wore a worried look, only making my stomach tighten. Caine had said as we were walking to the garage that he would fiddle with the surveillance so no one knew we were in there, but I was not convinced that would work, given how tense he was, not to mention always looking over his shoulder.

I tried hard to ignore what was behind the wall on the other side of the garage once more. *That fucking cellar.* But seeing it pounded guilt and sadness into my gut. Knowing well and true that their lives were going to end very soon... or already.

I swiped my fingers over the twisted metal and the blood stains—heavily stained blood marks—that were scattered over the passenger and driver seats of the car. Granted the blood was dry, and clearly had been for years... *six years.*

I swallowed around the lump in my throat, letting my imagination set the scene. My heart dropped and I could feel my tears building. I shouldn't feel remorse for the shadow man, but I did.

Two people had lost their lives in the very car I was puzzling about. Except, only one made it out, breathing. The shadow man. Or H, as they keep referring him to. Hux-something. I pushed aside my wandering mind, turning my attention to the dashboard on the passenger side. It had marks and scratches all over it, from what I gathered... fingernails.

I twisted my neck around to look at Caine again and he nodded, then lowered his head. The memory was clearly splitting through his mind, it was almost as though he had been there. Had he? Maybe that was why he had said *we*. I doted on him, losing a sibling wouldn't be a good feeling, whether you're blood-related or not.

I trailed my fingertips over the rest of the rusted carnage and stared at the bent wheels, and then the crushed bonnet, and the smashed windscreen. I peered inside through the passenger window. There were damaged CDs, earphones, books, and ripped-up notes from a journal that were spread throughout the car.

It took me a minute to realize that I remembered the shadow man scribbling in a journal the other night. Pieces of the puzzles were starting to form and make sense. I needed to know more, stat!

I didn't hesitate. I pried at the crumpled door. It didn't budge, so I gave up and leaned in through the broken window.

"Be careful. I don't need you adding to your wounds." Caine shuffled closer, but I shrugged him off and yanked one of the torn-up pieces. With shaking hands, I un-scrunched it and began to read, my heart pounding out of my chest at each word.

My regret will forever be losing you. The truth is too bitter for me. It should have been me. My love, in eternal rest, at my doing. I am not strong enough to continue life without you. What is life worth living if you are not here with me? You were the air—

"Come on." Caine tapped at the screen of his phone again, interrupting my deciphering of the shadow man's letter and ushering me back with urgency. I collected the rest of the notes and scurried back to him.

In seconds, we were out of the garage and making haste through the hallway, leaving no opportunity to be caught.

You were the air I breathed. I cannot stay here anymore, my wounds are a constant reminder, bringing me pain in each breath I take, a pain no one understands. I am so sorry, my love. Please forgive me. I promise I will be with you again. When I end it all, I will see you again.

H.

I read the rest of the note from earlier, paraphrasing over the last part for the umpteenth time while gulping down another mouthful of toast that Caine had just brought up from the kitchen for me, miraculously without choking. Eating was great, sure, but it came with a shit ton of pain. Each bite made me feel like my face was ripping open. Caine was quiet and hadn't whispered a word other than when he demanded I took my pills that I didn't take earlier.

Words failed me. *Pain. Wounds? When I end it all. Maybe that was where he had gotten all those scars from; the accident? Or maybe from the suicide attempt?*

I stopped reading to peer at him, he was sitting at the bench in the corner of his room eating crackers, staring at me, not at all as creepy as the shadow man always did. I could tolerate Caine's doe eyes on me without wanting to squirm.

"I'm just going to… read these," I stated, though my tone sounded like I was asking. His brows danced as he took another bite of his crackers, and I went back to the scrunched letters, laying out the rest of them on the bed. Most of them were torn, and needed sorting. They were from a journal, the rip on the side was evident of that.

I wondered what had happened in that accident, coming up with a lot of theories but quickly shoved the visions aside. It was clear that the letter was an apology to the woman Caine had mentioned from the accident, whoever she was. *Goddamn, I feel like an FBI agent running through murder scenes, trying to figure out the plot.*

The shadow man had blamed himself for her death, and I gathered that he kept the car in the garage as a reminder. *As punishment.* I hadn't yet figured out what it had to do with me, so I dug a little further. I fiddled with another pile of shredded mixed-up letters for heaven knows how long, but I managed to get the detailing right.

I pinched the bridge of my nose to relieve the pressure that was building, my head wasn't pounding as much but my body ached more than before. Maybe I needed more food. Though, I didn't feel like eating any more than the singular slice of toast.

'Empty promises'

I called for you in the forest. Where your voice told me to meet you.

You answered. I saw you. But you did not take me.

I offered my all. I held my head under, where the water meets the dark.

My heart was taking its last beat for you. But I woke.

Will you tell me who she is?

The girl who pulled me above the water.

The girl who took me from you.

H.

My throat narrowed. The letter was from his failed suicide. *Had someone saved him?* It couldn't have been one of his brothers as whoever he was talking about was a woman. *Wait... was this... me?*

I turned my attention to Caine again with a despairing glare, tapping on the letter. He was now neck-deep in a bottle of red wine. *Crackers and wine, a great mix.*

"What does this part mean? Is this what you meant by something to do with me?" He nodded, but didn't offer a speech. *Why does he seem so cold all of a sudden? Something isn't right.*

My brow furrowed. "But I'd never met him until those nightmares. I don't understand," I deadpanned.

He guzzled at the red liquid in the bottle, swallowing several gulps before coming up for air and staring at me with a face of a wounded puppy. My head raced with inconclusive thoughts and emotions.

"I've never saved anyone before. If I saw someone drowning, and I saved them I think I'd bloody well remember. You've got the wrong person. That's not me. I... " I stuttered, cutting myself off as I noticed that Caine had moved. He was panting heavily, pacing the floor with a great amount of guilt and sorrow over his face.

"What's happ—"

Caine was quick to cut me off, gesturing his hands in the air.

"I'm sorry," he croaked as if something bad was about to happen. Unease hit me like a bull at a gate.

"For what?" I mouthed. Inaudible from a hitched breath, and then I jolted, hearing slow footsteps echoing through the hallway from behind the door, before coming to a stop. My eyes widened, seeing shadows of two feet creeping from under the door.

I drew my hand to my mouth to mute my gasps, dreading the next chapter of my fucked up life. A moment passed from hearing my heart in my brain, though it felt like a century, and then the shadow man filled the void of the door. I lost all feeling in my legs, dropping to the floor like a sack of potatoes.

"No. Please... " I fitted into a wallow of sobs. *Not again. Not again.* I twisted my head back to Caine, seeing that he had his eyes pinned at his feet. *Traitor!*

Without the opportunity for a breath between sheds of tears, pain ricocheted through my body as I was being thrown over a shoulder and sauntered down the corridor.

Can't this mother fucker just leave me alone?

I trembled, blinking for light but none came, grimacing as the shadow man sat me down on top of the piano. He lit an old weathered candle from a shelf on the wall and the shadows in the room flickered under the dull light, realizing that we were in the room he had played the piano in—the first time I tried escaping.

I quickly glanced around, seeing that it looked like a library, there were books everywhere, some even on the floor. He moved slowly and didn't speak, nor did I. I was far too terrified. I thought only the worst... would I be in trouble for stealing his key and escaping? I squirmed, bunching the sheet tightly in my grip against me. *Clothes would be great right about now. Actually, no—scratch that, a hospital would be great about now.*

He placed the candle on the piano's shelf opposite me, lighting up the sheets of music. The grand piano was big and old, it had remnants of black paint smudged over the keys from his fingertips.

My brow furrowed, suddenly registering that there was not a sliver of anger in his body language. He was... calm? *Too calm.* Less than thirty hours ago he had me hanging from his ceiling like a puppet, and was as mad as anything, carving me up like a Thanksgiving turkey, before bleeding me into a bucket and taking me to the lake, where I was *supposed to be killed* and then offered to whoever... or whatever it was in the lake, for whatever reason.

Why would he have thought I was the one who had stopped

him from killing himself? The Whitlock brothers had all seemed pretty certain that I was the one, so what about the other hostages? It was starting to make sense, those women *did* look like me. Dark or black hair, pasty white skin, freckled faces, and green eyes.

It was a pattern. A toxic pattern. *He is a fucking psychopath.* Even after all that, I still wanted to understand him. He was like a magnetic force that I couldn't run from, making me need and long for answers. Intrusive thoughts swam through my mind... *denial. Why did I still want the shadow man after all that he had put me through?*

I couldn't help myself, not even having sex with him in a carcass-infused lake with open wounds was enough of a deterrent. I stared at him for too long without taking much notice and a single tear involuntary freed from my eyes.

He is so fucking... beautiful.

Gah!

"Don't try to understand me, pet," he spoke softly and my heartbeat slowed in an instant. I drew in a breath and summoned every inch of courage from my body. I wanted to hear the truth... from him. I wanted everything.

"But I *want* to understand you. I'm not scared of you," I whispered. I was sure I sounded convincing enough.

"You should be."

To prove a point, I shifted closer to him, hovering my ass over the edge of the piano. The sheet pulled from tension ever so slightly and let my thigh slip free—the biggest cut where my stitches were sewn into was on full display. The mindless tug to know more about the reason I was behind all this was much stronger than my loyalty to my life.

He dropped his head to where my leg was poking out, before looking back up again and drawing in a big breath.

"You're playing a dangerous game here, Esmeralda. Don't fucking test me," he staggered the words, as if to threaten, but I didn't care.

"I read your letters, so I know a little bit, but not enough," I admitted thoughtlessly. The man was unpredictable, I shouldn't play with fire like that.

He tensed. Air hissed through his teeth, and then he planted his hand on my cheek. I flinched, expecting a slap but then I melted into his touch for reasons I didn't understand. He whimpered, raising his other hand to the other cheek and the heat of his eyes burned into mine. Though I couldn't see them, I wished I could. I sobbed, I wanted to lose myself in his eyes... I wanted to understand him. Even more so now that I had been told I was the reason he was this way.

"Why do you test me? Do you not understand that I am a killer? A monster? And you are my prey?" he asked, holding my cheeks with light pressure.

"If you truly wanted me dead, I would be. And I wouldn't have tape all over my body mending my wounds. You even said yourself... that you can't understand why you haven't killed me yet. And yet, your brain is running a million miles an hour, wondering why you didn't kill me at the lake. You had every chance to. But you didn't." I spoke with only a fraction of courage. He seemed to be eating his words.

"What did my letters tell you?"

"Too much and not enough,"

"I see."

I pushed again. "Please. I want to know why. I *need* to know why."

He sighed epically. "For six years... I have been hunting you. Because something has been hunting me—*for you.*"

CHAPTER FIFTY-FIVE

HOLY FUCKING JESUS-MARY-AND-JOSEPH

The shadow man tugged me off the piano, and I stood. *He's only just put me here and now he's taking me off again... can't I just sit?*

He lifted up the cover of the piano and reached inside of it, pulling out a journal before lowering the lid back down again.

I was quick to figure out that it was the same journal as the one he had been writing in after returning from the lake, before he passed out. *I'm glad I didn't take it from him then, he would be cross with me if I had.* It was old, brown leather-bound, and had a *H* embossed in black on the cover. His initial. *Hux—* something.

I squinted, seeing some kind of runes scribbled at the bottom, ancient Greek maybe? Like his ring. I wondered briefly if maybe he was a witch or something, but the thought quickly vanished. There was no such thing. *Esme, come on, that's ridiculous.*

He opened the journal and trailed his finger over a Polaroid photograph of a young blonde woman. She looked my age, if not younger. She was beautiful, standing in front of a car holding her arms out like a starfish and laced with a big glowing smile.

It took me too long to realize that it was the same car as the one in the garage. *Oh, shit. It was her.* There looked to be a poem under the photograph, but I couldn't make it out.

"Is that the girl from the accident?" I muttered.

"Yes," he spoke tenderly, a tinge of grief in his voice.

I smiled through the corner of my mouth, trying to show my attentiveness and ignore the pain that shredded through my cheeks. *Holy hell that hurts to smile like that.*

"She was beautiful. What was her name?"

"Samantha," he sighed.

I let a moment pass before asking more questions. I had to remember that he was unpredictable.

"Are you a writer?"

"I dabble." He was quick to answer, but short in his response. I drew in a staggered breath.

"What is... hunting you?"

He held the book toward me. "Everything you want to know... is in here."

"You want me to read it?" I asked, confusion flooded my tone. He nodded and sighed again. I didn't know why, but I enjoyed the thought of him reading to me, but he seemed not at all interested in telling me anything, only showing.

I creased my brow, the man was pouring with pain and grief. *Unhealed.* I couldn't help but feel as though I was overstepping a boundary, discovering things I had no business in knowing. Though, for some reason, I was caught in the middle of it all. So I guessed that meant that I did in fact have every ounce of business working out why.

I shuddered from a weird sensation, listening to the shadow

man's words repeat in a timeless loop inside my brain, giving me the impression that we had met before—I was certain that we hadn't—but he was certain that we had.

"The moment you showed up in my head."

"The girl who pulled me above the water.

The girl who took me from you."

It was far from my comfort zone, but I was considering that maybe there was some kind of spiritual connection, considering the voices, the black fog, the static cracks, the chills, the hallucinations. I knew I had lost my mind, but that thought was absurd.

I shook my head and brushed away the thought, and then took the journal from his grip, holding it tight against my chest.

"Can you play me something?" I asked without thinking.

He spun around before taking a seat on the chair, and found the keyboards of the piano. He held his fingers there for a moment, as though to cue a request. I thought of the only song that had been in my head since I heard it, his lullaby.

"The one you were playing the night I tried... " *escaping.* I didn't need to say the word, he knew what I meant. "P-please?"

His knuckles clenched and his breath shattered against his mask, holding himself still for a moment. With a crack of his neck, he began to play the melody. I couldn't control myself, tears instantly trembled down my cheeks without warning and no sign of stopping soon.

The notes were as beautiful as I remembered them. Painful, but beautiful. He rolled himself into the song, losing himself entirely. As though the lullaby was healing him, taking great pleasure by playing it. But he didn't sob like he had done last time.

I watched him play, studying the pattern of the keys, and sat down on the chair beside him. He didn't stop playing, nor did he pay much attention to the fact I had taken a seat next to him. He was in his own world. I adjusted myself and let my fingers follow his rhythm, our melodies matching in harmony as he took the low keys, and I took the high.

His head tilted slightly toward me. I of course couldn't see his facial expression, but I could feel it. I was certain that he was smiling, because the heat of it radiated off of his body.

I tittered and couldn't help but return another painstaking smile that reached my eyes as I looked directly at him. The sexual, joyful tension between us was electric.

"I want you to read the journal Esme," he commanded.

"O-okay."

He had broken the silence. Along with my grin. I opened the book, seeing that there were pages missing, they must be the ones that I had taken from the car. A few had been torn in places with some of the paper left behind from a tear with some words intact, but I couldn't make out what they said.

I skimmed to a page I was able to read and took a deep breath. I started to read the first letter but was interrupted.

"Aloud, please, pet," he grumbled and then continued another melody. Still in minor keys, slow and dark.

'The Voice'

I heard a voice. In my dream.
Or at least, I thought I was dreaming.
It spoke of the accident. Last night.
It asked me if I wanted the pain to go away. I said yes.

But I woke up. In pain. Memory coming back in full swing, I had killed her.

H.

The year was written in numerals. I couldn't read them to save my life but I was sure it had number seven in it. It would make sense if it did, as that would bring it to 2017... six years ago.

"This was dated quite some time ago," I whispered, but he didn't respond. *So the voice from the lake is real?* I hadn't imagined it, and I wasn't going mad. I turned the page, clearing my throat to read another.

'Siren'

I heard her voice again.

I think it was a she. Or an it. I don't understand what or who she is.

It's like I'm always high before I hear her, intoxicated.

I need more.

She said it knew the past was eating away at me.

She said she will make it all go away.

I asked what she... it wanted from me.

At first, it said nothing. But the more it spoke to me the more it asked for.

It said to meet it where the darkness and water gathered and it would all go away, the pain, the guilt, the regret, the memories.

But only if I give my all. My trust, my soul, my flesh, my blood, my bones.

It wants my everything.

It wants me to die. I guess, anything is better than this feeling. I have already lost it all.

I am scared, but I want it all to end. I need it all to end.

H.

I frowned, there it was again, the needing to 'end' things. His suicide? Was the voice in the lake asking him to sacrifice himself to her... it? My head wandered with theories but didn't come up with anything that resembled reality. I didn't understand. *This is paranormal, this isn't real.* But it had to be, because I had heard her too.

Wasting no time, I took a big breath in and read another with great speed, becoming very intent on learning more about the man beside me. And in turn, myself.

'Assimilate'

I understand her now. I want her to take me. I know she can, she told me she can.

She makes me feel good. Until I wake up.

I cannot stand the dry inhale, I cannot stand the rain pounding on my skin anymore. The guilt. The pain.

My scars will always be my constant reminder of what was, and what could have been.

I'm left ugly from the lacerations and the bitter eternal rest that I cannot undo.

My punishment.

A lesson, to never love again. She said I am not worthy of love or a voice to speak with. I am broken.

I am afraid. I am lost. But I don't want to feel anymore. Every feeling I have reminds me of Samantha.

I just want it to all go away. I don't want to wake up anymore.

H.

My heart tightened, remorse striking me without warning. *Left ugly...* the man was riddled with scars, but it wasn't just physical, my assumption was that he knew his heart grew to become ugly too. *I am not worthy of love, I am broken.* I assumed that was why he wore a mask... and paint. Hiding from the world around him.

In the glimpse of my eyes, I could see a tear rolling out under his mask. Reading seemed to both heal and rile him equally. I could honestly say that I didn't know if it was from the song, or because I was losing myself in his letters and my thoughts. I hated being an empath at the best of times, but the darkness in his letters, and his pain ricocheted through my body for him. I was feeling all of it—I was feeling *all* of him.

"Do you want me to stop?" I breathed. Though I wasn't asking for his sake.

He shook his head. "No," he croaked through a tear. His body was tense, unwilling to let out a fitful amount of tears in a release.

The next page I could read was torn and I recalled the shape of the tear on the side, knowing for sure it would align with one of the letters that I had found in the car. The suicide note.

Who took me from you? I will find her and destroy her. And anyone who looks like her. Unease reared its ugly head. Because we had finally got to somewhere deeper into his fucked up past where it somehow involved me, and why I had so much to do with it. I turned through some more pages of scribbles... aggressive scribbles. Singular pages, singular words.

"*DEBT.*"

"*SLEEP.*"

"You want to go to sleep?" I questioned with a great amount of confusion. *Wait... didn't Eli mention something about a debt?* God, my head was fogging up. *This is a lot to process.*

"Yes. But it's much more than what you think. It's a place."

"A place where... ?" I pushed.

"A place where it all goes away. Light, sound, pain, regret. All thoughts. Everything," he said dryly. My brows furrowed. *Was it always this hard to get answers from these fucking people?*

"You mentioned a high before you see... her. Do you mean drugs?" *Or did he mean death?*

He didn't reply instantly, taking a moment to swap between melodies. "I guess you could see it that way. Keep reading.

"FIND HER."

"BRING HER TO ME."

My eyes cracked wide open, the realization hit me like a ton of bricks and I gasped so loud that I coughed. That quote was identical to the one I had heard at the lake when we were... *not the time, nor place to be thinking sexual thoughts, Esme.* The voice had also said *"mine."* I scratched at my head and swallowed the lump that was growing in my throat.

Holy fucking Jesus-Mary-and-Joseph... these are *about me!*

CHAPTER FIFTY-SIX

FALLING

I nudged away a tear of my own and continued reading out loud.

'*Her time to die*'

It happened again, the voice. She's mad. Very mad. Controlling my every thought since seeing the girl in my head the night I tried to find eternal rest.

I cannot choke the shadow down anymore. It is too strong. It is not how it was, how she appeared.

It said to me, "Aren't you forgetting something? The debt you owe to me.

You, are mine. And yet, you are not here. And why is that?

It is <u>*her*</u> *fault, you know that don't you?*

I told you to give her to me. And your debt will be paid.

Only I can pull you out of this. You want it to go away, don't you?

At the beginning of the ritual, you promised me your all.

You belong to me. I kept my oath, my blood for you.

But you did not come to me, did you?

You went to her.

My blood runs through you, you can feel all that I feel, and I you.

It is getting harder to ignore me, isn't it?

The longer you take, the louder I get.

I can take your pain away. And I can give it.

That wreckage is a constant reminder, isn't it?

Don't you want me to take it all away? I can if you do what I asked.

Give her to me.

My shadows run through your veins like thick tar, I can feel your pain.

Aren't you forgetting something?

The debt you owe to me, you are not paying.

I offered you the freedom you so desperately desired, and she took that from you.

She took you from me.

You want to see the other side, don't you?

Your debt.

Her.

Bequeath.

Bequeathed.

H.

"Oh my God," I breathed.

He snuffed and I saw another stream of tears coming down from under his mask.

"Close... but no, pet," he muttered. *What? This is so confusing.* His breath was becoming more shallow, but he continued playing the piano through his tears. The tunes somehow became more beautiful, eerie, and heart-wrenching. He was unraveling. I read another journal entry, mirroring his tears and sympathizing with his pain.

'Something Unholy'

I brought a girl into the lake today, and I took her life, like the voice told me to. At least... I thought it was the right girl, the one that pulled me from my demise.

It looked like her. Black hair, freckles, green eyes. I did what it told me to do. I did things I never thought I would.

Now the blood is on my hands for my debt.

I watched a girl's life drain away... for my own selfish needs.

Am I a monster?

The voice told me it would end for me if I offered her over. And I would go to sleep. But I am still breathing.
I killed for the voice, like she asked, but is it not enough?
When will I be pain-free again?

H.

I continued through my cries, droplets landing over the ink of the pages. The numerals noted somewhere around 2019, maybe 2020, and the next in 2022.

'Hunter. Hunted'

I need to hide my true self, for I no longer recognize who I am anymore. I am a monster.

I know I must become like it... her. A shadow. Careless. Soulless.
I need to become the mask I hide behind.
I need to become what hunts me.
The hunted, becomes the hunter.

H.

I took another breath, holding my hand on my heart. I didn't know how much longer I could go on with the letters. This is too much.

'The Debt'

I've searched and searched. I need to find her.
She is the offering. My offering.
For my freedom.
I will not stop until I find her.

H.

My breath hitched and my throat narrowed more than the last, my throat was hurting from reading and crying. I turned the pages of scribbles, finding another entry that was dated with numbers and not in numerals. It was marked *this* year. February of 2023. Exactly when my nightmares first started happening.

'Her'

I found her. After all my years of searching, I finally found her.
Esmeralda Jane Pierce.
I knew it was her the first time I laid my eyes on her.
She is responsible for pulling me from my demise.

H.

I hurried to the next, it was marked April of 2023.

'Butterfly'

She has no idea I have been watching her, the way she paces her room in those jeans, and that baggy shirt covered in stains.
I find myself watching her in her classes, walking home, following her. Just out of sight as she has coffee with her friend.

I love seeing the way her body reacts when I am near, the shudder her body repulses. I know that she can smell me, she will eventually catch my scent even when I am not near. Just like I can smell my own shadow.
She doesn't know that I watch her as she loses herself drawing those butterflies in her room. Much less brushing her hair in her sleep, or when I stroke her throat, inches from taking her life... but I don't.

I will wait.
She will come to me.
Stupid girl, she has no idea the carnage I will bring to her for what she has done to me.

I cannot wait to watch her life drain away for me.
Then I will finally be free.

H.

I trembled. Everything swinging into my core like a truck.

"So you *do* think I did it? You think I pulled you out of your suicide frenzy?" I muttered, feeling a sense of anger. He didn't respond.

He has lost his marbles. I had never met this man in my life, I didn't think... If only I could say for certain because I have never seen his face, not fully. But on the other hand, I knew that I had never *saved* anyone from drowning.

"I've never saved anyone in my life, this is not me. You have the wrong person," I bellowed.

"No. I don't. Keep going," he demanded weakly. My stomach knotted and bile threatened to flow.

"You *are* a monster." I hated saying the words. I hated believing that it might be true, I knew he wasn't a monster, not really.

"I—I'm n—fuck, read the fucking note, Esme!" He scowled.

I continued reading with another sob, noting just how much my head was throbbing. The letter was dated recently... *I think.* The last date I remembered was my birthday in May, so it mustn't have been much later—*while I was here.*

'Dissolving'

I tried to take her life tonight. I took her to where the water met the dark, like every other offering for the last six years.
But, her touch.
It's so... cleansing. I do not understand.

I have looked for her for so long. To kill her. The

taste of my freedom, now chained to my bed as I watch her.

She stares at me, I stare at her. Both of us trying to work out the other.

I cannot fathom the words of what happens when we touch, it is like splitting into a new aura. A static charge.

And now I can't say for certain if she is part of this twisted game, or something more.

I relished splitting through her skin to make her bleed, like I always do. Hearing her cries. I offered her blood in the water, like I always do.

But to submerge her for the final offering, like I always do... To clear my debt. To be without the pain from the wreckage I caused... almost a distant memory when I am near her?

I could not.

Something has changed. She... is changing me.

She is altering me into something... or someone I once was.

H.

I gulped, hard and loud. Confirming that it was the journal entry from the night he took me to the lake. And when he had said to touch him, and I did because it was as though it healed him. He felt that charge like I did—*and still do*. It was very clear that I had him in a chokehold in ways that he couldn't understand.

"Are you... Falling in love with me?" I shuddered. He didn't say anything. There was another letter. The last one.

'*A crossroad...*'

How is it I have the instinct to love her but I am hardwired to kill her?
Her touch, her lips... There is more. She is more. Esmeralda. My swallowtail. My nemesis. My rain.

H.

I shivered, and then he held the last note of the melody with his foot on the pedal.

"I need you to understand something. Because maybe if you do, I will understand it too. I saw your face a million times in my head the night I had tried to take my own life. *Your* face, and only your face. You became my every breath, every thought, every sound, and every feel. A fucking nightmare on loop. My purgatory. You, Esme, are the offering. The gift for my freedom. I have waited for so long for this moment. And yet, you're like a flame... and I'm the moth. I can't sleep. I can't breathe. But I cannot leave this fucked up world that I live in until—"

"Until I do." My voice croaked, cutting him off. I knew exactly where he was going with it.

"Yes," he nodded and then sighed. "But I can't."

My stalker, my kidnapper, my killer... just told me in his own way, that he was in love with me. My heart pounded out of my ribcage. How the fuck was I supposed to process this?

I propped myself off the stool and shook my hands out

vigorously as if to throw away all my illicit thoughts. Telling myself that there was no fucking way on God's green earth that I felt the same way.

I shifted behind him and he turned around to face me. I didn't think it through, acting completely on lust-filled adrenaline I dropped my sheet and it puddled on the floor around my feet and a pleasured groan formed from his chest, taking in all of me. Willingly at his disposal, for reasons I couldn't fathom.

"Tell me you feel it," I demanded under a rigid breath. I *needed* to hear him say it. I *needed* to hear him admit that he was falling in love with me. Without hesitation, he bent down and scooped me up. I wrapped my legs around him, and he lowered me onto the piano once more.

My feet landed on the keys of the piano, playing a misaligned tune. A breathy moan fled from my lips as he squeezed his warm fingers behind my ass and gave me a slight tug, scooping me in closer to the edge of the piano. He kicked away the stool and with hasty speed, he pried my legs apart.

"Yes, swallowtail. I feel it," heat pooled between my legs and in an instant, his fingers met the slit of my pussy, pushing between them carefully but with great hunger. "I feel you, all of you."

There was no denying how much I wanted him right then and there. I wanted him to claim me, but he stilled. As though he was processing. But what for? I leaned forward and trailed my finger down his neck, tracing along each of his shadows as the candle flickered on his black skin. Feeling the scars that penetrated his skin. I followed each muscle down to where the V of his hips sang against his jeans.

"I do, too," I admitted.

"Fuck," he hissed, drawing in a gasp through his teeth. He

rolled his neck back from the sensation of my soft touch. I shifted my hand back up and I curled my finger under the edge of his mask and he growled, grabbing my wrist in reflex. I flinched. *Wrong move...* he shook his head.

"Sorry," I muttered.

I needed him, *now*. I placed my hands on his old worn belt and unbuckled his jeans. They fell to the floor, freeing his cock. It stood to attention from him, proud and pumping with a glossy tip... for me. Its veins were thick and protruding, and his piercings gleamed under the candlelight.

I bit my lip in anticipation, both of us panting from our own puddles of desperation. Our need for each other splitting through the air.

Like lightning.

I traced over his veins, feeling the cool metallic rods of his piercings, wincing from the thought of how painful they would have been and rolled my thumb over the wet tip. He banded his finger under my chin and I met his eyeless gaze, but all I could offer him was a nibble at my lips and a whimper. Unable to process a single thought, word, or movement.

He collided with my pussy again and I cried out, "wait!" I panted the words. He stopped, barely able to soothe his own breath. I couldn't hide my sadness. All I wanted was to kiss him... to look into his eyes, his soul, to feel him, and to... *shit.* Love him.

"If I'm not allowed to see you. Can I at least know your name?"

He sighed deeply as if he hadn't told anyone his name for a *very* long time. Like he said, he needed to become the mask he hid behind, to become voiceless. I waited, scanning the eye holes of his metallic mask to find any hopes of light.

"Huxley. My name is Huxley."

Huxley... Huxley.

H.

The heat between us was truly undeniable. I felt as though, in that moment, I was glowing on the inside. Buzzing. And he was weakening, to me. I twirled my tongue at my lips where I wished he was and tipped my pelvis. He noted the invitation and shoved himself inside me, hard.

The air thinned and I folded for him in an instant. Would he always be able to do that? It was like magic. I crashed in waves as my pussy tightened around him, gripping him so hard that he couldn't move.

His hand moved to the small of my back and he squeezed hard, pushing even deeper into me. I could feel the piercings on the head of his cock penetrate somewhere that gave me a dull ache. Intensifying the stars around my head.

I was in ecstasy.

I screamed and howled, panted, and cried, shuddered and squirmed. I felt every inch of the orgasm as it tore through me like I had placed my hand on an electric fence. He thrust into me like I held every answer he had been longing for, for his entire suffering.

Like I was the cure.

The undoing.

Waves of pleasure rippled through me, and I climaxed again, again again, and again.

"Oh, fuck. Please. More. Huxley!" I begged thoughtlessly for him, more of him.

"Shit. Say it again," he ordered, arousal pounding him.

I wanted him deeper, and he delivered it. I needed everything he had even if it killed me, and saying his name out loud was a new rollercoaster of pleasure. Heat filled my core as my body responded to my desire.

"Huxley," I moaned breathlessly and he pushed himself harder. I whimpered through each of his thrusts, letting him consume me and fill me entirely. He tugged at his mask, bringing it to sit under his nose like the time before, and took to my mouth. I clenched and swelled around him as he drove his kiss into me and built his own orgasm, his body soon reacting, with one final thrust.

"Fuck, Esme. Fuck, fuck," he panted between my lips and held himself firmly against my body as he released himself, his warmth filling my pussy.

I felt his seed penetrate the top of my belly with such need and desperation. Claiming me entirely. The sound of his climax and possession he held over me took charge over my body, making me coil once more. Our breath formed into one... as did our molecules.

Shit.

It was there and then that I knew, and finally admitted that I was in love with a murderer. *My murderer.*

We dazed on the piano together for a moment, my body trembling uncontrollably along with his, staring at the ceiling before I finally had a breath to speak.

"Huxley?"

"Yes, my swallowtail?"

"Are you in love with me?" Granted, I didn't need to ask that. I already knew, and he had already said that he felt it too. But he didn't actually say it, not really.

"I think you know the answer to that."

That was a confirmation of my question.

Yes.

CHAPTER FIFTY-SEVEN

DOING IT HIS WAY

"Y ou studied butterflies, yes?" Huxley asked, pacing along the wall of his bookshelf.

"Entomology, yeah. I *was* nearly finished studying." I pursed my lips. I was so close to my finals and finishing college, but that was a very distant memory now. *Not that it was long ago.*

What in the life of Esme?

"Is that why you made all these?" he asked impishly, pulling out one of my favorite study books from the shelf on the wall. *The Papilio Palinurus – The Emerald Swallowtail* by Dr. W.K. Fresuold.

He opened the book and pulled out a plastic slip. I gasped, seeing that he had a ton of *my* butterfly drawings from the apartment, and from when I had been drawing on the terrace. *I knew it... the thief.* I frowned because of how much I had underestimated Huxley's knowledge of me.

"You... " I tried to find something offensive to say, but words failed me. I pushed the frustration aside and snatched the book, along with my drawings from his hands.

He snickered and crossed his arms over his bare chest. *Goddamn him and never wearing a shirt.* He was wearing his cape though... which also grew on me.

"I had been watching you for a while, but you knew that already. Your favorite color is emerald green, as are your eyes, your accessories and your favorite butterfly. Your shifts at the café were always 7 a.m. until 4 p.m. on Tuesdays, and 2 p.m. until 9 p.m. on Saturdays. Sundays you spent at church— sometimes in two different churches. Mondays, Wednesdays, and Thursdays you were deep in your studies, often finishing at home until very late. I think your go to comfort foods were peanut butter and jelly sandwiches, and black coffee... which you always managed to spill, given how stained your shirt always was. Actually, you are a very clumsy person, you always seem to fall over thin air. How am I doing so far?"

I nodded, not offering much else. Was he a true stalker or was I just that fucking easy to work out?

"Oh. How could I forget? You were born in May. It only makes sense why your favorite butterfly would be the Emerald Swallowtail. Green is quite simply put, the most *ravishing* color on you. I regret tearing that dress off you. I'll have more made for you," he said, stepping closer before trailing his finger along one of my art pieces that was in my hand.

"Because green really is quite beautiful, like you. *My* little swallowtail." He hummed "*my*" with a hint of possession, actually... a lot of possession. The butterflies in my stomach swirled like mad and my cheeks flushed crimson. I tittered, biting my lip to stop myself but my body just couldn't, making my grin stretch even further up my face.

Why do I feel... giddy?

"I love watching you squirm when you're nervous. You've just discovered how fucked up I really am, and yet... you're smiling."

I shrugged my shoulders. Trailing off, back into the memory of our sexually heated encounter only moments ago and the fact that the man was in love with me. My eyes widened, only now realizing that he had deposited his semen into me. *And on more than one occasion.* Until I had become a prisoner I was a virgin, and very much *not* on birth control. Which only meant the possibility of one thing... s*hit.* I shuddered, not letting another minute go by.

"Huxley?" I muttered in a panic.

"Yes, pet." He tilted his head, in the way he always did.

I ran my fingers over my mouth nervously, still trying to make sense that I was having a civil conversation with a psychopath. One that may very well have his baby growing in my gut.

"You, uhm. You know... inside me. Does that mean... ?" I stuttered, unable to comprehend the words. I think my hands did most of the talking than my own voice. *What a conundrum.* He chuckled deeply with an edge of darkness.

"You're only just now coming to terms with me releasing in you? Be that as it may, I'm sterile. I don't need my DNA floating around in dead bodies... you know, just in case." He added that last bit a little too easily—like it wouldn't hurt—but it did, and I let out a sigh.

Killer...

"I like claiming you," he purred, grabbing my cheeks. I melted to his touch, it was so... heavenly.

"I... like that too," I confessed thoughtlessly.

Killer.

Red flag.

Stop sign.

Caution.

Ding, ding ding!

Nope, through one ear and out the other, huh, Esme? Moral compass not here, me stupid. I scoffed at myself, I had gone utterly insane.

"Mmm. Maybe it wasn't an accident."

"What?" I murmured.

"Seeing you." He paused before continuing. "Maybe we were *meant* to meet. Maybe we were... made for each other." He spoke his confession like a question. I nodded, my mind absent of many words. I just wanted to see him. Under his mask. *How can I be in love with a man I've never seen? This is absurd.*

A minute or two passed as my head twisted and tormented me. Everything about it was so wrong... but so right. *But what happens now? What happens with the voice in the lake? The ritual, the offering, the death? What... is actually supposed to happen next? Can we be normal?* I pulled out everything in my being to burn the question.

"This voice in the lake... I mean, I know I heard her... it, whatever but... can you show me?" I asked in barely a squeak.

I wanted to see the voice thing, was she human? Or just a figment of his imagination that worsened over the years and was some kind of A.I speakerphone. I didn't understand it, but I needed to. Things like that didn't exist... not really. Do they?

He gulped, as though a sense of embarrassment.

"You don't believe me, do you?"

"I do, well I'm trying to. I've heard the voices myself. I

know it's there. But, I want to understand it more. I want to see what you see. I want to feel what you feel, so I can understand, well, you."

Huxley stilled and in an instant, the air felt cold and thin between us. I shivered.

"I can't do that," he snapped.

"Why?" I scowled at him. *Why the fuck not?* He moved me until I was at arm's length.

"You're forgetting that I still very much have very little power over the need to watch your life drain away, pet. It's who I am. And I will never change. My debt is written and I need my hell to finally end. Consider it like selling my soul to the devil." He paused for a moment, trailing his gaze over the cuts on my body before he continued. "And this time... I won't be able to hold back like I had done many times before. Because I can't hold *her* back."

"Then don't," I stammered without thinking. *Did I really just say that? Yes, I did.*

He tilted his head as if shocked by my response. He didn't reply so I trailed off. I guess, maybe I did know what I was doing. Offering myself to my death. If it meant my own freedom, I would do it. Because in reality, how could I come back from all of this?

If he let me go, what would I do? I had been through the mincer for christ's sake—I was a diabolical mess. What would my life be like outside? I'd be nothing, simply put. And I sure as shit wasn't going to stay in—wherever *here* was—in his personal prison, regardless of the way I felt about him.

So if he was falling in love with me, I needed to put a stop to it all, *now*. Before he falls any deeper and does not follow through with the sacrifice. Unless I killed myself first. But where would that leave him? Wounded, empty, living a life in a facade, and killing more innocent lives to fill a shitty void.

I couldn't take back the lives he had already taken, but if I was truly the piece of the puzzle for the whole madness, then I had the power to stop any more from happening. I knew that everything took place at the lake, so that was where we needed to go. Maybe I could reason with her? *That sounds insane.* I took a big breath.

"You say it's by a ritual right?"

"Yes," he admitted quietly with a nod.

"In the water?"

He nodded again.

"With blood, obviously." I was short and strong with my replies. There was no time for weakness. Besides, I had no damn clue how this freaking witchcraft bullshit worked, I'd read enough of Huxley's journal to make some sense of it all. I held out my hand and waited, gesturing it in a give-me action. He pulled his knife out and fidgeted with it as though he was feeling hesitant and confused?

"If you do this, we do it my way, okay?" he croaked.

"Okay."

He grabbed my chin, holding my contact with him, and then I smiled, I didn't know why... but I smiled, ear to ear. Ouch. I grimaced through the pain, and then he placed the knife against my lips and my eyes flared open, regret swam in my veins. *Why am I so foolish? Always with the brain malfunctions. My mouth? Why?*

I squeezed my fists together until I was certain my knuckles were white as the metal penetrated my skin. Heat and pain hounded through me but I stayed under his hold. He kept the pace, re-opening my welt from the corner of my lip outwards along my cheek—line for line.

A trail of blood followed the tears, and he repeated the laceration on top of the other one. He finally stopped and in an instant my body reacted, fitting into a sob.

Huxley rummaged around with something on the shelf and walked back with a rag in his hand, he quickly tugged it over my mouth and secured it behind my head. Deja vu hit me. The cloth felt wet but I accepted it anyway, *we do it his way.*

"So I don't hear your screams," he confessed softly. I felt a sense of numbness over my mouth but it quickly diminished and was replaced with splitting pain as he gave the knot one final tug.

The rag nuzzled into the welts tightly and the bleeding flowed a little faster. Or at least I thought it was blood. I shuddered and then he pulled out some chains and several ropes from another shelf. *Does he have these in every room of this place?*

He started to bind the ropes around me in the same perfect patterns as he always did. I lost my breath for a second and started to see double. *What the?* Suddenly the room started to spin. I blinked my eyes, but it didn't help.

I think I said something, but I couldn't be sure if it was the cloth that muted me or something else. Huxley sighed.

"It's so you can't move. I need you paralyzed, and unconscious," he said. *What?*

Why? The words didn't come out. Saliva pooled in my mouth and fuzz surrounded my eyes, what the hell did he do to me? I swayed, falling into him and he stroked his hand along my spine. "It's easier for me that way."

Terror roared through me and in an instant I regretted

everything I said. But the heaviness peaked and the darkness finally wrapped around me like a glove. *Oh, no—I'm not passing out again am I?!*

Yep.

The sound of his whimper as he threw me over his shoulder was the last droned sound that I heard.

CHAPTER FIFTY-EIGHT

THE MANIPULATOR

D *rip.*
Drip.

I blinked my eyes weakly, *what is that sound?*

Drip.

The sense of feeling heavy was the second reaction to alert me. *Am I... upside down?* I tried, but couldn't move my body. My heart beat pounded in my head, it was so loud. What happened? He had drugged me with something, but what?

The smell of pine pulled me entirely from my state of unconsciousness. I opened my eyes, seeing that it was dark. There was a hint of moonlight present; nothing like the time before, but still able to cast light to my location. I couldn't move my body. *Ow, my head!* I was indeed suspended upside down, and the ropes were pulled vigorously at my wounds that Caine had taped.

Drip.

I grumbled something but all that followed were just inaudible, muffled, wet sounds. The blood had been rushing to my head for God knew how long. I could feel it draining down over my cheeks and then my forehead before finally hearing it drip into the water.

What the fuck was I thinking? I can't do this. This was fucking insane.

My brain felt like it was going to explode, and there was a dull, burning ache radiating through my body, but it was only mild, assuming that the drug Huxley had given me was to blame. I was completely vertical and my limbs were curled into a pretzel.

The ropes held me by my waist and my knees, linked to chains. I couldn't tell exactly as my arms were secured behind my back and my ankles bound to my wrists. I was merely *dangling* above the lake, my head no less than two feet from the water. The fog had cloaked the forest, and the moonlight was reflecting over the water.

I could hear more shackles clinking and treading water nearing slowly. It sounded almost identical to when Huxley was threading a chain through his hands as it clinked over his rings. I frowned, not able to see where it was coming from. *Why did he have to paralyze me?*

A moment of time staggered by, hearing the sounds until two horns and the tip of Huxley's mask finally appeared in the corner of my vision. He was walking through the water beside me.

He sighed and then turned into my full vision. I could get a better look at him. He wasn't wearing his cape, only his jeans and his mask. I liked him better that way, more... human-looking. Even paralyzed, I could still appreciate him in all his glory.

I grumbled a bunch of wordless noises again as he held his hand under my head, seeing that my blood was dripping into his palm. *Fuck, how much was my mouth bleeding?* He was indeed holding a chain in his other hand, and I couldn't tell exactly, but it looked like it reached up above me, connecting to another set of shackles that I was hung by. *Chains... and ropes?* I guessed it had to be strong, considering I was hanging over a lake, using the trees as my harness point.

My head spun and thumped, I was fucking terrified but I think only because I couldn't move or scream, nor could I beg for my freedom... *if* I was to ask for it. He was gentle, and calming. He had only drugged me so that I *couldn't* beg for mercy, but was that for his sake... so he said.

I am now an easy kill for him... it... her? Completely paralyzed and voiceless. I can't hear anything yet, maybe she only comes out when the moon is full or something?

The blacks of his paint swirled around him even more, and his pink and white scars became more visible. With not an inkling of words, he began to let the chain slide through his hands. I whimpered against the bloody cloth, not really able to do or say much else in response from my body lowering slightly. He gripped and released it again, repeating in slow segments.

I couldn't deny the sense of feeling like he was stalling, or getting cold feet. My head was only millimeters from the water before he stopped again, taking a breath. Suddenly, he let go and my head was under the water.

Muted screams and bubbles of air were all I could manage, I had nothing. He held me there for a moment and then pulled me back above the surface. I filled my lungs with air, coughing for a breath. *Why did he stop? Come on. Get it over with. Jesus fucking Christ.*

He tensed and then yelled loudly, vibrating the water and startling me. I winced as the pitch almost blew my eardrums out. He punched every inch of air from his lungs. Suddenly a force of wind ripped through me, and the thick black smoke returned over the forest, and then over the lake like it had done once before. *She's here.* I held my breath feeling the familiar static voice echo, it was loud, and... furious?

"Aren't you forgetting something? The debt you owe to me." Her tone was muffled, but powerful.

"No. I won't let you. Just take me, please," he begged back. I could hear that his tears had returned.

"She is here right now, I can feel her. She is so pure." In an instant, her voice became hellish, possessive even. Giving the sense of a soul-sucking monster, like it held so much darkness and lies.

"I can't. Please!" Huxley belted another cry.

I blinked the fuzz that was washing over my head, I didn't know how much longer my body could hang this way without passing out... or dying. My head was throbbing and I didn't notice before, but my wounds were too, gravity was doing everything it could to mess with me.

"You don't want me to have her, do you?" She hissed again with every ounce of jealousy possible, like a snake. Her tone was vaporous. *"You want her for yourself. You love her, don't you?"* she added. The visual of smoke like fog thickened, closing around him, and me. I suspected that I was hallucinating because those things didn't happen in reality. *This isn't real. This can't be real.*

But it was.

"You won't take her!" Huxley snapped, backing away to the water's edge, still holding the chain that held me above water.

I couldn't pin what he would have running through his head. Was he really going to fight her... for me? If he was going to take her, that meant he truly did mean what he said when he felt it too. But what does that mean for him? Another debt?

"Unfaithful little serpent. You're forgetting that I can make you do it easily. You are too weak. Just like you are without your mask. But you already knew that, didn't you? Did you really think that she would ever love you? You are pathetic. Unlovable."

Her voice paused, and more of the static buzz ripped through the air, piercing my ears far greater than Huxley had done a moment ago. For a second, it sounded that perhaps she was... growling? Rumbling with anger, or something.

"I'm only going to ask you one more time, my dear. Give her to me. Then you will be free."

It was silent for a moment and then Huxley bellowed out again and abruptly tied the chain around a tree so I wouldn't drop into the water. He sobbed and began to tread his way back through the water again, stopping at an old pillory. *What? Was that there before?*

I blinked again with furrowed brows, I hadn't seen it before, but then again, it was always dark so maybe it was always out of sight. I winced as I watched him cut through his skin deeply with the knife three times before locking his head and then both hands into the pillory.

Crackles sounded through the air like an old record, louder, crisper, shattering from near and then far, left then right. It was truly terrifying. I could barely hold myself together, everything in my body was pounding.

"I'll die first!" he screamed loudly... in pain. *Invisible pain.* Again, and again.

Her wrath.

My tears mimicked his as I faintly watched him torment

himself, fighting a war that I couldn't fight for him. What debt he had with her was far greater than just an offering of freedom. He was a slave to that thing, and he wanted out.

Huxley had wandered down a dark paranormal hole—one that deserved to stay in the ethereal realm where it belonged. But like me, his curiosity had peeked, and created a binding contract when he offered himself to her for his freedom of pain and suffering.

A payment: his blood, bones, flesh, soul, and whatever else he had mentioned. Only somehow *I* had stopped the sacrifice, thus becoming the debt he owed that weighed heavily on his shoulders.

For six years.

I had a bounty on my head... for revenge.

"If you do, your debt will fall to her." Her tone had completely softened, like that of an angel. She really did remind me of a siren, her melodic voice was so celestial... luring, even. *How can it change so much?*

Was she a demon? *The devil?*

Or greater?

"No, please. I—"

"Then you leave me no choice. You'll see. I will make you suffer a million deaths until you pay your debt. I will hail upon you a wrath that you cannot survive. A pain you cannot handle," she sounded again with every ounce of jealousy and loathing through her tone—again, changing in an instant.

My heart pounded to his screams and cries, I couldn't be sure what she was doing to him, or how, but he sounded as though he was in a type of pain that even I didn't know... *and I had been butchered meat.* Moments passed of hearing him, he never once bent or broke to submission. He stood his ground to her orders. Fighting for me.

"Please. Just take me with you. Let her g—" Huxley muttered, and then a blood-curdling scream roared like someone had pierced a knife through his back. His pained screeches echoed throughout the forest for a while longer before he eventually fell heavy against the pillory, drifting into a state of unconsciousness, as was I.

I was holding on by a mere thread of hope. How long could a weak, wounded, bleeding human hang upside down for? I didn't have the answer, but I knew it could not be much longer, my eyes were almost closed, and my brain was painfully dizzy, like I had just come off a rollercoaster ride.

Through faded vision I could see that the black air, void, deathly shadow... whatever it was, was diminishing. *What about me? What's going to happen to me now?* Panic set in again but not a limb or muscle in my body would move at my brain's request. Unconsciousness began to cloak me again.

Come on, wake up, Huxley!

Wake.

Up.

My eyes felt heavy but I tried to fight them, realizing that each time I blinked, there was a change. *Wait, is my chain slipping? Is someone lowering me?* Suddenly, something blindfolded me and a pair of arms cradled my body, and *not* the arms of Huxley. I tried, but screaming, kicking, or wriggling didn't work because none of those orders from my brain to my body registered. All I could do was muffle a tune that sounded like a drunken, disorderly noise.

Acting on adrenaline, I tried to smell who it might have been, but the blood had clogged some of my nose, and I couldn't make out a scent. Whoever was holding me unhooked my bonds with a sharp knife.

I laid my eyes heavy again, my body holding on by a single percent of strength and hope, only partially aware that I was being carried somewhere. Without warning, I was launched into an opening without so much as a sliver of courtesy, my body crash landing into what I imagined to be a trunk. Defenseless. I couldn't move or scream, but I *could* cry. *What the fuck is going on? This feels like Deja vu.*

A moment of silence haunted me until the voice laughed, and then spoke.

"You're mine now, bitch," he hissed, and then the boot slammed shut, vibrating the thud into my eardrum.

Fucking Damon.

CHAPTER FIFTY-NINE

HIDDEN

I ntense ringing in my ear and heat tugged at my state of unconsciousness. *Why am I so hot?* The feeling of forcing my body to wake up was familiar, because almost every time I woke up, I had gotten there by passing out. I hated it.

I made sense of a presence near me and as the ringing sound slowly washed out I could hear crackles of a cigarette being drawn in. The fiery heat splitting through paper like it was right next to my ear.

My head pounded violently, but yet again I was not given the satisfaction of moving my limbs. How long did this paralytic last? *Where the fuck am I? Where is Huxley?* I blinked, it was dimly lit and all I could see was a cherry red cigarette sparkling before me, followed by a pungent cloudy exhale.

Heat stung my eyes and I coughed and gasped for a wad of fresh air. I soon felt the sensation of being sweaty, noticing the air was hot, and thick, and my toes were tingling. Why did they tingle? *Maybe the drug is wearing off?*

I opened my eyes again. Damon was standing before me with

his cigarette in the side of his mouth and a devilish grin that didn't reach his eyes. I looked down to see that I was not only tied by rope to a fucking chair, but I was also chained *and* padlocked to the floorboard.

I summoned all that I had and tried squirming; surprised that I managed to make a small movement against the taut ropes, but it didn't come without the pounding at my head to worsen. *Okay, it's definitely wearing off... I wonder if I can speak?*

I tried to go with *let me out*, but the rag around my mouth muffled my words. Though I didn't need words, my facial expression was enough. He said nothing. What in the ever-loving fuck was I doing with Damon? His signature unsettling, devilish laugh broke from his mouth. Whatever intentions he had for me was utterly terrifying. Given the last time I saw him, he had tried to mince my reproductive organ before storming off like a toddler having a tantrum.

My breath staggered, everything about him was more haunting than Huxley. *"I am ten times worse than he will ever be. I don't hesitate."* Damon's words hit me in my memory. I swallowed down the thickness at my throat, relieving nothing. I tried moving again and was able to tilt my head slightly, seeing that we were in a little cabin.

A *tiny*, wooden cabin—and *no* windows. Only barely lit by a flickering candle or two on the floor in the corner. Panic continued to havoc in my veins, becoming more aware of my surroundings. *Holy shit it's terribly hot in here.*

Too hot.

He stayed silent, watching me pull myself to the here and now. I trailed my thoughts into any, and all possible theories on where we might be and why he had taken me. Jealousy was my first suspicion, but I feared that *this* was far greater than petty sibling rivalry over a girl.

He had said that I was his now, when Damon closed me in the trunk. *Why? Come on, Esme. Think.* What were the last threads of memory? I think I remembered hearing the car driving, but I couldn't be certain of how far the drive was. It could have been minutes, hours, or days even, and knowing Damon... it would be the furthest away from anyone possible. And now I was—*here*—wherever *here* was.

Great! I decided at that moment that I would rather take Huxley's promised death for me than be stuck with Damon. I didn't think I could hate a person more, back to square one because of the fucking ass hat. I stared at him with a deathly glare, and he laughed again. I was slowly becoming more apparent with my body and everything that was happening to it, it wasn't good, because nausea threatened to hurl from my mouth. Pain was thundering in with great force, most of it in my head. How long I had been held upside down was anyone's guess.

I winced, and scrunched up my face, feeling the rag had stuck to my wound. My heart skipped a beat as Damon began to circle me, like a vulture. I could smell him past the metallic tang of my blood that had clotted my nose as the air wafted, the masculine woody low tones of his cologne mixed with hate, revenge, leather, whiskey, sweat, and cigarette.

He said nothing, did nothing, only circled me for long enough that I spun dizzy. The heat of the cabin was starting to coincide with my breath, giving the sensation of a slow suffocation. I started slipping into heaviness again, and I closed my eyes. *No! Fuck.*

Tsss.

I screamed into the cloth from a sudden, sizzling blow of hot pain over a torn open wound on my arm. I looked up, seeing that Damon had pressed the end of his cigarette into my skin. It pulled me entirely back into consciousness once more, and tears freed from my eyes.

Have I not been through enough? I wish I didn't scream, because it makes my brain hammer and the room to spin. What is happening to me? This feels like vertigo, and with a really intense headache.

Damon crossed his arms and tensed.

"Wake up," he hissed. The burn of his vindictive voice was just as sharp as the one he left on me. He was ropeable. For what? I observed him standing before me, his cold gaze was lifeless. Loveless. His lean yet masculine torso glistened from sweat in the candlelight, and his chest was expanding to his corrosive breath. If Damon wanted any more reactions from me, he certainly wasn't going to get it, I had nothing left to give... even if he forced it from me. I had gone through too much. *Too much.*

He yanked the cloth that was over my mouth down and I whimpered from the pain, feeling as though parts of my skin tore right off with it.

"Ah," I cried out, surprised that I could mutter out something more than a grumbled squeak or slur. A brutal grin pulled at his lips as he trailed his thumb over the resurfacing blood on my cheeks. I flinched to the torment. *Yes, I can feel movement coming back.*

I shifted to pull my head away and put all my energy into forming a sentence.

"Get the. Fuck. Away from. Me," I hissed, unintentionally

dragging out each word as I struggled to pronounce them. *God I sound like a stroke victim.*

"Oh, good, you can speak again. I simply can't do any form of torture when my hostage is mute," he mocked.

"What do you w-want, Damon?" I asked.

"You just won't die will you?" He furrowed his brow, curling his lip in disgust and continued. "I want to play with my new toy, without limits or rules. Besides, we never finished where we left off. "

No—I won't. And certainly not on your watch.

I sighed, I had bigger problems than a void to deal with, I had a Damon to worry about. Huxley's voice echoed in my head, *"and this time... I won't be able to hold back. I can't hold her back."*

Sadness started to flood me, the void had said she would hail upon Huxley a wrath he cannot survive for not offering me to *her.* A pain that he cannot handle. Unease tore through my stomach, coinciding with bile. *He is going to suffer... for me... again?*

I couldn't help but agree with her in one sense; that she was right. And that frustrated me painfully. He *was* too weak. He *couldn't. He wouldn't.* But my body was proof that he would always try... and that was what made him a monster. It was part of him, whether he accepted it or not. Mask on, or mask off. He enjoyed hurting me. He *enjoyed* being like her.

I finally pulled my attention back to Damon, who was taking a little too much pleasure in staring at my naked body before him. I would have thought I would be used to it by now, but I wasn't. *Ugh.* Revolt curled my lip at the memory of him forcing his body on mine, and his knife on my private area. I hated the fucker.

Spit swarmed in my mouth somehow climbing over dehydration. I saw an opportunity, and without hesitation, collected the liquid over my tongue and spat it at him. *Well... it landed next to him. But it still counts, fucker. Take that!*

He barely moved an inch, only leaning over slightly to glare at the hoagy on the floor beside him, before turning his dark eyes to mine and arching a brow.

"I'm going to pretend I didn't see that," he scoffed and trailed off, pacing back and forth in the cabin. He made the room spin but I held my own, somehow. "It seems my... *brother* has some kind of obsession with you. He just can't fucking kill you," he snapped playfully and tutted.

"Oh, brother. If only we could go back to the way it was before he had that accident. Uncle Soren was kind enough to take us all in. One by one over the years. Little lost, helpless, and homeless boys... and Ruby." Damon paused again to light up another cigarette and take a swig of whatever alcohol he had from a flask in his pocket. "Such a great life we had. Then *your* man decided to try and kill himself. That's when *our* lives changed."

My man? My eyes followed him as he paced circles around me, popping in and out of my line of sight. I hadn't a single clue as to why he had to share his life stories with me.

"He's not—"

"Shh, I'm speaking," he cut me off. I had tried to deny my relationship with Huxley, he wasn't my man. As much as I wanted that, it simply couldn't happen. "As I was saying... *he* had become hungry for death, desperate to kill for his freedom. Then he got *us* involved. He made us fucking suffer through his bullshit, living a life we didn't want, for him. So, eventually, we made a little corporation that worked for everyone. And do you know what we did?"

"No."

"Come on, not even one little guess?" He pushed.

"I don't know, Damon," I stuttered, wanting no part in his stupid games.

"Fine, I'll just tell you then. We find the girls, we fuck 'em, and he kills 'em," he sighed pleasurably with a groan. "We had it good. We got the babes. We didn't even need to woo them. Nothin'. We got what we wanted anyway, regardless of what they said... mmm, so much pussy. But that wasn't even the best part." He leaned forward, blowing his cigarette smoke into my face *again*. I coughed but didn't show emotion.

"I learned something about myself. I liked to hurt people. Torture innocent little lives for my enjoyment." Damon's tone was etched with jealousy and rage.

"What the fuck is your deal?" I snapped, the nausea really taking charge, and then he convulsed in laughter.

"Mmm. Aren't you a little fire-breathing dragon? You never used to be. But you see, he has changed, Esme. And I don't know if I can let that happen," Damon continued, though I almost didn't hear him at first as the ringing in my ear was whistling again. "We let him fill his delusions while we got to have our fun. *But...* then it all went to shit because he actually found you."

Why is he telling me this? I wanted to ask but my face asked for him.

"You're still not getting it are you? If he kills you, so does the *corporation* and my addiction along with it." He laughed again, mockingly, using quotation fingers as he said corporation. I turned my cheek away, I couldn't bear to look at him anymore. "I like to hunt for victims, I like to hurt people, I like to kill people, and I *love* fucking... *dead* people," He roared with a curled lip.

A small hint of bile reached my mouth, and the acid stung the part of my cheek that ached. Tears began to stream, heavy and with no sign of stopping. *Dead people? Dead people? This was vile, putrid.*

"I have that cunt to blame for my addiction. Six fucking years of his crap. Six fucking years of isolation and deranged behaviors. But once I got a taste for it I couldn't stop. So maybe, if I take away the problem, he will eventually forget about you. And we can go back to the way it was. I'm sure someone else will fill his fantasies."

"You're a pig," I spat again, and he shrugged.

"Yes, I am. And now you're mine. Little piggy."

I pursed my lips. "Fuck y—"

I couldn't finish the rest of my scowl because the familiar gun I had once been acquainted with was at my chin before I had the chance. The cool metal planting on my skin sent my body into a shiver, an odd sensation given how hot I was. But I wasn't giving in to him, no matter how much he scared me.

Act... don't react.

The weapon had a unique smell to it. It was not a rusty scent, instead, it was like a wet steel kind of smell. I couldn't put the words to describe the rest of the smells. The whites of my eyes grew larger as his thumb gently pressed the hammer of the weapon down, followed by the infamous sound of a bullet rotating in the chamber, and then clicking into a loaded position. Hair spiked from my body in an instant.

"I'm going to enjoy fucking the smart ass right out of that mouth. Fuck it until you foam. Fuck it until you can no longer breathe. And then I'll throw you around like a pitbull has found a stuffed toy to play with," he mocked in a predatory demeanor through his teeth, keeping his eyes on mine with a cocked brow. I trembled, feeling very sorry for myself and hopeless.

There was something different about a gun than there was a knife, like your life was less valuable. He began to trail it up closer to my mouth, and forced my lips to part with a firm nudge. I followed his command because that was what you did when you had a gun pointed at you. You do as they say, right? I gulped as the barrel smoothed its way through my lips, wincing from the pain as my cheeks cracked open a little more to the pressure, and immediately weeping blood again.

I cried out, feeling the heat of my breath steam over the metal and recirculate around my mouth. I didn't want to give in to crying, I really didn't, and not because the fucking jackass didn't deserve my tears, but because I knew crying would make my head pound more than it already was.

He held the gun in the void of my mouth and then teased the belt of his jeans with his other hand, inclining that he was going to pull himself from his pants. I thoughtlessly dropped my eyes, regretfully seeing that his pants were very taut... and throbbing. *Fuck.*

"Even with a gun in your mouth. You're fucking mental," he threatened and pushed it further into my mouth, leaving me no choice but to whimper as my cheeks stretched more. I shook my head slightly, as that was all I could. Damon pivoted the gun in the same direction as he pivoted his head. "Yes. So mental. You're too fun to just... *kill*. That's all he wanted you for. You are worth nothing to him."

An involuntary tear threatened to leave my eyes, but I argued against it and then a rogue grin turned his lips, making the dimples protrude. "Oh no… " He laughed, rolling his head back. "You like the son of a bitch."

"Mm-mh," I muffled my denial, unable to say much else over the gaps between the weapon and my lips. Granted, that was a lie. A big fat one, and he knew it too. He could clearly see right through me.

"No, you don't. You *love* him. And he loves you, doesn't he?" His tone was contemptuous like the word was a sin. *"That's* why he couldn't kill you. Pathetic."

He pulled the gun from my mouth in a scoff and I licked at my broken flesh, tasting the fresh blood instantly over the broken skin. It hurt, but it was nothing to my head. Of all people, I wished Caine would come to my rescue, I knew he was good— great—at mending me.

"Mhmm, mmm, mmmm. This changes things now. I think it will destroy him if I destroy you. What do you think?"

"He's already done that," I snarled, dropping my head to avoid eye contact again.

"Not as much as I can. Hurting him, making him suffer will be a far better reward for me than fucking lifeless bodies."

Finally, that tear that I fought so hard to not let fall came crashing as I let that truth swarm me like bees in a hive. *How could I have been so foolish?* Damon was right, I was mental. I was broken, faulty, and obviously very defective. Huxley had really fucked me up, physically, mentally, and emotionally.

My body was covered from head to toe in old, and fresh wounds, some under repair with tape glue, others with a needle and thread. I had been drugged, drained of blood on more than one occasion, hung like a puppet, and chased through the woods. I have had my virginity and dignity taken from me, my body exposed and humiliated, starved, drowned, chained, tortured, caged. I have had glass plunged through my feet... that I almost forgot, because above all else, it was *not* the worst thing to have happened to me since it all began.

My chest tightened. I looked down at my legs that were tied to the chair, some of the surgical tape Caine dressed my wounds with was still on, but the rest had fallen off... or been ripped off by the rope I was hanging by at the lake. They were red, raised, bruised, and ugly to look at.

I was ugly to look at.

But at least the infection was gone, which only made me more frustrated because it was just another thing that stopped me from dying after being so close to being killed.

Fuck my life.

CHAPTER SIXTY

ON FILM

I had been sitting in the same position for at least twenty minutes, watching Damon as he paced the floor of the cabin that felt like a sauna. I didn't have a watch, but I had counted over a thousand mississippi's in my head. He had lit cigarette after cigarette as if he were a chimney.

With each passing minute that had gone by, the more the drugs wore off, becoming further apparent that I was in a *very* bad way. My face had started to feel tight and numb, as though I couldn't move it. And it wasn't because I was having a brain-to-body malfunction. Something bad was happening, but I didn't know or understand what.

I had brief thoughts that maybe I was having a stroke, but I was only twenty-one, that wouldn't be possible, or if it was... only very little chance of it happening. But then again, maybe it *was*... *I mean,* I did hang upside down for an astronomical amount of time, dripping blood and was still very much healing fresh wounds from an infection that was caused by swimming in carcass infected waters after being sliced up like grandma's Sunday roast.

Yeah, a stroke would be the most logical answer to my problems.

I frowned, seeing Damon's facial expression change, the feeling that he had just worked out his plan for me had just popped into his head.

I studied him for a minute and he pulled out a phone from his pocket and then placed it on the floor in the corner so that it was sitting horizontally. He tapped a button, bringing up the camera, and flipped it. Relying on one or two candles wasn't going to cut it for a video but I could still see my feet, carnaged legs, folded belly, flattened breasts by the ropes and whatever else was left of me. I hadn't seen myself since catching my reflection in the car before Caine had found me. I was in a bad way then, but *now?*

Don't ask.

"Say anything stupid, and I'll put a bullet between your eyes. Got it?" he growled with one hundred percent honesty, flaring his nose and gesturing to the phone. I nodded my submission straight away, knowing this fucker had a phone gave me a good dose of hope.

Beads of sweat trickled down his forehead, it was really fucking hot. But adrenaline had spiked too high, there was no bowing to the darkness... *yet.*

He grinned once more and tapped the record button before walking slowly around me like he was the main star of the show. Dreading his next move now that he had the incentive to piss someone off. I shrieked as his knife met my neck, right under my chin where he had held the gun. I remembered Damon's knife like it was only yesterday... was it? A week? A month? Who knew.

Damon trailed the knife along the nape of my neck slowly as he positioned himself behind me, taking along a chunk of my hair with him. I sniveled, sniffing back the flow of tears. He groaned.

"Now, I'm going to make sure that you, and every other cunt knows... that I own you now," he whispered loudly in my ear before jolting upright and glaring into the camera.

"You hear that, brother? Your little bitch is *mine* now. And you wanna know something else?" He paused, shoving his knife straight into my thigh at a vertical angle with everything he had, plowing it right into a wound that Huxley had already cut open.

Flames of pain flooded me, a hollow unknown noise was the first sound that came from somewhere very deep in my body. Finally reaching my throat, I screamed, hard and loud. I trembled and white static smacked my vision, uncharted territory. This pain was excruciating.

"You will *never* find her," Damon added. "Revenge on my brother is so much more fun than fucking the rest of those helpless souls, living or dead. I loved claiming their tight little assholes, penetrating them so fucking hard that their organs rearranged, and then waiting just a few minutes after they die so I could fuck their still-warm bodies. And then again, when they're stone cold. So why go to all that trouble for him, when I can do all of that with you for twice the glory? God, I could cum right now, just thinking about it."

I gulped down the bile that kept pooling in my mouth, and suddenly I began to heave. What would I throw up? Nothing. Day old toast? Chunks of foam slivered from my mouth down my chin. I thought Huxley was sick, but Damon was a beast no human could compare to. I cried, hard. I prayed in my head for Huxley. But what if he couldn't break free from the pillory?

"Huxley! Please. Help me, please," I cried out for him, and without warning, the knife was yanked from my thigh and swung across my face, splitting the skin along the arc of my cheekbone with the tip of the blade.

I was seeing stars once more. My leg throbbed in the absence of the weapon and blood dribbled down it—with a sustained injury like this, there was not a single chance in hell I would be alive by the time someone found me. I trembled at the reality. *I am going to die in here, and it will have all been for nothing.*

"Silly girl. What did I say?" he hissed, and then squatted before me.

"Do you have any idea how many times he has tried to kill you? He even gave you the opportunity to run at the lake the first time, but... " he said, and I snapped my glare at him. How the fuck did he know about Huxley walking away from me? His grin was like I had just turned on the devil and given him ammo.

"Oh... you didn't know I was there, did you? Watching. You are pathetic. The both of you are. You really just couldn't stay away, could you... *pet*?" he said mockingly, using the words Huxley had said to me. "You wanted his cock, didn't you?"

I shook my head not having the ability to offer much else. How fucking dare he use Huxley's pet name on me? The very tang it left on my soul ruffled me.

"You weren't ever really scared of him, huh? He wasn't *scary* with you. You like his darkness... what he *allowed* you to see. You like what it does to you. You'd be happy to be buried to the sounds of his name. And you like the pain he brings you, hmm? You see something in him that he buried years ago. I know that he see's that too because he fucking changed, and I can't have that. He weakened. It all makes sense now," he muttered.

"What does?" I whispered in a mere squeak.

"You are his rain," Damon tutted before continuing, all smart ass activated in his tone. "I've never had that... because of him. Someone to claim for myself. Someone that would beg me for more, someone to—"

"Love?" I answered for him. "No one could ever love you, Damon, you're an empty soul," I finished the rest of my sentence with as much breath as I could muster. He grunted and rolled into another laugh. *This mother fucker and his sneering laugh. I hated him so much. Everything he did annoyed me now.*

"Meh," He shrugged. "So long as I have you, my brother is suffering. The same way he has made us suffer. And that gives me great pleasure." Damon winked as he adjusted himself, and his dark eyes glared at me through his long brown lashes.

His deep blue eyes pierced through my soul with no signs of life left. He was a jealous, homicidal psychopath. And a necrophiliac. A dangerous combination. Damon pushed my knees apart and began to secure them with another thread of rope so that they were pried open, and non-closable.

"Ah!" I yelped as his knife found the same area that he had tried to torment earlier, *my labia.* "What are you going to do?"

My head pounded through my cries as he lingered there with the sharp edge just applying pressure.

"I'm going to carve my initials into your skin silly, show him that you belong to me. And then I'm going to fuck you. I'm going to fill this little cunt with my cum while he watches. I'm going to mark *my* territory. Don't forget to smile!"

I bellowed the most spine-chilling screams, and wriggled against the ropes to my best ability, pushing through the pain and torment of my throbbing head as Damon began to slowly slide the knife over my pussy's skin. I tried so hard to clench my legs together but failed miserably against my restraints. He let out a wry cackle.

"Hmm someone has already beat me to it." He paused for a second, on purpose. "Oh... right. *Me.*"

The sick fuck, no—there was a better word for men like Damon.

C.

U.

N.

T.

CHAPTER SIXTY-ONE

D.W

S tars floated around my head and I shuddered, and then the tangy taste of blood pooled over my tongue, almost as fast as it was over my thigh. Feared and heated sweat trickled down my forehead. I rolled my head back to try and diminish the pain that consumed me, but it was no use.

Damon broke into a fit of laughs and pushed down harder with his knife against the sensitive skin inside the fold of my pussy, twirling it in a pattern. I begged and pleaded for him to stop but it only fueled him to drive harder. *What the fucking fuck is going to happen to me?*

"Fuck, you're going to make me cum if you scream like that again. That sound is just too nice. You... in pain, is my favorite noise you make," he snarled erotically.

I couldn't be certain of how long it lasted, but immense amounts of air hurried into my lungs when he stopped. I shivered, becoming aware that Damon had carved the initial of his last name. *W.*

"Now... the other side." Damon's tongue rolled over his lips. Arousal was well and truly at his disposal.

I worked hard in catching my breath but the unwelcoming sensation of blur at my eyes again hit me like a drunken sailor. Now that he had stopped, I could feel the rest of my body. The stab wound on my thigh was trickling uncontrollably. I couldn't look, because I knew that if I did, I would be wearing a layer of bile along with the blood.

I shook my head in disbelief, and the snot and tears blew out with a cough, though I wasn't certain they were tears that time. *Why is my face so numb?* Unable to speak a single word, I fitted into a shock of tremors as he started to carve another pattern on my other labia... my left one.

The pain plunged my mind into a state of near unconsciousness, only able to hear the ringing in my ear and blurred lines in my vision. The scraping and carving of the knife finally stopped again and I shouldn't have looked, I really should not have—it was the initial *D*.

"D.W... *fuck*," he groaned under his breath, taking a step back to admire his handy work. "That pussy looks fine wearing my name."

I ignored him, barely processing his words. My chest was aching from heaving and the snot spouting from my nose made it hard to breathe. I caught sight of his erection throbbing vigorously against his jeans, if it throbbed any harder it was going to tear through them.

"It's a pity, really. Because, no matter how many times I do this, no one is going to see it, in the flesh anyway. Pardon the pun, 'lil piggy."

I stared at him emptily, barely holding on. I needed to fight this, if I passed out what would happen to me? *He will fuck me. Though, what is worse? Being awake while he rapes me... or will it be a blessing to be insensible while he does?* I blinked away the sweat that trickled into the groove of my eye, pushing away my intrusive thoughts.

"Well, that is before the maggots and humidity decompose your flesh, leaving you as nothing but an empty corpse," he prowled his vicious words as he wiped my blood from his knife with the cloth that was around my mouth.

I gulped and panted slowly. It was inevitable. I was going to die at the hands of Damon, and the only thing I could think of was how much I wanted to be in the arms of Huxley. I would rather die a thousand deaths for Huxley than one for Damon.

Denial was a fucking bitch... *love* was a fucking bitch. I was *in* love with the shadow man, my God damn fucking shadow. If I was to die then and there, then I wanted the whole world to know that I loved him. The camera was still recording so I summed everything in my being and let it out.

"I. Love. *Him*," I sobbed, barely able to format the words, but nonetheless, they came out clearly.

I dreaded the next reaction Damon would give me. Would it be the bullet to my head? Or would I get another initial carved somewhere else? Not that it meant anything now. Huxley wasn't in the cabin to stop him. He would never find me. I was only fooling my damn self. He probably wouldn't even come looking for me.

Maybe Damon was right, that Huxley would just fixate himself on another helpless victim. Suddenly, I felt a shift in my body. Like my heart sank. *Is this... heartbreak? Is this what that feels like?* Damon laughed, as if he knew my exact thoughts.

"Too late for that now, bitch. You're mine, not his." He offered me a wink before rolling his head around a circle, loosening his shoulders like he was about to run a marathon, and blew a rapid blow of air.

He pulled a key from his pocket and unlocked one of the padlocks that were secured around my ankle and the shackle on the floor. He left the chain wrapped around it and repeated the same process on my other leg, and then started unthreading the ropes binding around my legs.

Both legs freed and I grimaced from the sudden movement, but I didn't close them. As much as I wanted to, there was no way I could move my leg without the gash spouting, it had only just lowered to a steady trickle.

Damon was quick with his movements and yanked my left leg across to the other side of the chair, twisting my limb with the pressure, and then locked it into place at the shackle. I cried out, I was now cross-legged.

The pain intensified and the alarm bells in my ears rang loud again. I was hurting in three different places. My thigh from the stab, both legs from muscle stretching like a pretzel, and the burning sensation on my pussy as both of my labia were now colliding.

He loosened the rope that was around my stomach and untied my wrists. I couldn't tell if I was still immobile from the drug Huxley had given me or because I had been bound for so long, but I could barely move, a slight wriggle was all I could bear. Damon pulled me upright and as he did my body automatically turned the opposite direction, untangling my legs.

Immense pain flooded my thigh, and I knew for certain if I looked at it the blood would have picked up the pace. The muscles in his arms swelled against his skin as he held the weight of me, not that there was much of me left. I shivered, and was now facing the back of the chair.

"Sit," he commanded.

"But I... " I felt dizzy even speaking a few words, but pushed them out. "I can't move my legs."

"Then fall," he said with a grin. Damon let go of me and my body swayed slightly with my weight on one leg. How I didn't collapse there and then like a bag of concrete I didn't know.

My head pounded with fog and vertigo, taking my breath away. Damon scoffed impatiently and pushed me. I managed to land on the chair with my legs to the side. He padlocked me in place to the shackles on the floor. I sobbed again and buried my forehead into the chair, letting myself drift slightly.

He grabbed my hip and pulled me back slightly so that my ass and pussy hung off the edge of the chair and then tied my legs from where my knees and thighs connected, looping the rope under the chair and pulling them tight. He sectioned off a few rows around back so that my breasts pressed firmly against the back of the chair before tying my wrists behind my back. I was pinned tight, unable to move, in a prime position for anything to happen back *there*.

"Mmm, *fuck*," Damon groaned. I shuddered from his arousal. "He wasn't joking when he said you looked good in ropes. But now you're bound for me, and not him. I couldn't think of anything better. And your ass at that angle... ah, fuck me. I can't *wait* to tear it open. I do love a chubby bitch, more to carnage."

"Rot in hell!" I spat but it only made him smirk with glee, I could hear it in his voice.

"I hate that I didn't get to be the first to rip through your canvas, though I will be your last. Crimson is my favorite color, and a knife is my favorite brush."

He ushered to face me and pulled himself from his jeans, freeing his erection. The veins were pumping hard against his skin like his arms were. My mouth dried and I was very unready for what he was about to do to me. "*I'm going to fuck you. I'm going to fill this little cunt with my cum while he watches. I'm going to mark my territory.*" Damon's corrosive words punched me in the gut.

"Now… you're going to be a good little slut and open wide for me," he said with a cocked brow.

I curled my lip but did as I did he slammed two fingers into my mouth, shoving right to the back of my throat. I gagged on impact, feeling the tear on my cheek again. Saliva pooled under my tongue and dripped out of my mouth.

"Rules. If you clamp down on me, I hurt you. More than I did to that little cunt of yours, and this spot right here… " He pressed on my thigh, right next to the stab wound, only with enough pressure to make me react. But it was enough to send circles in my head. "Do you fucking understand?" He hissed, pressing his thumb under my chin against the fingers in my mouth.

I cried out and coughed for mercy. All I could proffer was a gargle. His antagonizing blackened eyes pounded through my nearly lifeless ones, but through the glass of tears and defeat I nodded, submitting to all the weakness he desired against my will.

And with that, he yanked his fingers out and shoved his length in, grabbing the sides of my head as he rolled his head back against his thrusts. The tip of his shaft hit the nether of my esophagus and my throat swelled to take all of him. I gagged hard, though I had experienced him in my mouth before, he penetrated with much more effort. I panted whatever breaths I could rummage through my snot-filled nose as he pulled and pushed himself into building his climax.

I accepted it without the opportunity of rejection or denial. Unless I wanted a bullet to my head... *which now that I think of it, I wanted.* Very much so.

Used and abused.

But I had to hold on to the glimmer of hope that maybe, just maybe, my shadow might come looking for me. After all, he was the best stalker I knew. He had found me once before.

Lathers of white started to collect around my lips and his moans were aggressive and feral, like a wild animal. He was pulling my hair as balance, tingling the scalp, but that was the least of my pains. I needed to focus on my breathing, and the only way I knew I could manage that, was the thought of Huxley.

I pinched my eyes closed and let my mind wander. I imagined him finding me, I imagined that he needed me living more than he needed me dead. Because the truth was, I *needed* him, no matter how much death was at my doorstep for him. No matter how much the darkness cloaked him.

I was *the* offering. *His* offering... for his freedom. I wanted him to see Damon's video more than ever. And if he was right, it would destroy Huxley entirely, watching Damon hurt me like he was. Was my suffering enough motive to *never* stop looking for me? Would he turn the world upside down to find me? He had stood up against the shadow for me, so that gave me hope that maybe... just maybe, he would.

I battered my eyes to Damon pulling himself from my mouth, and then staggered somewhere behind me. I prepared myself mentally for his excessively large, warm cock to fill my entrance, but I could only elicit a feral scream as if my soul had exited my body for what *actually* inserted me.

The familiar cold, metallic sensation rippled through my folds with great force.

The barrel of his gun.

CHAPTER SIXTY-TWO

JUST LET ME ROT

I cried out hard to the torment that I never thought I'd experience in my entire life, my brain felt like it was splitting into two. Damon twisted and twirled the gun's shaft in a rhythmic pattern, teasing and caressing *the* spot in my pussy.

Denial and self-pity swam through my veins. It did something to me I didn't think could happen, for reasons I didn't understand. *What the fuck?* I scolded myself again, trying to think of anything else other than the possibility of me enjoying it, but the pressure of it hitting the knot was impossible to ignore. *Oh, no... fucking hell no.*

I needed a plan, stat. *Just think of Huxley doing this, and it will be over quickly. Don't show fear or pain, Damon likes fear and pain.* The vision of Huxley was quick to power into my mind, and the thought of it sent an involuntary breathy moan to part my lips and my muscles to mindlessly contract around the weapon.

"Mental. Fucking mental," he growled as he pushed it deeper, causing me to squirm as his finger collided with my clit.

I grumbled from my stupidity and more tears plummeted down my cheeks. He couldn't see me, and he couldn't hear me, so I cried in silence, this time from my own betrayal and confusion—I was turned on. *By a fucking gun.*

No. I'm not.

I couldn't believe that.

I wasn't turned on, my G-spot was just being penetrated and my only thought I could possess was the man that gave me my first orgasm. That's all it was. Nothing more. *Fucking hell, just saying that in my head is wild. This is ridiculous.* My pussy really did have a mind of its own. It was controlling my head and had been since my birthday. I hated that. I hated that *so* much.

After twenty-one years I had finally been shown pleasure, how to receive it, how a clit works, and to want and desire pleasure, to crave it and *need* it. It didn't take a rocket scientist to diagnose all of it as fucked up. *This is why I can't go back.* I could never live my life again. Not without mourning my*self* every second of every day.

I don't want to rot here.

I want to be of use.

Use me.

Use me to pay your debt.

Then I can be free of this.

Just come and find me.

I frowned, realizing that I was praying—not to *Him*, but to my shadow.

"Squeeze," Damon hissed, interrupting my trance. *Thank the Lord... no, fuck the Lord.* But what did that mean? To squeeze.

"What?" I merely whimpered.

"Tighten your pussy," he snarled as he pushed the gun harder against my inside of belly. *Oh.*

I squeezed hard, feeling every curve and edge of the barrel rubbing against my internal walls. I moaned and squirmed to the heavenly pressure, almost entirely ignoring the stinging sensation from his knuckles brushing up against the cuts on my labia.

"That's it, squeeze that little cunt, Esme."

"Oh, shit," I stuttered. *No! Don't moan, you stupid girl.* Fear and arousal swarmed through my veins. There was no fucking way I would live with myself if I had an orgasm from a gun. But did thinking of Huxley make it any better? I hadn't the answer.

"Now soften," he ordered. I did and he swirled my clit with his finger. "Good slut, I need that muscle in fine form."

His vindictive praise left a sour taste on my tongue. In a blink of an eye, he removed the pistol and unlocked the connection of my ankles from the D bolt in the floor, and then tipped my chair over. My cracked, weeping cheek was planted flat on the wooden boards, my neck was bent in a painful position, and my ass was right up in the air. And just when I thought it couldn't get any worse, it did.

"Ow," I bellowed. Feeling my pussy stretch and take an astronomical amount of pressure. I choked on my own hitched breath to the rush of Damon's cock, *and* his gun as they thrust into me.

My head was doing circles. I was messed up. I should be in a hospital for my wounds and a psych ward for my insanity. Who the fuck was I? I had completely lost sight of myself. Esme?

No. Not Esme... slut. Whore. Pet. Diamond. Swallowtail. Cunt. Freak. Piggy.

Just a few names that come to mind. *Maybe he should just leave me here to rot.*

Damon slid two fingers along the swollen fold of my pussy,

and in the very corner of my vision, I could barely make it out but he collected a stream of blood and my juices before drawing them to his mouth. His long tongue glided up his fingers and lapped up the concoction of which was me. A deep, feral growl formed in his chest.

"Fuck, you are delicious. You taste like my sweet revenge and his karma." He pulled the gun and himself from inside me, leaving a hollow emptiness and squatted beside my face. "Taste yourself," he muttered, putting the gun to my lips.

I shook my head to my best ability, because the whole conundrum had gone way too far. *No.* I wouldn't suck off a a fucking pistol. But did I have a choice? No. He tapped at my lips to open, the movement causing me to inhale rapidly through my nose. There was a smell: my sweetness, it intoxicated my brain. Damon saw this as an invitation, slamming the barrel in. The mixture of metallic, sweetness, and wetness swirled over my tongue.

I didn't know why, but I puckered my wounded cheeks and slurped up the liquid that had ventured down the barrel of the gun. Swallowing the contents as though it were a drink of water from a straw. My eyes widened, realizing what I had done. *Was I that thirsty?* Maybe, but a chance at liquid was the least of my problems, and Damon's face was just as shocked as mine.

"Fuck, you swallowed yourself too. *Shit.*" His last word sounded as though he was on the brink of climax. He threw the gun onto the floor and ushered behind me again, shoving himself inside me with haste. I cried out in defeat, only having the option to take all of him as he grabbed my waist, and then thrust hard allowing himself to unfold.

No! I said, but the words didn't quite reach my lips. He moaned and hummed as he deposited his warm liquid in my pussy, filling me so much that it pulsated around him and spouted like a fountain, dribbling out of my pussy and pooling down my belly.

He finally stilled, leaving me disgusted with myself. I felt dirty, and incredibly unwell. He fixed himself back into his jeans, before flipping my chair back to where it was and padlocking me back to the floor. Seeing the wound on my leg had returned to a weep again, instantly making me fuzz in the brain. He shuffled to his phone, hitting the stop button on the camera.

"Now, if you'll excuse me," he snapped in a low tone as he put the phone, and gun into his pocket and then walked to the door behind me.

"Wait! Where are you going?" I called out.

"Oh, come on, you're a smart girl. We're in the middle of nowhere. However, would I send this to him without any signal? But don't worry, when I do I'll burn it so he can't trace it. And then leave you here to rot. Chow," he taunted.

"Wait no! No! Damon? Please don't leave me here," I sobbed heavily. "No!"

And with that, he was gone. The wind from him closing the door almost blew out the candle in the corner, but the blue little flame held itself together, much like I was. My *only* shred of light. And my only hope.

I couldn't explain the feeling, but the second he was gone my body softened, and in an instant the darkness surrendered itself to me and I faded into a heavy state of what I could only gather was heat exhaustion.

CHAPTER SIXTY-THREE

HEAVENS DOOR

D oes death have a sound? If it does... I think I can hear it. I had only been hearing the sound of my own heartbeat and an occasional whistle of birds, everything else was a ringing in my ear and complete numbness... stillness.

I couldn't explain what was going on in my head, there was pressure and cloudiness. The pitiful stinging of my skin between my thighs burned like a fire had been lit under my flesh, another reminder that I was nothing but *property* to a deranged man... who was nowhere to be seen. At least my stab wound had stopped leaking... still so very painful, but my body had reacted well, all things considered.

That fucking morbid asshole.

The illicit dull ache at the tip of my female organ, right near my stomach made my chest hurt. It was raw and bitter. I crumbled, letting all my senses flood me into a heart-wrenching state of overwhelm. At least no one would see me die. And no matter how much I cried out, no one would hear me. The cabin was practically soundproof, it was very well structured so nothing could get in or out unless you had a key or a battering ram. It didn't have windows, nor gaps, not even a tiny ant would be granted entry... or exit.

A pungent smell of nearly blown-out candle vapor violently hit my nose, a painful reminder that I was alone, and almost in complete darkness. I eventually lured the strength to open my eyes again, drawing them to the tiny flame on the candle wick as it fought for survival... like me. I watched it fade and glow again, before finally subsiding to darkness and into nothing but a puddle of dried wax on the wooden beamed floor.

I sobbed for however long time allowed me, letting it swallow me like an unholy realm. Because what else do you do when you're staring at the same four walls with nothing but the sound of the tick-tock thump in your brain from your own heartbeat? Nothing but wallow in your own vicious mind. The silence was loud and painful. And when you have been through hell, it was very easy to fall into a pitiful shit show.

Damon had darted off into the sunset like Usain Bolt, never to be seen again—*the coward*. I knew for sure that I was going to die in the cabin. *Alone*. Unless by some miracle, Huxley found me, if that was possible.

The thought of him suffering ached my heart. I wondered all the ways of how the void would hurt him, or rather, what she would *make* him do to himself. She was strong, like she had a direct link to his veins and mind. She had said that she could feel him, and all that he felt. But was she just false perceptions?

I trailed off remembering that he had roman type numerals on his journal, and rune-like lettering on his ring. She was like a siren, or an ancient goddess maybe. Able to manipulate and tangle her thick venom under your skin and right through your veins.

It was often that anything to do with her, he appeared high on a drug, with instant personality changes. The hallucinations had clearly been hard enough for him to control as it was, especially at dusk. It made sense as to why he was like a wolf under the moon at sundown... because when the sun goes down, the darkness rises. As far as I could gather, sleep and eternal rest lived there: in the dark. And if you don't pay up your end of the bargain, guess who comes knocking?

I shook my weary head, pushing aside the ridiculous theory. Hallucinations. A Goddess? A GODDESS, ESME? *Am I living a lie?* Maybe I was still unconscious from hitting my head at the bar on my birthday? *Am I even real?* I blinked hard as if to double-check that I was human, and doing human-like things... my theory confirmed... I was *definitely* human. Of course I was, I had memories. I had a past before all of... *this.* I washed back into the recollection of what my life was like back at home... *before* the shadow man.

Home.

My mornings were spent making coffee and burning breakfast toast with Tilly. Laughing on the couch under her warm crocheted blanket, watching stupid movies. I didn't realize how much I would miss school, but I did. Even the café, and my shitty ass boss. How could I miss that? I missed drawing butterflies in my room, spending hours preserving them before putting them in beautiful little shadow boxes and hanging them on my wall.

I even missed the smell of everything. City traffic, my pillow, Tilly, the apartment, coffee, heck even the smelly old lady in the apartment underneath us. I missed everything I did. Right down to listening to Imogen Heap painfully loud in my room. I started to hum the lyrics to Speeding Cars, my ultimate favorite song of hers.

I remembered coming home from college one day screaming with excitement and showing Tilly, Imogen's music that I had discovered that day. I would give anything to be back home with her, even if it meant being forced to watch that stupid fucking movie *Fifty Shades of Grey* and listening to her sexual encounters without scoffing at her profanity.

My poor Tilly. My heart broke. But I couldn't think of that, I needed hope. So I decided that maybe... he hadn't killed her, knowing that it would hurt me. I needed to hold onto a fray of hope at the very least—for her sake.

Not even Huxley, nor Damon, nor any of the Whitlock brothers have hurt me like the pain I feel right now for Tilly. And not in the physical sense. This is emotional pain and one that is much stronger than physical.

I mourned a long time, and sadness and more beads of sweat cloaked me. I had no tears left to sob. Then, with heavy eyelids, I let myself drift once more, welcoming the darkness like an old friend.

I fought every cell in my body to force my eyes open again, which was getting harder and harder to do each time. Because were they really open or not? I couldn't feel them. My face was still numb and my hands were tied behind my back, not to mention the darkness was so dark, I couldn't tell if they were open or closed... I was blind. Physically or mentally? I didn't know.

My breath was weak and my body felt wam. Another pitiful reminder of the hellfire that was my reality. When I finally discovered that my eyes *were* open, I could see a faint but blurred ray of light, reflecting on the walls from the door frame behind me. *Daylight?* But the vision was gone as fast as it had appeared, and I fell apart like a broken record for what seemed like hours.

I hated waking up.

I tried to cherish the memories that pained and comforted me... some feeling like a hallucination that I was actually experiencing. Others were like a nightmare that I was certain I had experienced. I was losing the lateral difference between reality and fiction.

And I had started talking to myself.

I knew I was losing my mind... *lost my mind.* Because despite how much I wanted to be home and reverse the clock back to how it was. I wanted to be in the arms of Huxley, more. *He* was my ultimatum.

My shadow.

I talked with my imaginary self again, having not much else to say other than hearing her sing lyrics from the song *The Sound of Silence* by Simon and Garfunkel.

Hello darkness, my old friend. I've come to talk with you again. Because a vision softly creeping, left it's seeds while I was sleeping. And the vision that was planted in my brain, still remains.

Within the sound, of silence.

In restless dreams, I walked alone...

I didn't hear the rest, because, like the light in my eyes, the border between day and night fell in pattern. And I faded along with it. At least then—and *only* in the night—I could breathe a little easier, away from heat intoxicating my lungs. I collapsed my head forward over the back of the chair, and darkness and silence swallowed me whole all over again.

I woke again, greeted by a more intense ray of light than the time before and sweltering heat. Like my body was engulfed in flames, realizing quickly that my breath was barely existent, struggling to split oxygen from moisture. My head pounded and my throat was hoarse, my mouth failed to pool saliva for me to swallow, no matter how many times I asked it.

I managed to stay mostly awake, and it had taken me too long to make sense that the lines were daylight reflections beaming through the tiniest of gaps in the door. I counted the ray streaks on the wall to pass time. But I was sure they were just deliriums.

The shadows with time, recoiled a 180-degree pattern before fading into nothing again, my proof that another day had passed.

I grumbled as I came to once more. I didn't want to wake up anymore. I was done. Exhausted. Praying to whoever would listen to me, to just let me die. God wasn't on my side, or so I thought. *Fuck that monotheistic piece of shit.* I was always loyal to Him... there would be no way He would let me die this way... *if He was real.* The Bible had been wrong all those years. I sighed mentally, maybe Satan and Death *were* real? *Who cares, you're a goner anyway.*

I had counted consciously three times that the subtle pattern of light had moved from one side of the cabin to the other. The heat of the summer's day heating the cabin, made a regular sauna feel like a fucking fridge. My brain fog had only gotten more defective. As, despite the outrageous heat, the sweat had stopped sprouting from my skin somewhere along the way. Evident that I was dehydrated and deteriorating.

I had been in the cabin for *three* days.

The tingling sensation that had begun over my face, had spread midway through my arms and legs, trailing down my spine to the tips of my fingers and my feet. And for some strange reason, my face didn't move the way that it was supposed to, even when I had tried to scrunch my face up. It felt... saggy?

If that wasn't bad enough, the voices in my head had gotten so haunting they became my only friends. Hearing them teetering in and out in echoes, like the one in the lake. Some were close, and some were far away, almost like someone was calling out for my name. But I knew for sure that they weren't. I had to pay my deliriums no concern because that was all they were.

Talking to myself had become a hobby and somewhat pleasurable. I had started seeing things that weren't there. I had seen the horns of Huxley's shadow. I had even hallucinated being in my old room at the apartment. And strung out a vision of where he was climbing into it from the window, only this time I welcomed him in. He had even taken off his mask and lay beside me, telling me about his day in the lab. For some reason, my brain chose to think of him as a biochemist... just a regular guy who liked to sing and play piano with his wife... *me*. We kissed, loved hard, and then he brushed my hair to sleep.

But then, I woke up. It was a kick to the guts. *Now I*

understand why he wrote what he did in that journal. He didn't want to wake up anymore—I feel that. I know that pain now.

Because I don't want to wake up again either.

I had never felt so hollow and broken in my life. I felt empty without him. But I eventually got tired of arguing with myself and drifted into gloom again, imagining his voice calling for me.

CHAPTER SIXTY-FOUR

HEARING THINGS

My breath crackled, like phlegm had built up but no strength to cough it up. It sounded like a rattlesnake was stuck in my chest. I stirred but remained heavy within my body as a dull, distorted voice echoed in my brain, no different than it usually did.

My head pounded to the rhythm of my heart, which was slower than it was the last time I had woken. *Which was however long ago now.* I lost count after counting to three days. All I knew was that I had been here long enough for a human body to shut down.

I knew I was dying. Everywhere hurt. Everything ached. Everything was numb. I had lost control of my body, and now it was apparent that I was sitting in a puddle of my own filth. Not that I had any memory of shitting myself, I couldn't be certain of when I had eaten last. *How embarrassing. Though, truthfully, I didn't have the energy to care.*

I tilted my head slightly, hearing the same vocal note echo again. I sighed—*damn these fucking apparitions*—no wonder they drove Huxley mad. It was a strange sensation, like it was far away, but by the time it had reached me, it was nothing but a faint murmur. I hated arguing with myself that they weren't real because I think living delirious beliefs was worse than hearing them in the first place.

I stirred again as I heard it for the umpteenth time, making sense that it really did sound like a siren. I sighed in defeat, knowing for sure I was on my way to death. Had the hallucinations really come that hard? The voices always sounded so realistic.

"Esmeralda!" A warped voice hooted. *SHUT THE FUCK UP!* It was much clearer this time, and closer. I fluttered my eyes but the blurred fuzz wouldn't budge. I tried to pull myself together, but all I could manage was a faint moan, which consumed all of my energy, making me fall into darkness again. I welcomed it, for it took my pain and phantasms away.

I blinked from the odd sensation of the blacks of my eyelids suddenly going red. Yet another string of light bellowing into the cabin from behind the door. Light?... *Jesus? Heaven!*

I could see an Angel or mythical being float down from the ceiling, casting a beam of white light. My life flashed before my eyes, only realizing that it wasn't *my* life. *They got it all wrong. The myths.* It did *not* flash before your eyes, much to their beliefs... your life—as how you *wanted* it to be—did.

I was certain, because all I saw in my flashes was my future with Huxley, and *nothing* of my past. It was like a camera scrolling on screen, flashing from one memory to another. Living in his mansion, I was sleeping peacefully in his bed.

Another playing the piano with him. We wed, gosh he looked beautiful in a suit. All the brothers except Damon were there. Ruby and Tilly were my bridesmaids. There was not a chain, rope, lake or shadow in sight. He lived in happiness with me without his mask... without his shadow.

Then he was in the garden holding a pink blanket, cradling a baby. A daughter. *Our* daughter. Feeling a sense of honor in taking a murderer's last name, Esmeralda Jane Whitlock, and to birth his child. The visual took my breath away.

I suddenly coughed, spluttering briefly back to consciousness, I was fading. But the Angel standing before me was in no hurry to take me. *Why?*

I took a wounded breath and closed my eyes again in a drift to dream of my shadow... if I couldn't die in his arms at least I would die with him in my brain as my last thought. Albeit, it made no sense, to fall in love with and dream of a murderer. But he wasn't just *any* murderer. He was *mine*. I was *his* to consume. I wanted nothing more right now than for him to hold me as I took my last breath.

I will die here alone, in moments to come... I think.

I was sure I could feel it. I felt truly sad if it was possible to feel sadness before you died. And no one other than Mother Nature itself would find me, as my carcass would eventually be consumed by insects and other flesh-eating creatures long before anyone found me. And then those insects would eventually diminish six feet underground, then maybe a tree would blossom from my flesh.

That theory made me happy. *The circle of life.*

Although mostly cruel, there is beauty behind it. Like those girls in the lake. They too will recycle back into Mother Nature. New life will form, grow, and live. Like Alison Krauss from the movie Bambi quoted.

Even when you can't see it, inside everything, there is life.
After the rain, the sun will reappear, there is life.
After the pain, the joy will still be here.
There is life.
For it's out of the darkness, that we learn to see.
And all that we dream of, awaits patently.
There is life.

I rattled in my chest again, hearing soft voices from the white light that was an Angel before me, almost like the pearly gates were calling. I made mild sense of my body being nudged and tugged: the Angel was untying me to take me to heaven. It became apparent that my arms were no longer bound behind me, and my limp body was being cradled like a newborn infant in the being's arms. My hair was tenderly brushed away from my face.

I wondered what Angels looked like, but if I were to open my eyes would it disappear and not take me to the abode of God?

Because that was something I remembered my mother telling me as a child, with the Tooth Fairy and St. Nicholas, if I stayed awake they wouldn't come to me. And so, I summoned with what curiosity and little strength I had left to pull my nearly lifeless eyes up to see the light, to see heaven. What I saw was no white-winged, halo-wearing mythical creature, and there had been no pearly golden gates, or harps being played.

It was an unfamiliar face.

A *man* with pale skin and two big, bright, amber eyes as soft as lambs was burning into mine. He was glowing like a hypnotic realm. I had never seen a more beautiful and terrifying being in my entire life. He was panting heavily as though he had searched the earth below and the sky above for me.

With a deep barely existent, shallow breath my body stilled and fell heavier than the last. I never thought I would relish my last breath, the solace it brought me as the welcoming scent of pine, blood and moisture filled my nose.

A tear formed under the gleam of his eye, trailing down one of the deeper scars on his face that was buried from his brow and down to his chin.

"I am yours to the very end. I will set this right, I promise. And then you will be *mine*," his voice whispered tenderly, with need and desperation. Like an angel. Almost identical to the way Huxley spoke to me in my hallucinations. But it was again, just another helpless delirium.

Wasn't it?

Wait... I've seen that scar before.

And then, a glowing green amulet pulsating against his bare chest flickered between my eyelashes, letting it become the last thing I saw. The darkness closed in on me without permission, and I accepted it gladly.

Because I knew that my beloved shadow... had come for me.

The hunted... become the hunter.

CHAPTER SIXTY-FIVE

HEAVENLY BEEPS

I stirred, expecting pain to whomp me heavily... like it always did. But it didn't. I was in heaven. At peace. *I made it.* No pain, no worry, just bliss. I drifted back into my inebriated state, following the sounds of my steady breath and another noise I couldn't make out. *Huh?*

I felt a sense of weightlessness and yet... groggy. I felt like I was floating on cloud 9, dizzy and drunk. *Is this what heaven feels like*: bouncy, light and airy... and—

Beep.

What the? I didn't think heaven made those noises. What the hell was it? *Oh, crap.* Maybe I was in hell? No, that didn't check out either. A spike of curiosity surfaced in my brain with a need to make sense of the beeping sound, bouncing through my ears. I tried to make up a scenario of my mundane whereabouts. Only catching visuals of a wedding. *What? I didn't marry anyone. Did I?*

Suddenly it hit me. That it was my treacherous imagination, fooling me into believing that the only thing that burned the scene in my mind was what I *wanted* my life to be like. Morphing it right into a memory. *A fake memory.* That was far from the truth.

Beep.

I stirred again, my senses coming in full swing, and my true memories stapled me like a freight train. The cabin. Days. Unbearable inhumane heat. Pain. *Oh, the pain.* A gun in places I never wanted to admit. Grief. *Dying?* Then two big beautiful amber eyes etched a mark into my brain.

The eyes of my shadow man. I had been in his arms as he cradled me like a baby.

Beep.

I jolted upright from the repetitive beeping sounds and squinted from the lighting, noticing that it was daylight. Something I hadn't seen in a long time. I was in a bed. I planted my hand against my chest to soothe my abrupt flutters and I winced. *Ouch!* There was a pinching ache and a tugging sensation at my hand.

I looked down, seeing an IV pierced right in the little blue vein on my hand, wrapped in a clear bandage. The IV led to a heart monitor beside me—that would explain the beeping noises. There were other cords and tangles coming from my body. Yellows, browns, blues and reds. My eyes widened realizing that some were on my head as well as my chest.

I panted, taking a second to process as my breath escalated in fear, the monitor beeping faster. Where was I? Where was Huxley? What had happened? Dizziness provoked me, but the adrenaline fought it off. I twisted my head around to try and identify where I was. I gasped and tried to shoot backward, seeing someone was by my arm, but my limbs malfunctioned. It was a woman—the maid.

"It's okay, honey," her soft voice hummed.

"Wu- ha? Whu?" I slurred. What in the ever-loving fuck did I just say? That should have been *where am I? Where is he?* Why was it so hard to speak? Had I had a fucking stroke? My voice was slow and broken, like the time I had my molars taken out; the needle in my gums had made my lips and tongue do absurd things, and I couldn't speak clearly from the numbness.

"You're safe," she said. I glanced around the room again, soon realizing that I was in Huxley's room, in his bed. It was different from how I remembered. Not everything was black. There was no cage, no chains, and no frame in the center of the room to hang people by ropes. The only telltale was the view from the window... the pine tree backdrop. One I would *never* forget.

"Wh-uue... " I slurred again. *Where? Where is Huxley? Gah!*

"I understand you're trying to speak, Esme, but you must steady. Your heart rate is going out of control," the maid exclaimed.

I frowned, and then panic set in hard and fast, watching her fill something in the tube that went through my IV. The beeps slowed in an instant. I pulled in a heavy inhale until I was dizzy again and blew out my frustration. *I was safe.*

My heart had dropped to a pace similar to the way it was when I had awoken. Hopefully, now that I was calm, she would fill me in on all the details. But she ushered off to do something near a medicine cabinet. Huxley's room was incredibly different, there were books on shelves, lamps beside the bed, a *second* bed, a medicine cabinet, and a wheelie trolley *full* of medical equipment. Like the one full of food that she had brought into my room when I was held there.

She ushered back with a yellow folder and placed it in my hand. It had a name I didn't recognize in big letters on the front.

Miss. Vicky Kollens
DOB: 18th January 1997
Allergies: Nil
Blood Type: B Negative

Who the hell was Vicky? I tried to speak again using every inch of concentration.

"Ver-k-key?" I squeaked.

The maid gestured to open the folder. I did and pulled out a sheet of what I assumed to be MRI scans. There were a few pages, with black-and-white radial images. I furrowed my brows in confusion, looking up between them and the maid, and then back down again. I had no idea what I was looking at, but I did notice that there was a thick, black blob on one section of the image.

What does that mean? Who is Vicky? Why am I looking at brain scans for a Vicky Kollens?

The maid leaned in, dote laced in her eyes.

"I'm sorry. I really am. It was lucky he found you when he did. You've had a brain bleed Esmeralda," she whispered tenderly.

"What?" I breathed, surprised that the word had come out exactly how it was intended. I took a further minute to process. That would explain my muttering. I mean it made sense, I *was* hung upside down for God knows how fucking long and locked away in a sauna for five days... *stabbed and left to rot.*

Realization rippled through me and I jolted my hand to my

thigh over the wound. Discovering that it had a thick padded bandage on it. I breathed down the panic, looking back at the maid again.

"You will make a full recovery. But... "

"B-t?" I copied the *but,* stuttered but audible and she hesitated.

"We had to put you into an induced coma to help you. You were in a really bad way." Her sweet voice was genuine and sympathetic to my situation, letting me truly believe that I was in no danger.

Suddenly I felt dizzy again. *How long have I been in a coma? Where is Huxley? Did he see the video? Where is Damon?* At this rate, I had more questions than answers, and I wasn't getting anywhere fast. A brain bleed? *Shit.* What else was there? And who was Vicky?

"W-who. Vicky?" I asked, and then blew out rapidly. She sighed and fluffed down her uniform nervously.

"We needed a file while we were in the hospital... so that you were not... identified." *Oh.*

"Oh?" I breathed. I was in the hospital? In public? Why did I not remember? Is that part of having a stroke? How long was the coma? And as though she saw the light bulbs above my head spark with questions she pulled out a clipboard from the bedside table.

"You've had other traumas... only if you'd like me to read them out?" she asked hesitantly, with every shred of sadness in her eyes.

"No," I confessed. I only wanted to know the answers to the questions I had in my head. I didn't need to hear the other traumas, I already knew of those. I was a pin cushion. Cuts here, wounds there, knives, guns, glass, rope, oxygen deprivation. I'd had it all. I'd had it everywhere.

A specific memory washed over me, how could I forget? The knife to my pussy. Mindlessly, I squeezed my thighs together with no pain. *Nothing.* Other than the odd sensation of a tube between my legs that I hadn't noticed earlier. I lifted the blanket and trailed my eyes down, seeing that I had *two* catheters in.

I trailed off. *A brain bleed? Don't people die from those? What about the cuts?* I pulled my wandering attention to take a good look at myself. The wounds Caine had dressed were merely purple scars, some darker than others. I trailed my finger to the burn mark on my chest from Ruby, which was nothing but a white smiley face now. Further up feeling the raised skin on my neck, no pain, just scars. Lifting closer to my mouth and feeling my cheek, a tender but healed, raised cut trail.

Unease riddled me—I had been there long enough for my wounds to *heal. You'll be okay. You'll be okay.* Sadness hounded me and a tear freed from my eyes.

"You're going to be okay, miss." The maid stood beside me again with a genuine smile on her lips. She comforted me in more ways than I could admit, but there was only one need that I truly desired. *Him.*

"Ho- l-long. Been. Here?" I paced my sentence, asking her how long I had been in Huxley's room.

"Three weeks," she admitted.

I swallowed back my nausea, having no recollection of anything. I cocked my head, fixing a little more demanding approach.

"Huslee?" I asked, unable to pronounce the *x* in his name.

"Let's not worry about him just yet, okay? You've been

through enough. Let's keep you calm and steady. I don't want your condition to worsen. Okay?"

"O-kay," I replied. I was bedridden anyway, so I figured that I would eventually get my answers.

"Are you hungry?"

Hungry? Shit I hadn't had the thought. Come to think of it, if I have been here for three weeks, and not eaten over a week before that... then it has been a solid month since I've had food in my mouth.

That was more surprising than learning I had been here for three-quarters of a month. I laughed involuntarily to my cognizance, the smile reached my eyes and heat flooded my body in happiness, and then I wailed unintentionally. My body's response to the chronic overwhelm of feeling every possible emotion in as little as five minutes. But... in the answer to her question, yes. I was fucking starving.

"Yes, I am," I admitted slowly, holding my belly. Though, that didn't even scratch the surface. I suspected I could eat a whole horse. Maybe after I ate, and regained a little of myself then I would ask more questions. But for now... food, and rest. And a book. The maid nodded, happy to be of service. And put her hands up, gesturing to wait.

"I'm going to have to remove these cords from you, so you can eat like a normal woman again, okay?"

I nodded and she put on some blue gloves, and in a blink of an eye she removed the needle from my hand and then attended to my stomach. *Huh?* I didn't even realize I had one there. It was thick, but to my surprise it didn't hurt when she removed it.

After she cleaned me up and fiddled with a few things she finally came back to my bed.

"I'll fetch you something. Okay? Please, do not move. It is

paramount that you do not move. You aren't ready. You are safe here until I return, okay?" she demanded.

I agreed, not really paying too much attention... for my mind had wandered back to Huxley again. My thoughts were easy to wonder at the best of times, but under whatever juices she had filled me with to steady my erratic heart made it much worse.

"Wayet," I called out, frowning because I meant *wait*. I wanted to pass the time reading, I hadn't for so long, and there was a full shelf ready and waiting. It would be nice to touch, smell, and read again. "I h-har. Bo-ook?"

I pointed to one of the novels on the shelf so she could understand me, seeing as my words were not english. I knew that reading would stop me from trailing off, or from trying to get out of bed to find Huxley. She smiled and scampered to the full bookshelf, calling out a few names of authors. Some I knew, others I didn't, until she stopped at one that I did know and brought it to me.

I smiled so loud that you could hear it from the moon. It was bliss. A taste of normality. Leaving the bed was the last thing on my mind.

The second I opened the book and dove into the first page, I drew in the inebriating smell of old paper, musky notes, and someone's blood sweat, and tears poured into the words. I sobbed happy tears and fell heavily into the pages of a romantic book of poems.

CHAPTER SIXTY-SIX

I DON'T WANT TO BE HERE ANYMORE

I am yours to the very end. I will set this right, I promise.

Huxley, my name is Huxley.

I have the instinct to love her, but I am hardwired to kill her.

You are my pet, my swallowtail.

And then you will be mine.

The shadow man's soft, hypnotic voice and the vivid memory that etched my brain of his eyes glowing against mine, gave me comfort as I stared out the window. I felt a sense of Deja Vu as the sun gently kissed my pale skin, soaking up whatever vitamins it had left to radiate before it set.

My forehead created a hazy, sweaty mark where it rested on the thick glass, as did my hand. Just like it had done all that time ago in the room below. I had been looking out the horizon far too long, empty, thoughtlessly staring at literally nothing.

I stayed that way a while longer, watching the birds flutter for bugs on dusk, and the stars to slowly start sparkling. The sun shifted into stunning shades of orange, reds, and purples before it finally melted behind the pine tree horizon. And just like that, the darkness was reborn.

I don't want to be here anymore.

You'll be okay, you'll be okay.

My throat narrowed and the waterworks jerked from my eyes for the millionth time. Because I knew for sure that Huxley was down there in the forest suffering some kind of hell. *Because of me.* It was always this time of day that he struggled the most. Was that why he hadn't come to see me? He knew where I was. He saved me. He fucking saved *me.*

Flashes of memories burst through my mind—which had been happening a lot lately—making me dizzy. I had been through so much in such little time. I nearly died because of him, and on more than one occasion. Had I been left another second in that hell-bound cabin, I would have.

No wonder I had a brain bleed, or was it being held upside down for too long the cause? I couldn't be sure. But despite all that, I was still here, physically... for the most part. Mentally? *No* —I was not in a good way. *Ruined.* Fucking traumatized. And still very much absolutely clueless about what was next for me. All I had was the feeling of the blind leading the blind.

I shuffled slowly to the bathroom, swapping between bracing the wall for balance and managing to walk unassisted. I hadn't been to the toilet since this morning when the maid removed my catheters. Today was the first time I was able to get up and stretch my legs since waking up three days ago.

As my days passed, I learned that the maid used to be a live-in nurse at an old orphanage. She knew her way around a needle and was surprised at how well I could walk. I guess I had a lot of fight in me. I also learned that she was Soren's sister. Stephanie didn't speak all that much, but when she did I felt a sense of calm and did not have the need or want to peer over my shoulder.

I took care of my business and she peered her head around the corner. I rolled my eyes dramatically, the privacy was non-existent. *The last time I checked, I wasn't a paraplegic.* I could still remember how to pee on my own. I bit my tongue, because in her eyes, she was just looking out for me. Which was another thing, I didn't need to learn how to walk again, or talk, or eat, or anything. All things considered.

Stephanie had shown me my MRI scans better than the last, explaining the brain bleed, which I knew I had, but she forgotten to mention until then that I also had a fucking stroke. A stroke! I really fucking should have died, I would be much better off dead than in the mess I was now. *In fact, I really didn't want to be here. I am nothing like I was.*

I don't want to be here anymore.

"Sorry. Are you okay for a shower... while you're in here?" she asked sweetly, but her voice was muffled out mostly by the noises in my head.

The medication she gave me was strong, so making conversation and focusing on more than one thing was hard. Especially when most of my thoughts were a vicious cycle of hallucinations, death, and vivid memories. *But yes. I could use a shower... a long shower.* I was sure that the stench from me was no better than the deathly impurities at the lake, but the maid had been good to me, cleaning me with a warm soapy cloth and keeping me as hygienic as possible.

"Y-yes please," I said in a drony tone, it was more of an auto piloted reply. I had gotten better at speaking, but was a long way from my words being clear.

I tugged off my signature black silk robe that I had been fortunate enough to have been gifted yesterday morning, nuzzled snug in a gift box with the tag embossed with the initial - *H. Of course.*

I stood into the warm shower and immediate relief hit me, feeling like my sins were washing away down the drain as the water softly rolled over my back. I glanced over at the robe on the floor, unconsciously huffing at the darned thing. Stephanie never left my sight, not unless she was fetching meals—and even then, she worked quicker than speeds of light... so, had he come when we were asleep? But if he *had* been in the room, he would have said something, wouldn't he?

I thought of all the things I could say to him; *I hate you*, was the first that came to mind for what he had done to me. But that was a lie. Because regardless of everything he had done, I knew I could not live my life without him in some way. And I knew I could never *live* with him.

We would never be compatible. And that was what hurt me the most. Because he would spend every second of every day, fighting to *not* kill me. Our life was *not,* nor would it *ever* be, the way I had imagined it would be in my dreams. There would be no wedding, no romance in the garden, no ring on my finger, no smiles, and no happily ever after. So no matter what angle I wrack my brain, or how long I torment myself doing so... he is, and always will be, a *monster.*

He will always hunt me. He will always love to hate me. He will always hate to love me.

He is, and always will be a monster. My monster. My shadow. If I can't live with him and I can't live without him. Then I will die for him.

I DON'T WANT TO BE HERE ANYMORE!

I tried to hold my tears back but out of my control I heaved into the most depressing fit of sobs I had felt in my entire life. Whimpering and howling, crumbling like pastry as the warm water penetrated my skin. *I hate this, I hate this so much.* Why me? It took me too long to realize that I was screaming. Loud, and hard, my body trembling to accommodate the vocals.

Stephanie stood by watching sympathetically as though it were either a regular occurrence or something she expected. Every howl from my lungs brought a new haven, I leaned into the bellows more, and let my body revolt this new wave of sensations as it healed me in ways that I couldn't understand.

I roared until dizziness won me over and clouded my vision. My head throbbed. Shit, what did that mean? Did I overdo it? I sat down on the plastic chair in the shower, letting myself catch my breath and balance. And then I realized that what had just happened was *my* trauma response.

"Thank you," I mouthed to the maid without sound, I knew my words would be completely re-wired. She knew I needed that relief. I wondered for a moment if maybe I would have speech therapy? *I can't go on like this.*

You'll be okay.

"I'm going to hook you up again. Only for a moment, then you can go back in," she said, and then dried my finger and placed a little clip onto it. "You're okay, I promise. I'm under strict instructions to keep you calm. I know you feel better after that, though."

She blew a sigh of relief, like her life was dependent on mine as the monitor showed that I was steady. Which was crazy considering how intense those screams were. If my heart went too much off rhythm, I guessed maybe I would have another stroke? I didn't know how it all worked exactly. She released my hand and smiled.

"C-can I. Haaa... a min-et?" I pleaded with every inch of sadness that riddled me to have a minute alone, just wanting to sit on the chair and engulf myself under the water a while longer.

She nodded and stood back behind the door frame, occasionally peering at the watch around her wrist, counting my chest rises and falls. I stared off into the abyss... at absolutely nothing but the wet tiles on the wall and a spec of air. I let my mind drift, and allow every thought only of him to penetrate my mangled brain.

The echoes of his beautiful piano melodies sang in my mind, getting me through another day without seeing him, feeling him, smelling him, hearing him, or tasting him. I mindlessly drew my tongue over my lips, as if I would taste him on mine. But, only the cracked skin sensation and unbrushed teeth was what came back at me.

By the time I had finished with my shower, exhaustion laid into me heavily and I staggered back to bed with Stephanie by my side. Falling into a nightmare-filled sleep. Only seeing, feeling, smelling and hearing *that fucking voice...* the void. Fuck her.

She was hard to tune out, but when you're in your most unconscious state of asleep but awake in your dreams, you simply could not omit her. She always managed to find a way to bury herself into your mind, as though she had the ability to control your thoughts and make you believe things that were not real.

"He will never love you. I can make it all go away."

The way she howled those words in my brain was like the

chill of a thousand swords piercing through a single rose. The void was a lethal, manipulating bitch, but I knew the way Huxley truly felt about me, regardless of what she said. Yet I knew I'd never stand a chance against her either... I *have* to succumb to her.

I don't want to be here anymore.

She will make it all go away.

You'll be okay. You'll be okay. I had to keep telling myself that.

I stirred and woke early, long before the sun would, with a dire need for water. I felt as though I had not slept in months. No thanks to the fucking voices getting louder. I was going to need stronger medication if sleeping was going to become a nightmare.

I staggered to the bathroom to fill a cup of water as the one I had the night before was empty. I gasped and dropped the glass into the sink from the terrorizing visual before me. The mirror was broken... held together by tape. *That wasn't there before.* How did it break?

I craned my neck around in a panic, seeing Stephanie was still in a fitful sleep in the second bed. I turned back, noting there was blood smeared all over the mirror, and some dripping from the sharp edges...

It looked like a punch mark? I frowned, trying to make sense of it, and how it got there, and why. I leaned in closer and the waterworks trickled from my eyes. My heart wrenched seeing faded streaks of black paint, realizing it had been Huxley. *Is he here?* Why did he punch the mirror? Was he okay? Was I okay? *Am I awake or dreaming again?* Had he come in for me, only seeing her instead?

My head twisted into thought, how was he in the room

without me hearing him? The possibility of him fighting an invisible war with the void sent me into a shudder of woe, only adding to my tears that started as just a trickle. But the mirror wasn't the only broken thing in my line of sight.

It was also my reflection. One I wished I hadn't looked at. *Is that really me?* I didn't recognize myself. I hadn't seen myself since when I tried to escape, the reflection in the car? No. *That's not me.* I couldn't tell you who she was.

I was a bag of bones. How much weight had I lost? I couldn't tell you, but I was the weakest and palest I had ever seen me be. I ran my finger over the purple scars on either side of my cheeks, trailing the memories of the pain like it was yesterday. My eyes wandered over my body, taking in and absorbing the mess I truly was.

I had been minced like a serrated pork rind, carved and ready for a meal. I barely had any skin that was left unscathed. Every scar, every cut, every wound, the stab, the stroke, the burn, the brain bleed, the markings on my womanhood, the sexual trauma, the glass shatters on my feet... everything had a fucking story to tell. My body was a notebook. I hated that mirror. I hated all mirrors.

There is no coming back from this. I don't want to be here. I don't want to be here.

I don't want to be here!

You'll be okay.

Through my sobs, I blew out a heavy blow of air against one of the biggest pieces of the mirror that was not broken, leaving a streak of fog from my breath. I scribbled thoughtlessly on it with my fingertip, not really comprehending what I was writing.

'Are you okay?'

No...

I fell into yet another heavy sob. I *needed* him. I *needed* to avenge—not just myself, but him. I couldn't do *this* anymore.

The heaviness hounded me and I scurried back to my bed without the water I wanted, cradling my pillow, and cried myself back to sleep.

CHAPTER SIXTY-SEVEN

MIRRORS... I HATE MIRRORS

"This is beautiful, Esme," Stephanie praised with a grin like the Cheshire cat. She was sweeping her finger over one of my drawings in her hand.

"Th-anks," I stuttered, though I wasn't sure if it was from my stroke or the fact that I was chewing on a buttered dinner roll. I chuckled at the mess I was making, but it quickly silenced. Happiness was short-lived lately, and I wasn't one for talking much anymore. It was too draining. My misery was too strong.

I didn't need to speak often, having only a few words to say it was better to just keep my mouth shut. Besides, how could I speak when I had a million words in my head that weren't mine? I couldn't hear my own, not over *hers*.

But, the sense of peace and hints of normality that drawing was giving me, was better than I could have ever anticipated. I didn't know I could draw—it felt nice, it felt *me*. And I welcomed it like I would a newborn child.

"I take it you like butterflies?" she asked. I frowned, I guessed I'd never really taken much notice of them before, but they were beautiful I had to admit. And for some reason that was all I had been drawing as of late. I didn't know why. "You should study to be an artist. You have a knack for it."

My brow furrowed. *Study...* I was certain I had been to college before. But I couldn't piece down the rest of it, like a story with blank pages. But I do remember that Stephanie had said the loss of memory was normal, and I should get it back. I wondered what else I had forgotten, coming to terms with losing who I was hurt my soul. But in all honesty, maybe that was a good thing.

I tried to hide the sadness I was showing, surrendering to being part vegetable. I could barely walk, I staggered. I could barely speak a full sentence. And I could only make out *some* of my past. I didn't *want* to feel sad anymore. *Why am I still sad?* I had been given a brand new stack of Faber Castell colored pencils, and a sketch pad to draw in. I was even given a pair of earphones and an MP3 player to listen to music on.

Albeit the thing was ancient... but Beethoven, Schumann, Mozart, and Shubert were hit favorites of mine to keep me company as my pencils somewhat put my mind at ease. Music was nice. At least the music was louder than *her*.

I assumed the device belonged to Huxley, given that it was engraved with the letter *H* on the back. He clearly had good taste in music, and I could see where his influence was from when he played on his piano.

I sighed. All in all, drawing had tired my mind out. My energy was usually quickly diminished anyhow but far worse after drawing or reading. I even had an afternoon nap earlier, not that it achieved much. Mental exhaustion was a bitch. I had fallen asleep to Mozart, thankfully I woke not long before dinner.

I had stuffed my face well, leaving nothing but a crumb from my roll.

The sun was about to set again, though the sky wasn't as pretty as the last few nights. It was only orange... and gloomy. Evident that there was a storm coming in. A smile turned my lip but didn't reach my eyes. I loved thunderstorms. Lightning flashes, rain, and crashing vibrations were the most beautiful of natural disasters. I brushed the crumbs off me and moseyed to the window, finding a nice spot to lean on and watch the border between day and night recede.

Grumbles of thunder cracked in the distance, sending a vibrational tone up my spine. It was electric and exciting. But it wasn't quite dark enough to see the full effects from the flickers of lightning. I had an odd sensation in my gut as I stared at the pine trees, thinking of only *him* as always. There was something aching, and not something that medication would cure. I brushed it off and watched the storm pass on for a while, before needing to sit back down again.

"St-st. Epha-nie?" I called out her name, or at least tried to anyway. I decided that the tug that I was experiencing had gone on long enough. I knew that I needed a shower. *Alone.*

"Yes, Esme?"

"Can I. Hhhave. A sho-ower? Alone?" I pleaded softly. I hadn't been able to have a minute by myself, not even to take care of my defecation needs. She hesitated a while, but an insincere smile broke through her pursed lips.

"Fine. But you yell for me if you need me, okay?" Stephanie commanded. I nodded, but she stood her ground.

"Okay?" her voice was stern.

"Oh- k-kay." I held my hands up in submission, whatever it

would take to shut her up and let me get in there alone. She rolled her eyes and went back to reading her book.

The shower was hot and electric over my skin. I sat on the chair as my breath hitched, pleasure hit me in the pit of my belly like the thunderclaps outside. *In through the slit and swirl the little bud.*

How was my little sensitive button... so sensitive? I thought of Huxley and his miraculous, pierced length in every orifice. *Why am I doing this?* I didn't have the answer, but I had a need that I couldn't refuse. I continued circling to each delicious thought of him... how he stroked himself in the surveillance room, to footage of me. My temperature rose instantly and my cheeks flushed from the memory of my first orgasm. It was so wrong, but fuck it was hot.

My climax was on the edge and in four swirls of my clit I came undone like I was a wound-up thread on a bobbin. I caught my breath and found myself again, completely ignoring the pummels happening in my head. It was pounding, but I didn't care—the ecstasy was worth the pain. I figured if I had another stroke, it would at least be during an orgasm.

I rolled my hips with the rhythm of my touch and found my breast with the other hand, coaxing another sensation to ripple over me. My blood was pounding through my head as it rushed to my pussy, and my clit swelled from the thought of him inside me, fucking me hard without mercy. *This is by far the best thing I've done since I woke up a few days ago.*

I stopped suddenly, seeing that the shower-head was removable. *Hmm.* Curiosity sparked the better of me and I pulled it down, then turned the heat lower. I sat back down, propping my foot up against the wall of the shower in the most ungraceful way, and held the water's pressure toward my clit.

Fuck.

I had been sleeping on a gold mine for twenty-one fucking years. *This is incredible.* I was sure there were far better words than that, but I was burning up and short-circuiting. The flickers of the water vibrated the sweet spot and I fell apart again. Stars circled my head and my belly warmed to the sensation. I felt satisfied, but only by a pinch. I tried for another orgasm but the pleasure wasn't being transferred from my clit to my brain, it was just empty strums of my fingers.

There was still an emptiness. A missing part of the puzzle. I knew no matter how many orgasms I had or tried to have. It wasn't him.

I need him.

I scoffed, giving up entirely on the cum fairies. I switched off the shower and grabbed my toothbrush. I blew my warm breath over the mirror, still seeing the words that I had written. I asked myself if I was okay... but I wasn't. But that was for a different reason than the last time that I asked. I hated the mirror... because I hated what looked back at me.

I didn't know how many times I'd said it... that I didn't want to be in this world anymore, but every time it happened, it became louder in my head.

I leaned forward to spit out the contents of minty foam and bubbles, suddenly gagging for a breath at the sight of what was in the bottom of the sink. Blood, and something else I couldn't put the thought to. *Skin?*

I examined my body for injuries in a panic—was it me? *Self harm?* No, I was completely intact... the flesh wasn't mine. My stomach churned, I could taste my dinner surfacing. I shrieked in my head, but my mouth stayed shut. The sink was filled with clots of blood, and flesh.

And right on the edges... were two, black, smudged handprints.

I choked on the inhale of panicked air as I limped my way to the window. *Is he here? How did he get in again without me knowing? Without Stephanie knowing?* There was nothing outside, other than bolts of lightning and rumbles of thunder. I craned my head around, Stephanie was still reading a book, and was now listening to the music player. Stuck in her own world, and thankfully not up my ass for once.

I gave up on the idea of where he could be, tiring out from my orgasms, and shuffled back to my bed. I opened up the bedside drawer, fetching the drawing pad and pencils to draw what I had in my head.

My heart froze for a moment, before slowing only slightly, seeing that there was a note... left in blood and black paint streaks. *He has been here!*

'I am broken. I am incapable of love.

It is too late for me. For us.

For her.'

My shadow was hurting. The void was killing him... like she said she would.

I need to get the fuck out of here... and find him. I need to end this.

I don't want to be here anymore.

CHAPTER SIXTY-EIGHT

GREEN DRESSES AND AMULETS

I had tried to stay in bed, but I was too antsy to sit still after the first few hours. But, I needed to keep my cool. Otherwise, Stephanie would know something was up; I wouldn't get my chance to break out if I lost my wit, so being completely relaxed and stable was my ammo. I had thrown the art pad back in the drawer and had limped my way back to the window, and haven't moved since.

I stared at the trees as they cracked up to light from the storm, which was much closer now, and louder... more aggressive. I wracked my brain for a logical plan, only coming up with none. There was no way I would survive walking from the mansion to the forest, let alone to the middle—to the lake... where *she* was. And where I hoped *he* would be.

I jolted and then screeched a frightful yelp from the crack of thunder that hit something near the mansion. Everything turned black in an instant.

"Fuck. We've lost power," Stephanie cursed before speaking again. "Are you okay?"

I huffed at her unintentionally. *Why does everyone, including myself, keep asking me that?* "Yes." *Wait... it has only been me or her asking that question... damn these voices.*

"I'm going to have to get the generator going. I need to watch your monitor. You've been up and down all evening," she said. Her voice of course concerned, genuinely worried about my wellbeing. I hated being attached to that monitor so often.

In the corner of my eye, I could see from her silhouette that she was fumbling with something under her bed. A smile turned my lips but I hid it, biting them in the process. It couldn't get any better, a storm and her leaving the room in one go? *There was a God!*

"O-kay," I responded inconspicuously. Though, I wasn't good at it.

A bright light flared from a phone, and then her face lit up as she dialed a number, scoffing at whoever she had called didn't answer. I didn't even realize she had a phone. She had never been on it. She dialed another number and muttered something. No answer I presumed.

"Shit," she hissed.

"Who? I asked. Unable to string out the full sentence of who it was she was trying to call. *This better not fuck up any of my plans*. Not that I had one, other than get the hell out.

"Soren at first, then Eli and Caine. Those idiots won't answer their fucking phones. I need that generator going."

"Hhhu- sley?" I murmured Huxley's name. FUCKING HELL I HATE THIS! What about Ruby? *What about Damon? Or Soren.* She laughed, though it was insincere, completely ignoring me. I wondered if he even had a phone.

"I'll call Soren again... Honey? Yes, I'm okay. We need the generator going... you're where?... oh, for fuck's sake, Ren. Fine.

Okay. Okay. Yes. Bye." Stephanie pouted, tapping the red *end* button, and the light disappeared again.

"Everyone's at the club. Fucking idiots. In this weather? I'm going to have to get the generator going myself. You're not going to do anything stupid are you?" She scowled.

"No," I whispered, merely a squeak, but it was clear. *Yes... I am.* That was the biggest lie I had ever told myself, and it made my heart flutter with both excitement and fear.

"I mean it, Pierce. You're not in a good way. I know you... wander... where you shouldn't sometimes." Stephanie was genuinely concerned. But fuck her right now, she had no idea what I was going through. No idea how much I would put myself through for this man. *Okay, fine. She has some idea.*

"Remember what I said." Stephanie reminded.

"I remem-em bee." *I remember. I've had a brain bleed, how silly do you think I am? I'm safe here.* Was what I wanted to say to put her mind at ease, but those words would never leave my mouth.

Lying was hard, but at least I sounded convincing. Being untruthful was just not exactly in my nature. But I think I pulled it off, she darted out the door quicker than I had the chance to blink. As she left I noticed there were no locks on the door anymore... why?

It was finally was my chance, and I couldn't fuck it up like every other time I had ever tried to escape. Though, this time I'd be running *to* him, not *from* him. *Make that make fucking sense.*

I was a walking, breathing destruction, my reflection would always be a constant reminder of what I had been through. Who would want to live the rest of their life like that? *Not me.* On the plus side, it gave me the extra mental shift to go through with...

it.

Death.

Acting entirely on adrenaline, I headed for the door, sliding my way along the wall blindly in the dark. I gasped, something green and glowing caught my eye as I staggered passed Huxley's closet. I stepped into the area, smelling him in an instant and seeing a bowl of jewelry, glowing on a pedestal tucked to the back. I broke into a smile that I knew for sure reached my eyes. It was his amulet.

Has he left it here... for me?

I put it on without hesitating and a breathy moan parted my lips as the cold periapt sat against my skin under the robe. I felt like I had a piece of him on my skin, making the tear from my eye flow down my cheek—because it was *his*. The necklace was big on me, it had dangled over his chest when he wore it but with my short torso, it hung above my belly, which was now glowing green and my only light source.

I pulled it out of my robe and caressed it with my fingertip tenderly, remembering his kiss on my lips. *I am doing this for him. It's time.*

I turned on my feet to leave, only again becoming bewildered at what was before me. *What the actual fuck?* There was a stunning, emerald green, silk dress hanging right in front of me. Almost a replica version of the one he had me wear to the ball. *Green is my favorite color.*

Suddenly, without warning, a memory hit me like a lightning bolt: remembering that I loved butterflies—*green butterflies*—and that I studied them in college. That was why I drew them so much. It made sense now.

I drew in through my nose, inhaling everything. Him... all him. But why the dress? Maybe he was waiting for me? *Could he be?*

Fuck it.

I stepped into it, tying up the straps behind my neck and smoothed the dress down. It was tight around my belly, so it cinched me in nicely. Not that I needed it these days, not with how skinny I was. But I at least knew that he would like that I would die pretty for him. My heart danced from the excitement of hopefully seeing him again. I couldn't wait to tell him that I was ready. Ready to accept my passing for him—for his freedom —*and my own.*

But, I was more excited to tell him that I loved him, the real words, not just an '*I feel it too.*' I realized that I had never said those words before. *Love.* Actually I have never loved anyone before. I wondered if he would say it back to me. *Come on, Esme, focus.*

Shit.

The corridor was mostly dark, only able to rely on listening out for footsteps if anyone was around to stop me. I heard soft rumbles of thunder from far away and trickles of rain. I braced along the wall, pacing faster than my normal steps, but no faster than I could manage—I wanted to make it there alive. I needed to die *in* the lake, not *before* it. I decided there and then that I would head to the garage first and find a car... *again.* That would at least get me to the edge of the forest, and I could walk the rest of the way. *I hope.*

My heart raced in my chest and my head throbbed as I shuffled my way through the garage, using only muscle memory and swinging arms. The glow of the amulet was helpful, but not enough for such a large space. I finally found the car I had tried to escape with last time, it was parked in the same spot... as was the key, good.

The headlights came to life and the engine roared for me,

seeing that the garage was almost empty, nothing like it was. There was an SUV missing, the one Damon had put me in I presumed. *The fucker.* No motorbike either, as well as a few other sports cars.

Huxley's crushed-up car was still there, pained memories shoved in the corner with it. Then I found the cellar door... *No, no distractions, get the fuck out.* But I was dumbfounded; the door had been cemented shut. Did that mean no more girls? No more slaughter? I guessed it made sense—he found me. He didn't need to kill anymore. His twisted journey was nearly at its end, and mine would soon be too.

Shit.

How would the garage panel door open? The power was out. I banged my hands on the steering wheel and sobbed, not wanting to accept that I would have to walk. But as though a different God was watching, it began to open and the garage lights flickered back on, blinding me on impact. Either Stephanie had gotten the generator working or the power went back on.

I didn't think, and I certainly didn't hesitate; I slapped my foot with everything I had on the pedal and gunned it the fuck out. The wheels chirped and the scent of burning rubber fueled my nose, hitting an energetic, thrilled nerve I didn't know I had.

The shiny sports car hounded me up and out of the mansion at great speeds, and churned up the grass as I fled across the garden in the pouring rain. *How in the ever-loving fuck do you drive this thing?* It was faster than I could comprehend the direction in which I was going, which made me dizzier than I should have allowed my body to get.

I pulled slightly at the wheel, heading straight to the forest. I didn't have time to flick the wiper blade to brush off the rain on the windshield, I had no clue where the switch was anyway.

Alas, in moments I reached the woodland. I hit the brakes and fled in my fastest of slow paces, straight into the trees.

The aroma of pine was putting me in a turmoil of strength to keep going as my wobbly legs carried me through the broken sticks, branches, and rugged dirt. The moonlight and cracks of lightning lit the way and booms of thunder radiated up my spine. The soil was wet under my feet as they pressed into the ground. Every step was blanketed with desperation and need. Like I was speed walking for my life, like I had done all that time ago. Only I was speed walking to my un-life, *willingly*.

The rain was cold against my skin, but I knew the deeper I went into the trees the more sheltered I would be. My adrenaline started to wear off and I began to slow even more, I had pushed myself too hard, too fast. Soon coming to the fact that my head was pounding, and a ringing in my ear whined. Periods of dizziness threatened my vision and balance.

I winced and let out a deep sigh, leaning on a tree for a breather. I pulled myself together with all the strength I had to reboot my energy, I had such a way to go that I couldn't let up now. *Come on, body. Get me to the lake.* I imagined what it would be like to be cradled in Huxley's arms again... with a different necessity. My head against his chest, wearing the dress and his beautiful amulet. His scent, his eyes, his warmth, his... *him*. I wanted all of him. Everywhere, deeply.

'*I am broken.*'

His deceptive voice that echoed in my mind gave me the push that I needed, and my heart rate slowed once more, as did the pulsations in my head. Using the trees as guidance, I kept my pace. Trekking deeper and deeper. My feet pinched from the blows of the sharp, cold, wet earth, noticing that it had stopped raining for the time being. Perhaps the storm was starting to pass? The thunderclaps receded in the distance and the lightning was only barely visible over the tops of the trees.

'*I am incapable of love.*'

His nonexistent voice echoed in my brain again. No, you are not, I just needed to show you.

CHAPTER SIXTY-NINE

OUT OF THE DARKNESS... WE LEARN TO SEE

The smell of pine was starting to diminish as the familiar twang of blood and rotting corpses bombarded my nose. I was getting closer. It should have revolted me, only it was a welcoming invitation, not because I liked the smell. *Because I didn't.* But because where there were dead bodies and water, there was the shadow man—*my shadow*—and the empty viscera that awaited me.

I had no fucking clue where I was going, but I went on a whim wherever my nose led me. My feet were numb, my head hurt, and my arms were covered in nicks from sharp branches. The storm had completely passed, and the trees were starting to thin out. I pushed through my aches and pains as I held onto the glowing periapt as though it had a magical possession of strength and willpower.

The familiar ringing in my ears was growing stronger the further I walked—it was *her.* Making me painfully dizzy. I knew for sure that I was close. Shadows and flickers of light between the branches from the moonlight accompanied me through my treacherous journey. I was seeing brain fog. Or was it regular fog? I wasn't certain, I couldn't make sense of much anymore.

I just needed to keep pushing. I was exhausted, it had been hours, at a guess. Suddenly, the ringing stopped. Little static voices echoed in my ear, whispering almost inaudible nothings. Humming so softly and tenderly like a mother would lull a crying infant.

It was her, I knew it... it was the way she haunted, the way she got under your skin. I could make out a few words, but not the sentence. "*Mine,*" she sang. "*You belong to me.*"

But the sounds faded again and the ringing pierced me once more. Perhaps her voice was not clear because I had not bled in the water. Who knew, it didn't make sense to me, it didn't need to. *Blood, water, darkness, freedom.*

I pinched my cloudy eyes to make sense of my vision as I was seeing two of everything. I was feeling beads of sweat trickling down my forehead; it was weakness, knocking at my door.

"*It's okay, my dear. No need to fear me,*" she hummed again, and the feeling of dizziness and losing my sense of balance struck me harder. *Can she control me this way?*

I drew my hands to the sides of my head, trying to diminish the vibration of pain. *Bang, bang, thump, twang.* It was like standing under Big Ben's bell. I limped further, the scent of rotting flesh was becoming more and more pungent. The stench made my stomach churn. I looked around my surroundings, I had to squint to see it but right in the very furthest of my vision, was a reflection of water and the black fog that smothered it.

My heart pounded and my tears fled from my eyes without patience. I felt every emotion tear through my veins. *After many hours, I made it. I was finally here.* I scurried to the water's edge, panting, and whimpering with desperation, and more pain that radiated my body, mostly my head. I looked up, taking in how beautiful the moon was, in its bright and full form, shadowing between the clouds and onto the lake.

"He will never love you."

"He is broken. He will never stop trying to kill you."

The voice rang her tune. I turned my head left, but nothing... no one. I turned my head to the right and my heart shattered. Nothing. *No one.* Just me, the black fog, and her manipulation.

"He is incapable of love."

"I can make it all go away. Just one... more... step."

But she was wrong, I knew he loved me. But he will never *love* me the same way I loved him... not fully. He was a monster. And the void will never stop making him suffer until I am nothing but fish food.

The eerie ambiance rose high and the chill was powerful. I shuddered as it split through my core. I stood at the fringe... waiting, my toes digging into the sand-like terrain and cool pebbles. The bottom of my dress was now frayed from snagging twigs, branches, and the rugged ground. I froze, mindlessly staring into dead space which was death's doorbell.

My body on the outside was frozen, but everything inside was doing flips, turns, and tumbles. My mind empty of thoughts. Panting, and heavily overstimulated with the stench of demise from the countless bodies of innocent girls that filled the bottom of the lake before me... and quite possibly Tilly.

I looked down at the glow of Huxley's amulet, radiating as bright at the moon as it rose and fell with each of my breaths. *If only he was here.*

Come on, you can do this. For him.

Just... one... more... step.

I swallowed hard, but the nervous swell in my throat didn't budge. How the fuck did people kill themselves so willingly without fear? I was a nervous wreck internally. I didn't know what to do, how to act, or how to feel. All I know is that I wanted to. *Because I don't want to be here anymore.*

"Don't you want to set him free?" Her voice whirred. An invitation to the depths of her viscera.

I closed my eyes and mustered everything in my core. *This is the moment.* I craned my head, finally able to move my limbs again, and looked for something sharp, finding a nearby stone with serrated edges and grabbed it. *This will do perfectly.*

I collected my dress into my palm, lifting it slightly, and blew a heavy unsteady exhale. *I can do this.* I took a step forward, dipping my feet into the water. Instant shock repulsed through my body to the chill of the water. How was the water so cold? It wasn't the last time. Though, I *was* in a heated sexual state of affairs with a bad case of tunnel vision.

"He is broken. He is incapable of love. He is nothing without me," she howled again, closer this time.

I walked further in, feeling a slight swirl of warmth circulate me. I started treading water, blowing through each breath as I struggled to stay above. The dress had absorbed the liquid and was pulling me back, but I stayed bopping above the water.

At least I would until I was ready.

My head pounded loudly and I started to sob... because *he* wasn't here.

I propped myself onto my back to stay afloat and pulled the sharp stone to my palm, holding it there for only a moment, letting myself blink and absorb what I was doing. The moon shone a shade of blue, and diamond-like stars twinkled in the trees, soothing my nerves in an instant. If you looked hard enough, they looked like perfectly scripted pentagrams. But they didn't last long, grey clouds took over their beauty.

"You can give him everything he desires." Her voice was electric, with a suction-type power within it. It sounded like she was merely floating above me like a cloud, nearing. *"You can set him free, darling."* She was a lure, a siren.

My chin wobbled to my sobs and I instinctively pushed the stone hard into my palm. I didn't feel the pain at first, but it finally caught up with me and then the blood trickled down my hand, creating a whirlpool into the water. I lowered my hand, dropping the stone, and rolled back over, treading water. A strange wave of sensations hit me... weightlessness—the ringing stopped and my thumping became motionless. I looked up again, feeling the rain pour over my face.

"I can feel your heart, don't be frightened. You're safe with me. You know I can make it all go away," she sounded again, almost like she was beneath me. *"You are ready to sleep, my dear."*

I blinked, not really making sense that this was happening. I had gone completely fucking insane. She started to hum, like a lullaby. Identical to the one Huxley had played me on the piano. Even though the melody was the same, the message was different. I felt like I was tripping on some kind of drug, chasing it for more.

"You won't feel anything."

Her voice was soothing, like it was a hand, a guide, a passage of comfort. So I listened to her.

"Come now, I am here."

I took a breath and clutched my bleeding hand around his amulet before closing my eyes. I swallowed, and then another time because the first didn't budge the lump in my throat. I was scared, terrified. But not of dying... I was terrified of losing *him*. I would never see him again, or tell him that I loved him. But knowing that I was doing *this* for him, was enough to let me succumb. I heaved and cradled all that I had of him as my heart shattered and broke into a million pieces.

I don't want to be here anymore.

Without hesitation I drew in a final breath of wisdom and rolled my body forward, letting my back face the moon. The water enveloped me and I blinked away the blur, seeing the amulet shining under the water. I felt a tug of heaviness pulling me from below, and weightlessness receding.

Not a sliver of fear or trepidation ran through my veins. *I won't feel anything.* I was on cloud 9. It was calming. She was right, I felt no pain. Only the sense of his freedom warming my belly. *She will make it all go away. I can set him free.* I could hear my heart slow as it echoed around me in the water, it didn't scare me like I thought it would. I counted each beat as it began to fade.

I didn't fight, beckon, or pull myself back up. I let my imagination take charge, and what it would be like to kiss him one last time, hearing a combination of his sad, beautiful piano melodies and the lyrics of *There is Life* by *Alison Krauss* repeat in my mind.

'After the rain the sun will reappear.'

'For it's out of the darkness we learn to see.'

I felt the blackness pull for me, and my life the way *I intended* fled across the lids of my eyes. I let it consume me. Letting my mind carry me to a place in his arms.

'And out of the silence that songs come to be.'

And then I felt it... my heart was taking its last beats for *him*, and my soul was about to leave this earth. And my diminished, delusional brain let me see him *one last time.*

He cradled me. Smiling, ear to ear with his amber eyes. And even underwater he could speak to me. *"I promise the water will bring you back to me. When I have become the man you needed me to be. Then, I will be yours... to the end."*

The illusion of Huxley comforted me. He nearly blended into the shadows of the water. *He was the shadow... my shadow.* And learning to love him, I come to understand my shadow... because no matter where you are, day or night, even when you couldn't see them.

They are always, there. My shadow.

Fractured into a sensation of one last kiss, his twisted journey was at an end.

As was mine.

CHAPTER SEVENTY

ESME

We shouldn't always underestimate the power of our own imagination, should we?

'And all that we dream of awaits patently...
There. Is. Life.'
-Alison Krauss

"You

Saved

Me."

THE HUNTER. THE HUNTED
HUXLEY

'My Rain'

I am still her beloved remorse.
I will always hate to love her.
I will always love to hate her.

She will always be my rain.

The void told me to give my nemesis to her.
But she never said I couldn't bring her back.
And as she collapsed into me through her death
and again in her moment of wake, I knew that
this would be the start of something new.

H.

To be continued…
Because there is always another story.
'After The Rain'

MY MORALLY GREY DEDICATION

This is for my once-upon-a-time vanilla husband, who dipped his toes into the dark side for me, revealing a side of him that he never knew existed.

My morally grey husband.

I am proud to be yours. Claimed by you. Owned by you. Devoured by you.

Thank you from the bottom of my very unstable corrupt heart, and for inspiring me to finish this story.

Thank you for being my possessive book boyfriend, telling me I'm pretty, buying me books and coffee to feed my addiction.

More importantly, for show me that I can be me. You inspire me to be the best primal bad bitch in her feminine energy era that I can be.

Thank you for understanding my weird pansexual ass, and understanding my unhealthy addiction to masked men (and women...thanks Madeline Te Whiu!)

And lastly, thank you for loving me before, during, and after I discovered my true self, the changes you followed me through, guided me to, and pulled me from.

I am forever devoted to you.

Always.

I love you, my King.

- Love always, your Princess Queen xx

ACKNOWLEDGEMENTS

Hello, my darkling. Firstly, I'd like to thank you, *the reader*. You've come along with me on this wild journey, finding yourself now smack bang in the middle of my chaos. However you found me, I am forever grateful for allowing me to fuck with your mind, *just a little*. I want you to know how much you mean to me. Every like, comment, share, recommendation, breath and thought. I see you. I hear you. I feel you. I love you.

I'd love to thank my beta readers. You have all allowed me to pass on this story for a second time, giving me your eyes to check over everything where mine failed me. I appreciate every single one of you, and I hope you realise you're stuck with me for life now, right?

My deities. My girls. My coven. You have all been with me from the very first video I posted on TikTok in 2023 about my new debut novel I was writing, and stuck like glue since. For believing in me when sometimes I thought I didn't have what it takes. For holding my head up when the haters and cancel culture died to destroy me from the inside out and pushed me to where I am today.

My PA, Misha. For going above and beyond for me and my chaotic little hobby that I now call a career. For working your ass off with my endless requests. You have no idea how much you mean to me, even just as a friend to talk to when time is rough. Thank you babe x

My editor, Brittany. BRITTANY!! FUCKING BRITTANY! Where have you been hiding? I wish I found you when I first started this career. You are a fucking GODSEND! I truly mean it. I am certain on many occasion I had you questioning your career choice with me; your endless supply of messages, sweaty face emoji's and GIFS was evident of that. I am proud to call you my editor, from here on out. I won't hesitate to kidnap you either, you're *mine*, bitch.

Bree. Miss ma'am, you're a fucking needle in a haystack. You deserve the world and them some. I appreciate you tremendously. Never stop being you. Thank you for your endless support, and for being my proof queen. I love you x.

Lastly, I'd like to thank myself. Like I always do, and will never stop doing. For learning to grow, develop, change, and master this life of writing. For accepting that this career has its ups and downs, its good and ugly, its easy and hard, its victory and defeat. And for *always* finding strength to come out on top of it all.

With all that said, I have two tattoos on my leg which I would like to read to you. I want you to take them with you in your brain, for you never know just when you, or someone you know (or don't) needs to hear.

"She wears strength and weakness equally well.
She has always been half goddess half hell."

"Just like the moon, she must go through stages of emptiness
to feel full again."

ABOUT THE AUTHOR

Layla Moon is an Australian writer, she lives in Perth with her morally grey husband and three children. Plus the four legged children also. Her favourite thing in the entire world (on days that aren't her husband) is music, wine, books, coffee and biscuits.

Apart from having a sick obsession with metal music, she likes to write and entertain the minds of many. She has a heavy sense of humour, no filter and a bubbly nature. Above all else in this journey...

She has found her true self.

Because it's only when you risk failure, that you discover things. And Layla can"t wait to discover more in this path she calls 'writing'.

If you would like to stalk me, my information is on the next page.

TikTok

Instagram

LinkTree

Made in the USA
Columbia, SC
13 August 2024